# SPINDLES

## Stories from the Science of Sleep

Edited by
Penelope A. Lewis & Ra Page

First published in Great Britain in 2015 by Comma Press.
www.commapress.co.uk

A CIP catalogue record of this book is available from the British Library.

ISBN   1905583699
ISBN-13    978 1905583690

This project has been supported by the Wellcome Trust.

## Supported by
### **wellcome**trust

The publisher gratefully acknowledges assistance from Arts Council England.

Supported by
**ARTS COUNCIL
ENGLAND**

Set in Bembo 11/13 by David Eckersall
Printed and bound in England by CPI Group (UK) Ltd, Croydon CR0 4YY.

# Contents

# CONTENTS

# Introduction:
# What is Sleep?

WE SPEND A THIRD of our lives sleeping. That's more time than we spend doing anything else, which suggests that sleep has a fairly important biological function. But what exactly *is* sleep? Why do we do it?

Although scientists (and indeed writers) have been addressing this question for over a century, the last ten years has seen more breakthroughs than any other period of research. The findings have been surprising: Yes, sleep allows our tired bodies time to rest, but, as it turns out, sleep's main impact is on the brain.

Contrary to popular belief the brain doesn't switch off when we sleep. Instead, it goes through a highly structured architecture of sleep states. The easiest way to understand this, and the most objective way to consider what sleep is, is to look at the brain's electrical signals as measured with non-intrusive electrodes on the scalp through an electroencephalograph (EEG). When we are awake, brain activity measured on the EEG looks like a shallow, squiggly line, moving up and down almost randomly.

Wake

As we fall asleep, patterns of neural firing slow down and begin to be more synchronised. The amplitude of these oscillations becomes a bit larger as more neurons start to contribute to each wave, by firing slightly more in unison.

### Stage 1

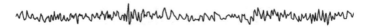

As we move deeper into sleep (Stage 2) brief periods of high frequency activity called 'sleep spindles' begin to appear over localised areas of the brain's cortex.

### Stage 2

Spindle

These spindles are characteristic of light sleep, and tend to occur over areas of the brain that have been intensively used during the preceding day of activity (e.g. over the motor cortex in someone who has been learning to play the piano). These are not dreams, exactly (their actual nature is discussed in Manuel Schabus's afterword to Claire Dean's story), but their name was too suggestive of 'spinning' and 'yarns' for us not to use it as our title.

As we move deeper into sleep, neural firing slows down and becomes even more synchronised. Now the bulk of cortical neurons act together in synchrony, firing action potentials, then pausing, then firing again, with a frequency of about one per second. This can be regarded as the deepest phase of sleep, and is often called 'slow wave sleep' because the EEG recordings show high amplitude, slow oscillations that correspond to the firing then pausing then firing. One way of thinking about this to to imagine the brain is like a tabletop with a hundred metronomes sitting on it. When we're awake they're all tick-tocking in fast, short swings, and they're all out of sync with each other. It's a kind of chaos. In deep, slow wave sleep (Stages 3 and 4), however, they're all swinging in unison: in long, slow arcs. This unison is a mysterious and dramatic phenomenon – so many different parts of the brain acting in synchrony, like the waves of the sea crashing and rising, crashing and rising, against the shore: slow, rhythmic, mysterious...

Stage 4

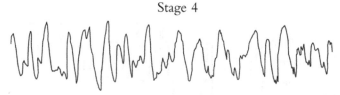

We don't see these kinds of waves when we're awake, probably because the waking brain has to process so many different types of information, it cannot afford the luxury of synchronisation.

After a period of deep, slow wave sleep, the brain typically moves back up through shallower, faster wave sleep and into the much-discussed, but little-understood, Rapid Eye Movement (REM) stage. This stage is characterised not only by brief, rapid eye movements which occur under closed lids but also by paralysis of all voluntary muscles. Part of the mystery of REM is that, paradoxically, although we are sound asleep during it, the EEG reading looks very similar to the one recorded during wakefulness. In other words, there is little synchrony between brain areas, which appear to be processing lots of different types of information at the same time.

REM

Interestingly, although we dream in all stages of sleep (and indeed whilst awake – namely, daydreams), REM dreams tend to be more vivid, emotional, and bizarre. For this reason, REM is thought to be important for emotional processing.

Typically, a healthy sleep may involve dropping down into slow wave sleep and back up to REM four or five times a night, with each cycle taking approximately 90 minutes to complete, with more time spent in very slow wave sleep in the earlier cycles and more in REM sleep in later cycles. The classic 'hypnogram' for a healthy night's sleep might therefore look something like this:

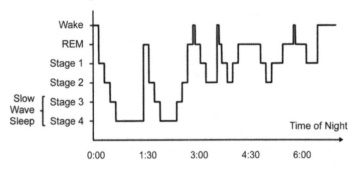

Just as brain activity in sleep follows a precise structure, so does our daily cycle of sleeping and waking. The sleep-wake cycle is controlled by a combination of circadian rhythms and sleep pressure. Circadian rhythms are the 24-hour oscillations in body temperature, hormone secretion, and other physiological processes that are driven by the sun's daily progression. 'Sleep pressure' is a bodily need for deep sleep. This sleep need is driven by physiological processes in a manner very similar to our need for food or water. Sleep pressure builds up while we are awake, and reduces rapidly when we are in slow wave sleep, hence it is highest in the evening when we go to bed. This is the reason why we tend to spend more time in slow wave sleep at the beginning of the night – later on, the sleep need has been satiated and the brain can concentrate on other types of sleep (specifically REM).

That's how science and the EEG define sleep, at least. Literature, and popular storytelling, have approached it quite differently. Over the centuries, sleep has gone from being viewed as a mystical, death-like, even supernatural phenomenon – preserving the innocence, beauty, or glory of the sleeper until the waking world merits their return; (*Sleeping Beauty, Snow White*, the indefinite sleep of King Arthur and Merlin, etc.), to being a place where nightmares and anxiety abound, exposing hidden truths about the sleeper's waking life – revealing guilt (Lady Macbeth), presaging doom (Clarence's dream in the Tower, *Richard III*), and so on. Were it not that we have bad dreams, however, sleep would be regarded by most writers as an elemental force for good, a restorative, recuperative act: the 'honey-heavy dew of slumber', as Shakespeare calls it, 'balm of hurt minds, great nature's second course'.

Since Freud, of course, the importance of dream interpretation has grown and grown, influencing whole swathes of 20th century storytelling, from the stream-of-consciousness prose of the modernist novelists, to the visual 'psychic determinism' of filmmakers, ranging from Buñuel and Hitchcock to Gilliam and Burton, where every image, like every dream ingredient, has meaning. Horror films have occasionally reached back to a pre-modern regard for sleep, where – through nightmares – sleep opens a door to demons (*Nightmare on Elm Street, The Haunting, Dreamscape,* etc). But otherwise Freud's influence remains palpable; indeed some argue that you have to go back to the writers *before* Freud to see clear, untainted, scientifically relevant depictions of what sleep is, and what its disorders and disruptions can do: Dickens' character Joe, 'the fat boy', in *The Pickwick Papers,* for instance, gave us the medical name for 'Pickwickian Syndrome' (also known as 'Obesity Hypoventilation Syndrome'), whilst Chekhov's heartbreaking story 'Let Me Sleep' showed us the psychological effects of sleep deprivation.

It is possible that Freud's dream theories, though scientifically outdated, continue to exert an influence over writers' imaginations – if only by preventing current authors from going near the subject of sleep, it being such a well-trodden territory already. But *now* is the time, more than any other, to engage with sleep! Science is finally starting to answer some of our age-old questions, and to revolutionise the way we think about it – not just as an opportunity to rest and recharge but as a dynamic period of (subconscious) learning, problem-solving, cleansing and reconstruction. It is with this new knowledge in mind that Comma Press has commissioned the 14 authors gathered here to respond to emerging research by collaborating with scientists working in different areas of this increasingly expansive field. In turn, the scientists in question have responded to each fictional 'response' in the form of an afterword.

So, back to the science.

What does sleep *do* for the brain? We don't yet have a complete picture, but *some* of sleep's functions are beginning to reveal themselves. For instance, sleep almost certainly plays a role in resetting the brain so that it is prepared for a new day of activity. Among other things, deep sleep is thought to cleanse toxins from the brain and reset pharmacological balances (Xie, 2013). This appears to be especially important for brain health, as the decrease in slow wave sleep which occurs as we age is highly predictive of atrophy to the frontal lobes, as well as gradually increasing impairments in memory and cognitive function (Mander, 2013). Additionally, connections between neurons which have been strengthened during the day are weakened or 'downscaled' during deep sleep, providing a homeostatic function that prevents the brain from becoming overloaded and makes space for new learning (Tononi & Cirelli, 2006). In fact, sleep works a kind of magic on memories, strengthening them, protecting them against decay, integrating new learning with older knowledge, and re-coding them in a more robust manner that helps to prevent interference (Rasch & Born, 2013). How does this work? A large part of the memory processing in sleep can be attributed to the reactivation or 'replay' of memories which occurs in most stages of sleep. Thus, newly learned memories are neurally 'replayed' meaning the same neurons that were active during wakefulness spontaneously activate again during sleep, like a kind of mental rehearsal of the learned information. (Note, these 'replays' should not be confused with dreams – it might be that some especially strong replays *surface* in dreams, but this probably only happens in a minority of cases.)

Because the brain is in a highly plastic and receptive state during sleep, the 'rehearsals' in each replay have an even stronger effect than actual rehearsals during wake. These rehearsals allow memories to be re-coded into different structures of the brain. Sleep often leads to creative insights into previously unsolvable problems. Because both creativity and problem-solving require the manipulation and recombination of existing knowledge, it seems plausible that memory replay also underpins these processes. This problem-solving power of sleep is explored in Sarah Schofield's story 'Benzene Dreams' and Bob Stickgold's afterword to it. The story takes its title from the 'discovery' of the Benzene molecule, by August Kekulé in a dream-like reverie – one of countless scientific and artistic problems that have been 'cracked' by dream-state problem-solving.

Memory replay, in sleep, is also thought to impact on the emotional content of memories. Specifically, if you have experienced something traumatic or negative, replaying this memory during REM sleep is thought to help you to separate the content of the memory (what happened) from the emotions attached to it, so that you can remember it without feeling so upset. Indeed, one day we may even be able to treat problems related to trauma and PTSD through sleep, by manipulating replay (as imagined in Adam Marek's story, 'Left Eye').

Technological developments such as the lightbulb, the TV, the laptop and the iPad, together with a modern 24/7 lifestyle, have done a lot to harm our sleep patterns by disrupting circadian rhythms and allowing people to dose themselves with bright light and stimulating activities that keep them awake late at night. Two stories here, Lisa Blower's 'Trees in the Wood' and Sara Maitland's 'The Rip Van Winkle Project', explore the effects of sleep deprivation and recent discoveries about the circadian clock, respectively. The latter story was consulted on by Russell Foster, one of the scientists responsible for discovering the hidden photoreceptors in the eyes which set this clock.

There is also considerable scepticism in the research community towards the emergence of certain smartphone 'apps' that make all kinds of outlandish claims about sleep improvement (see Andy Hedgecock's 'Counting Sheep'). But despite all this, there are undoubtedly reasons for optimism in potential technological applications of this research. The real hope is 'Sleep Engineering', that is to say the emerging science of how we can manipulate the sleep we get to our advantage. Perhaps the simplest example of this comes from the manipulation of memory replay in sleep. It turns out that we can trigger the selective replay of memories we want to target. This is done by pairing smells or sounds with target memories (like a voice reading a list of vocabulary words you want to remember while you also view them on a screen) and then re-presenting these sounds and/or smells while people are asleep (Oudiette & Paller, 2013). The brain is an associative machine, so when it is exposed to a sound or smell that was linked to something else (like the memory of a picture or idea) then that memory also becomes activated. This reactivation has been shown to strengthen memories and also potentially cause them to recombine. So, by selectively choosing which smells or sounds we present in sleep we can choose which memories to strengthen through reactivation, or indeed which attached emotions to strip away from a traumatic memory.

Sleep Engineering is not just for memories and emotions, however. We can manipulate the brain oscillations that occur in sleep, boosting some and suppressing others. At the moment this is mainly useful for research into what different frequencies of sleepful oscillation do, but once we gain a better understanding of this, selective enhancement and suppression could revolutionise the impact of sleep on our health and cognition. For instance, we can boost slow wave sleep by playing brief 'click' sounds at just the right point on a slow oscillation (timing them to coincide with each slow wave peak). This sound encourages neurons to fire in synchrony and thus enable us to prolong the duration of slow wave sleep (Stages 3 and 4). This could have particular benefits for older people, for whom the length of spontaneously occurring slow wave sleep has decreased. We can also manipulate REM sleep by enhancing or suppressing some of the key oscillation frequencies which occur in this sleep stage through the application of weak electrical currents to the scalp (Marshall, 2011), but more work needs to be done to understand the impacts of such manipulation.

Much more can be learned from the continued study of sleep – from making early diagnoses of neurological disorders with the help of sleep disorders (as in Annie Clarkson's 'A Careless Quiet'), to adopting more holistic responses to depression (see Martyn Bedford's 'My Soul to Keep' and Lisa Blower's 'Trees in the Wood'). Other disorders, such as narcolepsy, sleepwalking, and sleep state misperception (explored in Deborah Levy, Zoe Gilbert and Lisa Tuttle's stories), continue to shed new light on still largely unknown aspects of brain function.

In medieval and early modern Europe, a bedstead, with its linens and hangings, often accounted for a third of a household's wealth. Beds were placed at the centre of household life, and considered to have great importance. The conjugal husband-wife relationships that provided the core of the family were cemented in bed, through sex and pillow talk; the day's dealings and next day's decisions were often discussed in bed, and beds were also, of course, where children were conceived and born (Ekrich, 2005). Most importantly, beds were revered as the stage for sleep – a transitional state that was regarded as both necessary and treacherous, a passage of great vulnerability, from which the sleeper might not necessarily return. Perhaps it was this strong association with death that gave sleep such a key role in myth and fairy tale, as well as afforded it a special status in religious practices: the prayers said before sleep were similar to those said on the deathbed (Handley, 2012). People did not resent the time they spent asleep, but were instead fully aware of its impact on their efficiency the next day. In fact, poor sleep was sometimes interpreted as divine punishment for moral transgressions. Research into pre-modern sleeping patterns (by one of this book's consultants, Thomas Wehr) has even suggested that humans are naturally inclined to have *two* sleeps, divided by a short period of wakefulness which changes in length, according to the seasons. Science fiction writer Ian Watson (with Wehr's approval) here explores the idea that the miracle of consciousness developed in this small inter-sleep window (not the hearing of an inner voice, but the awareness of thought as something made up of different voices).

The medieval, spiritual appreciation for the importance of sleep has been largely lost in the present day. The prevalence of lights, drugs, environmental noises, and social pressure to be awake 24/7 is taking its toll on our sleep. We are often out of sync with the light-dark cycle, and are thus in a constant state of circadian disruption. However, an awareness of these problems, combined with the developing science of Sleep Engineering, should mean sleep has a better future. As we start to understand what it does and how it works, we can begin to manipulate the sleep that we do manage to get for maximal benefit, and truly start to harness sleep's mysterious power.

*PAL & RP, Manchester 2015*

# References

Ekirch, R. (2005). *At Day's Close: A History of Nighttime*, Weidenfeld & Nicholson, London.

Foster, R.G., Provencio, I., Hudson, D., Fiske S., De Grip, W., Menaker, M. (1991). 'Circadian photoreception in the retinally degenerate mouse (rd/rd)'. *Journal of Comparative Physiology* A 169 (1), pp 39-50.

Handley, S. (2013). 'Sociable sleeping in Early Modern England, 1660-1760.' *History: The Journal of the Historical Association* 98, (329), pp 79-104.

Handley, S. (2012). 'From the Sacral to the Moral: Sleeping Practices, Household Worship and Confessional Cultures in Late Seventeenth Century England.' *Cultural and Social History* 9 (1) pp 27-46.

Mander, B., et al. (2013). 'Prefrontal atrophy, disrupted NREM slow waves and impaired hippocampal–dependent memory in aging.' *Nature Neuroscience.* 16, pp 357-364.

Marshall, L., Kirov, R., Brade, J., Mölle, M. & Born, J. (2011). 'Transcranial electrical currents to probe EEG brain rhythms and memory consolidation during sleep in humans.' *PLoS One* 6, e16905.

Miles, P. & Pitcher, H., trans. (1982). *Chekhov: The Early Stories.* New York, Macmillan.

Oudiette, D. & Paller, K. A. (2013). 'Upgrading the sleeping brain with targeted memory reactivation.' *Trends in Cognitive Sciences* 17, pp 142-149.

Rasch, B. & Born, J. (2013). 'About sleep's role in memory.' *Physiological Reviews* 93, pp 681-766.

Tononi, G. & Cirelli, C. (2006). 'Sleep function and synaptic homeostasis.' *Sleep Medicine Reviews* 10, pp 49-62.

Xie, L. et al. (2013). 'Sleep drives metabolite clearance from the adult brain.' *Science* 342, pp 373-7.

# My Soul to Keep

## Martyn Bedford

SHE ROLLS ONTO HER left side, towards the camera. I note the time – 03:12:57. Strands of hair are snagged between her lips; a bare foot has emerged from the duvet and peers over the edge of the bed like a periscope. She swallows, crinkles her nose. As always, she smiles her Mona Lisa smile. According to the readings she is in REM, but her eyelids barely flicker.

*Sleeping Beauty*, the tabloids call her.

Even in the greenish night-vision lighting, Charlotte's features are flawless. It's easy to see why she captivates so many people. When she is facing the camera, I could gaze at the monitor for hours. When she turns away, I long for her to turn back. Awake, she never struck me as beautiful. Her grey eyes were almost always dull, her mouth a thin stripe that scarcely moved when she spoke. If you ask me, though, her beauty, her hypnotic appeal, isn't physical – it arises from her apparent serenity. She looks perfectly at peace with herself.

Dr Aziz tells us not to 'project'. But what alternative is there, with Charlotte?

I search her face for the faintest sign that she is aware – subliminally, unconsciously – of today's significance. Of course not. All I would see, if I saw anything, is the reflection of my own awareness. To Charlotte, it's simply one more night followed by one more day; although even that distinction is lost on her. She sleeps, she smiles. That's all.

The first time we met, she was just another patient. This was 15 months ago.

Dr Aziz brought her along to the lab around 8.30pm. 'Charlotte, this is Kim, one of our Sleep Technicians,' he said. 'She'll be looking after you tonight.'

The girl's 'Hey' was so automatic I wondered if she'd understood why we were being introduced. She wore a blue T-shirt that said FUN in big yellow letters, ripped jeans and green converses; her straight, dark hair hung to her shoulders and looked unwashed.

'You at uni, Charlotte?' I asked, once it was the two of us. We were sitting in easy chairs in a corner of the lab while I filled in the paperwork. I knew she was a student; I was making conversation to relax her. It took more questions to get her to say which university, which course. 'Oh, one of my sons is there. Sam. But he's in his final year, so you –'

'Do I go to sleep now?' she said, eyeing the bed as if noticing it for the first time.

I set my pen down. Went over the procedure which Dr Aziz had already explained to her: the acclimatization period; the attaching of the clips and electrodes.

'You'll go to bed about ten.'

From her appalled expression, I might have told her she had to stay up all night.

Charlotte had presented with depression near the end of her first semester at uni and was referred to her GP by student counselling, then to a Cognitive Behavioural Therapist. There'd been issues with anxiety and an eating disorder when she was 15 but, this time, the indicators suggested the onset of a Major Depressive Episode. Depressed mood for most of the day: tick; markedly diminished interest or pleasure in all activities most of the day: tick; psychomotor retardation: tick; fatigue or loss of energy: tick; diminished ability to think or concentrate: tick; feelings of worthlessness: tick; thoughts of her own death: tick. Less typically, the symptoms included heightened appetite and increased eating – which should have provided a clue to the particular nature of her depression. 'Excessive sleep' had been noted as well, but her doctor hadn't probed any further into that. It was her CBT therapist who realised Charlotte had a serious sleep disorder, as well as a serious mood disorder – and that the two might be interrelated. She referred her to a specialist: Dr Aziz.

'Why are there so many clips and stuff?' Charlotte asked, that first evening.

I talked her through the function of each attachment: brain activity, eye movement, muscle activity, heart rhythm, breathing function, blood-oxygen level... I might have been hypnotising her, the way her eyelids drooped. 'Don't worry – you'll get used to them.'

'They won't keep me awake?'

I couldn't help laughing. 'They'd be pretty pointless if they did.'

'Uh, yeah. I guess.'

She looked so lost in her confusion. I hadn't warmed to her up to that point. I can't say I exactly warmed to her, then, but I glimpsed her vulnerability. When you see the person inside the patient, you can't help noticing the person inside your professional self. *What if she was my daughter?* I recall thinking that, as I prepped her. Not that I have a daughter.

'I'm liking the pyjamas, by the way.'

She looked down at herself, as if trying to figure out why she was wearing pyjamas at all, or how they came to be patterned with tiny snowflakes. Like stars in a purple sky. 'Will you be watching me the whole time?' she asked.

'I'll be in the next room, yes. There's a monitor.' I indicated the camera. 'But I'll mainly be keeping track of the data feeds and making sure –'

'It's okay. I mean, I won't even know, will I?' She yawned, raised a hand to her mouth. Her pyjama sleeve slid down her forearm, the veins startlingly blue beneath the pale skin. 'You could draw glasses and a moustache on my face and I'd have no idea.'

She was asleep in four minutes; fast, but not untypical in hypersomnia. Nor was I all that surprised by the difficulty in waking her the next morning. The real sign that she was a special case came with the Polysomnography. Everyone, even a hypersomniac, is technically awake at numerous points during a period of sleep – a few seconds here, a few seconds there. But analysis across the range of PSG measurements showed this wasn't true for Charlotte. She slept for nine hours, eleven minutes without waking once, even for a nanosecond.

03:47:09. Security messages me: Charlotte's mother requests admittance, will I authorise? I authorise. She isn't due till ten, for the press conference, but I can imagine that she would want to sneak in early rather than cross a picket-line of camera crews and photographers. I listen for her footsteps in the corridor. I don't appreciate company at work. That's why I've been on the late shift for the past two or so years, since Sam went to university. I'd rather be alone through the night, here, than at home in an empty house. People ask if I'm ever lonely, but there's a difference between loneliness and solitude.

In the doorway, I conjure a smile. 'Hello, Evelyn.'

She steps into the observation room, pink-cheeked from the cold night air, her black coat glittery with rain. Her hair is as dark as Charlotte's but chopped into a severe bob and threaded with grey. 'I couldn't sleep,' she says. Realising what she has said, she laughs, a little too loudly. 'God, that's ironic, isn't it?'

Has she been drinking? 'Actually, it's paradoxical. Not ironic.'

Evelyn blinks at me.

'Sorry,' I say. 'My ex was an English teacher.'

I detect a flinch at 'ex'. You'd think it would be a point of connection; but, whereas I've been divorced for five years, she's been separated from Charlotte's father for six months. We orbit the same planet but on different parabolas. I suspect the real problem between us, though, is that I spend more time with her daughter than she does. Evelyn shrugs off her coat but remains standing, one hand on the chair I've wheeled out for her. With a vague gesture in the direction she's just come from, she says, 'There are more of them tonight.'

She must be referring to the Sleep Camp across the street. 'Yeah,' I reply, 'some new ones were arriving when I came in.' This is their solstice, I suppose. Behind the barriers, in their makeshift bivouacs, Charlotte's devotees will sleep with her – as close as they can, anyway – as the final hours and minutes of her 365th day tick down.

'Can I sit with her?' Evelyn asks. In the lab, she means. 'Please, Kim.'

I should refuse permission. I should remind her, politely but firmly, that we're outside the agreed visiting hours – that I'm prepared to let her stay with me in the observation room, but that's all. *Dr Aziz will have my guts for garters*, I should say. What I say, instead, is:

'Come on, I'll take you through.'

The morning following her first PSG, Charlotte remained sleep-drunk for some time after I managed to wake her. Even a shower and a change of clothes didn't lift the drowsiness and disorientation. I wondered how much longer she would have slept if I'd just left her there. Her notes indicated that, at home, she was typically asleep by 9pm and awake by 8am, if uninterrupted. During the days, she would have naps, totalling 5–6 hours. But patients are unreliable at self-recording, often conflating Total Sleep Time with Time In Bed. Just as insomniacs can overestimate how much they're awake, so some hypersomniacs exaggerate their propensity for sleep. Not Charlotte. She understood her sleep architecture only too well.

'Would you like some breakfast?' I asked.

I might've been speaking Chinese for all the response I got. I ordered toast and cereal. By the time it arrived, Charlotte had come round. As we ate, I outlined the day ahead. The Multiple Sleep Latency Test: At two-hour intervals, she would be asked to go back to sleep, enabling us to profile her 'onset'

– or how long she took to drop off. In between these times, she'd be given various boring, repetitive tasks to assess how easy or difficult it was for her to remain awake while performing them.

'This will be with one of my colleagues. I go off-shift at eight.'

'You work 12-hour shifts?' Charlotte bit into a triangle of toast.

'Four days on, three days off, yeah.'

Still chewing, she said, 'Just watching people sleep.'

'Or not sleeping. Most of our patients are insomniacs.'

'Isn't it boring?'

'As a Sleep Technician, it kind of goes with the territory.' The previous evening, she hadn't been remotely conversational. Already, I think I was aware that such moments of sociability – of normality – were, in fact, abnormal. For her. 'What about you?' I kept my tone light, teasing. 'Don't you get bored spending so much time asleep?'

'No.' Emphatic. Her mouth was lip-glossed with marmalade, but she either didn't realise or didn't care. 'Being *awake* –' she started to say, then stopped.

I tried to mask my interest. Weetabix, a sip of juice. Then, 'Being awake, what?'

But this young woman had done the rounds of counsellors, doctors, therapists; she saw me coming a mile off. 'Shouldn't Dr Aziz be the one to ask those sorts of questions?'

On the monitor, Evelyn positions a chair at her daughter's bedside and sits down. She knows not to hold Charlotte's hand, or stroke her hair, or kiss her, but sits close enough to do all of those things, if she chose to. She visits four or five times a week but, because I work lates, her dealings are usually with the day team. Occasionally, she'll arrive as I go off-shift, or leave as I turn up. Three times, she has come at night to sit with me in the observation room; but the last of these nocturnal visits was months ago.

She has never asked to enter the sleep-lab itself out of visiting hours. Until tonight.

She's talking to Charlotte; softly, but the mic picks up every word. My colleagues have told me about this: the long, chatty monologues, sometimes punctuated by weeping or pleas for her daughter to wake up. Dr Aziz has forbidden all non-clinical physical contact in case it interferes with the PSG channels, but he relaxed the rules on 'noise disturbance' when it became evident that Charlotte is entirely unresponsive to aural stimuli. Whether it's the bed-bath nurse dropping a stainless-steel bowl on the floor or Evelyn murmuring in her daughter's ear, the graphs remain stubbornly, relentlessly unaffected.

I mute the volume to grant her some privacy. And because I can't bear to hear it.

I speak to Charlotte myself at times: when I enter the lab to replace a dislodged attachment, or to adjust the feeding tube, or IV, or catheter, or simply to cover her when the bedclothes go walkabout. *Just clipping this back on your finger, Charlotte*, or *Let's tuck you in, shall we?* That sort of thing. Other stuff as well, if I'm honest.

'People in a coma can hear voices,' Evelyn once said to me.

Of course, Charlotte isn't in a vegetative state – she's asleep, not comatose. Cerebral and neurological functions are normal; there has been no brain trauma, or infection, or other identifiable cause for her unresponsiveness. Remarkably, it seems she put herself to sleep, and keeps herself asleep. It's inexplicable, but nothing we've tried – cold plunge-baths, loud bangs, loud music, pin-pricks, epidermal vibration, mild shocks, stimulants, bright light – has brought that sleep to an end. Yet it's conceivable that she might wake herself at any moment.

I watch Evelyn, watching her daughter.

When Will had pneumonia, I sat at his bedside through the night. It's what mums do. He sent me a photo-message yesterday – a selfie, with Angkor Wat in the background; week 32 of his gap-year trip. No text, just the picture and a smiley emoticon. I stuck another pin in the map on the wall of his old bedroom. I've seen Charlotte's bedroom in the newspapers and on TV; Evelyn keeps it exactly as it was the day her daughter entered the clinic long-term.

Her lips are still moving. Charlotte is still facing her, facing me, but her foot has retreated beneath the covers. She sleeps, she smiles.

*Where do you go to, my lovely?* What thoughts surround you, alone in your bed?

A year ago, she was unwell, desperately unhappy. But her perpetually tranquil smile invites us to assume she is happy, now; that she has attained a Buddha-like state of bliss.


I didn't see Charlotte again for six weeks after that first time.

At home, under her mother's supervision, she followed the plan drawn up by Dr Aziz. For a specialist in cognitive behavioural therapy, he takes an eclectic position on the treatment of depression – happy to stir biological and psychoanalytical approaches into the mix, if needs be. *With a patient like Charlotte, we might have to throw the kitchen sink in.* So he prescribed a cocktail of stimulant and antidepressant drugs, a new diet, physical exercises, the keeping of a sleep diary, prohibition of sleep outside night-time hours, increased daytime activity and bright-light therapy. She also saw Dr Aziz once a week for CBT, designed to challenge her perceptions about sleep. Hypersomnia patients often believe the only way to feel less tired is to sleep more; they have to be helped to think differently. Text-book stuff. Except that the text books for hypersomnia with depression, or depression with hypersomnia, are a work-in-progress. All we knew, pre-Charlotte, was that hypersomnia is the single most treatment-resistant symptom in depression; and that studies showed you must treat the sleep disorder as well as the mood disorder to achieve the best results for both.

Charlotte didn't improve on either front in those six weeks. She deteriorated.

'The root of the problem,' Dr Aziz declared at a team briefing, 'is that she doesn't sleep in order to feel less tired.'

'Why does she, then?' I asked.

'That, Kim, is the million-dollar question.'

With her consent, she was readmitted; this time, she would be with us for a week. Unprecedented. Hideously expensive. But, even back then, it was apparent that Charlotte's case was unique, opening up a ground-breaking area of research. He's a fine clinician, Dr Aziz, but he's even better at writing funding bids.

We played Scrabble, the first evening; a ploy to keep her awake until bedtime. In the 11 hours between Charlotte's readmission and the start of my shift, she'd clocked up 7.4 hours in short sleeps. *Rapid onsets; significant difficulty reawakening*, the handover notes said. *Marked avolition and anergia when awake*. Lack of motivation; lack of energy. Or, as my ex once put it: 'can't be arsed' and 'still can't be arsed'. (This was in the days when he still showed an interest in my work; when I still found his cynicism amusing.)

'There are two l's in "fuelled",' Charlotte said, after I'd taken a turn.

'Yeah, but I only have one,' I said. She frowned, then realised I was joking – that I'd tried to cheat. 'You should smile more often,' I told her, changing it to 'fled'. 'It suits you.'

She blushed, lowered her gaze. We'd been playing for about 20 minutes and she had already come close to nodding off two or three times. On her goes, she put down any old word, clumsily, seemingly uninterested in how many points it scored.

'We could switch the TV on, if you'd rather. Or watch a DVD.'

Charlotte placed some letters. 'You don't have to be nice to me,' she said, as if talking to the Scrabble board. 'I get enough of that crap from my mum. And Dr Aziz.'

'*Dr Aziz?* He hasn't been 'nice' to anyone since 2007.'

She didn't smile, or come close.

This was a typical conversation around that time. For me, at least. I gathered that Charlotte was even less forthcoming, less focused, with my colleagues – especially with Dr Aziz, on whom she had more or less shut down.

We were still unsure of the exact nature of her depression and its inter-relationship with her hypersomnia. Stress induced by the first-semester assessments at uni, social anxiety over living away from home and struggling to form friendships, the death of her grandmother the previous summer, the break-up with the boyfriend she'd had in sixth-form, losing her part-time job as a barista because she kept oversleeping and turning up late, the warning emails from her Progress Tutor about the number of lectures she'd missed, a bout of flu which wiped her out for most of the Christmas vacation . . . there was no shortage potential contributory factors in her depressive episode. But why did she sleep so much? And why, despite all the treatment, was she sleeping more and more?

'Why won't you let anyone in, Charlotte?' I asked, as I wired her up. This would've been the fifth or sixth evening.

'I don't want to *talk* anymore.'

'We're on your side, you know. We want you to get better.'

'No you're not. And no you don't.'

'No?'

'What you want – all of you – is to stop me sleeping.'

'Aren't they two sides of the same coin, though? You sleep, you get depressed; you get depressed, you sleep.'

'Is that what you think?' She shoved her fingers through her hair as if she wanted to yank it out by the roots. 'Jesus Christ.'

'So, *tell* me Charlotte. Please. Tell me how it really –'

'You want me to be 'happy', right?'

'Yes,' I said. 'Of course I do.'

'Then for fuck's sake let me *sleep*.' Her eyes filled with

tears; her shoulders shook. 'When I'm asleep, all the bad stuff goes away. Don't you see that?'

That week, her Total Sleep Time increased day by day. She became more resistant to being woken, more sleep-drunk and uncommunicative in the brief interludes when she was awake. In the final 24-hour period before we discharged her, her daytime sleep totalled 9.1 hours; that night, she slept for 10.5. This defied the laws of physiology. Sleep is driven by homeostatic and circadian rhythms: the more we sleep, the harder it is *to* sleep. And hunger or thirst should wake us, at some point, or the urge to go to the toilet. Not so, with Charlotte.

Ten days later, Evelyn phoned the clinic to report that her daughter had just gone a full 24 hours without waking. She was an emergency admission, then: if she didn't wake up, she couldn't eat or drink by herself. She remained asleep in the ambulance; she remained asleep here, in the lab, hydrated by a drip and with a feeding tube inserted into her stomach. No matter what we did, she slept and slept.

A new medical condition had been identified: Persistent Hypersomnic State, or PHS.

Before long, the whole world would know Charlotte's name.

Across the road, they've started chanting. I go to the window and peer through the blinds. It's just after 5am; the sky is still dark but the Sleep Camp is bathed by street lights. There are three or four times the usual number of tents, wigwams and yurts. On a typical night, the regulars and long-termers remain zipped away inside, sleeping or maintaining a silent vigil; but this is not a typical night, and the newcomers appear to be in the majority. The devotees sit cross-legged wherever there's space on the pavement, facing the clinic, eyes closed as if in worship, or raised towards the blacked-out second-floor window of the sleep-lab. Some hold up lit candles or the illuminated screens of their phones.

*Charlie*, they chant. *Charlie, Charlie, Charlie.*

It must be loud if I can hear them up here. What do they hope or expect? That, on the first anniversary of her entry into PHS, Charlotte will pick this moment to wake up? That she'll appear miraculously at the window above them, like a Living Goddess in Kathmandu, and let them gaze upon her beatific face?

A TV camera crew is there already; a couple of photographers. The 'true sleepers' in the camp must hate this. The noise, the showiness. Those who have been there all along, or who return again and again, have one declared purpose: to sleep in sympathy and solidarity with Charlotte. If you ask me, it's more than that – they seek whatever they imagine she has; they long to be hypersomniacs, too.

I step away from the window. On the monitor, Evelyn no longer seems to be talking. She might even have fallen asleep herself, in the bedside chair. As for Charlotte, she is in non-REM now. She smiles, as always.

*Charlie, Charlie.*

The Sleep Camp materialised after the Channel 4 documentary, broadcast to mark her 100th day. One tent, at first. Two 19-year-old girls. All the campers – regulars and casuals – have been female, aged from 15 to 25. The under-18s are rooted out by the police or social services, or by their parents, and packed off home. *A Sleeping Beauty for the 21st Century*, the programme was titled. Dr Aziz, with the consent of Charlotte's parents (still together at that stage), had allowed the film crew into the sleep-lab. A serious, intelligent documentary, was the intention; but, on television, human interest trumps psychological research every time. Even while the film was on air, our medical phenomenon had become an internet and social media sensation. By the following day, Charlotte's face – that mesmerising smile – was everywhere. She was the lead story on every news bulletin, every front page and home page. She trended. The only thing anyone was talking, commenting, Tweeting, 'liking' or trolling about. They loved her, they hated her; they pitied her, they blamed her; they accused her of faking it, they hailed her as a saint.

In the next few hours it will begin again, as the girl who has slept for a hundred days reaches another milestone: the girl who has slept for a year.

Not 'girl'; a young woman. Last month she 'celebrated' her twentieth birthday.

I log the data sets. It's what I do. What we do: round-the-clock Polysomnography, each 12-hour block of recorded information processed and analysed, every variation in the pattern and physiology of her sleep pored over for signs of change or clues to PHS. There never is any change, though. Charlotte's sleep is as remorseless, as featureless, as a desert.

At 05:41:22, I head along the corridor to the vending machine for my cappuccino fix. As the drink dispenses, the sleep-lab door opens and Evelyn emerges; groggy, distracted, her hair mussed up, she comes to join me.

'Can you hear them outside?' she asks, her voice raspy.

'Uh-huh.'

I expect her to make a disparaging remark about the Sleep Campers, or about the chanting, but, instead, she crumples into tears and I find myself enfolding her in my arms.

So, we had a rationale: *When I'm asleep all the bad stuff goes away.* And an implicit: *If I wake up, the bad stuff comes back.* That evening, more than a year ago – over a game of Scrabble – I coaxed a little more from Charlotte before she drifted into pre-sleep incoherence.

'What 'bad stuff'?'

She rubbed her face, as if cross with herself for crying. 'Everything.'

I check-listed some of the issues we already knew about but she just shook her head to shut me up. If she slept to escape all of that, why would she want to talk about it?

'I *love* going to bed,' she said, instead. 'Snuggling under the duvet, letting my head sink into the pillow, closing my eyes.' Her Mona Lisa smile surfaced.

'The cosiness?' The womb-like warmth and comfort and security, I left unsaid.

'The emptiness,' she said.

'Emptiness?'

'I lie there and empty everything out of my head and the sleep takes it away.' Her intensity was startling. In that moment, it really mattered to her that I understood. But my next questions irritated her, broke the connection.

'Do you dream?'

I knew she must, from the phases of REM, but she shrugged and said, 'If I do, I never remember them.'

'Do you think happy thoughts, then? Picture yourself in a happy pl–'

'I. Just. Sleep.'

'But, Charlotte, you can't sleep all the time. Can't sleep away the rest of your life.'

She didn't answer. Her expression said it clearly enough: *Why can't I?*

When we discussed this conversation at case conference, Dr Aziz hypothesized that Charlotte's sleep-craving was a surrogate death-impulse. With her previous therapist, she'd never spoken of feeling suicidal or considering ways to kill herself, as some depressives do. But she had wondered what it would be like to be dead.

'Can we infer,' Dr Aziz said, 'that Charlotte imagines death would be like sleeping?'

'The ultimate avoidance strategy?' one of the team suggested. 'All the time you're asleep, you don't have to *cope*. And if you're dead, or as good as, then you'll never –'

'Quite.' Dr Aziz managed a grim smile. 'There's a beautifully illogical logic to it.'

He would pursue that line in his consultations with Charlotte over the weeks ahead.

It never happened, of course. Within ten days of being

discharged, and after only one further therapy session (in which she blanked him), Charlotte went into PHS. Just when we'd unearthed a reason for her hypersomnia, we had no hope of reasoning her out of it.

'She's always been headstrong,' Evelyn says. 'Stubborn.'

Another paradox: Charlotte lacks motivation and energy, yet has the force of will to self-induce a year's sleep. Standing by the vending machine, I say as much to her mother.

'That's why they chant her name,' she replies. 'They think she's so fucking heroic.'

Her anger catches me off-guard. Is she annoyed with Charlotte's devotees, or with Charlotte? Or both? 'I hadn't thought about it like that,' I say, trying to be neutral.

'When Charlie had her eating disorder, we found out that she'd been going on this website – *Thinspiration*.' Evelyn's face is still blotchy from crying, her eyelashes dewy. 'All those girls, with their ribcages and cheekbones. Now she's the one being idolised.'

I retrieve my cappuccino and step aside so she can take her turn at the machine. For all that we've just hugged, we are more awkward with one another, not less. She presses 'Americano'. The cup drops into the slot and starts to fill.

'How d'you think they would feel if she woke up?' I ask. 'The Sleep Campers.'

'Let down.' She removes the drink before it has finished dispensing, seemingly indifferent to the scalding liquid splashing her fingers. '*How dare she betray us by waking up?*' As if it follows on naturally, Evelyn asks, 'You have children don't you, Kim?'

'Well, children – they're 23 and 21. Boys.' I tell her their names, and what they're doing now. She gazes along the corridor towards the door to the lab.

I break off. 'You ready to be swiped back in?'

'Do you miss them?' she asks. 'Your boys.'

'Ah, well. They have their own lives to –'

'I miss Charlie terribly, that's the thing. I want her to wake up for *my* sake as much as hers.' She turns back towards me, searching my face. 'Is that selfish of me?'

I hold her gaze. 'No, I wouldn't say it was.'

She nods but looks unconvinced. We walk back along the corridor with our coffees and stand together by the sleep-lab door. Through the viewing panel I see that Charlotte has turned over, away from us; her hair is draped across the pillow like a black silk scarf.

'How are you feeling about the press conference?' I ask.

'Oh, you know.'

I don't. I have no idea. The light on the security pad blinks from red to green as the door unlocks. I hold it ajar. She pauses, one hand splayed beside mine on the blond wood; her long, thin fingers next to my stubby ones, we make a bird with asymmetrical wings.

Evelyn says. 'I'll be notifying Dr Aziz this morning, so you might as well know.'

'Notifying him?'

We are speaking in lowered voices, conditioned to being quiet around someone who's asleep, even when it's Charlotte. Evelyn takes the weight of the door, her knuckles whitening, but I leave my hand where it is all the same.

'I'm withdrawing Charlie,' she says. 'I'm taking her home.'

A few days ago, on my cappuccino break, instead of returning to the observation room, I went into the lab. I sat with Charlotte for an hour. Sixty-three minutes, five seconds, to be exact. It would've taken some explaining if Dr Aziz had chosen that time to review the AV rather than simply reading the reports. The anniversary was looming – that might've been a factor; we were all in a state of heightened awareness. Also, I hadn't heard from Will or Sam in about ten days. Not that that's unusual, or any excuse for being so unprofessional.

'In the first few weeks after my marriage broke up – after

he left me – I dreaded going to bed at night.' That was one of the things I told her. 'The boys were both still at home, then, or I'd have slept in one of their rooms. So, what I did was sleep on top of the duvet, in a sleeping bag. Like he'd died and I couldn't bear to be in the space we'd shared for all those years, smelling him on the bedding no matter how often it went through the wash.'

On it went, my monologue. Pouring out of me. I'd never told anyone any of it.

How poorly I slept when I did finally drag myself to bed; how, perversely, I couldn't face getting up in the mornings. What was the point? Will and Sam, of course. But for them, I'd have lain in that sleeping bag half the day, not sleeping. Hating myself.

'Do you hate yourself, Charlotte?' I asked. 'I mean, *did* you, before this? Because you can't hate yourself when you're asleep, can you?'

Naturally, she didn't respond. I swept the hair from her face. Her forehead was cool and dry. Even once I'd withdrawn my hand I felt the ghost of her skin on my fingertips.

I can't recall everything I said to her in that hour, between the silences when I merely stared at her face. But I remember this: I sang to her. 'Scarborough Fair'. I used to sing it to the boys, when they were little, to soothe them to sleep. Now, I was singing it to Charlotte: a lullaby for the incessant sleeper. I swear that her eyelids flickered and her smile widened.

Afterwards, back in the observation room, I was convinced the graphs would show a momentary awakening that coincided with the singing. But, nothing. The whole time I'd sat with her, she had slept as deeply, as soundly, as ever.

Dr Aziz's office reeks of Evelyn's perfume. He has told me what I already knew, what he has only just heard himself.

'Can she do that?' I ask him across the desk.

'Why couldn't she? Charlotte has only ever been here with her mother's consent.'

I know that. Of course I do. I must be the least of Dr Aziz's priorities, just now, but he spares me the time even so. Evelyn, he explains, has raised enough money (by re-mortgaging the house, by signing a deal with a newspaper) to pay for her daughter to receive proper care at home for 18 months. Staff have been hired, preparations made. Charlotte's sleep will no longer be monitored. She'll be fed and hydrated, bathing and toilet will be attended to, along with regular medical checks. That's all. From now on, she sleeps in her own bed, in her own bedroom, until she wakes up. Whenever that might be.

'What about me?' The question is out before I can stop myself.

Dr Aziz frowns. 'Take a week off, Kim,' he says. 'Go somewhere nice. I'll have a new patient for you by the time you come back.'

I leave the clinic by the rear exit to avoid the press and the Sleep Camp. The walk to the bus-stop, the bus ride . . . none of it registers. But I find myself at the front door, letting myself into the house. It must've rained because my coat and hair are damp. I go through to the kitchen, only to stand in the middle of the room as if I've forgotten what I came in here for.

Breakfast, that's it. My routine after a shift: eat breakfast, take a shower, change into my pyjamas, close the bedroom curtains, read in bed till I'm ready to sleep.

I can't face breakfast this morning. Or any of it.

In the lounge, I slump on the sofa. I message Sam and Will. Sam won't be up, unless he has a morning lecture; maybe not even then. As for Will... I try to calculate the time in Cambodia but the maths is beyond me. I set the phone down on the coffee table. I'm still wearing my coat, I realise. At the clinic, the press conference will take place shortly. I picture the journalists assembling; Dr Aziz and Evelyn, in an ante-room, having clip-mics attached while a make-up person powders their faces for the cameras.

In the lab, Charlotte sleeps.

I imagine the day-team will have already removed all of the clips and electrodes and switched off the monitoring equipment. Later on, someone will detach the feeding tube, the IV, the catheter; they will bathe her, dress her, brush her hair. Then she'll be taken home and her bed will be empty.

For a time, I simply sit on the sofa. It seems like only a few minutes have passed but, according to my phone, it's 10:37. I must have dozed off. But I don't feel as though I have. Whatever, I take off my coat and hang it on one of the hooks by the front door, then fetch my bag into the lounge. I remove the large envelope containing the discs I brought home from work and select one at random. The remote isn't anywhere obvious, so I have to kneel on the floor in front of the TV and activate the DVD player manually. The tray slides out. I insert the disc and it slides in again. My knees click as I stand up and return to the sofa. The cushions are damp, but that doesn't matter.

After a moment, the screen flickers into life and her image appears.

She is lying on her left, eyes closed, face turned towards the camera. Smiling at me.

# Afterword:

# Hypersomnia

## Prof. Ed Watkins
University of Exeter

MARTYN BEDFORD'S STORY, 'MY Soul to Keep', provides us with an engaging story that elegantly combines an accurate digest of current scientific understanding with a modern take on the Sleeping Beauty myth. It introduces us to an extreme hypothetical case of hypersomnia and explores its ramifications. Whilst hypersomnia is a real and common clinical presentation, fortunately Persistent Hypersomnic State does not and cannot really exist and is only an intriguing product of Martyn's imagination.

Hypersomnia (from the Greek 'hyper' meaning 'over' and the Latin 'somnus' meaning sleep) involves excessively lengthy periods of night-time sleep, excessive daytime sleepiness and frequent daytime napping that occurs daily and persists for at least a month. It is most commonly associated with mood disorders such as clinical depression. For example, hypersomnia presents as a symptom in approximately 40% of young adults with depression and 10% of older adults with depression (see Kaplan & Harvey, 2009, for a detailed review). In fact, the combination of excessive sleepiness and increased appetite or weight gain occurs sufficiently frequently for it to have received its own diagnostic label of atypical depression, which occurs in as many as 40% of people who experience clinical depression. As suggested in Martyn's story, hypersomnia is more common in women with depression than men with it.

Excessive sleepiness is increasingly seen as an important mechanism that may contribute to the onset and maintenance of depression. There is growing evidence that individuals with hypersomnia who are followed up over time are up to three times more likely to experience a subsequent episode of clinical depression than individuals without hypersomnia. Moreover, hypersomnia appears to be associated with a more severe and more persistent course of depression. Several studies have found that it is the symptom that appears the most resistant to change even with successful treatments for depression. This suggests the importance of developing and evaluating effective interventions for hypersomnia.

Compared to insomnia (difficulties falling or staying asleep), treatments for hypersomnia are relatively under-developed and currently less effective. For example, there are evidence-based effective treatments for insomnia, both psychological and pharmacological. In particular, Cognitive Behavioural Therapy encourages patients to only go to bed when sleepy, to get out of bed if not falling asleep within 20 minutes, to remove distractions from the bedroom, and to promote relaxing activities in the evening – and it is often successful at tackling insomnia. However, pharmacological and cognitive-behavioural approaches to hypersomnia are still preliminary and have yet to be evaluated in large-scale clinical trials. It is also possible that excessive sleepiness may be harder to treat than excessive wakefulness: helping people to sleep typically involves removing barriers to sleep, such as worry, stress and poor 'sleep hygiene', whereas increasing alertness requires overcoming a natural desire to rest when sleepy.

Martyn's story highlights several topical issues within hypersomnia. As Kim notes, there is a debate as to the extent to which hypersomnia reflects an actual increase in the objective amount of time spent sleeping (Total Sleep Time), such as measured by polysomnography, versus a subjective perception of sleepiness and increased sleep (associated with Time in Bed) and experience of tiredness. Studies report mixed findings: sometimes patients with hypersomnia show elevated objective Total Sleep Time relative to healthy controls, but in other studies, there is no objective difference and there are only differences in reports of excessive sleepiness and increased time in bed for the hypersomnic patients. It may be that perception of sleepiness rather than actual amount of sleep is a key element in hypersomnia or that there are several distinct presentations of hypersomnia. Resolving the exact nature of hypersomnia is a priority for future research.

At the heart of Martyn's story is the idea that Charlotte's PHS may be an escape from her distress and from herself: *When I'm asleep all the bad stuff goes away.* The idea that hypersomnia may serve as an avoidance coping strategy is a scientifically reasonable and plausible hypothesis, which matches current theoretical understanding of depression. Psychological models of depression emphasise that increased avoidance contributes to the maintenance of depression. When depressed, people often reduce activities, withdraw from other people, and stop doing previously enjoyable activities. This can include spending more time in bed and more time sleeping. Trying to do things comes with the risk of failure and therefore it can feel safer and less uncomfortable to instead avoid these risks by doing less. Likewise, doing things can feel like it takes energy and effort. Often when people are depressed and already feel tired, they are concerned about conserving energy and not becoming worn out. Avoidance can therefore temporarily reduce unpleasant experiences, such as feeling upset and anxious, possible failure, fear of shame and embarrassment, and feeling tired. However, this temporary reduction in short-term distress can itself reinforce the avoidance, so that it becomes more frequent and gradually spreads out through the person's life. Unfortunately, this avoidance also prevents contact with positive, pleasurable, and rewarding experiences that can lift mood, such as enjoyable times with family and friends, which in turn, further maintains and fuels an ongoing depression. This avoidance model of depression is well-supported by the evidence and underpins successful psychological treatments for depression, in particular, behavioural activation, which focuses on identifying and reducing patterns of avoidance and replacing them with 'approach' towards potentially rewarding activities.

In this context, sleeping and spending time in bed are both powerful ways to avoid things going wrong by doing nothing. Moreover, bed can be a comforting place, with patients often talking of 'hiding under their duvet'. When asleep, there is a temporary loss of awareness of fears and concerns, producing relief from daily struggles (although such concerns can still manifest in dreams and nightmares). Further, because tiredness is a major feature of depression, the idea of trying to rest and 'recharge your batteries' is intuitively appealing to those who are depressed. Sleeping and spending more time in bed can then be seen as essential for recovery. Retreat into bed and into sleep can sensibly be hypothesised as an understandable attempt to reduce distress, albeit one that in the long-run is likely to prolong depression. Charlotte's PHS is this avoidance taken to the extreme. Whilst logically consistent with our psychological understanding of depression, it is important to recognise that there are strong biological reasons why hypersomnia cannot become permanent PHS. As noted in the story, sleep is self-limiting because sleep is driven by both homeostatic and circadian processes, so the more sleep one has, normally the harder it is to sleep and the extent of sleepiness is driven by chronological and social rhythms.

This suggests potential psychological interventions for hypersomnia based around reducing avoidance and replacing it with 'approach' (see Kaplan & Harvey, 2009 for a proposed intervention). For example, the therapy would focus on the patient increasing positive and stimulating activities to increase behavioural activation and alleviate the symptoms of depression including sleepiness. Psychoeducation would explain about normal patterns of sleep and explain how increased activity increases energy and alertness, at odds with potential beliefs that more rest is needed to reduce sleepiness. This would then be followed up by behavioural experiments to test these beliefs in which patients compare resting versus becoming more active over alternate days to learn which approach is more helpful. In parallel, pharmacological treatment of hypersomnia has focused on selecting antidepressant medication that does not promote sleep and the additional use of alertness-promoting medications such as Modafinil. More work has to be done, however, to develop and evaluate these interventions for hypersomnia specifically.

# References

Kaplan, K.A. & Harvey, A.G. (2009). 'Hypersomnia across mood disorders: A review and synthesis.' *Sleep Medicine Reviews* 13, pp 275-285.

# Left Eye

## Adam Marek

'WHY ME?' NANCY ASKS.

'You were recommended. A Squad Leader you worked with after Kandahar.'

'Dan Frume?'

'You remember him?'

'My work's pretty intimate. I remember everyone.'

'Intimate?'

'I mean, when you tuck someone into bed and then watch them sleep every night for weeks on end, you get to know them in an unusual way. You can't help but care about someone you watch sleep for so long.'

Hinderman looks concerned for a moment, but it passes.

'So who do you want me to work with?' Nancy asks.

'I'll come to that.'

'Okay. I have one condition though.'

Hinderman puts up his hand. 'I don't want you to agree to anything until you know what you're getting into.'

She regrets seeming too eager. It's obvious they can afford her. Look at this place. 'It's just, my last contract was terminated before it was completed. I can't have…'

'At Colder Hill, I know.'

How much does he know about her? A man like this, he could know everything. And yet, whatever he knows, she doesn't feel like she's having to persuade him. Maybe it's the other way round. Feels good; makes her see herself differently, legitimised, like this. The last three years since leaving Stanford, trying to prove herself, the validity of her work. Such a struggle to make people take her seriously, and now she's been flown out to Florida to meet a man who has thoroughly investigated her and yet still wants her to work for him. What's the catch?

The wall of black glass behind Hinderman turns turquoise as the lights inside the training pool ignite. Hinderman's office is level with the bottom of the pool, where there is a coral reef of submerged equipment: robotic arms, cross-sectioned station parts, experiment racks. Dad would have loved this. Hinderman sees her attention on the pool and swivels on his chair to stare at it himself. He makes a satisfied huff sound from his nose. Must be interesting for him to see it through her fresh eyes. How quickly we adapt to the sublime.

Three divers in EVA suits hit the surface of the water high above. Air bubbles fizz from the white fabric as they drift down. One of the three aquanauts waves, his face indecipherable behind his amber visor.

'All the directors' offices back onto the training pool,' Hinderman says. 'Completely impractical, the architect said at first, but I always wanted this view, and there are always other architects.'

'What kind of trauma are we dealing with here?'

Hinderman pinches his earlobe and holds it for long moments while staring at his desk, as if receiving a message from somewhere. 'Come on,' he says, 'let's go meet your test subjects.'

All the corridors are elliptical, the building shaped around the training pool. They walk past three thick frames on the wall, which display space suits from different ages – a baggy, yellowing Apollo-era suit, a bright orange shuttle-era suit, and a slim-fitting grey suit from Hinderman Industries' first sub-orbital commercial flight. This place is something else.

'What are your ultimate ambitions for your work?' Hinderman asks.

'Long-term? I'd like my own team. And then I'd train them to train other people. The process isn't complicated. All the work was in writing the algorithm. It's easy to replicate. I worked with six GIs at Colder Hill over the few months I was there. Was really starting to get somewhere, but more than 3,000 of them came back with some degree of PTSD. If we had more people.'

'But what's to stop someone learning your technique and then just setting up for themselves? How will you protect your project?'

'It would be possible to patent my algorithm, I guess. But I'm not interested in that.'

'Huh. So you're a… what's the opposite of entrepreneur?'

'I have the skills to help the most selfless people on Earth. It would be unethical of me to keep that to myself.'

'But what about quality control? Not everyone has your integrity. How would you protect your reputation if you've got a bunch of leptons bumbling their way through a technique with your name on it?'

She's not sure. Hasn't thought that far ahead. Has never dared look more than a few weeks into the future since she was 16, when Dad came back and everything changed. Hinderman is giving her a look because she isn't responding quickly enough. She doesn't want him to think she's unprofessional.

'That's all a long way off,' she says. 'One thing at a time. I'm still refining the process.'

'I think this will be as useful for you as it will be for me. Give you a different perspective. It might open up a field of possibilities you hadn't ever considered.'

Hinderman stops at the elevator and it recognises that someone is standing in front of it. It gives a single tone, a rounded throb that is gentle on the ear. Hinderman offers his eyes to the scanner. The elevator door slides open and they step inside and descend. Six floors down. Deep underground. What is she getting into?

There are six chimps, all housed separately in large glass-fronted cells. They have climbing equipment. Straw nests. Their muscular stink fills the lab. There is one technician, a Korean woman of about the same age as Nancy. Hinderman introduces her as Yuna and they shake hands.

Nancy finds it hard to look at the chimps. This is embarrassing. And so disappointing. 'I think you've made a mistake,' she says.

Hinderman walks to the centre cell, in which a chimp is standing just on the other side of the glass, looking out at them. With one hand the chimp is leaning against the glass. With the other he is holding a blue rubber dog bone, which he is chewing. The hair on this arm, from his wrist to the crook of his elbow, has been shaved off. The skin is grey-brown.

'This is Left Eye,' Hinderman says.

'I'm sorry but I think I've wasted your time.'

'He's been here for five years, but he's not been doing so well lately.'

'Mr Hinderman, my technique doesn't…'

Hinderman holds up his hand to silence her, and this time it irritates her. This man is an idiot. An idiot with unlimited resources is dangerous.

'Can you…?' Hinderman says to Yuna, and she offers her face to the scanner at the side of Left Eye's cell. A seam appears in the glass. A door. She pushes against the glass and the door springs open. When she makes three click sounds using something in the pocket of her lab coat, Left Eye drops the bone and comes bounding out. He leaps up into her arms. The thing has fearsome agility. Those able hands. Nancy backs away.

'It's okay,' Yuna says. 'He's never aggressive.' She touches the downy underside of the chimp's muzzle with the side of her finger, raising his face up towards her. The chimp's dextrous lips animate from a flat, puppet-like slit into a fleshy trumpet and back again with extraordinary plasticity.

Hinderman beckons Yuna to come forward, till she's right beside him and Nancy. This animal reeks of musk and medicine. Such brown eyes. Chestnut. She's never been looked at like this before.

'I've already spoken with my consultants, and your old supervisor at Stanford. Your technique should work. Chimps have similar sleep stages to us, apparently.'

Irritated that he would do that. No one is qualified to make that assumption. She shouldn't be here. This is a mistake.

'What are these chimps going through?' She resists the urge to touch the back of the chimp's hairy hand. Close enough to feel the heat coming off him.

'A level of unavoidable discomfort.'

'Why?'

'The needs of the future. For our crew capabilities to catch up with our drive capabilities.'

'You're putting chimps up there?'

'Not exactly, no.'

'Then what?' Hard to hold back the aggression in her voice. Why this ferocious feeling? She's making assumptions. Projecting. Foolish to do that. No, it's raw disappointment. Didn't know exactly what she'd been expecting when Hinderman's invitation came, but not… who would take her seriously after being involved with something like this?

'I'm rather disappointed at your reaction,' Hinderman says.

'This is way off path.' Measuring her words. 'And I'm not sure I'd be adding any value to your project.'

'Your contribution to the project could be the most important one. These little fellers need your help coping with the demands of the programme. The sleep engineering principles would be the same as everything you did at Stanford and Colder Hill. If it's your reputation you're concerned about, don't be. No one gets to know about any of this.'

'Then why would I do it?'

'Because we'd fund your research for the next five years. Because you won't find facilities like this anywhere else in the world. Because this is an opportunity to learn things that you couldn't learn anywhere else. And because Left Eye and the rest of these guys need you. Desperately.'

Hard to imagine that Hinderman was ever a child.

'Why is he called Left Eye?'

'It's just a name.'

Nancy isn't used to working with so many other people around. Left Eye is anaesthetised and flat on the bed. The size of his chest! Her hands are shaking. Had to use a child's plastic cap to map the electrode positions for the EEG on the chimp's head. This feels so odd. The chimp fur reluctant to part for her fingertips. So wiry. Hard to spot the red kohl pencil dots on Left Eye's mottled scalp. Has to put the cap back on and reapply the dots two, three times. All the while people watching. Hinderman in the corner with his fingertips on his chin. Feels like the first time she has done this. Like being back at university again. She squeezes the conducting paste onto each dot. Fumbles with the electrodes. They feel wilful in her fingers. Has to squeeze large blobs of glue onto the connectors to make them stick.

'You don't need to be so gentle,' Yuna says. 'He won't wake up.'

Nancy feels relief when all 22 electrodes are connected to Left Eye's scalp, and she has the easier job of applying the eye and muscle movement electrodes to his bare temples and his chin. At this stage, she usually says to the subject, 'You look like an electric Rapunzel'. She's good at being reassuring. Important that the subject is relaxed. It's reassuring for her too. Part of her process. Something deeply disturbing about working on a subject who has not consented. She feels like she's crossing a threshold. Desperate for touchstones of familiarity.

'You look like an electric Rapunzel,' she says to the sleeping ape.

Yuna frowns.

Nancy puts her hand on Left Eye's hot shoulder. The strength in him. That wizened baby's face. Moments of wishing she wasn't here.

'I'm not sure he's going to keep all these electrodes on when he wakes up,' Nancy says.

Step one is the memory test. The chimp sits on an upright chair. No straps are necessary on this occasion. Left Eye's compliance is a relief. Yuna has used a red headscarf from her bag to tie around his head, protecting the electrodes from his fingers. Nancy knows how itchy they can get. The chimp looks like a pirate. All the wires bundled in a ponytail and connected to the polysomnograph. It took almost an hour, all the while under scrutiny, to get all the electrode impedance lights turned from red to green. Finally ready to go. The people in the room – she doesn't even know who most of them are, there were no introductions – are uncomfortable from standing for so long, leaning up against workbenches. One squatting on the floor even. Is it really necessary that they're all here?

Nancy shows the chimp a series of 25 images on a computer screen: high contrast patterns of wavy lines, zigzags, silhouettes of simple shapes. She downloaded them from an online parenting site. They are designed to show to babies, before their eyes are properly developed. It's hard to think about Left Eye as anything other than a baby. It's the nappy, and the plastic wristband.

While the image sequence runs, she uses her laptop to play a series of 12 tones, each held for less than half a second. With a start, she realises she has forgotten the scent stimulus. The shakes return. She apologises to the room, unpacks the vapouriser, sets up the Bluetooth on her laptop. The vapouriser's red connection light flashes three times, then turns green. The room slowly fills with the sweet chemical smell of pear drops. On the screen of her laptop, Nancy watches the feeds from the electrodes. The seismic activity of a brain learning.

'Must be strange,' Yuna says, yawning. 'Compared to working with troops.' It's 2:20am, and they are the only people left in the lab.

'It is and it isn't. Everyone looks the same when they sleep. Like children.'

Yuna nods.

The lights in Left Eye's cell are off, but Nancy can see that he is asleep from the becalmed muscle channels on the EEG. He's in Stage 2, the short, dense weaves of sigma wave spindles showing his brain inhibiting his responses to external stimuli, keeping him in a subdued state of arousal. He's been dipping in and out between the early stages of sleep and full waking for the last four hours, and has not yet drifted into Stages 3 or 4, the slow wave sleep, which she is waiting for, so she can begin the stimulation process. This happens all the time with human subjects. Especially the first time they're hooked up. They're anxious and self-conscious about the need to be asleep. Sensitised by the unfamiliar bed. And with all the electrodes glued onto their scalp, they worry about rolling around and dislodging them. They just slip in and out of Stage 1. Often emerge in the morning thinking they haven't slept at all.

This was especially frustrating for the guys coming back from Kandahar. They approached the need to sleep with the same seriousness they applied to all of their duties – a state of mind that took weeks to overcome for many of them. One Lieutenant in particular, Ramira Gonzalez, who had just spent four months there defusing bombs, was so determined to conceal her inability to sleep that she would fake it, so as not to disappoint Nancy. She'd lie completely still for hours, pretending to snore even, while her EEG clearly showed that she was awake.

It's frustrating for Nancy, too, of course, to spend a whole night awake observing someone and not being able to run the process, but it happens often enough that she's learned to accept it as part of the job. But the pressure tonight is different. She imagines how disappointed Hinderman will be if there aren't results to show in the morning when he arrives.

They both stare at the EEG traces.

'Is that REM?' Yuna asks, pointing at a couple of spikes as they drift across the screen, left to right.

'No, not for a while yet.' Nancy shakes her head. 'So have you always worked with chimps?'

'I've worked with everything you can imagine. Ants. Cockroaches. Jellyfish. Toads. All the rodents of course. I've been working my way up the evolutionary ladder. Chimps are the top.'

'It must be interesting.'

'It's not for everyone.'

'No?'

'You know. My parents owned a farm when I was growing up, so I guess I learned to see animals in a very… *practical* way.' She tilts her head, maybe wondering if this was the right word to use.

'Here we go,' Nancy points at the screen. The EEG lines now show delta waves in widely spaced peaks and troughs. Left Eye is in Stage 3. Nancy runs the programme that begins the stimulation. From the speaker inside Left Eye's cell, the sequence of tones begins to play. The silver vapouriser beside the pillow on his trolley bed opens its mouth and puffs a breath of peardrop scent.

'So tell me,' Hinderman says when he arrives at the lab in the morning. He is carrying a cup of coffee for her. She takes it and sets it on the side. Doesn't tell him that she doesn't drink caffeine. Hasn't drunk any stimulants since her own battle with sleep began after they lost Dad. The prize of perfect sleep for her still, ironically, elusive.

It's 8:30am. She has been awake now for 26 hours. Yuna left at 4:30am, when Nancy said she needn't hang around. The poor woman had been nodding off in her chair. It takes a while to get used to this routine.

'I'm just running Left Eye's EEGs from the waking memory test and from last night through the algorithm. The results should be through in a moment.'

'But he slept okay?'

'Fairly erratic. I'm not sure what's normal, but he went into slow wave for long enough to run the stimulation.'

'Will you head back to the hotel for a few hours' sleep after you're done here?'

'Yeah.' Uncomfortable with him asking about her life outside of the lab.

'Are you safe to drive?'

'I'm used to driving half awake.'

On Nancy's laptop screen, the blue indicator bar shows that the algorithm is nearly complete. It finishes with the sound of a tiny bell being struck, and then a long page of data analysis appears.

'How does it look?'

Nancy scrolls through. There's a lot of detail to go through here, but for now she just scans for the top level information, which she can find quickly, the shape of the line-breaks at the key parts like a familiar map to her now.

'Sixty-seven percent,' she says.

'Oh.'

'No, that's good. That's really good.'

'Really?'

'In control subjects where I don't stimulate with tones

and scent during the night, memory replay fidelity while they're asleep is usually 15 to 30 percent. Replay as frequent as this has a big effect on the emotional valence. If this were a human subject, after five or so sessions of that quality, I'd expect a massive reduction in their stress levels... associated with the particular trauma memories we're working on. Impossible to tell yet how this'll go with chimps, but...'

'It sounds like a success.'

'It's encouraging. I didn't expect it to be so high.'

Hinderman claps his hands together and smiles. 'Excellent.'

'But this is all new, so I'll need to run it a few more times before we can know for sure how effective the sleep stimulation is.'

'Well, I'll see you back here later for the next one. We have a window available two weeks today and I'd like you to be ready for that.'

'Okay.' She doesn't know what she's agreeing to and she's too tired to think about it now. Nancy closes her laptop. Time to sleep. She's getting mild hallucinations – flashes of floor-level movement at the edge of her vision, which her supervisor at Stanford called *the black cats*. 'I'm getting the black cats,' being the usual way to tell your colleagues that you would be achieving nothing useful now until you'd gone to bed and had a few cycles.

Outside of the air-conditioned facility, even at only 10am, the sun has a dreadful weight, and the heat inside the Lexus that Hinderman rented for her is merciless. She starts the car and switches the air-conditioning to full-blast. Simple instructions to herself: get back to the hotel, take a few melatonin capsules, get horizontal. Try to get some respite from thinking about damn chimps till tonight.

In the toilet cubicle, Nancy undoes the top two buttons of her blouse and with a wad of tissue paper wipes her armpits. In the mirror outside, she comports herself before heading to the Conference Room. She arrives early, and for half an hour the room is all hers. She double-checks the connection between her laptop and the presentation screens on the side walls. She flicks through all her slides and rehearses in a whisper. Rationally, she knows she has no need to be nervous. Easy to talk about things you know well, and she has excellent news for the Board, likely exceeding their expectations. When she's prepared, she tries to relax by watching the activity in the pool at the other end of the room. Two trainees are practising repairs to a robotic arm. Bubbles rise from the sides of their helmets. Everything done in slow motion. One of them drops something that looks like a drill. It drifts slowly down. In space, it won't do this. Impossible to replicate zero gravity on the surface of the Earth. Training is all about approximating. There's no way to really know it till you're in it.

The Board Members start to arrive, pour coffee from the jugs on the trolley, and take their places. Hinderman is the last to arrive, 10 minutes late. He drops down onto his seat at the head of the long table and signals for her to begin by pointing his finger at her like a gun.

She explains how over the last two weeks she has performed daily memory tests on each of the six chimps, and nightly sleep stimulation. She has analysed the EEG data, running it through her algorithm, and for each of the chimps slowly refined a classifier – the idiosyncratic pattern of brain activity that shows the sleeping brain is replaying memories of the tests.

'You're able to see the chimp's dreams?' One of the board members interrupts her.

'No. Only that he or she is dreaming about the memory test.'

She explains that during the slow wave phase of sleep, the brain consolidates memory, replaying experiences from the day, transporting them from short-term memory in the hippocampus to the grand repository of long-term memory in the cortex.

'Sleep is like the passport of memory,' she says, 'And memories have to travel to survive.'

She shows diagrams comparing EEG traces from control chimps and sleep-stimulated chimps, describing how the tones and scents stimulate the brain to replay a memory multiple times during slow wave sleep. This forced reiteration of the memory encourages the brain to process it with ultra-effectiveness.

'In subjects with PTSD,' she says, 'There's an additional benefit, where the better processing of painful memories reduces the strength of the associated emotions.' The technique could have saved Dad.

She can see from the faces of the board members their surprise and satisfaction. Hinderman is all grin. He begins a round of applause that is quickly taken up by the whole room. This should feel good.

Afterwards, he puts his arm around her and squeezes. She keeps her hands in the pockets of her trousers.

'We need to get one of the chimps prepped for the launch on Thursday,' Hinderman says. 'Which of them has responded best to the tests?'

'Definitely Left Eye,' she says. 'The results from every one of his tests have been higher than any of the other chimps.'

Hinderman nods. 'Good. I'll need the tone and scent programme ready in a couple of days. You don't get to take anything up there without it being thoroughly screened first.' And then as he leaves her to pack up her equipment, he adds, 'I'm proud of you.'

When Nancy arrives in the morning, Left Eye's cell is empty. Yuna is chopping papaya and carrots on a board for the other chimps.

'He's gone already?' Nancy says. 'I wanted to say bon voyage before he went.'

'There's a lot of prep to do at Cape Canaveral before the launch,' she says.

'On Left Eye? What kind of prep?'

Yuna gives her a look. 'You know, it's best not to get emotionally attached to them.'

'But how can you not?'

'You just have to learn.'

'I didn't think I would. At first I found them a bit... uncomfortable to be around. But...'

'I know.'Yuna puts the knife down and wipes her hands on her jeans. 'You have to be prepared for when they come back. It's very different. When Right Eye came back, she was... she'd been so good natured and smart – just like her brother – but afterwards, she was uncooperative. Violent sometimes. We just couldn't work with her anymore. I was new to it then and I was devastated. You have to find a way to protect yourself from that. But the first time it's hard. On the other chimps too. The problems with Left Eye began when she was gone.'

'Is the experience of being up there so hard on them?'

Yuna looks at her. 'That's why you're here. It's up to you to help them recover when they come back.'

Nancy drums to Creedence on the steering wheel of the rental car and sings along. The flat landscape of sun-baked fields whizzes by, the ditches from which she saw an alligator emerge onto the roadside in her first days here, the silver eggboxes of industrial plants, the occasional lush orange orchard. It's 5am and the sky is a web of cirrus clouds. For once, the air conditioning is unnecessary. She got a call from Hinderman an hour ago to say that Left Eye was back.

The door to the lab recognises Nancy's eyes and opens for her. Yuna is slumped over her desk, using her rucksack as a pillow. Nancy tiptoes across the lab taking care not to wake her. The lights in the chimps' cells are off, but even in the low-level night-lighting in the lab, she can see the trolley bed in Left Eye's cell, and the silhouette of the chimp on his back. The relief of seeing that powerful hump of chest!

'Oh. Sorry.' Yuna's voice comes from behind her. She rubs her eyes with her knuckles and picks up her glasses from the desk.

Nancy touches her fingertip to the glass of Left Eye's tank and leaves a ring of condensation. 'Is he okay?' she whispers.

Yuna nods. 'He's been asleep since he arrived. The sedative should start wearing off soon though.'

Left Eye's splayed knees twitch, then relax back down again. Nothing to do now but wait till he awakes.

They sit and watch the outline of the supine chimp. Nancy opens a pack of dried mango slices and offers it to Yuna, but she says her stomach isn't awake yet.

Hinderman calls from his car on his way in. Says, 'Is everything… hang on, there's something in the road. Damn it. I'll call back.' Then hangs up. The sound of the call wakes one of the chimps. The motion-sensitive lights in his cell come on, and the light wakes the other chimps. As each one stirs, the lights ping on one by one in succession, till last of all, the lights in Left Eye's cell flare and now here he is sitting up. His hands are wrapped. Gauze mittens. The wrapping all the way up past his elbows. Splints. Panics when he can't bend his arms. Tries to touch his face, to feel the eyepatch. Nancy puts her hand over her own eye. A feeling of intense vulnerability shivers through her. Oh my poor baby. What have they done to you?

In the pool behind Hinderman's desk there is a new object. A huge, four-module facsimile of the Japanese space agency's docking port. Two aquanauts are in the tank practising evacuation. Hinderman hands Nancy a tissue but she doesn't want one.

'You're making a big mistake,' he says.

'I can't be part of this,' she says. Her cheeks are aflame.

'Of course you feel this way. I knew you would. It would be weird if you didn't.'

'I feel sick.'

He smiles. 'If it's any consolation, Dr Oshiro said it couldn't have gone any better.'

Nancy shakes her head. Can't make eye contact with the man.

'I want you to do something for me,' he says.

'What?'

'Left Eye's got a real bond with you. Will you put aside your own feelings for now and think about him? He needs you. All your results show that your technique will help his recovery. I need you to think beyond yourself right now, for his sake.'

'And get him ready for the next time?'

Hinderman sighs. 'There are a thousand impediments to overcome before we'll be ready for real life up there. Within a decade or two, the station won't be filled with a few dozen trained astronauts. It'll be filled with farmers and chefs and artists and news anchors. It'll…'

'But I'm not…'

'…It'll be filled with families. Imagine if your kid got ill up there. Would you want your child's operation to be the first of its kind? We're going to need surgeons, and we're going to need them to be as skilled as they are down here. Everything is different without gravity. We're having to learn from scratch. It's a completely different methodology. These chimps are no different to your soldiers. They're making a necessary personal sacrifice for the good of something that's greater than themselves. They need you to do the same.'

'The troops make that decision for themselves.'

Hinderman checks his watch, then sits up straight in his chair as if he's about to leave.

'When we first met, you said it would be unethical of you to withhold your skills when they could help – that's exactly what you'd be doing if you walked away. I need you to continue what you've started here. Where else would you go, anyway? You got booted out of Colder Hill for not producing results fast enough. You think any other military facility will be different? You're right at the start of your career, and I'm the only one who's going to give you the time and funding you need. You leave now, you'll be teaching at a university somewhere within a year and hating every minute of it. I'm giving you the opportunity to be the best you can be.'

'If this is the cost of life up there, then it's too high.'

'It might be hard for you to believe, but I care about every one of those chimps. It would break my heart if Left Eye went the same way as his sister.'

Impossible to read the truth of this in his face.

'You'll find someone else.'

'No. There's no one else I can trust with this. You're the only one. Take a couple of days, then come back to me, okay?'

Outside the hotel window, landing lights drift down to Hinderman Industries' runway. Another batch of sub-orbital tourists returning from a brief sojourn in the world above the clouds. On the bed beside Nancy, the paella on the room service tray is cold and untouched. She puts it on the floor, then undresses and slips under the thin covers. Cannot help but imagine what Left Eye is doing right now. In her mind the chimp is fully anthropomorphised. Confused. Hurt. And lonely. Missing her.

Wishes she wasn't here. Regrets that her pursuit has brought her to this place. Didn't know she was building a trap for herself. Angry with Dad. If he'd been able to cope, she'd be on a different path now. Free of this bind.

A phantasmagoria of memories lines up for processing. Hinderman's patronising grin. The aquanauts at play. The gentle ping of the elevator. The sound of Yuna's knife on the chopping board. Left Eye struggling against the splints. His grunts, which to her ear were full of disbelief. The treachery feels like her own. Would the chimp be better off if she stayed, more able to cope? Or would she make him a better, more compliant subject, cause him to endure even more test surgeries on the station? Couldn't bear to betray him again.

She switches off the bedside light. Puts on her headphones. Activates the vapouriser. Listens to the tones. Waits for sleep to transport her. Hopes that in the morning she'll have found the courage to stay.

# Afterword:

# Targeted Memory Replay

## Dr Penelope A. Lewis
University of Manchester

SLEEP ISN'T A PASSIVE mind-state. While we're under, our brains are very busy, and one of the things they are doing is replaying memories (Diekelmann & Born, 2010). Memories are spontaneously reactivated through the different stages of sleep. This means that the neural responses which built the memories during wakefulness (e.g. activity in the auditory, motor, and olfactory areas, as well as any other brain areas involved in the memory) occur again during sleep. Perhaps unsurprisingly, reactivation is associated with stronger memories that are more resistant to subsequent interference. Thus, replay in sleep is thought to strengthen the memories just as if we were practicing them during wakefulness (although reactivation during sleep is potentially even better, as the brain is in a more receptive state).

Striking research from Bjoern Rasch (2007) at the University of Friburg in Switzerland, and Ken Paller (2009) at Northwestern University in Chicago, has shown that while memories are replayed spontaneously in sleep, we can also trigger replay on demand, thus ensuring that the memories which we specifically want to target get replayed. This is done by associating sounds or smells with a memory while awake, then presenting these sounds or smells again during sleep. The brain is a highly associative machine, so experiencing such stimuli triggers activity in cortical areas that were linked to these stimuli during previous experiences. If the sounds and smells in question were linked to specific memories then these associative links will trigger memory reactivation. This type of memory triggering in sleep is called 'Targeted Memory Replay', or TMR.

In addition to processing memories, sleep is well known for altering our emotions. We all know that if we are upset by something then the best solution is often to 'sleep on it', but we also know that we should 'never sleep on an argument'. Evidence that emotional responses can be both strengthened (Lewis, et al., 2011) and weakened (der Helm, 2011) over a period of sleep abound, providing scientific support for both these (seemingly contradictory) age-old counsels, even though it is a bit unclear how sleep actually acts on emotions. One prevalent hypothesis from Matt Walker at Harvard, the 'Sleep to remember sleep to forget' framework suggests that reactivation of memories in sleep allows the emotional content to be stripped away (Walker, et al., 2009). This hypothesis relates specifically to REM sleep, where the pharmacological milieu (especially the low levels of a neurotransmitter called 'noradrenaline') mean the body cannot react to emotional events as it normally would during wakefulness. Without a bodily reaction, emotions will tend to lose their salience and become less upsetting. Thus, repeated replaying of emotional memories during REM is proposed to 'disarm' them by separating emotional responses from memory content. Although these ideas are highly compelling, scientific evidence supporting this theory is actually rather slim at present. Instead, as yet unpublished work by Maria-Efstratia Tsimpanouli and Isabel Hutchison, both at the University of Manchester, has shown that triggering the replay of emotionally upsetting memories during slow wave sleep, using TMR, leads to a reduction in subjective ratings of how upsetting or arousing the memories are. Although this is a new finding and in need of replication, we are hopeful that TMR of emotional memories during sleep could be used to help people who are haunted by upsetting memories that won't go away. Sufferers of Post Traumatic Stress Disorder are an obvious example of this, as are many patients with serious forms of anxiety. In 'Left Eye', a version of TMR is being used to reduce the trauma experienced by chimps who are subject to experimental surgery at a space station.

44

In his story, Adam Marek emphasises the similarity between humans and chimps in a very compelling manner. While TMR has never yet been used on chimps, their sleep has all of the characteristics required for it to work, so although the story is in some ways far-fetched this is not an entirely fanciful application.

Importantly, Nancy talks about 'replay fidelity' as being '67 percent' in Left Eye, which means she is using a state of the art technique which Suliman Belal has developed here in Manchester to identify when neural replay actually occurs during sleep. This is an important feature of the story, as it seems that she finds unexpectedly high replay fidelity in chimps, meaning her technique for reducing their anxiety has a really good chance of working. Although the story doesn't make it clear exactly how she measures the replay fidelity, this is done by using a technique called 'machine learning', to examine the electrical signals recorded from electrodes on the scalp. Machine learning essentially takes a fingerprint of what that electrical activity looks like when the person (or chimp in this case) is experiencing a particular memory while awake. Afterwards, the computer can screen through all of the data collected during sleep to see how often this pattern of activity is repeated – and how closely such repetitions match the original fingerprint. Because Nancy is using TMR, the task of screening the data will have been greatly simplified, as she will only have to look at the second or so of brain recordings after each auditory tone application to determine whether the memory associated with that particular cue has been replayed at that time. The '67 percent' in the story therefore refers to the proportion of times that the expected replay actually occurs after such a cue.

In Marek's story, of course, society is preparing for interstellar travel, for which living in space (and dealing with inevitable trauma in space) would be necessary. In reality, I suspect, society will need these techniques for processing trauma a lot sooner, and for situations a lot closer to home.

# References

Diekelmann, S. & Born, J (2010). 'The memory function of sleep'. *Nat. Rev. Neurosci.* 11, pp 114-126.

Rasch, B., Buchel, C., Gais, S. & Born, J. (2007). 'Odor Cues During Slow-Wave.' *Science* 315, pp 1426-1429.

Rudoy, J. D., Voss, J. L., Westerberg, C. E. & Paller, K. A. (2009). 'Strengthening individual memories by reactivating them during sleep.' *Science.* 326, pp 1079.

Lewis, P. A., Cairney, S., Manning, L. & Critchley, H. D. (2011). 'The impact of overnight consolidation upon memory for emotional and neutral encoding contexts.' *Neuropsychologia* 49, pp 2619-2629.

Van der Helm, E., et al. (2011). 'REM sleep depotentiates amygdala activity to previous emotional experiences.' *Curr. Biol.* 21, pp 2029-2032.

Walker, M. P., van der, H. E. & van der Helm, E. (2009). 'Overnight therapy? The role of sleep in emotional brain processing.' *Psychol.Bull.* 135, pp 731-748.

# A Sleeping Serial Killer

## M.J. Hyland

*I am accustomed to sleep and in my dreams to imagine the same things that lunatics imagine when awake.* – René Descartes

AROUND MIDDAY, ON A weekday in May, I was sitting at a table outside a café in Chorlton, writing and drinking coffee. I was alone. At the next table there was a grey-haired man with his wife and their dog, and the dog was tied to the leg of an empty chair.

The man and his wife finished a bottle of wine and, when she left, to meet her sister and to 'do the shopping for dinner', the man turned round to face my table.

– You look very engrossed, he said. You've hardly stopped all day.

He was right. It was 4pm.

– My name's Frank, he said.

– I'm Maria.

– You look like a journalist. Am I right?

– No, I'm a novelist and a lecturer.

He told me he liked books, that he'd recently read and liked a book by James Patterson, or maybe it was Andrea Camilleri.

On my table was a copy of *The Snows of Kilimanjaro & Other Stories* by Ernest Hemingway. I'd been re-reading 'Up in Michigan' and the *Paris Review* interview in which Hemingway named Hieronymus Bosch as one of his 'literary forebears'. The interviewer said: 'But the nightmare symbolic quality of his work seems so far removed from your own.' Hemingway replied, 'I have the nightmares and know about the ones other people have. But you do not have to write them down.'

Frank pointed to *The Snows of Kilimanjaro*, and said:

– I like Hemingway too.

– So you like the man who loved five-toed cats and hated his mother?

– Is that a story or a novel?

– No. Hemingway liked cats, especially Polydactyl cats, the breed with extra toes and he also hated his mother.

Frank nodded.

– I have a few things in common with Hemingway, I said.

Frank didn't ask what I have in common with Hemingway, the cats or his hatred of his mother, but if he'd asked, I'd have told him it was both.

My right hand was sore but I started working again and, as soon as I began, Frank stood and looked across at my computer.

– Are you writing a new novel?

– No, I'm writing an article about the science of sleep and dreaming.

Without warning, Frank picked up his glass of Chardonnay and his electric cigarette and moved his chair next to mine. To a passerby it would seem as though he'd always been there.

– You don't mind?

– Of course not, I said, but what about your dog?

– He's okay where he is.

– What's his name?

– Pretzel.

– That's a good name for a big dog.

Frank smiled.

– Why don't you ask Pretzel if he wants to come over here?

Frank went down on his haunches and whispered in his dog's ear.

– What did he say?

– Well, Maria, he said he'd be honoured.

Pretzel curled up under the table with his snout resting in a square of sunlight.

– I might be able to help with your article, said Frank.

– How so?

– I'm a psychotherapist.

– Do you interpret dreams?

– I also specialise in other areas, such as gestalt and…

Frank talked for a good while about his ability to 'unpack' the 'hidden human psyche' by using 'holistic treatments'.

– I can unlock what a client is hiding and get to their secrets, he said, sometimes at the start of the very first session.

– That's impressive, I said, but I'm not writing about dream interpretation – that's Freud's business.

– Okay, but you haven't told me what you're writing.

– All I've written so far is a rough draft based on a theory about the positive side-effects of persistent nightmares.

Pretzel was asleep.

– I think he's snoring, I said.

– Can you hear that? I'd love to have the hearing of youth.

I wanted to leave. The sun had switched sides and my hair was getting hot. I put my computer in my bag.

– You're leaving? said Frank.

The waiter passed by and Frank asked for another bottle of Chardonnay.

– And for the young lady?

– No, thanks, I'm fine.

The waiter left.

– Why don't you stay and tell me your theory?

– If I stay, I said, could we swap places? I need to sit in the shade.

For a while, Frank talked about his psychotherapy practice; that dream interpretation is vital to good therapy, 'so long as it's combined with holistic specialist treatments,' and so on.

When he'd finished talking, it was after 6pm. I stood.

– I'd really better go, I said.

– But you haven't told me what you're writing about.

Maybe saying it out loud might be a good test for my theory and so I stayed and ordered another coffee.

– What's the title?

– I don't have one yet.

– And the theory?

– I have vivid and violent nightmares, lots of them, and I've had them all my life, and my theory is that nightmares function as a cure, of sorts.

Frank raised his eyebrows.

– You look sceptical, I said. Do you want some examples?

– Only if you feel comfortable telling me.

– Sure. In the past week, I've had two fairly typical nightmares. In one, I met an old friend who said my ears were bleeding, gave me his scarf and told me to clean up the mess my blood had made on his clean floor. In another, I was strapped with ropes to a cot-bed and I said, 'I always knew I'd end up dying in a welfare hotel.' But these nightmares were mild compared to most.

– Why do they upset you?

– They don't upset me, or make me wake in fright, and that's the point of my theory, or part of the point.

Frank had his eye on the waiter and it was clear he wanted the wine more than he wanted to listen but I'd started, so, I'd finish.

– Shall I go on?

– Yes, yes, I'm fascinated.

– My nightmares started when I was very young and I think a lifetime of dark dreaming has done me a favour, might even have flushed my mind of the traits and tendencies that would otherwise have landed me in trouble. My nightly dark dreams have also functioned to salve, or at least soften, some of the worst blows and bruises of life and…

– I hope you don't mind me asking, said Frank, but did you experience childhood trauma?

A predictable question but I couldn't blame him for asking.

–Yes, and no. I witnessed more than I suffered, and yes it was dire stuff but that's a dull species of truth and it's far from the point of my theory.

– Keep talking.

– My father and brother and dozens of my paternal relatives have spent their lives in prison, psychiatric hospitals or sleeping on the street with a bottle, or a needle in their arm, and far worse. When I was a child, my nightmares seemed to inure me to this trouble and, over time, might have given me a knack for detachment.

Frank touched my knee.

– Do you mind me asking what kind of trauma?

– Trauma is an overstatement, but yes, my childhood was deranged, from infancy till the day I left home and I give my persistent nightmares some of the credit for the fact that I didn't end up in prison or become an illiterate junkie - the sort of fate my genes clearly had in mind for me. Does this make sense?

– But I don't think you can be cured by -

– Okay, I said, here's an example. When I was eight or nine, my father slashed our neighbour with a dog-chain and when the police took my father away, I didn't sob like my mother or hide behind the garbage bin like my brother did. I went to sleep and had a dream in which I tied my father to a chair and cut his head off with – I can't remember what.

Frank poured another glass of wine.

– And in my nightmares I sell counterfeit money, urinate on carpet in posh houses, and yet in waking life I'm an ordinary defective, no better or worse than most and I'm pretty sure my nightmares played, and still play, a part in this.

Frank frowned.

– I'm not sure that bad dreams could do what you say, Maria, and maybe you need to –

– Fine, maybe not, but isn't it possible – in theory –that

nightmares might act to purge fury and pain? Or satiate or sublimate the desire to enact base desires? Or act as a cleaning-house for the wounds that flow from trouble? A kind of sleeping therapy, if you like, without all the talking and the bills?

– Anything's possible, said Frank, I suppose.

– Maybe this will make sense. Even after an especially gruesome dream I wake in a mood of 'lucid indifference' and this cycle started when I was a child. From about the age of seven I was certain that I wouldn't end up like 'them', my family, and that my nightmares weren't a bad thing but a good and special trick that my brain played to make me tougher.

– Maybe you still have nightmares, said Frank, because you haven't faced your trauma and you need to do some work to repair the emotional damage.

– No, not at all. The very opposite might be true, that my nightmares have already done some of this work, as you call it.

Frank opened and closed his mouth and was itching to talk. He was a man more used to talking than listening. But I had to finish, I was too far gone to quit. Even though I might as well have been talking to Pretzel, Frank's idea that I needed his brand of psychotherapy pissed me off.

– The thing is, I said, I left home when I was sixteen, studied law, lectured at three universities and have written three novels so, all said and done, I think I've beaten the odds. And maybe my theory is bullshit, but if nothing else, it's fascinating isn't it? At least a little interesting that in my dreams I've murdered my brother, father and my mother and not once, but many times. While I sleep I'm a serial killer, and when I'm not taking revenge on my family, my dreams provide surrogates so I can push strangers over the railings of ten-storey car parks. So that's it, my theory: my dark-dreaming has functioned as a ventilation system, or something of that order, and re-wired my brain.

Frank put his hand on my leg and left it there. At last he had his chance to diagnose me.

– Don't take this the wrong way, Maria.

– Okay.

– I've treated lots of career-women with denial issues and I've helped them with a combination of therapies and I think you could benefit from some...

I checked my watch and made my face look harried.

– I'm sorry, Frank, but I really have to go now. The BBC awaits. I've got a book review thing.

This was a lie. I don't know why I didn't tell the truth or why I needed to impress this fool.

– That's a pity, he said and then he gave me his card: his name, Dr Frank D—, his email, business address on Deansgate and two phone numbers.

– If you ever need to talk.

– Thanks, Frank, you've been a great help.

– I come here most weekends, he said, usually with my wife, but if you're here next weekend, we could talk some more.

– Okay, I said.

– Sunday, for brunch, around 11, if you like?

When I got home, I searched for Dr Frank D— on Google and with the exception of a link to 'Serenity Place Clinic' which he shares with a hypnotherapist, an acupuncturist and a podiatrist, I found no papers published in his name or any other links to his psychotherapy practice.

A few days later an engineer from British Gas came to my house to service the boiler. I left him alone to work downstairs while I wrote upstairs in bed. When he finished, he called up to me from the kitchen.

– I'm all done down here.

– Do I need to sign something before you leave?

– Yes, if you could.

– Could you come upstairs? I'm working in the front bedroom.

He came up.

– This is my office, I said, this bed and these pillows. I laughed, and so did he.

– You just need to sign this, Mrs Hyland.

– I'm just Maria, not Mrs. I've forgotten your name.

– I'm just Richard.

I smiled and signed the form then told him I was writing about dreams.

– Do you mind if I ask you some questions about dreams?

– For what?

– For this piece I'm writing. I'm doing research.

– Okay.

I wasn't in a robe or pyjamas, but Richard didn't want to be too close to the bed and so he stepped back and leant against the far wall.

– Do you have dreams? I asked. Do you remember them?

– Never.

– Everybody has dreams.

– Nah, I never dream, but you should talk to my wife – every morning she wants to tell me all the dreams she's had.

– Does your wife have nightmares?

– Not really, she says they're nightmares but they're only dreams about work things and forgetting to file things or running late and that sort of run-of-the-mill thing.

– Are all her bad dreams about her job?

– Yeah, and the people at her work and cock-ups and people not talking to her and getting shafted and what-have-you.

– Is that because she's worried about her job? In the daylight?

– I don't think so.

His pager beeped and then his mobile rang.

– Sounds like you need to go, I said.

– I'm two behind, so yeah.

– Thanks for letting me ask you about your dreams. I hope you don't think I'm a mad woman.

– I've met worse.

– Thanks very fucking much. Do you mean worse, or weirder?

– Bit of both.

He laughed, and so did I.

In July, about two months after I met Frank, I sent him a short story which I'd written soon after that day in the café. I sent it by email (and used a fake Yahoo account) and I told him the story was a work of fiction based on my 'Nightmares as Catharsis' theory.

In the story a young man with a tattoo of Horace on his hand makes an emergency appointment to see his psychiatrist:

'Thanks for seeing me, Doc.'

'You said it was an emergency.'

'My nightmares are getting more vivid and I keep re-playing them in my head during the day at work. They're so real, like what happens in the dreams are things I've actually done.'

'Patrick, I'm not sure I know what you mean,' he said.

'Like I told you last time, I keep killing people.'

Dr Diffey looked at my bag which was down by my feet. I had no shoes on.

'This killing happens in your dreams, Patrick, so I'm not sure why–'

'Listen to me. I walk down a street with a big-bladed knife in my hand and, when I see an open window, I throw the knife.'

'What's your intention when you throw the knife?'

'To kill whoever's sitting inside the front room of the house.'

'And yet this is a dream, so why are you–'

'Because of what I told you. I want to do the thing in my dreams for real.'

'And who do you want to kill?'

'I've thought about killing you. I know where you have dinner with your wife every Friday night, except for that one week when you didn't go because the restaurant was closed for renovations...'

Dr Diffey got out of his chair and opened the window, which I thought was a bizarre thing to do. If I was going to kill him, I wouldn't do it in his office right in the middle of Deansgate.

'It's a little warm in here,' he said.

That was a lie and I knew it was a lie because he didn't sit down again but stayed standing by the open window and didn't take his jacket off, which is what you're supposed do if you're feeling warm.

'Doctor, the thing is, I keep rehearsing how to kill, exactly like in the dreams.'

'Do you have fantasies about killing other people? Your sister or your mother?'

He asked me about killing my sister because I live with her and she has MS and I've told Dr Diffey that I'm getting sick and tired or looking after her. She says she can't even rip the lid off a bottle of milk, those thin bits of foil on plastic milk bottles.

I once told Dr Diffey that I think my sister fakes most of her symptoms and last week I said I wanted to push her down the stairs when she said: 'It's too hot. This summer is too hot and it's crippling me.'

'No,' I said. 'I think about killing you.'

'Why do you think that is?'

Dr Diffey looked at my jacket.

'Is my coat in the wrong place?'

'No, Patrick, it's fine where it is. But if you'd like to hang it up, there's a coat-hook on the back of the door.'

'I want to kill you in my dreams and what-not because – it's hard to explain – but first of all, you're not really a doctor. You're just a psychoanalyst and anybody can be one of them. And second of all, you talk all the time and never listen. I try to tell you things – like I'm not the same "me" that's in those dreams – but you don't listen and you don't ask questions, all you do is make speeches.'

This was strange because today was the exact opposite of what I'd just said. I was the one doing all the talking and for once – for once in two years – Dr Diffey wasn't doing all the usual things. Usually, I'd be half-way through saying something and he'd lean forward and open his mouth as though he couldn't wait to have his turn to speak. Today was different and better and he wasn't opening his mouth every other half-second like an ugly fish.

In late August (or early September), I was back in the cafe where I met Frank and sitting at the same table – outside, in the corner, under the shade of the awning. I'd just begun some work for a PhD Student when he snuck up behind me.

– Don't you know all that typing will send you blind one day?

– Hi, Frank. Where's your wife?

– She's inside.

– With Pretzel?

– He's at home today.

He sat opposite.

– You don't mind if I sit?

– Of course not.

– How's your article coming along?

– Not too bad. You can read the beginning if you like.

– Why don't you read it for me?

– Okay:

Nabokov cursed his 'poor sleeping' and took 'a strong pill' to give him rest and got no more 'than an hour or two of frightful nightmares'. I've had nightmares all my life but, unlike Nabokov, I don't curse them, don't wish they'd quit, no matter how many, no matter how lunatic or foul. I'm grateful for them.

The insistent and hyper-real violence of my nightmares, the thrashing cruelty played out in the soft hold of sleep has, over time, stemmed the flow and force of my bad memories of the real thing, the kind of memories that might have sent me round the bend, or worse.

– Sounds interesting, he said.

– Thank you.

– I thought your short story was interesting, too.

– That's a nice thing to say.

– Is it autobiographical?

– Christ, no. The main character is a man, for a start, and I'm a woman, and I don't know any psychiatrists called Dr Diffey.

– Maria, I was going to try and contact you after I read the story, but I didn't know your full name.

– Oh?

– My wife and I were concerned.

– Were you?

– Well, the story sounds like a confession and a symptom of repressed rage and we both thought that -

– That's fascinating, I said, but I have to go now.

I got up, quickly walked away, left a full cup of coffee on the table, drove home, watched an episode of *Columbo*, then read until sleep took hold.

When I woke I did nothing: didn't turn on the radio, did no talking, didn't make coffee. I did nothing because I need silence to creep up on the night's dreams in the hope they might show themselves, give me a chance to see, even a scene will do. And, as usual, I wanted to know what my nightmares were made of.

Like Orpheus, we're built to turn round, to look back. We need to satisfy our curiosity whatever the risks, no matter the penalty inflicted by the Underworld. We wake and go back into the 'devil's throat'. The alternative is blind-folded oblivion and so what dangerous yet beautiful sense it makes; the urge to look back so we might unravel the warped things that came while we were down in the dark.

Afterword:

# Bad Dreams

## Isabel Hutchison
University of Manchester

'IT'S JUST A DREAM' is probably most people's response to the recounting of a nightmare. But are dreams truly random concoctions of our imagination, or is there more to it? Maybe our dreams reflect more about ourselves than we would like to admit. M.J. Hyland's mock-autobiographical short story addresses this very question. The protagonist is particularly curious about her dreams because of their violent nature. Unlike other people she asks, Maria finds herself committing crimes she wouldn't ever contemplate in her waking life. She sees her dreaming self as her dark alter-ego – similar to Mr Hyde – acting violently so her waking self doesn't need to.

Although Maria recoils in response to Frank's suggestion of using Freudian dream interpretation, it's easy to see why someone would interpret her theory as compatible with Freud's. In *The Interpretation of Dreams* (1900), Freud argued that dreams allow us to fulfil our deepest and darkest desires. When awake, our preconscious (or super-ego) keeps unruly thoughts at bay, forcing us to conform to social norms. While we dream, the suppressed thoughts disguise themselves in symbolism, giving rise to bizarre and cryptic dream content. In this case, a Freudian would try to reword Maria's theory in terms of her 'dream-self' acting out 'suppressed urges', so her waking self could be more civilized. However, though fascinating in its own right, Freud's dream theory hasn't stood the test of time. Not all dreams reflect a dreamer's urges, and a universal symbolism for dreams seems unlikely at best.

More recent theories on the purpose of dreaming provide a much more robust explanation for dream content, and may even help to elucidate the violent dreams our protagonist experiences. According to one of these models – the Threat Simulation Theory (TST) proposed by Revonsuo (2000) – dreaming allows us to rehearse dangerous situations; be that an attack by a wild animal or an upcoming maths exam. Dreams can be highly emotional, and most dreams are negative in nature, with fear being by far the most commonly reported emotion (Merritt et al., 1994). If facing our fears in our sleep could prepare us for the real thing, we could save ourselves a lot of trouble. According to the TST, the more threatening experiences you have in your waking life, the more common and threatening the encounters become in your dreams. Dream reports from children who have either experienced extreme trauma or have been brought up in a safe environment support this theory (Valli et al., 2005). Our protagonist – who admits to having experienced *some* trauma – is therefore likely to have especially threatening dreams. Patients suffering from Post-Traumatic Stress Disorder struggle with recurrent, traumatic dreams. The level of distress they experience often makes it impossible to sleep through the night.

However, the Threat Simulation Theory doesn't account for the many other emotions commonly experienced in our dreams. Recently, a more expansive theory on the purpose of dreaming has been proposed by J. Allan Hobson from Harvard. His idea is that dreams represent a virtual reality model of our world. Memories from past experiences provide material for the dream content, and we use this to generate future scenarios – in the absence of external influences - to prepare for waking life (Hobson, Hong & Friston, 2014). This helps us to update our knowledge, fix misconceptions, optimise our responses, and ultimately update our model of the world.

It would seem our protagonist's knowledge of her paternal family's crimes and her own trauma are so strongly ingrained in her personal model of the world that it has remained a part of it throughout her life. These dreams may even be triggered by experiences during the day – any seemingly innocuous activity, even watching an episode of *Columbo*!

What's interesting about M.J.'s story is the fact that she describes waking up from her traumatic dreams with a feeling of 'lucid detachment' – she has no fear of committing these crimes and sees them clearly and objectively for what they are. This 'stripping away' of emotion brings to mind the 'sleep to forget, sleep to remember' (SFSR) hypothesis by Walker & Van der Helm (2009). This states that while the memory of emotional events is selectively strengthened during sleep, the emotion *attached* to that memory gradually fades over time. REM sleep – during which the most bizarre and vivid dreams occur – sees a strong activation of emotional regions of the brain. This curious feature of REM sleep, along with a growing body of behavioural evidence, suggests that this stage of sleep is responsible for the processing of emotional memories. How – and whether – this 'emotion-stripping' of memories relates to dreams is unclear. According to recent, and as yet unpublished, findings from our lab at the University of Manchester, it seems we can enhance the strengthening of memory and simultaneous fading of emotion by exposing participants to memory cues (in the form of sounds) during sleep. Though we play the cues during slow wave sleep, the amount of REM sleep during the same night predicts the success of habituation to cued memories; in other words, those sleepers that get a lot of REM sleep habituate the most, while those with low REM sleep become slightly sensitised (i.e. more emotional).

The fact that the narrator of this story comes away from her dreams with a clear head and the determination to avoid violence and crime in real life suggests that, in her case, this 'overnight therapy' has been successful – perhaps she has enjoyed a high proportion of REM sleep (either way, Frank's concerns are probably unjustified).

It seems memories that are reactivated in slow wave sleep

are processed during subsequent REM sleep. How REM sleep mediates the strengthening and 'emotion-stripping' of emotional memories – and how dream theory fits into this – is still a mystery to sleep researchers. In a recent review, we propose that these two processes are separate (Hutchison & Rathore, 2015). During REM sleep, the hippocampus – which deals with recent memories – is disengaged from the neocortex, which stores memories in the long term. According to our model, recent emotional experiences are 'tagged' in the hippocampus. Slow wave sleep then transfers these new memory traces to the neocortex. Dreams may reflect the integration of these transferred memory traces with previous memories.

A major challenge facing anyone attempting to form a bridge between sleep-dependent memory processing and dream research is that, in order to study dream content, researchers must rely on entirely subjective (and fallible) dream reports. Efforts to predict dream content based on brain activity are slowly on the rise (Miyawaki et al, 2008), though we are still far from having a 'live stream' of our nocturnal adventures. For now we must both trust the dreamer's memory, as well as their honesty – and maybe not everyone is as honest as our protagonist.

# References

Freud, S. (1900). *The Interpretation of Dreams*. Franz Deuticke, Leipzig & Vienna.

Hobson J.A., Hong C.C., & Friston K.J. (2014). 'Virtual reality and consciousness inference in dreaming.' *Front Psychol.* 5 p 1133.

Hutchison, I.C., & Rathore, S. (2015). 'The role of REM sleep theta activity in emotional memory'. *Front. Psychol.*, 1st October 2015.

Merritt, J.M., Stickgold, R., Pace-Schott, E., Williams, Hobson, J.A. (1994). 'Emotion Profiles in the Dreams of Men and Women.' *Consciousness and Cognition*, 3 (1), pp 46-60.

Miyawaki, Y., Uchida, H., Yamashita, O., Sato, M., Morito, Y., Tanabe, H.C., Sadato, N., Kamitani, Y. (2008). 'Visual Image Reconstruction from Human Brain Activity using a Combination of Multiscale Local Image Decoders.' *Neuron,* 60 (5), pp 915–929.

Revonsuo, A. (2000). 'The reinterpretation of dreams: An evolutionary hypothesis of the function of dreaming.' *Behavioral and Brain Sciences*, 23 (6), pp 877- 901

Valli, K., Revonsuo, A., Pälkäs, O., Ismail, K.H., Ali, K.J., Punamäki, R-J., 2005. 'The threat simulation theory of the evolutionary function of dreaming: Evidence from dreams of traumatized children.' *Consciousness and Cognition*, 14(1), pp 188-218.

Walker M.P. & Van der Helm, E. (2009). 'Overnight therapy? The role of sleep in emotional brain processing.' *Psychol Bull.* 135 (5), pp 731-48.

# The Rip Van Winkle Project

## Sara Maitland

HYPNOS, WHO IS BOTH the God of sleep and its personification, stirs in his sunless cave. He relaxes briefly into his sleep inertia, then sits up, stretches his arms and fumbles out his ear-plugs which he places tidily on the rocky shelf beside his huge black-canopied bed. Now he can just hear the last quiet lapping of the river that flows through the cave while he sleeps; mortals believe it is Lethe, the river of forgetting. They are, as so often, very much mistaken. While Hypnos sleeps the gentle flow of the river distributes all the sensations, ideas and memories of the previous day through his brain which then sorts, retains or rejects them – consolidating, clarifying, organising and allocating them most usefully throughout his consciousness.

Morpheus, shape shifter, psychologist and bringer of dreams, swings down from his black horse, pats her flank casually, hands her reins to a waiting servant and goes into his house. The last hours before sunrise are his busiest time, for most vivid dreaming is done shortly before waking. Now he can relax – he drops his bag of tricks near the front-door, sinks into a deep armchair and with an amused grin re-reads a chapter from his well worn copy of Sigismund Freud's seminal work of 1900.

The lovely nymph Circadia, guardian of the deep rhythms of the turning world, rises with the first paling of the night and as the sky turns from indigo to peach she begins again and forever her beautiful rhythmic dancing in the birch groves of Arcadia. Even in the fullness of summer the light on the mossy ground is dappled bright and playful, and the individual blossoms of the thick cow-wheat under-storey turn towards her with joy.

A little later, though not enough later in her opinion, Sally Brampton, fourteen years old and grouchy with it, necks the first of the cans of Irn-Bru she has hidden in her bedroom cupboard. Her mother does not approve of her having sweet drinks in her bedroom but what the hell does the old witch know about anything? She needs the stuff to get her going, just like she needs her Nan's stolen sleeping pills to get her to sleep. The caffeine takes a while to kick in, but she can already hear her mother winding up into a screech about the school bus, about being late, being idle, being insolent. She struggles into her uniform trying to convince herself that the uncomfortable line where her bra digs into her flesh proves she is developing a tasty cleavage, and not as the stupid bat 'teasingly' calls it 'puppy-fat.' She is bleary, sulky, spotty and has not done her homework.

Matt Oliver, stressed about his GCSEs and how distressed his mother is going to be when finally he reveals his mock results to her, wakes to discover that when he fell asleep barely five hours ago, he had left the lights, his computer, his TV and his glasses on. The last is the most serious, as he knows he will have a thumping headache all day. Briefly he cannot face it and pushing his spectacles off his face, curls up again and tries to forget it all – the weariness, the hopelessness, the headaches, the bullying – none of which he can tell his mother about because she will look tragic and whine about his father leaving them. Then he realises she will whine if he doesn't get off to school on time and drags himself reluctantly out of bed. He is bleary, anxious, depressed and has not done his homework

A typical morning for all five of them.

As he comes to full consciousness Hypnos remembers what had been worrying him the day before and finds, with pleasure but not much surprise, that he now knows what to do about it. No hurry though – it is important and can therefore wait for a few hours until he reaches full wakefulness and effectiveness.

Eventually he gets up and does his morning exercises, although it may not actually be morning according to Apollo's brutal chronology. Hypnos lives in the dark to maintain his own steady inner day which happens to be set to 26.374 hours, rather than the more vulgar timing of the sun. There is a fierce simplicity in the hearts of the Gods which means that they act from their own core not from the hints or entrainments of the world. After that he gets dressed; being a God he sleeps naked; being a Greek god he takes his exercise naked as well; but in his waking time he wears a pair of striped flannel pyjamas with white buttons and a traditional plaited cotton draw-string.

Only after all this and a nutritious breakfast does he turn his mind to business. First he sends for his son Morpheus, even though just thinking about the youth makes him feel peevish. Over the centuries dreams have been given greater and greater importance and from his father's point of view the God of dreams has become rather above himself. Sometimes he even acts as though sleep was simply an occasion for what Morpheus insists on calling 'the processing of sub-conscious materials.' Really! Nonetheless Hypnos knows Morpheus will have to be consulted. Then, with considerably more pleasure, he decides he can justify inviting Circadia, whose loveliness will certainly cheer him up.

They arrive with gratifying promptness – Circadia gliding in and placing a daughterly kiss on his cheek; Morpheus manifesting suddenly from the ceiling, greeting his father with a distinctly unfilial nod, and saying somewhat truculently, 'So, what's all this about then?'

Hypnos draws himself together, notes his own paternal patience and long suffering good temper with some pride and begins his carefully prepared oration.

'My dear Children...'

'She isn't,' says Morpheus sneering at Circadia.

'My dear Children, for so you both seem to me, I have called this urgent meeting because of my deep concern about the state of the world. About the foolishness of mortals. About the profoundly worrying contempt and disregard with which they appear to hold us. This would seem to be directed solely at my jurisdiction – they still worship the gods of Power, Money, War and Sex. But it has come to my somnolent ear that they say things like, 'Sleep is for wimps,' 'Sleep is for cowards, for sluggards and time wasters.' They say people who want to go home to bed aren't made of the 'right stuff', aren't 'with the programme'. It isn't about money – they're bullying each other into working inefficiently and for far too long for free. Even when they aren't working they are up all night – shopping, something called 'onlining', even just staying awake to watch television shows they say are rubbish. I do not understand what is happening. I want to know why. That is why I have called you in.'

'CBT' says Morpheus.

'What?' asks Hypnos; suddenly he sounds old, frail.

'Nonsense,' says Circadia firmly. 'That's just silly. CBT, Hypnos, or to be slightly clearer, Cognitive Behavioural Therapy, is a treatment for their mental difficulties that doesn't really bother much about dreams. Watch my lips, Morpheus; it... is... NOT... all... about... dreams. It is not all about you.'

'Circadia,' replies Morpheus gently – and how can a voice be so soft and so cold? – 'what are you most afraid of?'

She looks away quickly, fixes her eyes on the middle button of Hypnos' pyjamas – the silliest, safest thing in all her immediate view; but even as she focuses her eyes she is hideously aware that this will not work. The God of Dreams always knows, always rides his black steed straight into one's deepest terror... and suddenly, inevitably, her birch trees are burning, burning, their delicate fingering branches are burning, the flames and smoke rising into the pure blue evening sky, and the grove of special ganglia at the deepest back of her eyes and their delicate fingering nerve branches like birch twigs that reach into her brain and deliver the light which no one sees to her suprachiasmatic nuclei are burning. Her eyes are burning and she will be blinded, completely blinded, eyeless and she will not be able to find the rhythm of waking and sleeping, doing and restoring, the deep rhythm of life to which she dances... and... and she will go reeling into the smoky chaos, blind, never sleeping, never waking, never knowing the shape of light and dark, of day and night, never...

...But she is tough and, for all she is immortally young and lovely she is more ancient even than dreams, evolved independently in every life form, secure inside the skull bones of birds, the eyes of mammals, the sap of leaves. In that powerful resilience she pulls back from the chasm of terror and reiterates, 'No Morpheus, no. I am not afraid of dreams. It... is... NOT... all... about... dreams. It is not all about you.'

'Bugger' says Morpheus nonchalantly as though it were all a joke.

'What are you two on about?' says Hypnos querulously.

'Morpheus, as usual, thinks that everything is about him and his dreams, but I don't agree. That's all.'

'But, if you don't agree with Morpheus, what do you think has caused this lamentable lack of, er, deference, this growing abuse of sleep, this... this... I mean it can't be about belief; everyone believes in sleep even if they don't believe in me – what is going on?'

'I've thought about it,' she says, 'I've thought about it a lot. And I think it is about electricity.'

'El-ek-triss-it-tee,' Morpheus makes a sound somewhere between an oath and a snort, 'Oh come on.'

'Well I don't mean electricity itself, I mean electric lights. You know what they are like, those mortals – if they can do something they always think it is clever to do it. Just over a century ago they killed the night, the darkness, and now there are children growing up who have never seen the Milky Way, who have never sat round a glowing fire and listened to old stories and learned to tell them, who are not afraid of the dark because they have never been in the dark, who are being made ill and stunted and accident prone and miserable because they are too tired, because they have broken the rhythm, because all the night business – even dreams, Morpheus, even dreams – is not getting done. Of course there is deep magic in light at night – fireworks, the Aurora, the Beltane Fire, meteor showers, even the full moon reflected silver on water, and mother coming in with a candle when you wake and the holy sisters singing through the darkness. But they... they are tired and fretful and sickly, because it is never truly dark for them and if it is not dark it cannot ever be light either; if they do not sleep deeply, they cannot be fully awake.'

There is a long pause.

Then Hypnos says, 'I still don't understand. If they are tired all the time, why don't they notice, why don't they just turn the electric lights off? Why aren't they out sacrificing black cockerels, or whatever it is they do now, at my altars?'

'Because they are stupid,' says Morpheus.

'I think,' says the nymph, a little sadly, 'it is something about them, something strange, something... perhaps... I don't know, but something we immortals got wrong for them. If they don't have something they know they need, they always pretend they don't need it; they always try to despise it. They suffer from anhedonia. I mean, everyone knows, that coffee and bitter chocolate at bedtime stops you sleeping so what do they make into the smartest, grandest, most highly rated, socially admired thing to end an evening feast with? *After Eight* mints and black coffee. Then instead of saying I'm tired now, I will turn the lights out and go to bed, they put lights in their bedrooms and say that being tired proves you are a weakling. Don't think I haven't tried. I've taught them and shown them – I've even revealed my secrets; the beautiful, elegant inner clock that is both wired in to their brains, intact, always present and at the same time is responsive, flexible, self-regulating. And those magical ganglia, not the old rod and cone ones that let them see, but the other more mysterious ones that are sensitive to light but not to sight, that tell their inner brains that it is daytime or night-time, time to wake, time to sleep. They know all that now – and they study it and research it and work on it and worry about what will happen on Mars where the light is red-shifted and the rotation too slow – and then, and then', her (exceptionally lovely) bosom heaves with indignation, 'and then they give their children televisions and computers and nightlights and music machines that fill their heads with noise; and they persuade themselves that it is somehow cruel and repressive to send the young people to bed, to sleep. They just refuse to get it.'

She pauses. The other two are silent. She says, apologetically, 'I am sorry. I do go on. But sometimes I despair.'

There is a longer, gentler pause; then Hypnos says,

'That all sounds sadly probable to me. What do you think, Morpheus?'

Like many gay men Morpheus has a sort of tenderness towards pretty young women who do not fancy him but are not in any way offended by his sexuality. So he shrugs his shoulders almost benignly and says,

'OK. Well, why don't we run with it?'

Hypnos is beginning to feel sleepy again; it makes him a little tetchy. 'Alright, alright; but what do we DO?'

Morpheus looks blank.

'We need to re-entrain them,' says Circadia, 'I think that we start with the teenagers.'

'Oh? Why?'

'Well, they are suffering the most. You know, no one pays any attention to that delay in their sleep cycle. Their grown-ups give them rooms which are entirely unsuited to sleeping anyway with all those lights just when they need darkness, and then they are dragged out of bed hours before they are ready and bullied and harassed about being lazy and wasting the day and being uncooperative or rude. And they get hungry and fat which makes them miserable as well as prone to Type 2 Diabetes, and they feel all stressed, and their immune systems are undermined and they can't concentrate and they are just weary, exhausted the whole time – and then they get blamed for it. I should think they would be all set up for what I have in mind – making them into sort of Ambassadors of Sleep, High priests of Hypnos. And teenagers do love to know better than anyone around them.'

She needs the two of them on-side. She glances round trying to gauge their response; Hypnos is yawning and Morpheus has begun to clean his nails with his pocket knife. There is nothing for it but a bold approach,

'So' she says, 'we are going to abduct them.'

Hypnos' eye-lids, which had been drooping, shoot up abruptly. Morpheus is sufficiently startled to jerk and cut his finger. 'Fuck,' he says, and then not wanting to admit to pain, says, 'don't be ridiculous. You know bloody well that's not allowed.'

'Well,' she says, 'they aren't going to complain and anyway no one will know we have abducted them – we are going to call it re-mythologising. Even the Olympians will like it.'

'You see in every culture there are stories about heroes and heroines who fall asleep for a long, long time – and wake to good things: Vishnu sleeping the world into existence, Adam sleeping so that Eve can be made from his rib, The Squirrel hunter of the Seneca Nation, The Seven Sleepers of Ephesus, the Harper of the Ring of Brogar, Honi M'agel... you can probably think of lots more. We do not kidnap the young people; we let them believe they are in their favourite stories. We take them somewhere they want to be and we make it dark all night so they sleep until they wake and then golden bright all day and we let them move to the rhythms of their own bodies until they come fully alive again.

'In fact,' she becomes suddenly efficient, whipping a small notebook out of a fold in her tunic, 'in fact I have selected two individuals we could start with: Sally Brampton and Matt Oliver. They are both in grave sleep-derivation trouble.' She summarises their situations.

Hypnos grunts, depressed, 'They sound pretty desperate cases,' he comments, 'Why them?'

'Well, good point. Sally is, underneath all that rubbish, genuinely articulate and remarkably astute – you can see it in her ability to supply herself with both sleeping and waking drugs with no one noticing. I believe she is a natural politician; a born leader of a pro-sleep campaign. But she has a crucial feature – secretly she still believes in the fairy stories, in Cinderella, Snow White and, most importantly from our point of view in Sleeping Beauty. She wants to be in the story; she wants to be the Princess. She would not admit it, but it's true.

With Matt it is a bit different, perhaps more of a risk but... with teenagers and art it is always difficult to be sure; mortals' creativity always seems problematic. They get deflected, distracted so easily. But I believe he is a contemplative, a potential poet. He is highly practised not just in living with mythic fantasy, but in taking control of it – it is about all he does do. And,' she pauses, glancing sideways, blushing slightly, 'and I think Morpheus will enjoy him.'

'Oh dear,' says Hypnos.

'He's over sixteen,' she says hastily.

'Oh Ho,' says Morpheus cheerfully.

'It is more of a problem though to know quite how to lure him in. I thought about elves, but he's a bit old for that or aliens, but somehow aliens without electrical power doesn't seem to me to work. And werewolves and vampires and zombies are creatures of the night themselves – we can hardly expect him to go to sleep in the dark if we have persuaded him he has been abducted by any of them. So I think it will have to be super-hero stuff and I don't know much about that.'

Morpheus suddenly re-engages. He grins and says, 'Vikings.'

'Vikings?'

'Yeah, or Celtic warriors. I use them quite a lot with sulky young men – they like the idea of being heroic and killing lots of things and history makes it safer for them, less guilty. I'm sure your lad would enjoy being carried off by pirates, especially if they are wearing horned helmets – very Freudian.'

Hypnos is entering his homeostatic sleepiness phase. He is not one to ignore its demands. He makes a show of decisiveness, 'Good. Yes. Excellent. Thank you, Circadia. I am very grateful. Get it organised, will you.'

And so it is.

A year later Sally Brampton – detoxed, fit, braless and fierce – is organising a strike in her school: No Registration before 10am. She has a beautifully researched and presented dossier of facts, an exceptionally efficient administrative team (although they giggle a lot and always meet in the dark) and a powerfully effective rhetoric. After her articulate and witty local radio interview the strike spreads to other schools; the matter is brought up in parliament; sleep becomes a topic of national and political importance. Teenagers' late waking needs are enshrined in the new Bill of Rights. Sally still dreams of the Sleeping Beauty, but now when her handsome prince slashes his way through the undergrowth and finds the castle and climbs the spiral staircase to her thick curtained chamber and sees her, exquisitely beautiful and sound asleep, he does not disturb her. He unbuckles his scabbard, strips off his princely garments, puts on a pair of striped flannel pyjamas with white buttons and a traditional plaited cotton drawstring and snuggles in beside her for a long, long snooze.

A year later Matt Oliver has discovered contact lenses, the local gym, post-modernism and sex. He has lost his listlessness, his suicidal ideation and his virginity. His boyfriend finds his striped flannel pyjamas with white buttons and a traditional plaited cotton draw-string hilarious but only in a rather touching and tender way. His mother likes his boy friend and is trying to acquire one of her own (although both the boys think she is a bit naive about online dating). He still plays fantasy games occasionally, but increasingly prefers chess and is developing what he happily knows to be the slightly nerdy hobby of restoring old clocks. He is a bit too fond of Wagner, but will grow out of that Nordic angst. He records his florid but profoundly satisfying dreams in a note book and broods on their meaning and significance with a healthy adolescent mixture of self-admiration and self-irony. Over the next ten years the notebooks will evolve into his extraordinary debut novel, which will have wide ranging influence among young people and will make him very happy.

Morpheus and Circadia become better friends. He visits her in her grove some mornings after his night ride is completed. He loves to watch her dancing in the dappled dawn light.

One day he asks her, 'What made you think of it?'

She looks thoughtful and perhaps a little shy. 'I kept trying to think about who were the losers from this electricity plague, because of course there have been lots of gains, lots and lots of good things too. And it seemed to me that turning our backs on the night, bringing the light, bright and busy into what ought to be the dark... the losers were us, the deep rhythms, the patterns of sleep, of life itself, and... and also the old stories: electrical lighting dealt them a mortal wound. Once people could be productive after nightfall something fundamental changed. You could read, work... Story telling is unproductive – there is no marketable commodity. It needs shadow and leisure and time to grow and shape itself. And of course, that was us too – because we are only stories after all, we gods and immortals and the deep dancing.'

Morpheus looks up sharply, but she smiles and says gently, 'I know, I know, Morpheus, but it is not all about dreams... So then I started to think that they were sort of the same in a way – that the old stories and the photo-sensitive retinal ganglia were alike. They both draw light in and then they do not use for anything obvious or practical or busy – not to see NOW with, but to re-set the inner clocks. And without that they do not seem to do well, those mortals. So it was just a matter of bringing them back together.'

'They still dream though,' he says stubbornly.

'Yes of course they do,' she says, reaching up and stroking his black horse's silky muzzle, 'of course they do. That is part of it, Morpheus – dreams are part of it. Grow up.' But she smiles her sweet smile and he laughs at himself. He gives her a quick hug, swings up onto his horse and gallops off. She returns to her dancing.

Hypnos sleeps. Hypnos dreams and because he is the God of sleep his dreams are his own; neither Morpheus' nor Freud's. At least so he believes. He smiles in his sleep and turns over, pulling the blanket of the dark more snugly around his head. He sleeps.

Afterword:

# The Circadian Masterclock

## Prof. Russell G. Foster, CBE, FRS
University of Oxford

THERE HAVE BEEN OVER a trillion dawns and dusks since life began some 3.8 billion years ago. During that time the earth's daily rotation from sunrise to sunset has slowed to almost exactly 24 hours – or 23 hours 56 minutes and 4 seconds to be precise. The physiology, metabolism and behaviour of organisms, including us, are aligned to this daily cycle through internal clocks which enable an organism to effectively 'know' the time and in many species the date. Those organisms that anticipate this predictable change in the environment, and synchronise their internal biology in advance of the changed conditions, will gain an advantage over both their competitors and predators.

The clock also stops everything happening within an organism at the same time and ensures that biological processes occur in the appropriate sequence. For cells to function properly they need the right materials in the right place at the right time. Thousands of genes have to be switched on and off in order and in concert. Proteins, enzymes, fats, carbohydrates, hormones, nucleic acids and other compounds have to be absorbed, broken down, metabolised and produced in a precise time window. Energy has to be obtained and then partitioned across the cellular economy and allocated to growth, reproduction, metabolism, locomotion, cellular repair. All of these processes and many others take energy and all have to be timed to best effect by the millisecond, second, minute, day and time of year. Without this internal temporal compartmentalisation our biology would be in chaos.

The mechanisms underlying circadian rhythms involve circadian oscillations in gene expression, protein modifications and ultimately behaviour. These oscillations are controlled by the signals of the core clock genes. To be biologically useful, these rhythms must be synchronised or entrained to the external environment, predominantly by the patterns of light and dark produced by the earth's rotation, but also by rhythmic changes in environmental factors such as temperature; food availability; rainfall and even predation. The key point is that the rhythms are not driven by a response to rhythmic external influences but are generated internally and locked on to (entrained) to external cycles, usually by light.

Circadian (*circa* about, *diem* a day) rhythms are innate and hard-wired into the genomes of just about every plant, animal, fungus, algae on the planet and even cyanobacteria (a type of photosynthetic bacteria). In humans, our daily patterns of sleeping and waking, eating and drinking depend not just on an alarm clock or how much exercise we have done or the adverts we see on television, but also fundamentally on what our internal biological clocks are instructing us to do. When left without time cues, such as deep underground or in experimental isolation chambers, our endogenous clocks still tick and still attempt to drive us. Our physiology is organized around the daily cycle of activity and sleep. In the active phase, when energy expenditure is higher and food and water are consumed, organs need to be prepared for the intake, processing, and uptake of nutrients. The activity of organs such as the stomach, liver, small intestine, pancreas and the blood supply to these organs need internal synchronisation, which a clock can provide. During sleep, although energy expenditure and digestive processes decrease, many essential activities occur including cellular repair, toxin clearance, and memory consolidation and information processing by the brain. Disrupting this pattern, as happens with jet-lag, shiftwork or even some teenagers leads to internal desynchrony of the circadian network and our ability to do the right thing at the right time is greatly impaired. Such disruption in sleep and circadian rhythms can result in major impacts upon our health, some of which are summarised as follows:

| Emotion | Cognition | Physiology & Health |
|---|---|---|
| *Increased:* | *Impaired:* | *Increased risk of:* |
| Mood fluctuations | Cognitive Performance | Drowsiness |
| Depression & psychosis | Ability to multi-task | Microsleeps |
| Irritability | Memory | Unintended sleep |
| Impulsivity | Attention | Sensations of pain & |
| Frustration | Concentration | cold |
| Risk-Taking | Communication | Cancer |
| Stimulant use | Decision-making | Metabolic |
| (e.g. caffeine) | Creativity | abnormailities |
| Sedative use | Productivity | Diabetes II |
| (e.g. alcohol) | Motor performance | Cardiovascular disease |
| Illegal drug use | | Reduced immunity |
| Dissociated mental | | Altered endocrine |
| processing | | function |

Although an individual's body clock and sleep/wake timing is profoundly influenced by genetics, sleep timing is not fixed through development. Under the influence of the changing hormonal environment of puberty, the clock often gets later from childhood through adolescence, reaching peak lateness in women at 19-and-a-half and in men at 21, meaning that young adults tend to want to stay in bed in the morning. With age, individuals move to an earlier phase so that by the time we are in our late 50's and early 60's our sleep timing resembles that of late childhood.

On average the circadian rhythms of an individual in their late teens will be around two hours delayed compared with an individual in their 50's. As a result the average teenager experiences considerable sleep loss, and asking a teenager to get-up at 07.00 in the morning is the equivalent of asking a

50 year old to get up at 05.00 in the morning. Teenagers are biologically pre-disposed to get up late and go to bed late, but this predisposition has been exaggerated because of the human invasion of the night by artificial light and because societal/parental attitudes towards 'bed time' have become more relaxed. Bedrooms have been transformed from places of sleep to places of entertainment, packed full of electronic devices – with 24/7 access to the internet which further delays the onset of sleep. Bed times are pushed later, but the alarm on a school day still goes off at the same time. It has been estimated that for full cognitive performance teenagers need about 9 hours sleep each night. Many get far less than 6.5 hours on a school night.

The scientific evidence of the importance of sleep is overwhelming. Elegant research has demonstrated the critical role of sleep in memory consolidation and in the enhancement of our ability to generate innovative solutions to complex problems. In addition, impulsive behaviours, lack of empathy, our sense of humour and mood are all markedly modulated by the amount of sleep we experience. Sleep disruption increases the level of the stress hormone cortisol. Just one lost night can raise cortisol levels by nearly 50 per cent by the following evening. The grumpy, stressed, moody, insensitive and angry adolescent is usually also a tired adolescent. Perhaps less intuitively, sleep loss is associated with a range of metabolic abnormalities. Young men who slept only four hours on only six consecutive nights showed a major impairment in their ability to regulate their blood-glucose, exhibiting insulin levels comparable to the early stages of diabetes. Allied studies have shown that sleep loss elevates the hunger hormone ghrelin and depresses the hormone leptin, which gives us our sense of feeling full. In view of these results, perhaps long-term sleep deprivation might be an important pre-disposing factor to chronic conditions such as diabetes, obesity, and hypertension – which are now alarmingly common in adolescents.

Sleep deprived adolescents are turning increasingly to stimulants to compensate for their sleep loss. Caffeinated and sugar-rich drinks are invariably the stimulant of choice. There is considerable individual variation in how quickly caffeine is metabolised, but the half-life of caffeine is between 5-9 hours. So an afternoon or evening caffeinated drink will delay sleep at night. Caffeine, of course, is not the only stimulant used by teenagers. Nicotine consumption also improves alertness, concentration, reaction times, and short-term memory. Tiredness increases the likelihood of smoking. Collectively, after a day of caffeine and nicotine consumption; the biological tendency for delayed sleep; and the increased alertness promoted by computer or mobile phone use, sleep is not easy! Sedatives may then be sought in the form of sleeping pills and/or alcohol. One 13 year old teenager I interviewed recently said that she had no problem getting to sleep at night because she used sleeping pills. Although alcohol and sleeping pills induce sedation, they do not provide a biological mimic of sleep. Indeed, some of the restorative benefits of sleep can be inhibited by these agents. Teenagers, like night-shift workers, are particularly vulnerable of falling into a 'stimulant-sedative feedback loop' using alcohol or sleeping pills to sedate the brain, followed by increasing levels of stimulants to promote wakefulness.

To improve both school performance and teenage health, several schools in the USA have implemented a delayed start to classes along with education relating to the importance and regulation of sleep (sleep education or sleep 'Cognitive Behavioural Therapy'). After the later start, academic performance and attendance increased, whilst depression and self-harm declined. Such findings are consistent with a small UK study at Monkseaton High School, North Tyneside. School start times were shifted from 08:50 to 10:00. This led to an increase in the percentage of pupils crossing an attainment threshold from 35% to 53%, and in those children classified as socially disadvantaged the increase was from 12% to 42%.

Whilst it is true that most school regimes still force teenagers to function at a time of day that is sub-optimal, a later start by itself is not enough. The population in general, and teenagers in particular, must start to take sleep seriously. Sleep is not a luxury or an indulgence but a fundamental part of our biology enhancing our creativity, productivity, mood and ability to interact with others. If you are dependent upon an alarm clock, or parent, to get you out of bed; if you take a long time to wake up; if you feel sleepy and irritable during the day; if your behaviour is overly impulsive, you are probably not getting enough sleep. Take control and try and develop a structured bedtime routine. Ensure the bedroom is a place that promotes sleep, ensure it is dark and not too warm; Stop texting, working on the computer and watching TV at least a half-hour before trying to sleep; Do things that help you relax and wind-down; Avoid bright light before bed which promotes alertness; Try not to nap during the day, which will delay sleep; Seek out natural light in the morning which adjusts the body clock and sleep timing to an earlier time; Avoid caffeinated drinks after lunch-time.

It is my strongly held view, based upon the available evidence, that the efforts by dedicated teachers and the money spent on facilities will deliver a more rewarding educational experience when adolescents, parents, teachers and school governors start to take adolescent sleep and circadian rhythms seriously.

# Benzene Dreams

## Sarah Schofield

DAVID SHOWS ME INTO his office.

'I think you need to stop and think before investing,' I say as I sit down. 'We're heading for trouble.'

David frowns. He perches on his desk and taps a pen against my file. 'Phil – you're sitting on a goldmine. Honestly, stop worrying about it.' He pushes a Starbucks cup towards me. 'Here. I got you one.'

'Sorry. I don't...' I stare at the cup.

'Oh, drink it. I've bought it now anyway.'

I move it closer and then slide it to one side. I pull myself nearer the desk. My chair is too low. 'Users will get angry. We'll be hijacking their dreams, David.'

'Not you. Not us. The advertisers…' He holds out a box of cherry bakewells. He has soft brown eyes. I feel genuinely worried for him.

I shake my head. 'It's invasive. The app is supposed to just be a bit of fun. I came by today to let you know I'm withdrawing the product. Thanks for expressing an interest, but –'

'Wait, just wait... My solicitors have already drawn up the paperwork.' He stares out of the window and I watch him staring.

'Please stop badgering me about this…' I look at the pot plant on the table. The pebbles over the surface look dry. I want to touch it to see if it's real.

'It's in the terms and conditions, isn't it? About the pop-up ads.'

I nod.

'Every user has to agree to it.'

The Dreamsolvr file is on top of a stack of files on his desk. The heading – *Dreamsolvr: solve your problems through dreaming!* – slopes across the manila.

'The commercial aspect. It doesn't sit comfortably…'

'Are you serious?' He leans back in his chair.

'There'll be legal implications. What if the app makes leading suggestions? Like what if a legal firm is advertising cheap divorces and someone gets a divorce when they didn't even want one and –'

David is smiling. 'Do you honestly think that any judge would believe your app could be responsible for regrettable life choices?'

'It's not funny.'

'It's ridiculous. The in-app adverts will be targeted; a symptom of other internet use, a user already looking online to solve a problem.'

'I'm saying this as clearly as I can, David –'

'Listen to me. Users will dream about these things because they're already doing them… Trying to find solutions on the internet, which the advertisers target and latch onto in the app ad pop-ups and –'

'Or are the ads causing them to dream about it and *then* search the internet, which then feeds the targeting of the adverts in later use? It's reducing the dreamer's gene pool. Giving people Benzene dreams.' I draw a circle in the air. 'Like a snake eating its tail.'

He is looking at me blankly. 'Don't you want to make a lot of money very easily?'

I stare at the coffee cup.

'This app, with my help, is going to make you a ton. Bigger than Candy Crush. Bigger than Angry Birds.'

I shrink back. 'Then this app won't solve problems it'll just create new ones. The same as the adverts.'

He flicks the file closed. 'I'm ready to go all the way with this. Are you with me?'

'You're heading for trouble. That's all I can tell you.'

'Why are you resisting? Is there something you're not telling me? Is there another interested party?'

I do not say anything. I try to remember where I am.

He sighs. 'Why don't you sleep on it? I'll call you tomorrow.'

I just manage to catch the train. I sit as it leaves the station and I spend the first few minutes of the journey watching an empty juice bottle roll back and forth along the aisle. We speed past the damp, grey city outskirts, buddleia blooming like mould from the brickwork. Further down the carriage a man is eating crabsticks one after the other from a packet. A small dog sits at his feet looking up at him. My eyes are heavy as I lean back in my seat. I enter some data on the Dreamsolvr app. I type quickly while the dream is still in my memory.

I am supposed to meet her in this National Trust car park. I'm leaning against the fence watching a man feed a handful of silver into the ticket machine which clatters out, rejected. I pat my pockets to see if I have any change.

A woman stands beside the stile at the far end of the car park. She is looking at me. I go over.

'Diane?'

'Let's get moving shall we?' She turns and I follow her up the pebbly fell path. We cross a bridge and climb over a gate.

'There were other apps we looked at; bingo and a dating one. But yours, with the dream element, goes deeper. It'll have a profound effect. You could make a huge difference in society. You'd be a hero.'

I scoff and she looks over at me. 'A silent one, of course.'

The path becomes more rugged as it rises, following the contour of the fell. A tarn glitters darkly below. Izzie and Sophia would love it here. I am wearing the wrong shoes.

'Just let me double check I've got this.' Diane turns to me. 'So dreaming is the brain's way of solving problems –'

'Yes, but it's not always completely –'

'And this app speeds up the process, by telling your brain to focus on specific problems?'

'Have you tried it?'

'But the dreamer, our app user, won't necessarily start having lots of zany dreams? The sort they'll bore all their friends and colleagues with and want to share on social media?'

'Not at all. It's in the non-REM phase… where your dreams are very ordinary. It sustains you there for longer, replaying those problems.'

'A dangerous tool in the wrong hands?' She looks across at me, and heat rises to my face.

I look at the footpath and continue, 'The app samples the dream data you've put in and eventually learns how to match dream elements with the EEG patterns it's read.' I glance over at Diane. She nods for me to carry on. 'You then tell it what you want solving in your life. It waits until you dream about that problem, then it stimulates your brain to keep dreaming about that one thing specifically, until… hey presto, you wake up the next day having subconsciously solved it.'

'How does it know the specific thing will show up?'

'It doesn't know anything; it calculates that sooner or later you will; you dream of thousands of different things each night.'

A man passes with a Jack Russell and I stop to scratch its ears. When I look up Diane has continued on the path without me. I run to catch up.

'I was wondering… Why did you want to meet here?' I push my hands into my pockets. I touch something cold and metallic. A dog whistle. The last time I wore this jacket Dynamo was alive. I squeeze the whistle in my palm inside my pocket as we walk along.

'This is… sensitive. We needed to be out of range.'

I stare at the steel sky.

'This conversation never happened.'

'Okay,' I say. I hunch my shoulders up against the cold.

'But there's another reason we came here.'

The path curves around the hill and opens up a view across the valley, sculpted like a heather-brindled slumbering beast. Beside the path, a rock face juts from the heather. Diane sits in the shelter of the stone and I perch beside her, the cold seeping through my jeans. A sheep's broken call echoes across the fell.

'Who do you see... or a better question, who do you never see in places like this?'

I clear my throat. 'I'm not sure...'

'The hard up, the deprived, the unemployed. Your app could open this up to people who would never even think to come. Never get to see it.'

'By manipulating their thoughts? That's not how the app is supposed to be used, just dropping things in –'

'Don't think of it as manipulation.' Diane leans forward. 'We all want a healthier, happier society. Your app will enable us to actualize our election promises. Increase the happiness quotient.'

'Quotient?'

She takes a packet of organic choc-chip cookies from her rucksack and holds them towards me. I don't want one but I take one anyway.

'We could pour a load more funding into TV campaigns for better, positive lifestyles, work motivation, healthier living, or we can draw those campaigns into a format that seems to have a more effective reach.'

'So people will dream about the gym because of your messages in the app and then they'll decide to go?'

'No, Philip.' She looks affronted. 'The other way around. If this is something their brain is already processing as a way to solve their own obesity, or... social inertia problem, we will facilitate the action quicker.'

'And it will look good for you because it's in your manifesto,' I say.

'Sometimes you have to take the ethical higher ground.'

Down in the valley, sheep cluster together, chewing on the patchy grass.

'You understand how sensitive this information is, don't you? To really effect change, society needs to be naïve.' We sit for a while and then she adds, 'You like it here; places like this.'

I turn to her. She gazes back, unflinching. There is a picture of me leaning windswept against a cairn on a Facebook profile, illustrating a life that people believe is mine. It has likes and comments from friends I don't really know. The photo replaced one of me with the old dog, Dynamo looking noble in the garden. My page is mostly made up of links to petitions; anti-fracking, Amnesty, news articles… that Izzie has posted and I've dutifully shared.

'You'd be doing something important for your country.'

My cheeks burn. Something glints across the valley in the heather. I blink, pretend not to have noticed it.

'They're like lambs. And your app will be the shepherd.' She touches my arm. 'We'll contact you in a few days' time. You understand how important it is to keep absolutely quiet on this.'

I wake on the sofa. Since getting home this evening, I haven't spoken properly to Izzie. I stand and creep up the stairs. Sophia's bedroom door is ajar. I sit outside on the landing, listening to Izzie reading her a story.

'He cut out the work again overnight and found it done in the morning, as before; and so it went on for some time: what was got ready in the evening was always done by daybreak, and the shoemaker soon became thriving and well off again.'

Izzie nearly trips over me as she slips out of the door.

When we get to the kitchen I ask, 'How many times?'

'Three tonight.'

'Those bloody interfering elves.'

'I find them creepy. I find it creepy how much Sophia loves them.'

I laugh and pour her a glass of wine.

'How did your meeting go?' she asks.

'Yeah, fine.'

She unzips Sophia's lunchbox and looks expectantly at me. I peel the Fairtrade label from the bananas in the fruit bowl and press it onto the back of my hand and then peel it off again.

After a moment she asks, 'What did they say?'

The bananas are speckled with black. 'I only bought these the other day,' I say. 'It's frustrating that the normal sort seem to last longer –'

'The meeting?' She raises her eyebrows.

'There's a non-disclosure agreement…'

She snaps a banana from the bunch and drops it into the lunchbox. 'Right.'

'Sorry, it's just…'

'No. Fine.'

The house is so still and my eyes fall to the corner where Dynamo's bed used to be. I'd crouch there in that spot for ages scratching his ears, his eyes half-closed, while pins and needles spread through my legs.

'We could always get another.'

I look over. Izzie is staring at me. I get out my phone and open the app screen. I read the Problem Suggestions and the pages of entered dream data.

'Since when have you known anything about sleep science?' she says.

I scroll through the app.

'Does your investor believe you designed it? Because I don't. I looked online and it's complex –'

'I did a course.'

She looks at me and I gaze back evenly.

'I swear sometimes it's like I don't know you at all, Phil.'

I have a sudden urge to get out. I go to the porch and

pull my trainers from the bottom of a shoe pile. 'I'm going for a run,' I call over my shoulder.

I sleep badly.

David is leaving messages for me everywhere: on my mobile, my email, my social networks. He is trying to arrange a meeting to sign over the app. I block him but somehow he keeps getting through.

I am reading *The Elves and The Shoemaker* to Sophia. She wants to hear it one more time, one more time. But as I turn the pages David's face morphs onto the little elves in the illustrations. He dances naked across the page. I need to get a grip. I need to contain this. I am so tired.

I try not to sleep. I make up my dream posts. I set my alarm to go off every few minutes so I don't start to unravel in a dream. I don't know how they would know anything more than what I record, but I can't be certain. I wait for the call.

Diane calls me. 'Apologies for the delay. We wanted to check a couple of details. But everything looks good to proceed. Can you meet me tomorrow morning? Bring the data files and we'll sign it over?'

I stand in the doorway of David's office.

He looks at me with puppy dog eyes. 'Are you going to sell me the app?'

'You can't have the app, David. It's for your own good.'

'What kind of figure would change your mind?'

'I don't…'

'Name your price.'

'It's just…' I walk across the office and stand beside him as he sits in his desk chair. 'I've missed talking to you. Is that weird?'

'Name your price.'

I sigh heavily. I take a pen from my pocket and make marks on a piece of paper that I do not understand. I place the paper on the desk in front of him.

David raises his eyebrows. 'Name it! Any price!'

'I just did.' Something is incorrect, spiking like a splinter under the skin.

'Name it! Any price!'

'I feel like we're shouting at each other through one-way glass,' I say. He smiles.

'You can't hear me, can you?'

'Is your other option really more ethically sound?'

I push my hands into my pockets.

'I mean…' He laughs. 'We're pretty much the same thing.'

'You and her?'

He shakes his head. 'They'll be watching you. After you hand it over. We, on the other hand, will leave you alone. And you'd get your fee.'

'It's not that simple – I think it's too late. It's gone too far to call back now.'

'You know I'm right, don't you?' He looks at me softly.

I sigh. We think about it together in silence. David smiles. He reaches into his desk and pulls out a dog whistle. 'So… I found this. It's yours.'

He puts it on the desk on top of my file. I look at it.

An idea begins to unravel. 'I could write some code. Something that I can use to check what they're doing.'

'Then you could call them back if they're going astray?'

'I'd be able to whistle blow if they started doing something unethical.'

David picks up the whistle and blows through it and there is no sound. 'A secret frequency. No one would know.' He puts the whistle down on the desk and we both look at it for a while. Then David says, 'Phil… I think I have an idea.'

'Let's get some fresh air. I know somewhere nearby,' I say.

While David stands and pulls on his coat I pick up the whistle and test it, blowing into it as hard as I can. There is no sound at all although I can feel the air rushing through the silver chamber.

Soon, we are strolling through the pine forest where I used to take Dynamo. I blow happily on the whistle and somewhere, far away, a dog starts barking.

I wake and pull out my earphones. It is 2am and I forgot to set the alarm to break my sleep. I am hot and my heart is leaping. I scan the room. I get up and sneak around, searching my house. I make up some dream data on the app. I lean in the doorway of Sophia's bedroom, my ears tuned to any tiny noise. Her favourite book is tucked beneath her pillow. I go to my computer and open the app programme. I begin coding an access key.

In the morning I drive into the city and park. I have put all the app data and documents into a Bag for Life and it bumps against my leg as I hurry along, looking for Diane's office block. I push open the door of a mirror glass-clad building and cross the empty foyer. I take the lift to the third floor and find Diane's office.

Diane sits behind her desk. There are photos of children. I wonder, fleetingly, if they are actually hers.

I sit opposite and put the bag down on the floor beside me. 'You've been checking on me, haven't you?'

'Your app is incredibly easy to hack. That will be our first fix.' She leans forward, her palms open on the desk. 'We were beta-testing your product. Checking there weren't any loopholes we'd missed.'

'You were beta-testing me,' I say.

She laughs and looks away.

'Any loopholes?'

She tilts her head. 'Can I be honest? I think you've created something that has grown way beyond you. It really is for the best that we take it over from here. That level of influence... in the wrong hands... For example,' she grimaces, 'that run you went for last week?'

I nod.

'Do you think you decided that for yourself?'

My forehead is cold and prickly. 'That isn't what it's for. It's for problem solving –'

'We also needed to check we could trust you. You're a wholly moral being, Philip. Look at you. It's adorable and terrifying all at the same time.' She nods at the bag by my feet. 'Really? Is that your idea of secure?'

'Hidden in plain sight?'

'For it to work, on a bigger scale, I needed to know you were reliable. That might seem manipulative. But you understand, don't you, Philip?'

I look down at the bag.

'Don't be alarmed, but when you get home there won't be any trace of the app left on your computer.' After a moment she adds, 'Get on with a new project, Philip. Forget about this one.' She stands and so do I. She reaches out for the bag and I hand it over. She transfers it to a briefcase as if I am no longer there.

So I go to the door. I turn back to her. 'Can I just ask one thing?' I pause with my hand on the door handle. 'About David?'

She looks up at me blankly. 'David?'

I leave the building and I run, heading for open space, my soles slapping against the pavement. I carry on running even when my breath is jagged and a stitch claws at my ribs. Finally, when I reach a leafy square off the main street, I slump onto a bench and rest my head forward into my hands. I wait for my breathing to settle.

I get out my phone. I scroll back and forth across the home screen but the Dreamsolvr app has gone.

I am overwhelmed by a sudden wave of longing.

I open my contacts and roll through until I find the dog shelter number. I stare at it for a while. Then I notice the contact listed directly above it. There is no surname. Just a first name.

I press call.

'David?' I say.

'Hi,' he says. 'Hello, Phil. Nice to speak to you, finally.'

'This is so strange…' I say.

He laughs. 'I know, Phil. I feel like I already know you.' Neither of us speaks for a moment. Then he says, 'She's got it, hasn't she?'

'Yes,' I say. I wait for him to say something but he is silent. So I add quietly, 'But I wrote an access key.'

'I could transfer your money. Right away…'

My ears are ringing. The phone is hot in my hand.

'Phil, you deserve this.'

And I am reciting the access key code to him. And it feels like I'm dreaming. But I know that I'm not and it isn't until I've given him the last digit that it occurs to me that I haven't thought this through. I can hear him typing on a keyboard. It will be re-encrypted, beyond my control, before I can get to a computer. The app spins out of my grasp like the tail end of a dream.

'Great. That's great, Phil.'

I try to think of something to say. 'We could meet up…'

David lets out his breath slowly. 'It's best if we don't. It's just…'

'Oh…' I scuff my shoe against a weed growing through the tarmac beneath the bench.

'It's for the best, Phil. Go home. Forget about all this.' And he hangs up.

I am light-headed. I slump back. I turn my face to the sun and close my eyes. My thoughts are jumbled but one image leaps into my mind; people invading my home, little hands pulling apart my computer, trampling dirty feet across everything. My work, my creation; all gone. I try to quell it with the thought of the money transfer. And then I realise he did not ask for my bank details.

I stand and walk back to where I parked my car.

I get in and start the engine.

I pull out into the traffic and head for the dog shelter.

Afterword:

# Benzene Dreams and Sharks: Be Very Afraid

## Prof. Robert Stickgold
Harvard University

NOW THAT YOU'VE READ Sarah Schofield's provocative short story, 'Benzene Dreams', it's time to separate the science from the fiction. There are so many crazy-sounding ideas in this story, I hardly know where to begin. But here's my list:

1. Dreaming is the brain's way of solving problems.

2. An app could speed up this process, even implanting suggested solutions.

3. An app could learn how to match dream elements with EEG patterns that it could read.

4. It could then wait for a particular pattern, and then keep your brain dreaming about it.

5. And when you woke up, you would have solved your problem.

Crazy-sounding, yes. But impossible? No. In fact, maybe even reasonable. Let me take you on a tour through what's going on in scientific research right now.

*1. Dreaming is the brain's way of solving problems.* The title of this story, 'Benzene Dreams', comes from a dream reported by August Kekulé, in 1890, describing his discovery of the structure of the benzene molecule. It is one of three dreams reported to lead to insights leading to Nobel Prizes. While such dreams (leading to Nobel Prizes) are rare, the ability of the brain to solve problems while we sleep is universal, and now well documented. In 2004, Ulrich Wagner and his colleagues at the University of Lubeck in Germany showed that students allowed a night of sleep after learning a rote method of solving a class of mathematical problems were two and a half times more likely than other students (who instead spent a normal day awake) to subsequently discover a short cut that dramatically reduced the time required to solve them. Their paper, published in the prestigious scientific journal *Nature*, was the first to present clear proof that the brain can solve complex problems while it sleeps. Since then, Ina Djonlagic in my lab has shown that the sleep brain is better than the wake brain at discovering complex patterns in large bodies of observed data. But even more generally, the concept of 'sleeping on a problem' is universally regarded as effective, and variants of this phrase can be found in numerous languages.

Whether this problem solving normally occurs in dreams is unclear, since we remember so few of them. But in a second study on discovering patterns during sleep, Murray Barsky in my lab showed that this pattern discovery depended on REM sleep, when we do our most intense dreaming. And Erin Wamsley, also in my lab, subsequently showed, using a maze-learning task similar to *Duke Nukem*, that while naps taken after maze training led to better performance after four hours, it was specifically those subjects who reported dreams related to the maze that showed the greatest improvement. The problem was that the dreams these subjects reported, while *related* to the maze task, didn't look like they would help. One subject reported thinking about a bat cave he had explored a few years earlier, and how they were 'maze-like'. While obviously related to the task, it shouldn't have led to better performance! My guess is that those parts of the brain that were dreaming were trying to figure out how maze-learning might help them in other circumstances (like when they go exploring caves), while other parts of the brain, whose activity isn't reflected in dream content, were practicing and improving their ability to actually perform the task.

Taken together, this is one crazy-sounding idea in the story that probably isn't so crazy. The dreaming brain is solving problems!

*2. An app could speed up this process, even implanting suggested solutions.* Well, this sounds even more crazy, but several labs have been able to speed up this sleep-dependent memory processing of memories formed earlier that day, and they can pick and choose which ones to enhance! Based on these findings, DARPA, the United State's Defense Advanced Research Projects Agency, last year put out a request for proposals on how to do this better, and I suspect they feel that it could be done with an app!

But these studies have shown that you can enhance already formed memories. This isn't the same thing as solving problems, although we know the sleeping and dreaming brain can do both. So can we implant suggestions for how to solve one's problems, maybe suggesting that you exercise more? I don't know of any labs that have tried this, but Ken Paller's lab at Northwestern University, outside of Chicago, has shown that they can reduce people's implicit social biases by triggering recent memories during a single nap, an effect still evident a week later (Hu, 2015). Based on their work and ours, I wouldn't reject the possibility of planting solutions in the sleeping brain. Hmm, I can almost see how to do it.

In work from Ken Paller's lab, subjects were taught the locations of some 50 objects displayed one at a time on a computer screen (Rudoy, 2009). As each object was displayed, a matching sound was played – *meow* for a cat or a *boing* for a spring. About 45 minutes after the training was completed, subjects were allowed to take a one-hour nap. But while they were sleeping, the researchers replayed half of the fifty sounds (without waking the subjects). Then, after their nap, the subjects were retested. While their accuracy at placing the objects decreased by about 10% overall, their accuracy placing those objects whose sounds were replayed decreased by only 3%, while that of the other 25 objects decreased by 18%. Replaying the sounds while subjects slept actually caused those specific memories to be reactivated and strengthened...

So how might I influence your decisions? I wonder....

'Welcome to the Center for Sleep and Cognition, here in Boston! Today's your lucky day. As payment for participating in my experiment, you are going to be given a pair of tickets to the event of your choice – an opera, a movie premiere, or a Boston Red Sox baseball game! The choice is yours. What's the experiment? We want to see whether or not watching a short video while we play associated sounds softer and softer will actually help you hear the sounds. To make it more interesting, the sounds will come from the opera, the movie, and Neil Diamond singing 'Sweet Caroline' (played before the Red Sox come to bat in the eighth inning of all home games). We'll show you film clips from the three events while playing their matching sounds softer and softer. All you have to do is press the button every time you hear one. Oh, and after we're done testing you, we'll let you take an 'undisturbed' nap before asking you which event you've decided you'd like to attend. Sort of let you 'sleep on it'. Ready for the test? Let's start!'

3. *An app could learn how to match dream elements with EEG patterns that it could read.* It'll be a long time before a mobile phone will have the power to analyse EEG patterns with this level of sophistication, but we have some data suggesting that you can find EEG patterns that indicate that the brain is processing that same maze task I mentioned above. Even more impressively, researchers in the laboratory of Yukiyasu Kamitani in Japan have used functional magnetic resonance imaging to see what sorts of things subjects are dreaming about! (Horikawa, 2013). It's not mind reading, but it's a start towards deciphering what the brain is dreaming about, while they're dreaming about it!

4-5. *An app could then wait for a particular EEG pattern, and then keep your brain dreaming about it, so that when you woke up, you would have solved your problem, and maybe the way the app wants you to.* Once you've gotten the other problems solved, this one is a piece of cake. It's nothing more than putting the pieces together, which sounds kind of scary.

But I don't think we really have to worry, or at least not about this possibility in particular. We are already bombarded with so much advertising aimed at getting us to buy things we don't really want, this is just ratcheting it up one more notch. Think product placement in movies. Think those 'beautiful people' paid to wander through pubs and clubs, wearing one product or another, or just talking to whoever they meet about this really exciting movie they saw last night. Think advertisements that use sex to sell cars, cigarettes, alcohol.

What we don't know is how effective dream manipulation might be. We don't remember very much of what we dream, even if we have what's considered exceptional dream recall. We probably dream at least five or six hours out of an eight-hour night, and remembering much more than half an hour of those would be exceptional. What we do know from scientific experiments is that it is very easy to subtly manipulate people so they make specific decisions without any idea that their decision-making was manipulated. When asked why they made a planted decision, they simply confabulate, convincing themselves of some explanation that makes sense to them, but which is totally wrong.

So looking at what we know and what we don't know, I guess we can't really say that such dream manipulation couldn't be more effective than I've been thinking. We can change your social biases while you sleep – for the better in the study of Paller's group, but changing them for the worse shouldn't be any harder. We can selectively enhance some of what you've learned, while leaving the rest more likely to be forgotten. And the U.S. military is pouring money into figuring out how to do all of this better (although I honestly believe that their goals – ranging from increasing the efficiency of their training programs to reducing the debilitating consequences of PTSD – are not ones we should be afraid of).

Okay, so now I've scared myself! I need to go sleep on this.

# References

Barsky, M.M., M.A. Tucker, and R. Stickgold, (2015) 'REM sleep enhancement of probabilistic classification learning is sensitive to subsequent interference.' *Neurobiol Learn Mem*, 122, pp 63-68.

DARPA (2015). 'RAM (Restoring Active Memory) Replay'. [10/2/2015]; Available from:

http://www.grants.gov/web/grants/view-opportunity.html? oppId=276181.

Djonlagic, I., et al. (2009). 'Sleep enhances category learning.' *Learn Mem*, 16 (12), p. 751-5.

Horikawa, T., et al. (2013). 'Neural decoding of visual imagery during sleep.' *Science*, 340 (6132), pp 639-42.

Hu, X., et al. (2015). 'Cognitive neuroscience. Unlearning implicit social biases during sleep.' *Science*, 348 (6238), pp 1013-5.

Kukelé, A. (1890). 'Benzolfest: Rede.' *Berichte der Deutschen Chemischen Gesellschaft*, 23 (1), pp 1302-1311.

Rudoy, J.D., et al. (2009). 'Strengthening individual memories by reactivating them during sleep.' *Science*, 326 (5956), pp 1079.

Wagner, U., et al. (2004). 'Sleep inspires insight.' *Nature*. 427 (6972), pp 352-5.

Wamsley, E.J., et al., (2010). Dreaming of a learning task is associated with enhanced sleep-dependent memory consolidation. *Current Biology*, 20(9), pp 850-855.

# Counting Sheep

## Andy Hedgecock

*Wednesday 12 March*

LINDEN ALWAYS HATED THE midweek team meetings, and today's was torture. He sneaked a sidelong peep at his fellow lecturer Lea: her mood had veered from irritated to combustible.

'So how do we transform our service?' Their Head of Department, Fay Niven, stood against the whiteboard like a TV weather presenter and swept an elegantly airbrushed fingernail along an archipelago of Post-it notes. The Humanities teaching team had endured an hour's discussion of the 'role enrichments' stemming from the imminent corporate restructure. Linden was sceptical, but he wasn't going to provoke the woman who decided which of them would be spared when the college began the inevitable cull.

He looked around the semicircle of plastic and chrome chairs. To his left there was Jamie, wearing his charcoal Pierre Cardin meeting suit and nodding vigorously every time Fay paused for breath. Next, was Sarita, crossing and uncrossing her legs in a forlorn attempt to get comfortable. Then Adam, leaning forward and fondling his goatee as if considering a chess move. To his right was Lea, slouched low in her chair, mouth masked by the collar of a leprous leather jacket, eyes hidden by two-tone curlicues of hair. She was furious, he could tell.

'I need you to focus, guys. So what do you reckon Lea?' Linden discovered a new and unexpected interest in the toes of his black suede brogues and silently implored Lea to camouflage her contempt, just this once.

'Look, I don't want to be unhelpful,' Lea broke the silence, 'but there's very little to say.' She pushed her glasses down her nose and peered at Fay over the top of the frames. 'I didn't join the college to be a bean counter, I came to teach.'

'Absolutely,' said Fay, her glossy fuchsia lips fixed in her signature smile, and her voice remaining serene. 'But I'm less certain why you constantly undermine me. So guys, how do we up our game and keep Lea teaching?' She tapped the board with its Post-its and crudely marker-penned think bubbles containing phrases like 'accepting change', 'lean thinking' and 'income generation'.

The session closed with an introduction to the new Auspex performance management system, an 'online dashboard' allowing regular autopsies on team performance. There were graphs and tables showing contact hours, average grades, student evaluation scores, retention rates and destination codes. Lecturers were to report their achievements against targets on the first Monday of every month, clicking on a colour-coded button. 'OK guys, we've decided on a comment by exception protocol,' Fay explained, 'if you display a red or amber indicator you'll need to input a note justifying why that's happening.'

Lea waved a bangled wrist in the air. Fay smoothed a lapel of her jacket and nodded.

'Fay, what will happen to the students while we're playing at being management consultants?' Linden looked towards Lea and willed her to shut up.

Fay turned her smile up a notch. 'This is an invest-to-save project, Lea. It's a tool to empower you to deliver the Principal's Focus on Learners strategy, to make sure everything we do puts students at the heart of our business.'

As the neat percussion of Fay's stilettos faded into the corridor, Linden took his black and white tartan scarf and yellow waterproof cycling jacket from the back of his chair. He hissed at Lea: 'What possessed you to have a pop at her?

She's never liked you.'

Lea shrugged. 'Fancy joining us for a quick pint after work?'

In the bar of The Narrow Boat Inn, Linden, Adam, Lea and Sarita were joined by a couple of mature students, Justine and Simon. Linden had nearly finished his pint of Guinness before Justine spoke to him: 'Would you mind if I talked shop for a minute?'

'No problem Justine, go ahead,' he said, trying not to stare at her swollen cheek and the bluish smudge under her left eyelid.

'Could you say Jeremy Bentham was a forerunner of the scientific socialists?'

Linden shook his head, setting out his objections to the idea – including Bentham's love of the free market and the *Panopticon*, his design for high surveillance buildings. 'But,' he continued, 'I can see where you're coming from, Justine. Bentham also came up with the *Felicific Calculus*, a formula for measuring and spreading happiness. He looked at stuff like the number of people affected, the strength of the feeling and how long it lasted. Well meaning, but ended up being regarded as a bit daft and dangerous.' He downed the rest of his pint.

Back home, Linden spread his mark books – one for each Sociology cohort – across the dining room table. Working on an A3 sheet he listed students who might draw unwelcome attention from Fay: infrequent submitters of assignments were shown in blue, poor attenders in purple, low achievers in green and those with significant personal issues in red. Several names appeared in all four colours. He was putting an asterisk against each of those when Cara appeared in her pink and grey checked dressing gown. She placed a coffee mug onto an open mark book.

'Thanks,' said Linden looking up briefly, 'I won't sleep if I don't sort this. The rumour is they'll cut at least one job per subject team, and this is the kind of stuff they'll look at.'

He picked up the coffee cup and winced when he saw the crescent moon stain on the mark book's gridded page. He started to count off colleagues on his fingers. 'Sarita had a bit of sickness last year, but her results were better than mine; Jamie is bullet proof, Fay loves him. She has complete contempt for… other people in the team, but they are popular with the students. Adam is a psychology specialist, but Fay could ask him to cover sociology. She never seems keen on me.'

'Linden,' Cara yawned, 'do you really imagine spending half the evening doing colouring-in will push you up Fay's league table?'

*Wednesday 19 March*

Linden arrived ten minutes before the meeting and browsed a muddled essay on symbolic interactionism. Lounging in a swivel chair in the third-floor staff breakout area, his attention drifted from the essay to a point beyond the floor-to-ceiling window. The relentlessly flat lighting of the open-plan offices and anti-glare coating of the glass conspired to cast the world outside into permanent twilight. A group of students were enjoying a fag break on the canal footbridge below. And there was someone in red skinny jeans and ankle boots: Lea was rummaging in her fringed tote bag as she walked onto the footbridge. She was going to be late.

By the time Lea arrived, Fay had apologised for the lack of a proper meeting room, made her introductory announcements, powered up the portable projector screen and displayed a website featuring the image of a mouse curled up in a nest.

'So pleased you could join us Lea,' Fay said without looking away from the screen. 'Maybe a colleague will bring you up to speed with the information I've shared so far.'

The only seats free were right in front of the screen: Lea hung her jacket on the chair and delved into her tote bag for a pad and pen. Fay watched impassively, until Lea looked up.

'Sickness is a barrier to delivering our Focus on Learners strategy,' she began, 'so we all need to take responsibility for our wellbeing. We're adding personal health indices to the Auspex dashboard and running staff development sessions on diet, fitness, mindfulness, stress and resilience. But today I want to talk about sleep and its role in effective performance.'

She pointed her wireless clicker at the screen and the display cut to a copyright page with the heading *Dormouse Sleep Management Programme*. 'This is an app you can download to your phone for a few quid. This stuff is from their sales website, but you'll get the idea.'

Fay flicked through sleep habit-tracker diagrams with their colourful spikes, spindles and histograms, explained the intelligent alarm clock function and demonstrated the sleep deficit indicators. 'You put your phone under your pillow and it records tossing and turning, checks if you snore or talk in your sleep, and works out the best time to wake you with music, birdsong or whatever you like.'

The group looked at a screen headed 'Apnoea Alert'. 'Breathing problems to you and me,' Fay explained. 'It's up to you, but it might improve the quality of your sleep. Vital for wellbeing and mental health,' she barely paused for breath. 'You can upload your data to support groups and compare sleep efficiency scores. It helps establish good habits and –'

'I'm sorry Fay,' Lea interrupted, 'our sleep is really none of your business.' She looked round the room for support. Linden dodged eye contact by gazing intently at the screen. The only sounds were the drone of the aircon system, the novelty ringtone of a distant phone and the relentless hum of students moving around the building.

'You turn up late to all my meetings, Lea, and you make negative comments at every opportunity. Fortunately, your colleagues seem more open-minded.'

That night, Linden set Dormouse to wake him at the optimum time, between 6:15 and 6:45, and furtively slid the phone under his pillow.

'What are you doing?' Cara's voice cut through the darkness and he froze: she wasn't asleep after all. She lay on her side, facing the wall.

'Something for work, a health monitoring scheme, it's daft, but Fay is keen.'

'You're terrified of Fay,' Cara muttered, keeping her back to him.

Linden climbed under the duvet and put an arm round her winceyette pyjama top: 'It's just that Fay decides who gets a place in the lifeboat, so I'd be stupid to piss her off.'

Cara didn't move. 'I really don't care how much you suck up to your boss, Linden. I'm just hoping you don't back the wrong horse again.'

*Thursday 20 March*
*Dormouse Sleep efficiency index: 72%*

Linden saw Lea on the other side of the bridge as he pedalled along the rain slicked asphalt of the cycle path. It was a damp, bright morning and erratic swirls of light reflected from the canal onto the weathered brickwork of the arch as he coasted towards her on his shabby old mountain bike.

Lea, jacket tightly zipped against the cold, leaned against the metal railings and flicked cigarette ash into the canal, its water tinted walnut and olive by shadows and pale sunlight. She grinned as Linden leaned his bike to dismount. 'Done any good toadying lately?'

'It's about survival, you should try it sometime.' Linden looked away from Lea to a convoy of mallards whisking the murky water as they took off. 'How's life?' he continued.

'Fine,' said Lea, 'apart from worrying about losing my job and sitting through an evangelical rally every Wednesday.'

'But you and Adam are OK?'

Lea adjusted her glasses and peered over the rims. 'Lovely bloke, cleverer than you and makes me laugh. Or were you really just asking about the sex?

Linden laughed.

'He was a git yesterday.' Lea opened her mouth in an astonished 'O', and blew a hoop of smoke towards him. 'I expected a bit of support from you, too – we're still supposed to be friends.' His sense of amusement evaporated with her smoke ring. 'I can't believe you let Fay get away with all that fake compassion. As for that bollocks about tracking sleep…'

'I'm feeling knackered at the moment, and I think Fay has noticed,' he sighed, 'so I'm giving Dormouse a go'. He pulled aside his scarf and rooted for his phone in the pockets of his high-vis yellow jacket. He held the screen of his phone to her and she leaned into him. He took in the familiar bouquet of Chanel Number 5 and stale cigarette smoke. 'I'm not all that interested, Linden,' she whispered, 'but if it makes you happy tell me what it says.'

'My sleep performance is at 72%.' He explained the implications of his moderate efficiency score and the way clustered spikes on the movement and sound graphs might correlate with disrupted sleep.

Unhurriedly and emphatically, Lea ground her cigarette butt on the railings. She regarded him, steadily and impassively: 'Or, of course, it could all be complete bullshit. Listen to yourself, sleep *performance*, for god's sake; who are you performing this sleep for Linden, who is the sleep supervisor?'

Linden shook his head. 'Fay wants everyone on the bus with this wellbeing thing. This is part of it, so why not give it a go?'

'I'm not a joiner-in, Linden, and you know this is dangerous drivel.' Lea took off her glasses and started polishing the lenses with a square of tattered cloth. 'I've done a correlation of my own,' she said, without looking up. 'The mutton-dressed-as-lamb end of our leader's wardrobe predicts serious confrontation, and she's squeezed into a pink minidress with matching stilt heels today. Tread carefully.'

As he cycled away from Lea she shouted after him, but her parting words were muted by the breeze and the cicada song of his bike wheels. She could do what she liked and take the consequences.

*Friday 28 March*
*Dormouse Sleep efficiency index: 70%*

The muffled, distant voice of Thea Gilmore singing 'Bad Moon Rising' nudged Linden into consciousness. He delved under the pillow for his phone – the clock read 6:27. He stretched his arms across the mattress and reached out for Cara. No Cara. Last night he had mentioned that her nocturnal pitching and flailing affected his sleep graphs. When he suggested moving to the guest bedroom she glared at him. He pointed out he was simply being honest and practical and, after a frosty discussion about the definition of honesty, Cara grudgingly went along with the experiment. So Linden spent the night alone for the first time since the month she found out about the affair.

Lying on his back he tapped the Dormouse thumbnail. Once again, the line graphs displayed the occasional burst of spikes indicating movement and louder noise, such as snoring. A bit of a downturn, he thought.

Arriving at work, he crammed his cycling gear into a locker and walked out of the changing room in his new pin-dot grey suit with paisley lining. It had cost a packet and drawn caustic comments from Cara. And, for all the expense, he wasn't convinced it lent him the air of modish engagement Jamie never failed to cultivate.

'Morning Mr Harper,' Fay's voice rang out from behind him. 'Looking very dapper today.' As they walked into the lift she lowered her voice and touched his arm. 'While I have you, I know you're concerned about last year's disappointing exam results. That was a challenging group, Linden. Decisions about our reorganisation will take attitude to change and cooperation into account. It's important to be seen as purposeful in this climate. Sharing ideas is important for professional development, but don't spend too much time with colleagues who aren't well thought of.'

She peered at Linden as if gauging his response. 'I don't want to make a big thing of this, but the decision-makers are watching all of us all the time.'

Linden spent much of the morning thinking about the implication of his conversation with Fay, and his lesson preparation didn't go well. He wandered to the refreshment hub, tapped 75 on the drinks machine and collected a scalding cappuccino. He saw Adam coming towards him from the departmental office. 'Hi Adam, are these paper cups getting thinner or is it me?' No response. 'Adam?'

Adam looked directly at Linden as he walked into him, knocking the cup from his hand. Coffee splashed onto sleeves, trousers, shoes. 'Christ,' Adam bellowed, grasping Linden's forearm to steady himself. 'Sorry mate, I didn't see you. I must have been in a trance. Hang on…' He fumbled in his jacket and produced a crumpled grey handkerchief.

'Hi guys.' Fay ambushed them as Adam dabbed at Linden's sleeve. 'The Principal wants to see a more transformational approach to motivation so we're using gamification to encourage healthy competition. We're going to award monthly prizes for the highest levels of achievement recorded on Auspex. What do you think?'

Whenever Fay cornered him, Linden felt like a schoolkid in the headteacher's office, but he knew he ought to respond: 'Why not, I think people would go for it.' He could sense Adam looking at him.

Fay nodded. 'Adam, I need a word with you about your student evaluations and attendance levels at some stage. You look a little under the weather.' She inclined her head and arched her narrow eyebrows. 'Been burning the candle at both ends?'

'I couldn't be bouncier Fay,' said Adam, 'Further Education's answer to Tigger.' Linden and Adam failed to avoid eye contact and Adam smirked. Fay looked pointedly at the coffee spattered on their shoes and trousers and then sashayed into the office.

Linden had always imposed his authority on groups of learners pretty deftly, but that afternoon he was having trouble kick-starting a discussion of Durkheim. The students acted like he wasn't in the room and talked among themselves. Overwhelmed with a vague sense of desperation, he decided to grab their attention by standing on a chair and bellowing over the hubbub. Order was restored, but Linden was on autopilot – his voice dampened, his focus blurred – even as he set a revision essay at the end of the session.

As he rode home Linden tried to recall how the group responded to the activities he'd devised. All he remembered with any clarity was the image of his final PowerPoint slide – masked looters with a blazing car in the background. Increasingly, his working days were a haze he passed through with less and less energy. Oddly though, there was no evidence his sleep was deteriorating, in fact his overall Dormouse sleep efficiency score had improved. His reflections stalled when he spotted a woman in a blue coat walking towards him in the towpath's pedestrian lane. He slowed down and sounded his bell as a precaution, but there was little risk as she was looking straight at him. Suddenly, when she was just ten feet away she stepped out into the bike lane. Linden clutched his brakes and skidded, his front wheel tilting and sliding to the right. There was a scream. He fell away from the bike and his left shoulder thudded against the grass banking next to the canal.

'Wanker!' She yelled as he moved his upper arm in an extravagant circular motion. Nothing broken, no cuts. His lycra leggings were untorn, his rucksack was fine, his yellow jacket was grass stained but otherwise undamaged. He picked up the bike and spun the wheels. 'It seems ok,' he said in measured tones, conscious of the need to avoid making a scene near the college, 'but why couldn't you see me? I rang the bell and I wasn't going fast.'

She moved towards him, thrusting her hands into her coat pockets as if to prevent herself from hitting him. 'You came out of nowhere, like a maniac. You complete twat.'

*Friday 4 April*
*Dormouse Sleep efficiency index: 68%*

'I haven't seen much of you over the last week,' said Lea. 'Did our leader give you the same 'watch out for the watchers and shun the slackers' speech she gave Adam?'

Linden was setting up an exercise on brands and power in one of the glass-walled classrooms at the centre of the building. He glanced at her, catching a glimpse of the top leaves of her tree of life tattoo above her halter-neck top. He shook his head, and resumed the process of placing A3 sheets, marker pens and packs of corporate logos on each table.

'There's no point in pissing Fay off.' He continued setting up the room. 'Things have changed at the college, Lea. The management don't tolerate eccentric behaviour these days. Just keep your head down and hope for the best.'

As he plugged the HDMI lead into his laptop he knocked over his paper cup. Water spilled across the past papers and handwritten prompt cards, and Linden stared at his carefully inked letters as they bled into incoherence.

When he looked up Lea was gone, he hadn't heard the click of the door.

Linden had hoped the session would be less fraught than yesterday's but, seconds after beginning his explanation of the session, he restarted a sentence that had warped into incoherence. As they worked on the brands exercise the students' voices seemed muffled and the room looked fuzzily focussed and depthless. No one asked Linden any questions, no one looked at him. Why did he feel so tired? Why did his self-awareness seem so muted? According to Dormouse, his sleep efficiency was pretty stable. He wondered if he was misreading the data, or overlooking some aspect of the app's functionality.

As he tried to wrap up the exercise, sounds outside the room interrupted the flow of his thoughts – raised voices, phones, the squeaking wheel of a maintenance trolley – and his comments tailed off without reaching their conclusion. His voice had no resonance: he was speaking from within a soundproofed bubble. He was sweating heavily. He tried to break through the stifling meniscus with a question. 'So how do the images that companies project affect our self-image?' His head swam and as he looked around the room, silently imploring someone, anyone, to answer. As he glanced from face to face his mind was engulfed in an avalanche of information. Diana, a black girl in a salmon-coloured vest top, looked back at him sympathetically: test average 81%; attendance 100% this year; a good B in last year's sociology mock in spite of a week off for an appendectomy; awarded Linden's lectures a median evaluation score of eight out of ten. Good bet for added value and destination data. He quickly looked away from her to the mature student Simon: already has nine GCSEs taken 15 years ago; an A in his mock; mean test score 78%; discussed a personal debt of £19,000 with tutors on four different occasions; median student evaluation score for Linden of seven out of ten. Linden rubbed his temples, but the information came faster. Ginger-haired, gap-toothed Kerry was staring out of the window: Type 2 diabetes; attendance 70%; grade prediction on the C – D borderline; mean test scores 38%; median evaluation score of four for Linden's sessions.

He headed for the door, trying to keep his breathing under control, passing slender and stringy haired Justine, the other mature student: current grade average C; seven GCSEs, all Bs and Cs; mean test score of 55%; median student evaluation score of nine; accommodated in a woman's refuge in the summer term; withdrawn from mock exams; predicted grade C.

He had no sense of rapport or empathy as the minutia of their lives cascaded into his mind. He reeled from the room, and leaned his head against the cool glass of the wall of the corridor outside. He couldn't ask Lea to cover his class, maybe Adam would step in.

Adam Greer, whose median student evaluation score was one point more positive than Linden's but one behind Lea's, was working in the breakout area, hunched over his laptop. 'Adam?' No response. 'Adam?'

In desperation, Linden closed the laptop lid. Adam looked up astonished. 'Christ, you took me by surprise. Linden, you look shocking, are you OK?' Jamie took over his class and Adam drove him home. Linden stared ahead, barely daring to look across at the driver's seat. As they drove along the inner ring road the world was occluded by veils of information – group baseline scores, grade averages, prior qualifications, attendance averages, student self-assessment scores, satisfaction scores... He shut his eyes but the numbers continued to pour into his consciousness.

By the time Adam's car pulled up outside his 1930s semi, he was drenched with sweat and breathing like a worn out foot pump. Cara was waiting at the gate, looking impassively towards the car. Adam must have phoned ahead.

*Monday 7 April*
*Dormouse Sleep efficiency index: 66%*

The weekend was over and Dormouse serenaded Linden with Bon Iver's 'Flume'. He stretched. No aches, no pains, no shakes, no sweats. 'Shit,' he said, remembering his bike was still at work. He'd have to walk. He checked his phone – it was 6:44. He stumbled from the bed and fixated on the Dormouse thumbnail, barely daring to check the feedback. No major change in the graphs – 66%.

His phone buzzed several times as he stared intently at his reflection and sloughed the shaving foam from his cheeks. He splashed water over his face and checked his inbox – a text from Adam telling him to stay away until he felt OK, and one from Fay saying Sarita was off sick and would he be coming in today? By the time he got downstairs, Cara was hunched over her MacBook Pro in her favourite cashmere V-neck, hacking out a proposal for a marketing campaign. 'Caz, look at this,' he said, flourishing his phone, 'My sleep quality has dropped and I'm getting more and more tired.' She said nothing but continued to stare at the screen. Cara Harper, Upper Second in Journalism and Media, earns about £40,000 in salary and dividends, served a suspended sentence for possession of a controlled substance ten years ago. He touched her shoulder. She screamed and jerked backwards away from the screen.

'Why the fuck are you creeping up on me?'

He felt lightheaded. 'I'm off to work,' he said eventually and headed for the door. 'I'm walking in.'

'Don't go back until you've seen a doctor,' she called after him.

The towpath was an ordeal: the thought of cramming through the reception area with students leaking data was too much to bear, so he paced to-and-fro under the birdshit-coated arch of the road bridge for ten minutes before heading for the college. Reception was unstaffed and automated: it was virtually deserted as he walked past the framed prints of athletes, celebrities, historical figures and allegedly inspirational quotations. So far his senses were uncontaminated by other people's details and numbers. He waved his staff pass at the proximity reader and clanked through one of the security turnstiles.

The clamour in his head began as he reached the department and fell in step behind a couple of first year sociology students. The one with three convictions for shoplifting and the one with an A grade average. He realised Ms Shoplifter was talking about him. 'He looked like shit yesterday... hope he's off sick... it would be a result if we got Sarita or Lea... Linden's right up himself and his lessons are really boring...'

*Shut up and sod off you thieving cow*, Linden thought.

Suddenly, he spotted Fay striding across the floor and walked towards her. First in Psychology, University of Central Lancashire, winner of the FE Management Rising Star Award... 'Fay, I need to speak with you urgently.' No response. He wondered if she had heard him. He was dizzy and breathless, and Fay walked very quickly. He followed her into a glass-walled meeting room in which his fellow lecturers were huddled in anxious clusters, like guests at a cocktail party whose host had forgotten to order the booze. Linden leaned against the back wall.

'We have a calamity.' Fay explained Sarita had phoned early this morning to say she was unwell, and had just now texted to say she had a doctor's note for the rest of the week. A timetable crisis was averted when Jamie and Lea agreed to cover Sarita's sessions. 'Thanks guys, very much appreciated ...' Fay's words receded from his consciousness as Linden was once again hit by a wave of numbers. Jamie Brewer, aged 28, average student attendance 94%, mean student test average 77% and median student evaluation score of 8. Lea Preston, 33, attendance 93%, test average 79% and evaluation score of 9. Adam Greer, 29, attendance 83%...

At the end of the briefing the group hurried from the room to their lectures. Adam and Lea speculated about Sarita's history of depression, while Linden walked behind them in silence. He felt giddy and sick. He had to get out of the building.

*Friday 11 April*
*Dormouse Sleep efficiency index: 65%*

Linden checked Dormouse after Fay's wellbeing call –
mandatory on the fourth day of sick leave.

Cara had packed her laptop and an overnight bag on
Wednesday and driven off to stay with her business partner
Kathryn. Not an issue. Linden could get on with his new
project without having to field negative questions. He was
going to come up with an updated and adapted version of
Bentham's *Felicific Calculus*, focusing on teaching effectiveness
rather than happiness. They could use it to model best practice
and help the college save jobs. But what metrics should be
included?

There were unruly piles of books and papers on the table
and the wall was covered with Post-its and Blu-Tacked A4
sheets. He had removed a print of Stanley Spencer's *Angels of
the Apocalypse* to make room for his charts, mind maps, tables
and equations. One sheet, headed 'Financial Viability', was
crammed with handwritten calculations of return on investment
and breakeven points. Another, labelled 'wasted resources',
included a flowchart showing the 'customer value stream' and
'learner flow'. At the centre of the wall were two league tables:
one showing student marks, attendance data and predicted
grades; and a second displaying performance data for every
member of the Humanities teaching team. There were
numbers for sickness, based on memory and guesswork; and
there were figures from Auspex for average grades by cohort,
mean test scores and median student evaluation scores. There
was a column for 'preferred teaching methodology', one for
'empathy with learners' and he was trying to come up with a
'conversion metric' by generating scores for destinations –
work, university or apprenticeships. The challenge was to filter
irrelevant data and identify a set of metrics that predict the
award of a coveted Ofsted Grade 1 for teaching. And a Grade
1 might mean additional funding and fewer lecturers for the

chop. What should the points tally for Linden and colleagues be based on? How could all these numbers be weighted to produce a definitive points system – an unambiguous league table with leaders vying for promotion and stragglers in the relegation zone?

Linden stood back from the wall and let his eye travel across the diagrams, spreadsheet grids and colour-coded post-its. Earlier in the day he had scrawled a formula in his hardback notebook: 'te = ((sc − at) / at) + (gr / (st − bs))'. He read it again: it wasn't right. He drew a series of diagonal lines through it.

The next time he crossed out a formula it was four in the morning and the sky was getting light. He was knackered. He walked upstairs, set the Dormouse alarm for 11:30 to 12:00, and pushed the phone under his pillow. He was so close: tomorrow he would find a solution.

*Monday 28 April*

On the first Monday after the Easter break, Linden clambered over a tubular steel gate with a sign reading 'Danger: no public access.' He walked along a gantry to the centre of the water pipe bridge thirty yards east of the college. From his vantage point he could see the canal towpath and footbridge.

He couldn't bear being in the house any longer: he couldn't drag himself away from his papers and Post-its, and his correlations and vectors plagued every waking hour he spent there. He had spent most of last week sleeping rough, resting fitfully and opportunistically in abandoned commercial properties further along the canal, but still the metrics crowded every other thought from his consciousness.

He peered through the safety rail, manically scrying the water as if the solution to his calculations lay beneath its surface. The canal modulated from coffee in the sunlight to hickory in the shadow cast by the footbridge, provoking an unexpected and fleeting memory of Cara's stocking tops.

Several hours later Lea was on the footbridge, lighting her fifth fag of the day. The fifth Linden had seen. She looked down at the water. Linden fished in his jacket for his hardback notebook and thumbed past tables recording arrivals, departures and lunch breaks. On the page headed Cigarette Breaks he added a tally mark in the 'Lea' column.

He took out his phone and thumbed through the 27 messages asking him to get in touch – from Adam, Fay, Lea and Cara. It was too much to resist: he opened Dormouse. The sound and movement graphs were neat dog's teeth rather than mountain peaks. Sleep efficiency 100%. Nothing added up, not even this. Numbers couldn't be trusted. He tossed his phone from the bridge into the turbid water below.

There was shouting. Down on the towpath a wiry man in a white t-shirt yanked a woman's head back by her stringy ponytail and slapped her. It was Justine, the mature student. Linden set off along the gantry and scaled the gate. By the time he reached the towpath Lea had stepped between Justine and her attacker and was flailing at him.

Linden pushed between the man and Lea, and took two hefty kicks to the thigh. As he fell he saw Lea take a jolting punch to her left cheek. Her head went back. She staggered and fell backwards down the bank.

Scrambling down to the edge of the canal, Linden grabbed Lea's legs and, with a desperate burst of effort, dragged her away from the water. She was conscious but her eyes seemed out of focus. Looking round he saw Justine sobbing as black polo-shirted college security staff dragged her assailant to the ground. Staff, students and passers-by began to mill around.

Linden limped back towards the water pipe bridge.

*Monday 5 May*

A week later Lea was back at work with a partially closed eye and a smoky bruise on her cheek. Adam accompanied her to

Asquith Road Police Station, to meet DS Chris Cataldo and a victim support worker. In a sparsely furnished interview room with a colour scheme of magnolia and gamboge, Cataldo powered up his laptop and inserted the memory stick containing extracts from the college's CCTV. 'I'm sorry you're going through this so soon after we spoke about the disappearance of Mr Harper,' he said.

Adam held her hand as she watched the incident play back as if through an icy mist. 'It's a short clip and the resolution is very poor I'm afraid,' said Cataldo, pausing the video and zooming in.

He spoke above the atonal clatter of the station – footsteps, raised voices and banging doors. 'Here's Mrs Andrews.' He pointed at Justine with a plastic stylus. 'Here's the charming and gallant Mr Andrews,' he said jabbing at a white t-shirt as if pricking a voodoo doll. The stylus hovered over Lea's jacket. 'Are you OK with this?'

Lea nodded. 'The quality degrades at this point,' he said, clicking his mouse button. The images of the scuffle were blurred. Part of the scene was occluded by an amorphous dark shadow and flickering flashes of yellow. 'And the colour balance is nothing to write home about.'

Lea leaned forward and asked Cataldo to rerun the few seconds in which she scuffled with Andrews.

'Stop please.' Her voice cracked. 'Can you zoom in…. thanks … can you get closer?' She stared at a magnified but grainy patch of colour at the centre of the screen.

'What is it? What's wrong?' asked Adam, his voice rising.

For a second she had thought she was could see the sleeve of a yellow, waterproof cycling jacket and black and white tartan scarf. Not possible, she told herself.

'Nothing. I'm sorry, there's nothing.'

Afterword:

# Sleep Supervision

## Dr Simon Kyle
University of Oxford

WE LIVE IN A WORLD where quantification rules supreme. So much of our daily lives is characterised by metrics and summary values – from calorie and step counts to number of Facebook 'likes', YouTube views and Twitter followers, through to work performance 'outcomes' and league tables. Of course, we expect such precision and nuanced analysis when making sense of our personal finances, but increasingly we are encouraged to measure and reflect on almost every aspect of human behaviour. On the one hand this 'quantification obsession' could be considered a *popperian* success; the ability to test ideas (hypotheses) with REAL, 'hard' data, as opposed to relying on instinct or intuition, helps guide decision-making and modify behaviour. But could there be unintended consequences of our desire to measure, track and learn more about ourselves?

In 'Counting Sheep', Hedgecock tackles society's obsession with measurement and performance. Set within higher education – a discipline enslaved by performance indicators – we are introduced to a struggling college facing threats of a possible 'restructure' (euphemism for staff redundancies and cost-savings). To improve college outcomes and rank staff members, the principal introduces a formal system of evaluations and performance metrics. Monitoring and performance enhancement initially begin in the workplace but eventually extend to the home environment through a focus on sleep optimisation (via the 'Dormouse Sleep Management Programme'), owing to the links between sleep, wellbeing and productivity. The protagonist, Linden, a man clearly hypersensitive to feedback and appraisal, becomes consumed by the urge to improve his work performance through sleep enhancement; an obsession which degrades his ability to work, sleep, hold down relationships, and ultimately his mental health.

While Linden may exhibit rare, excessive responses to quantification and evaluation, 'Counting Sheep' raises important questions about society's preoccupation with the 'quantified self', and sleep tracking in particular. With a recent surge in sleep apps, wearable technology and sleep sensor start-up companies, we are led to believe that tracking devices can provide us with reliable and objective insights into our nightly sleep experience. These include total number of hours and minutes slept; number and duration of awakenings; causes of these awakenings (e.g. noise, apnoeas); and the architecture of obtained sleep (e.g. 'light' and 'deep' sleep). Some devices also claim to optimise sleep-wake performance through environmental feedback (e.g. about light and temperature) and scheduled alarm awakenings to reduce sleep inertia. Nearly all of these devices (both wearable and smartphone applications) employ accelerometer-based technology to measure movement, the absence of which indicates likely sleep. Within sleep science, accelerometer-based tools (actigraph watches) have been extensively tested against gold-standard, objective sleep recordings – polysomnography – and the field understands their limitations. Movement-based assessments tell us virtually nothing about sleep architecture but can provide useful information outside of the sleep laboratory on sleep-wake timing, day-to-day variability in sleep-wake periods and, within acceptable limits of error, total sleep time and sleep continuity. In contrast, we know very little about the validity or reliability of popular sleep trackers. Indeed recent scientific reviews of commercially-available smartphone apps and wearable devices find almost no supporting data (Behar, et al., 2013; Lee & Finkelstein, 2014), although validation studies are beginning to emerge for select activity trackers in specific populations (de Zambotti, Baker & Colrain, 2015).

Do we really need to know if these devices measure what they claim to measure? Is it important? Surely daily sleep appraisals, even if not completely accurate, are relatively harmless? It turns out this may not be entirely true. Classic findings in psychology demonstrate the importance of expectations on subsequent behaviour, cognition and health, perhaps most clearly expressed in the placebo effect and its more sinister relation, the 'nocebo' effect (believing that inert or active substances will lead to negative outcomes actually increases the likelihood of such negative outcomes occurring). Similar mechanisms may influence our sleep-wake perceptions. In an interesting study published in 2005, Christina Semler & Allison Harvey recruited a sample of poor sleepers who complained of insomnia symptoms (problems initiating and maintaining sleep accompanied by daytime impairment). Over three separate days participants received feedback (positive or negative) on their 'sleep quality' via an alarm-clock interface. Participants simultaneously wore an actigraph watch to index objective sleep and – as far as participants were concerned – to guide feedback on sleep quality. In reality, however, feedback was random and unconnected to objective sleep. Each day, participants were also asked to rate their degree of sleepiness, negative thought content, monitoring for sleep-related threat, and use of safety behaviours (behaviours designed to avoid or minimise the consequences of sleep loss but that instead may have paradoxical effects). Findings indicated that on days where negative feedback was delivered, participants reported greater amounts of sleepiness, negative thoughts, sleep-related monitoring and use of safety behaviours, relative to days where positive feedback about sleep quality was provided. These differences were independent of objective sleep; that is, actigraphy-defined sleep remained constant across both 'positive' and 'negative' nights. Thus, sham-feedback about prior nights' sleep quality influences how we perceive, interpret and interact with the day. Moreover, the variables measured by Semler & Harvey are known to play a role in disturbing night-time sleep, setting up the possibility that misperception of sleep may trigger conditions propitious to the development of insomnia disorder.

A related study published in 2014 similarly provided feedback to participants, this time based on sham measurement of a daytime 'REM sleep signature', captured by an elaborate set-up of EEG, heart rate and pulse recordings (Draganich & Erdal, 2014). Students were randomly assigned to receive positive feedback (achieving greater than average amounts of REM sleep) or negative feedback (achieving less than average amounts of REM sleep). Primed with the importance of REM sleep for daytime function, participants were next asked to complete a battery of reaction time and performance-based tests, assessing different domains of cognition – including attention, verbal fluency, working memory and visual-motor processing speed. Regardless of actual sleep quality (measured for the previous night), those assigned to the low versus high REM sleep manipulation performed worse on tasks assessing attention and verbal fluency. Again then, priming poor sleep expectations was shown to translate into daytime impairment; and this time on objective tests. It is conceivable, indeed likely, that inaccurate sleep devices may be guiding important aspects of daily functioning, influencing them in both positive and negative directions. As we observe with Linden in 'Counting Sheep', such priming effects may be most pronounced in those with specific vulnerable predispositions; an idea that requires further empirical scrutiny in the evolving scientific literature on sleep sensors.

While caution should be encouraged in the absence of robust scientific data, it would be foolish to completely ignore the possible benefits of sleep tracking. For example, valid and reliable sleep measurements in the home environment could help to profile, identify and manage disordered sleep in novel ways and on a global scale. We may also learn new insights into dynamic factors that influence and regulate sleep, and be afforded the opportunity to assess differences in sleep patterns across culture, over time and in connection with major phasic events. For those keen to simply optimise sleep and its benefits, intelligent systems may provide evidence-based answers, but we must also be careful to avoid propagating excessive sleep preoccupation (or 'Chronorexia'; Van den Bulck, 2015). Indeed, it was noted over one-hundred years ago in the medical journal, *The Lancet*, that: 'Very often the surest way of keeping awake is trying hard to sleep. We do most things best when we forget ourselves; sleeping is no exception' (Sawyer, 1878). A wealth of literature in the cognitive and clinical sciences supports the view that mental phenomena can dysregulate biological functions, including sleep (e.g. Rasskazova, et al., 2014). In conclusion, therefore, it would appear prudent to list our demands of a potential (ideal) sleep supervisor – a supervisor in whom we trust, can rely upon for support, provides direction and mentorship when needed but also encourages a healthy dose of independence and scepticism!

# References

Behar, J., Roebcuk, A., Domingos, J.S., Gederi, E., & Clifford, G.D. (2013). 'A review of current sleep screening applications for smartphones.' *Physiological Measurement*, 34, R29-R46.

de Zambotti, M., Baker, F.C., & Colrain, I.M. (2015). 'Validation of sleep-tracking technology compared with polysomnography in adolescents.' *SLEEP*, 38, pp 1461-1468.

Draganich, C., & Erdal, K. (2014). 'Placebo sleep affects cognitive functioning.' *Journal of Experimental Psychology: Learning, Memory, and Cognition*, 40, pp 857-864.

Lee, J., & Finkelstein, J. (2014). 'Activity trackers: A critical review.' *Studies in Health Technology and Informatics*, 205, pp 558-562.

Rasskazova, E., Zavalko, I., Tkhostov, A., & Dorohov, V. (2014).

'High intention to fall asleep causes sleep fragmentation.' *Journal of Sleep Research*, 23, pp 297-303.

Sawyer, J. (1878). 'Clinical lecture on the causes and cure of insomnia.' *The Lancet*, 111, pp 889-890.

Semler, C.N., & Harvey, A.G. (2005). 'Misperception of sleep can adversely affect daytime functioning in insomnia.' *Behavior Research and Therapy*, 43, pp 843-856.

Van den Bulck, J. (2015). 'Sleep apps and the quantified self: blessing or curse?' *Journal of Sleep Research*, 24, pp 121-123.

# Thunder Cracks

## Zoe Gilbert

I'VE HEARD IT SAID, a strong wind can send a man's mind sailing out of his head. It's that way with horses. Perhaps a storm, the kind that shifts trees and blows out new caves, can do worse. A storm like we had, that autumn, might be enough to possess a person. It might send a girl's sense skittering out of her head and leave only thunder in its place. That would be one story.

But I said I wouldn't tell. I promised, and I've kept it. Nothing good would come of it, for folk would take the tale their own way, and she's only a girl still. Madden Lightfoot, my youngest stable hand, calm as can be now with the horses. Taken up where her father left off, so sudden.

I said I wouldn't tell, but I'd like to ask her, 'Do you remember, Madden? Or was it the thunder got in your head?'

★

At noon, while Madden and her father Pike were at work on the High Farm, the sky had turned to twilight, and the storm rolled in. By the time they had trudged down from the farm, the lower slopes and lanes were pouring new rivers to meet the gnashing sea. Madden shuddered at the might of the water, at the wind urging her towards it. Ever since, the west wind has rampaged, hurling curds of sodden sky against the earth, soaking it through.

All night, Madden, her little sister Clotha, her Ma and father have stayed awake, to watch the roof in case it should slip, to watch for water seeping through the walls. The storm filled them with a kind of fearful glee, and they did not think of resting. Now, after another day shut up in the house, Madden is dulled by the lack of sleep, but restless still, the throb the wind left in her matching the storm outside. It is dusk, but there is no light to fade away. There have been no shadows today. The roar that still echoes around the house is lulling. Clotha has given up poking at her sister with her bony feet.

All day their Ma has flitted in and out, to help neighbours scoop belongings from the torrent in the village below, or tie down the ones that might blow away. The gossip is that the waves have turned to monsters of scum and broken fish, and have churned the shore up so the rocks, when they can be glimpsed, are all in the wrong places. Madden longs to see this, to feel the sea's wrecking strength.

It is not only the shore that the storm has whipped cock-eyed. With the earth turned to loose mud, trees have begun to slide. All the copse at the riverbend is bunched together at the bank, her Ma said, and soon the trees will slither into the torrent one by one, like reluctant horses into a ford. This Madden also wants to see.

Clotha has relished these snippets of storm news, jinking about the house like a restless dog, pressing her ear to walls, holding out her hand as if hoping for drips through the roof. Madden stays curled in a chair. She cannot even hear the sea beyond the roar and smash of wind and rain, but she wants to crawl into the cave at the far shore end, and find what new passageways have opened and shut now. Her father showed her this cave, a hiding place that is never the same twice. He used to take her there, while her Ma was still nursing Clotha, and send her in while he kept an eye on the tide.

'What did you find?' he would ask when she came out, blinking, and he would make her draw the cave's shape in the sand, showing how it had changed since the last time. Then one day, after a wild spring tide, when the shape she drew in the sand showed a cavern that had never been there before, he sent her back in. 'Wait,' he said, 'until you can see in the dark.'

She had crouched in the nook of rock, hearing her breath echo, until there on the cavern wall, she saw. It was the shape of a horse, and a boy leading it. Small, but not a trick of the rock: carved in. Then her father was there, at her shoulder.

'Shift,' he whispered. He pulled a chisel from his pocket and she watched him chip around the boy's head, the stone ringing with each hammer knock. 'Come and look.'

Now it was a girl who led the horse across the cavern wall, with long curling hair like her own.

'Soon as you're old enough,' her father said. 'We'll get you as skilled with the horses as any boy. And if time comes I'm gone, you'll have my work, and take care of your Ma and Clotha.'

She pictures the sea churning sand through the cave, washing it away, so that the cavern is opened up again, the horse and girl showing on the wall. Then she watches the fierce water scrubbing them out.

'Stay awake,' Clotha hisses in her ear, pinching her arm. Madden rubs her eyes, hearing again the storm roar that had faded for a moment. She must not sleep. Clotha is hunting for drips again, but it is not the roof that worries Madden.

Her belly had turned cold as ice that day in the cave, for horses terrified her even then, and they still do. Now, at thirteen years old, she is apprenticed to her father at the High Farm, where he makes workers of the wild horses and knocks the farm-born ones into good shape. Not the son he wanted but his eldest child, and he has no inkling how hard she has to try not to run away from those beasts, to be still when she looks at their rolling eyes, their twitching shoulders. She cannot harness their might, the way her father does.

Instead, she dreams of horses every night, the thunder of hooves rolling towards her, and she thrashes awake just as she will be trampled. Worse than the terrors, the night wanderings she has not made since she was a child have come back.

Last week, Robin, the lanky, straggle-haired man who gives her father work at the High Farm, was waiting at the gate one morning.

'A word, in the house, Pike,' he said. When her father came out his cheeks were as red as embers.

'See this,' Pike said to her. He pointed to where the heavy iron bar, the one for keeping the barn door shut and the horses in, lay on the ground. 'Seeing as you took it down, you put it back up now.'

Madden stared. The bar was as long as she was. 'I can't,' she said.

'You did, so you will. The colt's out and the mare too.'

After she'd struggled with the weight of it long enough to sweat, burning with a shame that didn't seem to belong to her, he had taken one end and dragged it away. 'If those horses don't come back, if we can't find them ourselves, we'll bear the cost. Robin saw you do it himself, middle of last night.'

She didn't believe him, but climbing into bed that night, she found the mud on her sheets. Then, the shame she had not felt for years, since she had wandered in the night as a child, came sidling back.

'He's worried for you, that's all,' her Ma used to say then, coddling, when Pike shook his head. Her father's silence, his stony eyes, told her something else.

She must not sleep.

Thunder breaks again, a long cracking sound as though a piece of cloud has broken off, and somewhere nearby wood splits and creaks. The cave at the far shore end is roaring.

★

I said I wouldn't tell. Not this time. It bothered me bad enough that I told Pike Lightfoot his daughter had been up to the farm in the night and let out the horses. I only meant it were odd, and he should keep an eye on her. But there he stood and yelled at her with all the farm hands to hear. There'd been something strange about her that night, walking so slow but strong enough to take down the iron bar, looking at me but not looking.

Still, I'd almost forgot it when this storm came in. I'd the horses to think of, bolted after the fence gave in the night. I've seen plenty of storms blow in, blow havoc and blow out again. It can be a fine thing, in its way, takes off a skin of earth, washes out the grumblings and stinks that have been growing, and leaves us fresh as peeled apples. But this one, it were ruthless, never-ending. Enough to put thunder in anyone's head.

It were right up high on the hill I saw her, while I trudged out looking for the horses. Scrap of washing, I thought, flapping up there against the rock. Meant to pick it up and keep it for its owner. But when I got closer I saw it were a dress and inside it, Madden Lightfoot. She lay still as if she were warming herself on a sunny spring day.

I called out, loud as I could in the wind and the sideways rain. She stirred from the rock where she'd been laying and looked up, and then she walked right off, in the opposite way from me. I shouted some more, but on she went, like she didn't hear at all. Put me in mind of the way she'd been when I caught her by the barn the other night. Something not right. No sign of my horses, then, and I felt I should see the girl safe, so I followed.

The oddest path, she took, across the field, seeming to feel with her feet in all that mud. Then she climbed right over the field wall, even though there's a stile but a few yards away, and dropped down to go on walking on the other side. I went by the stile but I kept my eye on her. She didn't go fast, but steady in spite of that jostling wet wind. Two more fields she crossed in that way, straight over walls like she hardly noticed them in her way.

I were wet to my guts by then, and she'd not as much as turned to look at me. I were wondering what do to, if I should make a grab for her and get her home by sheer force. But she turned into the wood, pushed her way fearless through the holly thickets and there in the gully, up to her knees in a mire of leaf and black mud, she found my mare.

It seemed a blessing that – as if she were paying me back for letting the same creature out before. I had some trouble to get my hand knotted firm in the mare's mane, get her soothed.

'Is that what you're out for, helping find my bolted horses?' I asked. She stared at me but she didn't answer. Her look seemed to go through me. 'Might be time to get home now, get dry,' I tried. I were starting to feel a dunnock, talking with no answers. But then the thunder cracked, and the poor mare whinnied, and the girl gave a shudder, and all in a rush so sudden after her standing there so quiet, she ran at me and grabbed my hand. She were yelling something all jumbled. She caught me by surprise, pulled my hand so hard I lost my grip on the mane, and dragged me away from the mare. I had a struggle, then, running after the horse in all that mulch, and Madden Lightfoot went marching off, and I couldn't catch up with her until we were halfway back over the field.

She turned and saw me. Both of us were as draggled as trolls, but that odd, empty look in her face had gone. She seemed to know me again.

'You did me a good deed,' I said. 'Let me see you home safe.'

But she looked at the mare and shook her head. 'Please don't tell my father you saw me out,' she said, and she ran off down towards her house.

★

Clotha's squeal is what makes Madden look down and see the muddy prints she has left. Her ankles are thick with stuck on leaves, and her dress as brown as if it were made from a sack. But it is too late to clean up, there are voices at the door and her Ma sweeps in fast behind her, head down in a whisk of water and wind. She is in a wretched state herself, her hair twizzled into a soggy nest and her bluish face scratched all over, and everything soaked.

'Where d'you get to, and get like that?' she asks, and shakes her head at Madden. 'Your father saw you coming down from the field. He'll want an answer. Now see if you can get that fire up. I'd give my fingers and toes for hot water, if I could feel them.'

Madden shoves her feet into her boots to hide the mud, just as her father follows through the door, and hurls his sopping cap onto the floor. Her mind is full of that horse, and Robin there too with her, all of a sudden in the field. She wonders what she has done this time, if it was her let the mare out again. There's no time to puzzle out which would be least bad, to say she's gone wandering in her sleep, or that she'd purposely disobeyed, for already her father has his shoulder against the great oak table and is groaning with the effort as he pushes it towards the door. When he has it wedged there, he stops, and leans. 'We'll have no more of it,' is all he says.

Madden stays quiet. At least this way she cannot do it again.

'But the roof, Pike,' calls her Ma, from where she is digging out dry clothes from the cupboard. 'If it slides we'll be stuck under a heap of wet thatch.'

'It can't go on much longer, this storm,' Pike replies. 'Safer in here than out there.' He doesn't even look at Madden.

'Well, I'll keep awake, even if you can't stay up another night.'

'Me too,' Madden says. She cannot shake the horse out of her head and is afraid of it becoming a whole sky full of horses, thundering into her dreams, giving her terrors. If she stays awake, she cannot dream. She cannot wander.

Pike is the only one who climbs up to the sleeping loft, still in his wet clothes. Her Ma sits Clotha between her knees by the hearth while they dig for sparks.

'What shall we sing, to keep wide awake?' Ma starts humming a rambling tune.

Behind it Madden can hear the tick, tick of the dripping thatch, drifting in and out of patterns, now like a clock, now like a patter of running feet. The room is foggy with smoke from the fire where water flicks down the chimney. She thinks of the cave at the far shore end, all the deep, dark rooms it might have now, how the girl leading the horse might have been smashed right away by the sea.

Ma's singing has turned to a burble, and now it has become only whistling snores. Clotha's head is resting on her knee, mouth open. The wind growls at the walls. Madden's eyelids are heavy, heavy as the oak table she'd never be able to shift, too heavy to hold back a cloud of horses. Around the house, thunder cracks.

★

Back at the stable, and the mare safe, I remember I thought on Madden Lightfoot. Couldn't make head nor tail of it. Don't tell my father, she'd said. But I didn't like the idea of keeping it from Pike, if she were to go wandering about again, and something were to befall her out in that storm. It was still raging then, and I'd seen on my way back up to the farm how everything were shifted about. Trees down or standing where there were none before. Lanes gone and hedges washed away and all the landmarks made so they muddled the eye, if they were there at all. It gnawed at me, the thought of her out alone with that uncanny look about her, like it were another creature behind her eyes. So I made up my mind it would be a good deed, to pass by the Lightfoots' and have a word with Pike. I'd have to go looking for the colt, anyway.

Night had fallen by then, with scant moonlight behind the running clouds, but I made it back down to the house. I were waiting, thinking out what I'd say, when a boom of thunder shook the whole place, and then I saw the door open a crack, the glow from their fire showing. It shifted a bit more, then out she slid, Madden Lightfoot, and came walking right out into the night.

'Weather for staying indoors,' I said, or somesuch, as she passed near me. It were like she saw me but didn't hear. She were looking at me odd again, with no meaning in her face, and then went walking right past. I didn't like to shout, I remembered the way she'd shuddered at the mare's whinny in the wood, and grabbed at me so hard I lost my footing. I weren't afraid, quite; wary perhaps, but I set out after her.

The rain were easing, but the wind still whipped at us. She didn't seem to mind it. The moon when it showed between the clouds lit her way a little, though this time she didn't make for the wood but wandered towards the shore. Bitter, the air there, and stinking of the fish that the sea had smashed on the rocks. All the foam on the high waves showed pale, and the sound of it enough to make a man quake, but on she went, walking where the shore edge path used to be but were now just a mess of rocks and mangled turf.

At the end of the shore path she began climbing up the outcrop that hangs over the cave there. I struggled on the wet rock, all covered with seaweed flung up and mud flung down, but she got up nimble as a goat and when I heaved up beside her, the sight were a wild one. I'll never forget.

The middle of the rocky ledge had crumbled right away and a spray from the cave below came puffing up out of it like smoke. Waves smashed and boomed down there, and I shouted out for her to be careful but she paid no heed. I ran to where she was bending to look down, and above the rushing of the water I heard a panic whinny. I could hardly make it out, but down in the cave were one of my horses, thrashing in the water. There were nothing I could do for the poor beast. I held onto the girl to keep her from falling and together we stared down.

It was then I heard a yelling behind us and there was a man, clambering up the rocks. It were Pike Lightfoot.

'Madden!' he shouted.

He were slipping on those black rocks. A mercy it would have been if he'd never got onto the outcrop.

'Watch how you step,' I called, but that only made him gather strength, and then he were standing before us. The girl didn't say a word.

'Madden' he shouted again, but it were me he looked at. 'Give her to me.'

I wanted to tell him not to shout, not to fright her. 'I only followed her,' I said, 'to keep her safe.' I couldn't say, right there beside her, that something seemed not right. That she'd thunder in her head.

Pike were right up close, then, and nowhere to go with the hole right behind us. The wind were like a hand swiping at us. He grabbed hold of me, and the wave that must have come in below made a boom like it would blow us into the sky. The air split with it, and Madden gave a scream, and she pushed us away from her, me and Pike, with such a might that we both fell. I smacked the rock, but Pike, one quick tumble and he were gone.

I looked down into the cave but I could see nothing, only the swirl of that treacherous water.

Some while, I crouched there, between that staring girl, with her strange, quiet face, and the roaring from the cave. Whichever horse of mine had been down there had gone, and so had Pike Lightfoot. I were looking down again, when I felt her hand on my shoulder. She gazed about at the rock and the shore below, all those big, churning waves, and I saw her eyes had changed to knowing again. They had fear in them now. She said to me, 'Please, Robin, don't tell my father that I went walking in the night, will you? I'll make up for the horses I let out. Please don't tell.'

She trembled like a struck bell.

'I won't tell,' I said.

And I haven't told. For what good could come of it?

★

Her Ma is still snoring, and Clotha twitching in her sleep alongside, when Madden creeps into the house. The great oak table is shifted back from the door, and she wedges a stool against the door to keep it shut. She will say the wind must have done it, that she woke to hear it banging in the night. Her father will be fast asleep still up in the loft. Nobody need know that she has wandered in the night at all.

The dripping from the thatch and in the chimney has stopped. Even the wind has given up its howling and makes only weary whispers about the house.

Madden crouches beside the dwindled fire and pokes in new kindling, to make it warm for when the three sleepers awake.

Afterword:

# Sleepwalking

## Dr Paul Reading, MA, MB BChir, PhD, FRCP
The James Cook University Hospital, Middlesborough
President of the British Sleep Society

THE MYSTERIOUS PHENOMENON OF sleepwalking has fascinated physicians, scientists, artists, authors and playwrights alike for centuries. Although our neuroscientific understanding of sleepwalking remains rudimentary, the traditional view that sleepwalkers are somehow 'possessed' by dark supernatural forces of the night has generally been superseded. However, it is easy to understand how the often bizarre, complex and potentially dangerous behaviours exhibited by some sleepwalkers has led to such speculations and comparisons with the actions of zombies. Indeed, the outward demeanour and actions of a sleepwalker may well appear 'demonic' or 'unworldly', especially to an anxious bed partner who has just been abruptly woken from deep sleep.

Sleepwalking is a type of sleep disorder called a parasomnia that generally arises from the deepest stages of sleep. It is surprisingly common, affecting up to 10% of children on a regular basis at some point during their development. Sleepwalking tends to resolve spontaneously through adolescence but may persist or recur in around 2% of adults. An extremely wide spectrum of behaviours is reported, from the benign 'wanderings' of young children to agitated nocturnal disturbances more often seen in adults. The latter may engage in complex, even violent activities in a state of partial awareness even though subsequent recollection of the event is generally absent or, at best, extremely vague. The behaviour of some sleepwalkers clearly has an apparent 'goal' such as seeking out food or actively escaping an imagined threat. By contrast, in many, the behaviours are bizarre and out of character, occurring randomly and without obvious purpose.

Sleepwalking typically occurs within an hour of going to bed because this is when most people reach the deepest stage of sleep, so-called non-rapid eye movement (non-REM) or slow wave sleep. Following a period of deep non-REM sleep lasting 20 minutes or so, it is then normal to enter lighter non-REM sleep or perhaps REM sleep, the stage most strongly associated with vivid dreams. However, sleepwalkers have an abnormal tendency to shift very rapidly from deep sleep to an altered state of consciousness, somewhere between wake and sleep, in which they can appear responsive to external stimuli and are able to navigate away from the bedroom. Understandably, given its nature and the lack of animal models, there are significant logistical challenges when trying to investigate sleepwalking experimentally. However, several brain imaging studies have shown that the frontal areas of the brain remain asleep or 'switched off' in this state whereas most other areas appear awake and fully functional. Deactivation of the brain's frontal lobes helps to explain the unnatural and seemingly robotic nature of many sleepwalking events as well as the subsequent amnesia. It also probably accounts for the abrupt change in personality that many sleepwalkers exhibit and their inability to recognise familiar people even though most elements of visual processing clearly appear intact. Although sleepwalkers are potentially a little more clumsy compared to their levels of performance in the wakeful state, they can retain surprising levels of dexterity and motor control. Extreme examples of complex behaviours include phone texting, climbing ladders onto roofs, or even successfully driving a car in traffic.

The ultimate cause of sleepwalking is unknown although most authorities propose an abnormality of neurodevelopment or brain wiring in very early life that alters how the brain regulates and orchestrates shifts between the various sleep stages. It is traditionally considered a disorder of arousal, most simply characterised by incomplete awakenings from sleep. There is certainly a strong genetic component as sleepwalking commonly runs in families. The fact that the phenomenon usually improves spontaneously with age probably reflects the sobering fact that the deepest stages of sleep from which sleepwalking arises will naturally deteriorate or diminish as an inevitable and early part of the natural ageing process.

In those predisposed to sleepwalking, there are several factors that may act as precipitants or triggers for individual episodes. If sleep is particularly deep, perhaps due to a prior spell of sleep deprivation or an external factor, such as hypnotic medication, this will often increase the likelihood of events. Furthermore, once deep sleep has been entered, if an internal or external sensory stimulus partially arouses the subject, a sleepwalker may well exhibit an episode rather than simply wake up or enter a lighter stage of sleep. Remarkably, in a laboratory setting, sleepwalking can reliably be triggered by exposing potential sleepwalkers to a loud alerting auditory stimulus once they are witnessed to have entered deep sleep using cerebral monitoring. In the real world, such arousing stimuli may also include loud noises, typically snoring, but also excessive limb movements from either the sleepwalker or the bed partner, as well as uncomfortable or inappropriate sleeping environments. Internal arousing factors such as anxiety or excessive stress undoubtedly play a role in some and may influence the precise nature of any sleepwalking episode, particularly with regard to its emotional content.

Other than attempts to identify and reverse potential fuelling factors, there are no recognised or proven treatments for sleepwalking. Indeed, to date, there have been no randomised trials of any potential medications to treat this relatively common phenomenon. Anecdotally, some short-acting hypnotic drugs may trigger sleepwalking whereas longer-acting agents sometimes suppress episodes in individual cases. Limited evidence also suggests that the neurochemical changes produced by certain antidepressant drugs may suppress the tendency to sleepwalk.

Increasingly, courts of law are being asked to deal with cases of violent behaviours resulting in harm to people or damage to property allegedly arising from an episode of sleepwalking. In these situations, behaviours are proposed to occur involuntarily or automatically from a state of deep sleep. A defence of so-called automatism may be upheld depending largely on empirical background evidence and the precise details of the case. Not infrequently, excessive alcohol intake precedes the episodes and it may be difficult, if not impossible, for an expert witness or jury to be certain whether behavioural outbursts are indeed a result of sleepwalking or simply alcohol-fuelled. However, most authorities recognise that the secondary effects of significant alcohol intake such as sleep deprivation, increased snoring, or a full bladder may play a role in generating events.

In Zoe Gilbert's gripping short story we hear the bizarre and tragic tale of Madden, a girl in early adolescence previously prone to abnormal nocturnal 'wanderings'. The setting is clearly rural and far from modern, giving a wonderfully gothic feel to the narrative. The behaviours exhibited by Madden in her somnambulistic state are bizarre yet seemingly goal-directed, in part at least. Sequentially, over several episodes, she releases horses from their stables and then appears to locate them whilst in a sleepwalking state. Her staring appearance and actions are not natural such that the narrator is clearly able to distinguish this altered state from her wakeful persona. The single-minded yet inappropriate nature of her behaviour, directly striding across open countryside, avoiding simpler routes, would be typical for a seemingly determined sleepwalker, as would her lack of subsequent memory for any actions. The combination of perplexity and guilt when full awareness is subsequently regained is certainly reported by sleepwalkers in clinical situations. One might propose Madden's significant fear of horses has somehow influenced the nature of her episodes in the same way phobias and stressful events can commonly influence dreams and similar sleep-related phenomena. As an aside, although suggestive of a female horse, the word 'nightmare' has an interesting etymology, actually referring to a mythological demon, a 'mare' in Old English, capable of tormenting victims through frightening dreams. The intriguing physical strength and remarkable powers of location exhibited by Madden add to the 'supernatural' feel of her episodes as witnessed by the narrator. Whether sleepwalkers, like hypnotised subjects, are indeed capable of performing tasks beyond their expected abilities has yet to be studied experimentally, but remains an intriguing speculation.

To explain the timing of Madden's sleepwalking behaviours, it appears there was, literally, a 'perfect storm'. As a main risk factor, she was clearly significantly sleep deprived, partly voluntarily but also due to the prolonged tempest over several days and nights. Sleep, once finally achieved, is likely to have been severely disturbed both by the weather conditions and her pre-existing anxieties, potentially fuelling an episode of sleepwalking.

The purposeless tragic final act leading to the dramatic demise of Madden's father is compatible with a sleepwalking event. As bed partners of sleepwalkers may confirm, attempts to physically restrain an agitated sleepwalker may well produce a violent physical reaction during which there is no apparent facial recognition of the perceived assailant and no subsequent recall. It is intriguing to speculate on any judicial outcome if Madden's actions had led to criminal proceedings. From what we know, however, she very much appears the innocent victim of a severe sleep disorder rather than simply a young girl with thunder in her head.

# The Night Husband

## Lisa Tuttle

IT'S A STRANGE THING, magical, but ordinary. Everyone needs it, wants it, yet it is taken for granted. No one really understands it, yet we make rules, measurements and pronouncements as if we do.

My problem with sleep began in childhood, when my parents forced me to go to bed not when I was tired, but when they were tired of me. Once I had been kissed goodnight I was not allowed to get out of bed or turn on a light – no matter how bored and restless I felt. The only cure for that was sleep, they told me, and the sooner I stopped struggling against it, the more quickly the night would pass.

I spent so many long, lonely, boring, frustratingly wakeful hours that, in memory, they blend into one eternal sleepless night that seems to have taken up the major part of my childhood. I had various mental games and challenges to keep myself entertained, like any prisoner, and I told the time by my parents' unseen but distantly apprehended routines. First there would be the sounds of television or music or conversation going on in the front room, and although it was too far away and too soft for me to understand, and it was naturally frustrating to be so cut off from the things that interested my parents, still it was comforting to have this evidence that life still went on in the lamp-lit living room from which I had been banished. After a while, though, the television or music came to an end, and then there would be the softer, blurrier sounds of creaking floorboards, running water, toilet flushing, yawns and sighs, soft murmurings and the groan of bedsprings that meant my mother and father were going to bed. Then silence flowed through the house like a thicker, deeper version of the darkness, and I felt the whole world was asleep and dreaming, I alone shut out from this mysterious communion.

Until, amazingly, I opened my eyes to daylight. The night had ended, and somehow, although I could not remember how it happened, I had slept.

Growing up, I did not outgrow my difficult relationship with sleep. I never told my parents (why should I add to their feelings of guilt?), but those early years of enforced boredom in bed shaped the rest of my life. As soon as I was old enough to decide for myself, I stopped going to bed. I fell asleep on the couch or at my desk, sometimes in the bath, even occasionally in some quiet corner of the library or the Student Union. My difficulties with sleeping extended to sleeping *with;* relationships remained casual, temporary affairs well into my twenties. And then I met Alan.

The first time he fell asleep in my bed, instead of feeling annoyed or uncomfortable, I was charmed. I didn't wake him up and tell him he had to go home. I didn't fume and brood, and I didn't leave him there while I read a book or got on with something else. No, I just lay there beside him, not feeling bored or impatient or any of those other unpleasant things, but simply happy, lucky, pleased to be near him, watching the beautiful blank vulnerability of his face and breathing in his exhalations, almost as if I could sip sleep from his lips.

And then I slept.

It was as if he shared his sleep with me, and this was the best gift anyone could have given me, something I had been waiting for, without knowing it, all my life.

No one else could understand what I saw in him, and my friends and family thought I was rushing things when I asked this man I hardly knew, and seemed to have so little in common with to move in with me, but he gave me something I needed. For the whole time that he shared my bed, I slept like a normal person.

We didn't get married – that was a step too far, for both of us. He moved in with me, and I paid the mortgage (well, it was my flat) and we split the other bills. We kept our finances separate, and other parts of our lives, too. We got along well, in the sense that we didn't fight, but maybe we were careful not to have too many things to fight about. Money could have been a bone of contention, if we had let it. We didn't talk about politics (or we would certainly have argued) and I didn't care enough about his various sporting passions even to have an opinion.

My friends didn't get it, and he found evenings spent with them a big drag. Most of them were primary school teachers, like me, and into artsy-crafty sorts of things: knitting, making jewellery, vintage clothes, folk music. Alan was selling phones when I met him, later he worked for Littlewoods. He liked beer and sports and heavy metal. But you don't fall in love with someone on the basis of shared interests, even if they might keep you together after the physical ties fade, if they do. Never disregard the physical: it was enough to bring us together, and keep us together for nearly six years without the binding ties of marriage, kids or a shared mortgage. Although the definition of 'together' was pretty far stretched by our final year.

I think we both knew it was over for months before we finally admitted it to each other, so it was not only inevitable but even a kind of relief when he finally moved out.

A relief, until I went to bed and discovered I could not sleep.

At first, with no one to tell me to go or invite me to come to bed, I kept putting it off, and every night it was later when I found myself dozing off at my desk or on the couch. But if I got up and put myself to bed it was like a flash-back to childhood: right away I was wide awake, bored and restless, checking the clock every few minutes, fretting over the time

I was wasting, and before long I couldn't stand it, and was up working on a project, reading, watching TV, or else I got on the cross-trainer, hoping to wear myself out enough to sleep. I would have preferred to go for a walk outside – there's nothing like insomnia for triggering claustrophobia – but a woman on her own, walking through the streets of east London long after midnight… I was sensible and stayed in.

After a few weeks my work began to suffer as I forgot things, found it hard to concentrate, became short-tempered. Yet no matter how tired I felt in the daytime, at night sleep continued to elude me. I went to the doctor, who was sympathetic, and prescribed tablets. But although they knocked me out, I felt even worse the next morning, as if I'd spent the whole night involved in some bitter, yet curiously pointless, argument. My jaw ached from grinding my teeth, and I found my thoughts running in circles, fixed upon some particular phrase or scene, like a memory from my time with Alan – except we never argued.

I've always been inclined to avoid conflict. I hate quarrelling. I rarely gave my parents any trouble as a child, and while living with Alan I became increasingly adept at avoiding dispute, without realizing how much I was avoiding *him* as well, until at last there was nothing to come between us, but even less to keep us together.

I binned the prescription and resolved to get on with my life. I had managed on little sleep before I met Alan and thought I could do so again. But it seemed I had lost the knack. When I fell asleep, sitting at my desk, in full view of a class of giggling, whispering 8-year-olds, I could no longer pretend I was coping.

The word around school was 'narcolepsy' and I did nothing to correct it, for I had noticed that people were more sympathetic to someone who uncontrollably falls asleep when she shouldn't than someone who can't sleep when she should.

I was referred to a sleep clinic, where I was interviewed by Dr Bekar, a young woman with short dark hair, brown eyes behind spectacles that looked almost comically large on her small face, and a warm, sympathetic manner. I soon learned the limits of her sympathy, however. As an expert on sleep, she believed she understood my problem as I could not. She spoke of 'dysfunctional beliefs about sleep,' and tried to convince me that I was getting more sleep than I realised – not enough, obviously, but my own anxieties about not getting 'enough' sleep was a major part of the problem. Sleep was not the problem; only my attitude towards it. I had to change the way I thought.

I told her in more detail about my childhood experiences, and she listened patiently. 'Yes, no doubt that is when you developed your ideas about sleep,' she said. 'And it could be helpful to explore that at some point, but I think –'

I interrupted. 'I used to dream,' I told her. 'I may not have slept much, but I did dream. It was only because of that, that I knew I slept at all.'

'And do you remember your dreams now?'

'Well, of course not! I don't dream. I've told you I can't sleep. How can I dream if I don't sleep?'

'Everybody dreams,' she told me. 'Not everybody remembers their dreams.'

'I don't sleep,' I said flatly.

'No one can survive without sleep. You would be in much worse shape, both physically and mentally, if you had truly been awake the whole time for the past four days.'

'It's been longer than that.'

'It only feels that way. No, wait, please listen. I'm not making light of your problem – it *is* a problem, only not in the way think it is. From everything you've said, it sounds to me as if you are suffering from sleep state misperception. Sometimes, the brain can trick us – we think we're still conscious when actually we are sleeping.'

That sounded like sheer nonsense to me. How can you think you are conscious unless you are conscious to think?

Another name for it was 'paradoxical insomnia.'

I didn't buy it. As if you had to be a scientist to know the difference between sleep and waking; as if my own experience meant less than something she had read, based on studies of other people!

At last, seeing I would not take her word for what was wrong (or not wrong) with me, Dr Bekar suggested I come in for overnight observation, and a full set of polysomnography readings. Then we would be able to see exactly when, how long, and how deeply I slept. It sounded reasonable, but I knew it would be a waste of time. How could you measure something that didn't happen? I didn't sleep at home, so I was never going to manage the trick in a laboratory, all wired up to various machines. One sleepless night would not convince Dr Bekar that she was wrong – but if I had to go through the same farce several nights in a row to prove how unique my problem was, I would submit to it.

How anyone ever manages to sleep under those circumstances, in one of those places, I'll never understand. I certainly couldn't.

First, I was wired up – that took at least half an hour for the careful placement of electrodes on my head, face and chest, and the gradual creation of a surrounding nest of wires. Then another half-hour in which everything was checked and calibrated. I lay in bed and performed a series of surrealistic exercises on command:

Close your right eye, then your left.

Now blink both eyes.

Swallow. Again.

Now grind your teeth. Very good!

Turn your head to the right. Turn your head to the left. And so on.

Bedtime and lights-out, when the observations would commence, was left up to me: 'whenever you feel ready to sleep.' Sure. If I had waited for that magical moment, we'd be there forever, so I resigned myself to the inevitable at twenty-three-hundred hours (it sounded more scientific than 'eleven o'clock'). The final bits and pieces were hooked up when I was lying in bed, and then – darkness.

Back in the lab, I knew, the technician would be able to watch me through the window by infrared, but she would not do that very often. For most of the hours ahead, I was told, she would have her attention on the screens where my brain activity and other physical information (pulse rate, heart-beat, breathing, etc.) was displayed. If I happened to dislodge one of the connections ('Don't worry about it! Move around, get comfortable!') someone might have to come in and re-connect it, but otherwise I would be left undisturbed.

I was supposed to feel free to move about, but the fear of dislodging a connection, or getting myself entangled in the spiders-web of wires overhead, inhibited me, and from the moment the lights went out and I was plunged into darkness, I was gripped by a sort of helpless despair. Why was I here? Why was I putting myself through this suffering? Sleep had rarely seemed so impossible a journey.

It was a long, lonely night. The peculiar loneliness of knowing I was not alone, although without a companion, reminded me unpleasantly of those nights when I was a helpless, lonely child.

Finally it was morning, and the blessed relief of having all wires and patches removed; then I was allowed to have a shower, get dressed, and was even given breakfast before I went home. It would take several hours for the data that had been collected to be scored and interpreted, so I would have to wait until the next day for an appointment with Dr Bekar, who would go through the results and explain them to me.

I was looking forward to it, rather maliciously. Although I did not expect it would change her mind – I thought she might accuse me of deliberate sabotage, of keeping myself awake – she would be bound to offer me another chance. Not until they'd been able to monitor me for three or four consecutive nights would she take my complaint seriously, and even then might suspect me of taking daytime naps. But eventually she would be forced to acknowledge the truth that I had known for a long time: that it was possible to survive without sleep.

A fantasy played out in my mind as I lay awake at home that night: Dr Bekar's astonishment would lead to a more in-depth study which, although tedious, I must allow in the interests of science. Papers would be written, and I would be invited to appear at scientific conferences, and even on television. Others like me might come forward – how misunderstood we had been! – at last, our suffering was not in vain. Dr Bekar would write a book, and there would be a documentary made about my life – maybe even a docu-drama, something like that one starring Robin Williams – *Awakenings*. This one could be called *Sleepless*. Or would *Always Awake* be better? I thought of various stars who might play me, and was generous in my casting of the Dr Bekar part.

Embarrassing though it is to admit, the imaginary movie – and the actors who might play us – was still very much on my mind when I met with Dr Bekar again, and this combined with my usual tiredness to make me zone out a little. I didn't really absorb the import of what she was saying until she asked if I could compare the *quality and duration* of my sleep in the clinic to an average night at home. It was a strange question to put to someone who had not slept at all, but then I thought of how she looked down at her tablet before she put the question, and considered the possibility that she was working through a list of standard questions, so I took no offence and raised no objection, and said that the major difference was that in the clinic I was obliged to stay in bed. At home, after two or three hours of sleeplessness, I would usually get up and do something more productive. Or, if I was too tired to concentrate, I might watch a movie or TV show I'd seen before, until I dozed off in my chair.

'So, you never spend more than two or three hours in bed?'

I shrugged uncomfortably. 'Sometimes I don't get up

before morning. If I'm *really* tired. Then I think, well, even if I can't sleep, at least I'm *resting.*'

She looked down at her tablet again. 'Would you like to know exactly how long you spent asleep while you were being monitored?'

My skin prickled uneasily. 'What do you mean? I didn't sleep, not at all.'

She showed me charts tracking my brain waves – of course, they meant nothing to me without her interpretation.

'Here you are at lights-out. This pattern is normal wakefulness. You are quite alert, still, even though you're not physically active, and there are few stimulants in the darkened room. This does not look like someone who is ready to fall asleep. It's much the same picture, as you can see, for the first 33 minutes.

'Now you are calmer, although still awake. And here, at forty-six minutes, we see the beginnings of Stage 1 sleep. You see the difference? It's still very close to wakefulness, and if something happened to startle you at this stage, most people would not even realise they had been asleep.'

I frowned and fidgeted. 'Maybe because they weren't. *I* wasn't.'

She pressed on, determined, and showed me the peaks and valleys indicating what she called 'Stage 2, or light sleep.' This was still on the borderland of true sleep, and it was possible that I could have been conscious of myself lying in bed, which I might confuse with being awake.

Stage 3 – the slow waves detected by the polysomnograph left no room for doubt, according to Dr Bekar. Only two hours after I went to bed, I was asleep.

I wanted to ask why the picture of brain waves, produced by some machine, was a more accurate interpretation of my experience than my own memories. But I felt too angry to speak. It was more than my usual fear of argument. I knew scientists believed their machines. If anyone was mistaken here, all the supposed experts would insist it must be me.

She continued. Here, after an hour of deep sleep, the steady wave pattern (her 'proof' that I had slept) changed to something more like it had looked at the beginning. Even I could see that.

'That's when I woke up?'

'No. This is where you entered the REM state, which is associated with more vivid dreams.'

I huffed in disbelief. 'What? When the waves look like *this* you say I was awake. But when they look like this *again* – I'm not awake? I'm still asleep? How can you say that? Anyway, I know I was awake.'

'This is the REM state. It's very different from normal sleep. Well, I'm not sure it should be called sleep at all, to be honest, but it is not a waking state, either. It's something else. You move from sleep into REM, as you can see from your brain activity.

'The pattern you see here – it's not identical with the one we saw at the beginning, although it certainly looks much closer to wake than to sleep. The brain is active – but you're not awake. We know that REM is necessary – having too little of it is just as bad for mental health as having too much. But we don't know *why* because we don't understand what it's for. It might make more sense to describe REM as neither sleep *nor* waking, but a third state of consciousness.'

'And what *is* that state?'

'Let's just call it REM, shall we? We have no better name for it. It's still very mysterious to us, and is very hard to study. It may be as different from sleep as sleep is from wake. For now, we can only speculate as to its purpose. It may be connected with learning. Newborn babies spend something like 50% in REM, but that drops off dramatically as we get older.' She stopped and blushed a little. 'It is a very interesting subject – to me, anyway. But it's not really relevant to your case. You have no problem with REM – you seem to be getting as much of it as you need, even if we still don't know why you need it!

'So, getting back to your problem. On the evidence from your night in the lab, you *can* sleep, and you *do* sleep. If it weren't for your tiredness and your self-reported insomnia, I'd say that you are getting as much sleep as you need. Or at least that you can. You're not tired now? And you did not report feelings of tiredness after your night in the lab.'

'No, just excruciating boredom,' I snapped.

She managed to look sympathetic, although what she said was not. 'Well, you may have to get used to putting up with a little boredom, if you want to get a good night's sleep.'

In the end it turned out that the best scientific advice on offer was identical to the regime my parents had forced on me long ago. Instead of being active and doing something useful, I was supposed to spend many long hours alone in the dark every night. The more she spoke about the need to change my attitude towards sleep, the more I felt I was being preached at. Just because she was an expert on sleep did not make her an expert on *my* experience of it. The one encouraging thing that I took away from our meeting, and I'm not sure why, was her admission of ignorance about that mysterious third state of consciousness named after the rapid eye movements that signalled it.

I did not return to the sleep clinic. I did not take up the cognitive behavioral therapy prescribed by Dr Bekar. Just because my perception was different from hers did not make it wrong – I did not think I suffered from 'sleep state misperception' – even if there was something a bit paradoxical in my continuing insomnia.

Too often in the difficult, sleepless nights that followed, forcing myself to remain in bed (as advised), playing parent to my inner child, my thoughts returned to Alan. Should I have tried harder to work things out with him? Could we have stayed together? Was it my fault, or his, that we had not, or were my friends right and he was always wrong for me?

But if I could sleep with him, maybe I could sleep with someone else.

I decided to look for a new boyfriend, and with that aim in mind, signed up with a couple of dating websites, enrolled in a new evening class, and spread the word amongst friends and colleagues that I could use a helpful cupid.

Then one day I ran into Alan, outside what used to be 'our' Starbucks. It was the first time in months, and I did not recognise him immediately. He was older, shabbier, and somehow bulkier, more solid than in memory. I would have walked right past him if he hadn't stepped out in front of me.

He said my name. He did not look pleased to see me. He did not look friendly at all.

'Are you following me?'

My stomach fluttered at his closeness, then clenched. 'What?'

'You heard me.'

His mouth was set in a grim line.

'Of course not! Why would I follow you?'

'I don't know. You tell me.'

My fists clenched at my sides, but I gave him an appeasing smile. 'I don't know what you're talking about. I'm just going shopping – on my way to Waitrose. I don't even come here anymore, and I wasn't… I don't know how you can think… Since you left me –'

'You mean, since you threw me out.'

'I did not!'

'I've seen you, hanging about outside my flat at night.'

My stomach lurched. I wished I could flatly deny it, but there had been one occasion – well, two, to be honest – when, unable to sleep, I'd gone for a walk and somehow, not even meaning to go there… 'Well, I was curious to see where you lived, and anyway, that was months ago!'

'Months? I saw you last week.'

'No way!'

'Stop it. I saw you.' His look shifted, revealing something softer underneath. With a little shock, I wondered if he still cared. 'Look – you can tell me – if –'

'No, *you* look.' I was determined to have the last word. 'Maybe you've been following *me.*' I turned on my heel and walked away from him – even though that meant I was now headed back towards home, and would have to do my shopping somewhere else if I didn't want to risk running into him again. It was over with him; I had found someone new.

His name was Tom. I met him in the creative writing class I had signed up for on a whim. He was a little older than me, with cropped steel-grey hair and deep lines around his mouth and eyes. They looked like laughter lines, although he was always quiet and serious in class. Afterwards, some of us would go to the pub around the corner, and there I found out how easy it was to make him laugh. I liked the sound of his laugh even more than his deep, warm, slightly hesitant way of speaking. I liked him, and I thought he liked me.

One night we were the last two left in the bar and as he raised his glass to finish his beer I offered to buy another round.

'They're about to close – they want us gone,' he pointed out.

'Then let's go somewhere else.'

He smiled and shook his head. 'It's late.'

'Then how about tomorrow?'

The smile faded. 'You know, I'm married.'

'I don't mind if you don't.'

'Well… that's very kind of you. But my wife would mind.'

'She wouldn't have to know.'

My words hung there like a challenge. He said nothing, and I couldn't take them back. I knew they would still echo the next time we met. Our parting was awkward.

At home in bed I kept replaying the scene, as if I could still get it to come out differently. I couldn't stop obsessing over it, and naturally was wide awake when I heard the knock at my door.

I looked at the clock. It was almost two, an unlikely time for any visitor, but I didn't hesitate, or pause to put on a dressing gown. The flat was warm, and my long, floral-print night-dress was old, but modest enough for a meeting with my upstairs neighbour or whoever else it might be. Only at the last moment, as my hand was reaching for the dead-lock, did I have the sense to ask, 'Who is it?'

'It's me.' Tom's voice was unmistakable.

I opened the door and he came in. We looked at each other. I wondered why he had changed his mind, what he had told his wife, and how he had known where I lived, but I said nothing, fearful of breaking the spell, just took him by the hand and led him to my bed.

Naked, wrapped in his arms, I felt relaxed and happy for the first time in months, and fell quickly, deeply, asleep.

Yes, it was as quick and as unsexy, and as unlikely as that.

But it was irresistible, delicious, and I preferred it to anything else we might have done together. My sleep was deep and sound and lasted unbroken until my usually unnecessary radio alarm woke me in the morning.

When I opened my eyes, I found I was alone in my bed as usual.

But I was naked.

Looking over the edge of the bed, I saw my night-dress in a heap on the floor. The sight brought back a strong physical memory of Tom, but there was no sign of him as I drifted lazily around the flat in search of more evidence. He had not left a note. The door was locked, but not double-locked, which of course could only be done from the inside, or with a key. Those two small things were suggestive, but not proof. I might have forgotten to bolt the door. I might have undressed myself, half-awake or dreaming. In REM-state.

The more I thought of it in the waking state, the more I realised it must have been a dream. If Tom would not go for a drink with me, he would surely not have left his wife to come to my bed a few hours later. How had he known where I lived?

But if it was a dream, it was the best dream I'd ever had. I had dreamed myself to sleep.

I was so thrilled, I thought of going back to the sleep clinic and telling Dr Bekar the big news. I had gone direct from wake to REM, and then from REM to sleep. I could sleep! I had cured myself. The REM state was the key – REM state and obsessive thinking and sexual fantasy… But she'd never believe me, unless I could do it again. Scientific proof requires reproducible results.

But I could not figure out how to make it happen again. If it was something I had done, I had not done it consciously. Maybe it *was* real, and it was Tom who had let me sleep. The effects of my night with Tom (call it a dream or not) lasted well through the week, leaving me more alert and energetic during the day.

When the next creative writing class rolled around I was charged with anticipation. I arrived early. He was almost late, trailing in after the tutor, and although there was an empty chair beside mine, he took a seat the other end of the long table, then pushed his chair back, which made it hard for me even to see him, impossible to catch his eye. At the end of the 90 minute session he was the first to leave, managing to slip out the door while everyone else was still milling about. When I got to the pub, there was no sign of him.

There might have been some other reason for his late arrival and quick departure, but I had no doubt he was deliberately avoiding me. And his avoidance was too extreme to be explained by what had happened in the pub. I'd made a pass and he'd deflected it – big deal. It must have happened to him before. Men were generally flattered rather than horrified when a younger woman (reasonably attractive) expressed an interest. Even if he was determined not to give me any false hope, there was no need to act like that.

But… if it was *not* a dream? If he actually had come to my flat and… after such a risk, had he felt my falling asleep as a humiliating rejection?

I lay in bed that night wishing I could explain: falling asleep in his arms had been the greatest intimacy, the ultimate act of trust for me. If only I could make him understand… if only we could talk… around and around swirled the words in my head; careful, convoluted arguments, a verbal unveiling. If he knew who I was, would he accept me? I reminded myself that I had no right to ask him for anything. He was married; his wife, although scarcely real to me, was nevertheless a human being, an innocent victim, someone I had no wish to hurt. It was not even Tom I wanted, not really; my deepest desire was for sleep, that ordinary, mysterious state which had eluded me for most of my life.

The knock, when it finally came, was somehow no surprise. Yes, this was how it worked. I felt calm and reasonable as I understood the pattern: the mind went round and round, over and over the same ground, creating a path, until the man I wanted was compelled to walk that path, to my bedside. I was not asleep, but neither was I awake; I was in an altered state, and in this state, my dream could come true.

I got up and went to the door. But this time, when I opened it, I saw Alan.

Really, there had never been anyone else for me.

His expression was grave and sad, but loving, too. This was my Alan.

'We have to talk,' he said.

I went to him, and pulled him in, and stopped his mouth with mine, and led him back to my bed.

Love is strange, magical yet ordinary. Everyone wants it, needs it, yearns for it, yet takes it for granted. No one truly understands it, yet we speak and act as if we do.

When I woke in the morning he was gone. I wasn't worried. I knew he would be back.

# Afterword:

# Paradoxical Insomnia

## Stephanie Romiszewski

The Sleepyhead Clinic

INSOMNIA REMAINS ONE OF the most common medical complaints in society today. We know that getting a good night's sleep makes us feel better; we only need one bad night's sleep to be convinced. Research only corroborates this, and in fact tells us that long-term, poor sleep can have significant social, economical and health impacts. In this context, we love to blame poor sleep for everything, we scare ourselves with facts about the growing disruptions of modern life, and generally start fretting quite quickly when sleep does not come at night. Is it any wonder then, with all this pressure, that sleep is increasingly regarded as a luxury commodity? Just one more source of anxiety to add to the heap of other anxieties that make up modern life?

There is one subset of insomnia that is even more weird and wonderful than insomnia itself, namely 'paradoxical insomnia', or 'sleep state misperception' as it was formerly known. On the surface, sufferers of this condition display all the same symptoms that you would expect from an ordinary insomniac – difficulty in getting to sleep or staying asleep, broken sleep patterns, or just very poor sleep in general. Sufferers typically describe it as a problem that severely impacts on their personal, day-to-day lives. However, when these patients are studied objectively – by monitoring their brain waves at night in a sleep study – there is one very significant difference between an insomnia sufferer and a paradoxical insomnia sufferer: sleep is there. And it is more or less normal. Imagine then the shock of the sufferer, convinced that they've not slept well, being confronted with test results that they

159

absolutely have!

Paradoxical insomnia is poorly understood. There is little research in this area, as ordinary insomnia is rarely diagnosed using standard sleep tests (night-long measurements using EEG recordings, etc) because there is usually no sleep there to study – sleep tests like these only act as a tool to rule out other sleep disorders. A thorough medical history for the patient is usually all that's needed to diagnose insomnia and so without the regular use of an objective, diagnostic tool such as the aforementioned sleep tests, it is extremely hard to prove a case of paradoxical insomnia. If it is suspected, then a set of sleep tests might be conducted as an aid to convince the patient that they are indeed sleeping. And rather than alleviate the patient's anxiety over the issue, it can potentialy increase the patient's sense of frustration, as it does in Lisa's story. Around 5% of insomniacs are thought to actually have sleep state misperception. Some research (Krystal, et al., 2002) has shown that the sleep architecture of paradoxical insomnia is indeed different from that of normal sleepers – in short, deep stages of sleep are more disrupted by activity which is abnormal for that stage of sleep and consequently sufferers are more likely to experience 'hypervigilance' – extensive awareness of the environment and mental processes whilst their eyes are closed and in an otherwise a rested state. There are other theories (Feige, et al., 2008) that suggest paradoxical insomnia sufferers are actually interpreting the REM state (when more detailed dreams happen) as wake time – an intriguing theory, but one that has little evidential support.

But is it so shocking that this type of insomnia exists? Perhaps the explanation is simpler: maybe it's simply a product of culture and habit. How many times have we claimed we just didn't get ANY sleep last night and how many times has this *actually* been true? Is paradoxical sleep merely an extension of this inclination to exaggerate?

We know that we can't survive without sleep, so either insomnia is fatal, or, our bodies are so fantastically intelligent that even without us knowing we do get some snippets of sleep. We know that the latter is true because whilst insomniacs do tend to sleep less and the sleep quality is poor, insomniacs are surviving and are leading busy, productive lives with little or no other health issues. The most effective treatment is relatively straightforward with a bit of commitment and some perseverance, namely Cognitive Behavioural Therapy for Insomnia (CBTI) and involves building up a natural sleep drive and strict scheduling regimes in order encourage the body into consolidated, uninterrupted sleep, as well as reducing the anxiety and repetitive and unhelpful thoughts that can accompany and trigger the condition. This type of treatment is significantly successful in insomnia cases and has long-term effects.

Interestingly, research does show that this also works for paradoxical insomnia patients. How can this be if these patients do not have insomnia? There is clearly much to learn about this intriguing medical condition, and as such, us sleep specialists do not take it lightly. I, for one, tend to treat a suspected case of paradoxical insomnia just as I would a standard insomnia case and use CBTI. Results so far have been successful. Whilst I am at heart a scientist, I am at most a caregiver, and trying to enforce a diagnosis or scientific explanation onto someone who is going through such a complex condition is about as useful as a silent alarm clock. It is my job simply to try and help.

Lisa's story perfectly reflects the frustration that sufferers of this condition feel, as well as the sense of loneliness that comes with so many sleep disorders – disorders that affect people indiscriminately. It is also an excellent example of how science can only tell us so much, and that we are still very much reliant on our own feelings and perceptions of the world around us – in fact we favour them over the facts sometimes.

# References

Krystal, A.D., Edinger, J. D., Wohlgemuth, W. K., & Marsh, G. R. (2002). 'NREM sleep EEG frequency spectral correlates of sleep complaints in primary insomnia subtypes.' *Sleep*, 25 (6), pp 630-640.

Feige, B., Alshajlawi, A. N. A. M., Nissen, C., Voderholzer, U., Hornyak, M., Spiegelhalder, K., & Riemann, D. (2008). 'Does REM sleep contribute to subjective wake time in primary insomnia? A comparison of polysomnographic and subjective sleep in 100 patients.' *Journal of Sleep Research*, 17 (2), pp 180-190.

# Narcolepsy

## Deborah Levy

### 1

'DID YOU SAY SOMETHING GAYATRI?'

Anthony James sits at the kitchen table carving a small tiger out of walnut wood.

The tiger which is about the size of his thumb now has four legs but he has not yet made its face. Gayatri James is leaning on her elbows at an angle on the sink. She is gazing at the faceless tiger while her husband gazes at her.

'I said I want to go home for the winter', his wife replies.

'But I am your home, Gayatri.'

At that moment the tiger falls from his left hand. His lips twitch as his head slumps forward. His wife removes two small carving tools with their sharp blades and wooden handles from the table. His hair is white and abundant, his eyes are blue but now they are closed because he can feel the weight of a live tiger lying across his chest. After a while it lifts its heavy belly from his body and he can breathe again. He thinks he can hear their grey Siamese cat lapping up water from the dripping tap in the bathroom.

### 2

When Anthony James fills the kettle with water he notices how the stainless steel sink spins back to him a distorted version of his face. Three eyes, a face drowning in waves of approaching sleep as he moves his head from side to side to side.

'Gayatri', he says, 'This has been your home for three decades. You always said you wanted to live in a colder place. Kolkata was too hot, that's what you said.'

He reaches for a packet of chocolate and marshmallow biscuits called Wagon Wheels and unwraps the foil as he speaks.

'Then there were the monsoons between June and September. It's too hot and it's too wet in Kolkata. That's what you said.'

She is putting on her coat. It is snowing outside and the grey Siamese cat is sleeping on a chair.

'I would like to go home for the winter,' she says.

'But the snow is very light', he dips his Wagon Wheel into his cup of tea, 'it's just a flurry.'

3

Gayatri James walks slowly through the snow towards the Thursday market in the village square. A few energetic shoppers rummage through umbrellas and diamond studded mobile phone covers on the stall next to a pile of chicken thighs. Two women in identical anoraks that are zipped up to their chins, wait for a silver dish of potatoes to be weighed in kilograms. They lean in to each other as if joined at the hip, a blur of waterproof shiny material, four eyes taking in the middle aged Indian woman walking past them. Gayatri James finds herself bent over the lilies that stand in two buckets at the flower stall. Their petals are bruised with cold. She is cold too. Sometimes she wears a sari, sometimes trousers, but she always shivers in both. She can hear the twinned women talking about the Bulgarians who beg with their babies. They are thieves and gypsies. They are given houses as soon as they arrive. Nothing is too good for them. The man weighing the potatoes has joined in the conversation. His voice is low but loud, something about how Bulgarians ride horses and never learned how to drive cars.

Gayatri James points to the lilies. The flower seller wraps them for her, bouncing the flowers in his hand while she searches for change in her purse.

'I'm sorry to keep you waiting', she says.

He reaches for his sandwich and chews the bread extra slowly to pass the time. Gayatri James finally gives up looking for the coins that lurk at the bottom of her purse and hands him a ten-pound note. Now it is his turn to search for change. His fingers are frozen because he has taken off his glove to eat his sandwich.

Gayatri James says, 'I am reminded of eight small drawings by the Russian artist Ilya Kabakov.' She explains that the drawings show a man standing underneath a shower, he is naked but there is no water coming out of the shower. She says, 'I think his drawings are about a person who is always waiting for change, like you and me.'

The flower seller starts to cough. He lifts his feet as he tries to clear his throat and then slams his boots down on the fallen petals by his buckets. Gayatri James pats his back with her slim brown hand.

'Yes, you're right,' she says. 'That is how you pronounce the Russian artist's surname, Kabacough.'

She offers to hold his sandwich for him while he gets his breath back. He passes it to her and continues to choke. She waves it at the man selling handbags and rucksacks.

'Hello Igor.'

He waves back and then winks at the women who are buying potatoes.

'Morning Gayatri. How's Mister James today?'

'He's carving a tiger.'

'Another one? Well he's a nocturnal beast himself, isn't he? Has he had a haircut yet?'

'No. He likes his hair.'

The flower seller is now tugging her hand to remind her to return his sandwich.

'An arranged marriage was it?' one of the women quips.

Gayatri James swaps the sandwich for the bouquet of lilies.

'Yes, in a way it was.' She smiles at the women. The snow falls lightly on their identical anoraks as they wait for their potatoes to be weighed.

'It was hard work snaring a man like Mister James.' She walks towards Igor's stall and examines a suitcase while she speaks.

'I had to ride my horse through a dark forest in the monsoon rain to find him. In this forest lived a species of deer with four horns and many white-eyed buzzards, also known as hawks. They flew above me as I galloped through the dripping trees and they guided me to the shore of a deep wide lake.'

She runs her finger along the faulty zip on the suitcase.

'On the other side of the lake I glimpsed a hut built on stilts. Of course I knew I would find Mister James in that hut, but first I had to cross the water. How much is this suitcase, Igor?'

He tells her it is seventeen pounds but he will sell it to her for twelve. She shakes her head and asks him to remind her where she has got up to.

'You have just seen the hut built on stilts but you are standing on the wrong side of the lake.'

'Yes. But then I saw a beggar floating on a tree down the lake and this gave me an idea. I said to this holy man, "If I give you all my tobacco would you swap it for your tree?" He agreed and so I built a canoe and rowed in a frenzy across the clear tranquil water. It was full of carp as thick as my thigh. I caught two of them and smashed their heads under my boot. But I did not eat them despite my hunger. I knew I would need them to barter for a love that was bigger than a carp. At last I arrived at the hut and found my man lying in his pajamas on a mat.'

She lifts up the suitcase and prods the buckle of the strap.

'Mister James was guarded by six tall women armed with spears. I think they were Bulgarians. They were civil and distinguished. Two of them had PhD's and one of them was something big in engineering. When I offered them my very last box of green tea as dowry, they refused. Mister James is an exceptional man and they were not going to give him away easily. Of course when I threw in the fresh carp they relented. There is not a woman I know who can resist barbequing a fish on a fire of hot coals. Mister James was mine. Yes, it was a marriage arranged by a force bigger than us both. The wheels on the wagon of fate were turning but who was driving the wagon?'

When Gayatri raises her face from the suitcase, the two women lower their chins and scowl at their shoes. The man weighing potatoes throws in an extra large King Edward. It disorientates the scales but he can't be bothered to start all over again. Igor searches in his pocket for a felt tip to write the price of the suitcase on a tag but can only find a tattered five-Euro note.

The snow falls lightly on them all.

Gayatri reminds Igor to send her regards to his wife. She has to rush now because she is taking herself off for a sauna at the Recreation Centre.

An icy wind blows under the door of the changing room as she slips out of her sari and folds the pink and green material neatly into a square. Gayatri James takes off her earrings and then three bracelets and places them inside one of her shoes. She rolls off her tights which are made from a fabric that promises to tame her spreading stomach, until finally, naked and shivering, she walks barefoot towards the shower. The first trickle of water is cold so she steps back to fiddle with the shower switch. At last the water is less cold but not warm so she dares herself to wet her hair. Still shivering, she wraps a towel around her body, picks up the small plastic bag she has

left on the hook outside the shower and steps into the heat of
the wooden sauna. It smells of trainers and armpits. She climbs
to the top bench, spreads out her towel and lies on her back.
Someone has scratched the word ARSE on the wooden
ceiling with a pair of tweezers.

As the heat begins to warm her spine she gazes at her
breasts which are small but fallen, at the many folds of her
belly, the scar on her knee and the chipped orange nail varnish
on her toes. After a while she drinks from a bottle of water.
She starts to sweat. She opens the plastic bag and takes out a
small glass bottle of almond oil which she rubs into her arms
and then around her heart, moving down to her stomach,
between her thighs and onwards towards her shins and feet.

She is now glistening and hot. And then she mixes some
eucalyptus oil into what remains of her bottle of water and
sprinkles it on to the coals. She is happy to have found a warm
place in a cold place.

4

'HAPPY BIRTHDAY, ANTHONY!'

Gayatri James lights the candles on the birthday cake she
has baked with self-raising flour for her husband. A vase of
lilies stand nearby.

'Make a wish Ant.'

'I'm too old to make a wish.'

'Shut your eyes and think of something you want.'

Anthony closes his eyes. It's not so much dark behind his
eyes as grey. He searches inside the grey for a wish. The grey
changes to deep red and then to the green of parakeets. He
thinks he wishes to sue the Royal Bank of Scotland but
forgets what it is that so enraged him at the time. And while
he is on the subject of time, there is the matter of his new
watch. It stopped the day after he bought it. He replaced the
battery but the hands remain frozen and this is a secret
torment. When sleep attacks him it is comforting to glance at

the time when he awakens. So now he wishes he had actioned the guarantee that came with the watch. Something else comes to mind. He wishes he had shopped around for a tariff that represented better value than his current energy provider. He is the victim of woeful misrepresentation as a direct result of telephone selling. He wishes that the regulators were more enthusiastic about laying a glove on the power industry. And then there is his wish to eat more meat. Gammon is always reasonably priced but his wife doesn't eat pork or beef or lamb. She is not vegetarian because she eats chicken but now she has stopped eating chicken and tells him that all chickens everywhere should be kept alive to lay eggs. After a while he realises that his main wish is to resume carving the face of his tiger.

'I've made my wish, Gayatri. Can I open my eyes now?'

Anthony James wonders if his wife knows that he peeped his eyes open when he made his wish. His eyes were open and he saw her plunge her little finger into the centre of the cake and then delicately insert her finger, covered in icing sugar, in to her mouth.

'Yes, Ant. You can open your eyes.'

When he officially opens his eyes he looks at his watch and shudders when he discovers, again, that the hands are paralysed, they haven't moved for months.

'I have been wondering Gayatri, if you bought the suitcase when Igor reduced it by a fiver?'

'And where would I be heading with this suitcase?'

'Away from me and the missing messages in my brain,' he says.

'I don't want to run away from you Ant.'

'I'm glad you found a warmer place in the sauna anyhow,' he says.

'I did not go to the sauna.'

'Yes you did. You oiled your body but forgot to oil your hair.'

'No', she says, 'I bought some lilies and came home to bake you a cake.'

'I no longer know if I am dreaming or awake or if it really is my birthday.'

She hands him a small box wrapped in lime green tissue paper, the colour of his favourite parakeets. He opens it to find a perfectly formed jewelled watch to replace the one that has stopped.

'Sometimes wishes do come true,' he says. 'If they are modest wishes they stand a chance of not being crushed by the wagon wheels of fate.'

He wraps it around his wrist. The hands of his new watch flicker like a pulse.

'May I ask you Gayatri, was I dreaming that you told the market traders you galloped on a horse through the monsoon rains to find me?'

'Not you were not dreaming,' she says. 'The only thing I lied about was the carp.'

'But you did not to go to the sauna?'

'I'm flattered you dreamt about me naked in a warm place,' she says.

5

Anthony James spends the rest of his birthday day making the tiger's tail longer and then carving its face. He holds his new animal in the palm of his hand.

'What do you think?' He smiles at his wife. 'I've painted his chin and stomach blue.'

Gayatri lifts the tiger from his hand. The head is large in proportion to the body, a big head with a fierce expression that she knows intimately. She has seen the tiger before. She recognises it in the same way she recognises the face on all the animals he carves. The tigers face resembles her own face. Its eyes are her eyes, except this tiger has three eyes. One of them is closed but serene, as if it is slumbering in a tree, purring on the exhale of breath.

The open mouth, carved crudely from walnut, is his mouth. Its plump belly is her belly.

'Do you like him Gayatri?'

She passes him back his tiger.

'It's one of your best', she says. 'I like the three eyes.'

That night she makes a pot of dhal with extra cumin and garlic. They eat it sitting round the gas fire while the Siamese cat purrs on her lap and the radio broadcasts news of the sort of weather they can expect in the next few days.

It will be bitterly cold but the snow will fall lighter on Saturday.

'Do you still want to go home, Gayatri?'

'No, this is my home. And anyway, I have become very fond of the market traders.'

Her husband guffaws and then gently chides the Siamese cat who is now licking the dahl from his wife's spoon.

'Let your hair down for me, Anthony James.'

Balancing his bowl on his knee, her husband lifts his right hand to the top of his white head where his abundant hair is moored in a neat bun. He deftly removes a pin and his hair falls down past the woolen collar of his cardigan until it rests on the last vertebrae of his spine. When Gayatri James leans forward to kiss his forehead, his warm skin smells of wood and he is wide awake.

Afterword:

# Seized by Sleep

## Prof. Adam Zeman
University of Exeter

NARCOLEPSY IS ONE OF the most distinctive disorders in medicine (Dauvilliers, Arnulf, & Mignot, 2007). Its name means 'seized by sleep', highlighting its ubiquitous feature – sufferers are constantly sleepy, irresistibly so at times, dropping off during meals and conversations, while sitting in a class or playing in an orchestra, even while making love. Its second cardinal feature, 'cataplexy', is no less remarkable: emotions, most notably laughter, cause a partial or complete loss of muscular power: the head nods, the knees buckle and, in a full-blown attack, the sufferer falls to the ground, fully conscious yet, for some seconds, quite unable to move.

This odd combination of symptoms was first described in the 19th century, and christened 'narcolepsy' by a Parisian physician, Gelineau in an article in the *Gazette des Hopitaux de Paris* (Gelineau, 1880). During the following century, other elements of the disorder were recognised. In addition to sleepiness and cataplexy, sufferers are prone to hypnagogic hallucinations, vivid, dream-like experiences occurring on the cusp between waking and sleep. One other prominent symptom is also loosely related to dreams: people with narcolepsy are exceptionally liable to sleep paralysis, the sometimes terrifying experience of awakening unable to move a muscle. During these episodes the sleeper's 'dream' may project itself into her surroundings, with hallucinations, for example of an intruder, or of an assailant who may be sitting astride her chest, impeding her breathing, adding to the terror of the experience.

This 'narcoleptic tetrad' – sleepiness, cataplexy, hypnagogic

172

hallucinations and sleep paralysis – was well-known by the time I reached medical school. Another symptom, which can greatly trouble people with narcolepsy, was underemphasised. They are bad at staying asleep as well as staying awake, so that their nights are typically broken, with long intervals of wakefulness: the salutary 'circadian' cycle of activity by day and rest by night is thoroughly fragmented.

Narcolepsy is rare – but not very rare. It affects around 4/10,000 people, making it about half as common as multiple sclerosis. I see about 50 patients with narcolepsy in my sleep clinic in the South West tip of England. It most often starts in the teens, closely followed by the twenties, though it can begin at any time of life. It is associated with a particular, inherited, 'tissue type' (HLA-DQB1*0602), though this tissue type occurs quite commonly, and most people who possess it never develop narcolepsy. This suggests some genetic contribution to the risk of developing this illness, and indeed with a close affected relative the risk of the disorder rises from 4/10,000 to 1/100, implying that most patients with narcolepsy *don't* have affected relatives.

What biological sense can be made of this baffling collection of problems – days punctuated by sleep, nights punctuated by insomnia, loss of muscular power with emotion, vivid dream imagery at the onset of sleep, paralysis on awakening? An early insight into the nature of narcolepsy came from studies showing that in addition to falling asleep rapidly, sufferers enter much more quickly than usual into dream sleep.

'Rapid eye movement' or REM sleep, during which we dream prolifically, is usually delayed around 1-2 hours after sleep onset. During those hours we typically dip down through a series of deepening stages of sleep, enjoy the night's longest period of restorative 'slow wave sleep', and only then re-ascend the sleep ladder, eventually reaching our first REM sleep period. These cycles recur several times, with decreasing amounts of slow wave sleep and increasing amounts of REM as the night passes. But in people with narcolepsy, REM sleep is trigger-happy. Rather than awaiting the first REM period after 90 minutes of non-REM sleep, the narcoleptic sleeper plunges rapidly into REM – the hypnagogic hallucinations of narcolepsy are the subjective correlate of this 'sleep-onset REM'. Indeed people with narcolepsy sometimes report the sense that they have a second dream life running constantly in parallel with their waking life – and the two quite often get confused.

Other features of narcolepsy, also, begin to make sense in the light of the dominance of REM in the condition. During polysomnography, the overnight sleep study performed to diagnose a range of sleep disorders, REM sleep is recognised by several complementary features: brain wave activity resembles that of the waking state; the eyes dart rapidly about – but despite their striking activity in the muscles of our eyes, most of the body's muscles are markedly *inactive*. In fact, during REM sleep our muscles lose their normal 'tone' because they are effectively paralysed, by an active mechanism within the brain designed to prevent us from acting out our dreams. This 'REM atonia', it turns out, underlies both cataplexy and sleep paralysis. Cataplexy occurs when the atonia of REM sleep cuts into wakefulness, induced by emotion; sleep paralysis occurs when the normal atonia of REM sleep persists into wakefulness, with or without the accompanying experience of a dream (I should add for reassurance that most people who experience sleep paralysis do *not* have narcolepsy – it is an occasional, isolated, oddity for many of us, often running in families).

The underlying cause of narcolepsy came to light relatively recently. The cycle of sleep and waking is controlled by a set of chemicals produced by cells buried deep in the brain that send them widely throughout the brain (Pace-Schott & Hobson, 2002). These chemicals are 'neurotransmitters' – substances released by one cell to increase or decrease the electrical activity – the 'firing rate' – of the cells with which it makes contact. The chemicals in question are mostly quite familiar ones – like noradrenaline, also involved in the 'fight or flight' response; dopamine, which goes missing in Parkinson's disease; serotonin, boosted by Prozac – or Ecstasy; histamine which, elsewhere in the body, fuels your hay fever; acetylcholine, the chemical enhanced by drugs for Alzheimer's disease.

In the late 1990s a biochemist decided to go hunting in one of these deep brain regions, known as the hypothalamus, for novel neurotransmitters (de Lecea, et al., 1998). He identified a promising candidate which he christened 'hypocretin' – 'hypo' because it came from the hypothalamus, 'cretin' because it resembled another brain chemical called 'secretin'. He had no idea what it did, but a series of subsequent discoveries, in which serendipity played a large part, revealed that animals lacking the 'receptors' that detect hypocretin both slept too much and lost muscle tone when excited – they had narcolepsy. In 2000 it was shown that people with narcolepsy have very low, often undetectable, levels of hypocretin in their spinal fluid, and, by implication, in their brains (Nishino, Ripley, Overeem, Lammers & Mignot, 2000).

The current working understanding of hypocretin's action in the brain is that is stabilises the system controlling sleep and waking – it helps us to stay awake when awake and asleep when asleep (Sakurai, 2007). In its absence the brain flips inappropriately between the two states. Hypocretin also, specifically, biases the brain away from entering REM sleep. The otherwise baffling features of narcolepsy make sense given what we know of that hypocretin has these effects, and that it is missing from the brains of sufferers. But why should it go missing in the first place?

The answer is not yet known for certain but two clues point in a particular direction. The tissue type associated with narcolepsy, the catchily named HLA B*0602, plays a role in the body's immune system, hinting that immunological processes be involved in narcolepsy. This suspicion, and specifically the idea that narcolepsy might be an auto-immune disorder, in which the body attacks one its own components, was fuelled by a recent observation, made first in Finland, then echoed elsewhere in Europe. A particular formulation of swine-flu vaccine, Pandemrix, used in 2009, triggered a small but definite 'epidemic' of cases of narcolepsy, some of them unusually severe (Miller, et al., 2013). Vaccination, like infection, can set off auto-immune processes if there is some molecular resemblance between part of the vaccine and a constituent of the human body.

Narcolepsy can be a severely debilitating disorder: work, play, relationships all suffer greatly when repeated, uncontrollable bouts of sleep begin to punctuate the day. Emotion becomes problematic when it triggers paralysis: people with narcolepsy often have to learn to keep a straight face. Poorly controlled, untreated narcolepsy makes driving dangerous – indeed, illegal. But if narcolepsy is one of the most distinctive human disorders, it is also one of the most satisfying to treat.

The traditional approach to treatment is with stimulant drugs for sleepiness, and antidepressants for cataplexy. In the UK the usual first choice of stimulant is a drug called modafinil, which, used first thing in the morning and at midday, usually reduces sleepiness without entirely abolishing it. Many people with narcolepsy benefit from the addition of twice-daily dose of an amphetamine, for example dexamfetamine. Both drugs sometimes cause unpalatable side-effects and neither is always effective. Strategically placed, planned, naps can be a useful complement to stimulants – sleep is refreshing in narcolepsy, so that, for example, a half-hour lunchtime nap can recharge the batteries for the afternoon's work.

Antidepressants reduce cataplexy, not because it is in any sense a symptom of depression, but because antidepressants, as a group, tend to reduce REM sleep and REM-sleep related phenomena of which cataplexy is one. Again, they have their side-effects and their efficacy varies between sufferers.

For many people with narcolepsy the traditional combination of stimulants and antidepressants does well or at least adequately, allowing more or less normal activity to resume. But the improvement is usually partial, and, in a substantial minority of sufferers, inadequate to the demands of everyday life. Over the past decade or so a new treatment has become available which is creating a tricky dilemma for the British health system.

Xyrem, sodium oxybate, works very differently to traditional treatments for narcolepsy. It is taken at night, before bed and again around three hours later and promotes sleep, rather than opposing it. It enhances and consolidates nocturnal sleep with remarkable benefits both for daytime sleepiness and cataplexy. It is probably the most effective drug I have used for any chronic disorder: people speak of its life-transforming effects, resume education, get back to work, find time for their hobbies, rediscover laughter. But although it is not particularly expensive to make, drug development costs and the workings of the market place have made it extremely expensive to buy. National Health Service commissioners and hospitals are being forced to decide whether £10-15,000 a year is too high a price to pay for productive wakefulness. Not surprisingly, the answer has varied across the UK, prescribing is patchy and the treatment controversial.

As one gains experience in medicine, and the basic demands of diagnosis and treatment become less challenging, clinical encounters become more sociable – there is at least a little time to get to know one's patients. I have very much enjoyed getting to know people with narcolepsy. What matters to them, of course, goes far beyond their illness. I love Deborah's fictional account of narcolepsy both for bringing it to life through the story of Anthony and Gayatri – and, simultaneously, for putting it in its place. EO Wilson has written that science offers explanation while art provides understanding. A similar distinction has science creating 'likeness' while art conjures 'presence'(Martensen, 2004). Anthony and Gayatri become present in this understanding story which reminds us that love very often turns out to matter most.

# References

Dauvilliers, Y., Arnulf, I., & Mignot, E. (2007). 'Narcolepsy with cataplexy.' *Lancet,* 369, pp 499-511.

de Lecea, L., Kilduff, T. S., Peyron, C., Gao, X., Foye, P. E., Danielson, P. E., et al. (1998). 'The hypocretins: hypothalamus-specific peptides with neuroexcitatory activity.' *Proc.Natl.Acad. Sci. U.S.A*, 95, pp 322-327.

Gelineau, J.-B.-E. (1880). 'De La Narcolepsie.' *Gazette des Hopitaux de Paris,* pp 626-628 & 635-637.

Martensen, R. (2004). *The Brain Takes Shape*. Oxford: Oxford University Press.

Miller, E., Andrews, N., Stellitano, L., Stowe, J., Winstone, A. M., Shneerson, J., et al. (2013). 'Risk of narcolepsy in children and young people receiving AS03 adjuvanted pandemic A/H1N1 2009 influenza vaccine: retrospective analysis.' *BMJ,* 346, f794.

Nishino, S., Ripley, B., Overeem, S., Lammers, G. J., & Mignot, E. (2000).'Hypocretin (orexin) deficiency in human narcolepsy.' *Lancet,* 355, pp 39-40.

Pace-Schott, E. F. & Hobson, J. A. (2002). 'The neurobiology of sleep: genetics, cellular physiology and subcortical networks.' *Nat.Rev.Neurosci.,* 3, 591-605.

Sakurai, T. (2007). 'The neural circuit of orexin (hypocretin): maintaining sleep and wakefulness.' *Nat.Rev.Neurosci.,* 8, pp 171-181.

# Voice Marks

## Claire Dean

I THINK HE'S UNCONSCIOUS, I don't think he's dead, she said.

The print only took up a small space on the gallery wall. Sky filled two thirds of it and the man lay at the bottom, eyes closed. It looked to me as though all the rubble had been saved for other photographs nearby. It could have been a picture from another time and place, except that he was lying in the middle of a road.

She said she knew the photograph, that she'd asked me to meet her at the gallery because she needed me to see it. Years ago, when she was sorting through her dad's books she'd found it – the exact same photograph – inside an old geology book. It had been torn from a magazine and tucked between pages listing types of millstone grit. At the time, she didn't know if it was just a scrap used as a bookmark, or if it meant something to her dad. She hadn't known what to do with it, so she'd tucked it back in. She had no idea where the book had ended up when the house was sold. It was seeing the photograph on the wall with its title, *Sleeping Knight #1133,* that made everything clear. It's incredible, she said, how one memory can pull another up. Now she knew who he was.

The room was empty apart from the pair of us and the young attendant, who was trying to look like she wasn't watching us. Lines of black and white photographs taken during the Korean War were followed by Birmingham back-street portraiture. I edged towards the next photograph, hoping she'd follow. It felt like we were intruding on the dying man, staring at him for so long, whoever he was.

She hugged her coat around herself. Her face was pale and her eyes puffy. Working nights at the sleep-lab made her own sleep patterns erratic. She stayed with the photograph. I moved back to her side.

When I was ten, she said, I woke from a nightmare and ran to my parents' bedroom door, but then stopped. On the other side of it, my mum was speaking to someone. I crouched in the dark in the hallway, carpet tufts gripped between my fingers, and listened. Dad was definitely asleep – I could hear his heavy breathing – but Mum was telling someone off. Don't lie down, she said. No, you can't lie down to sleep. Wake up now. Come home. Come home to me.

Terrified, I crept back to bed, but I could still hear Mum's voice as I pulled the blanket over my head and hugged my bear.

People always assumed my parents were happy, she said, but during the day they moved around one another without touching. I didn't see it until I was a teenager. Didn't understand it until I was married myself. They got on with everything quietly, but they were two cars on separate tracks of an old wooden rollercoaster. Like the one at Blackpool where we holidayed every September, leaving just before the illuminations were switched on.

She stepped closer to the photograph, fingers raised. I was worried for a second that she was going to touch it.

I can't be certain Dad knew its title, she said, but he used to tell me about a sleeping knight. He always liked to go for a walk after tea, before bed, and sometimes he let me go with him. His favourite walk started from the top of the lane, where a gap in the wall led up into a straggle of woods. We followed fox paths out onto the moor. There was a brook we had to jump over that appeared and disappeared in the long grass as though playing tricks on us. After that, heather stretched right up to the clouds.

Dad could name everything – plants, birds, trees, rocks. I got merlins, cotton grass, peregrine falcons and sphagnum moss from him. When we reached a particular gritstone crag, Dad always stopped and said, he's still in there. This sleeping knight wasn't one of Arthur's army, Dad said he was from another time. Once, I asked him what the name was for the bright orange rings that spattered the stone. They're voice marks, he said – the marks his voice leaves when he shouts out. Whenever I asked after that he said, lichen. It's only lichen.

It wasn't just once I heard my mum talk in the night, she said. There were other times, and even though it unnerved me so much, I got into the habit of creeping to the door to listen. I learnt at that age that the night is a different world. Dad snored through it all. He had a thunderous snore.

She turned away from the photograph to me, just for a moment. I've felt it, she said, someone's name coming to my lips without warning; the compulsion to speak it aloud. Have you? She didn't wait for me to reply. Mum must have held his name in all day long, she said, and then at night it spilled out of her. She called for him and no one replied.

It didn't surprise her that she could remember her mum's words. It's the spindles, she said. When I got back into bed and slept, the spindles worked like bridges, carrying my mum's words from one part of my brain to another. Keeping them somewhere safe. All the names of rocks, the trees, the birds Dad gave me crossed the bridges too.

Her eyes closed as though she could fall asleep standing there. I reached out to take her hand, but pulled back as she began to speak again.

People don't realise we can hear when we sleep, she said. Not during the spindles, though. They seem to protect us from being woken as the memories are moved. Perhaps they protected Dad. He might not have heard Mum's words. But he must have known, she said, why else had he hidden the photograph? It could have been in that book for years, sandwiched between rock types.

She let her fingers trace the figure of the man in the air, just above the photograph's surface. My mum must have been the one to cut it out, though, she said. She can't have hidden it very well. How long must she have searched when it went missing?

Her hand dropped to her side. She lost him twice, she said.

Another couple had entered the room and I moved to leave a little more space between us.

Last night, she said, one of the participants in the study, a student in his early twenties, confessed to me that he was nervous about being watched as he slept. All I could do was reassure him it was his brain we were watching as I hooked him up to the EEG. People worry they'll dribble, or pass wind, or talk in their sleep, she said. It's exposing. Sometimes the brain does give up its secrets, but sometimes sleep is burying them further away inside our heads.

She took a step back, but didn't look away from the photograph. I remember his name, she said. I might be the only person alive who does. It feels like if I said it out loud I could wake him up.

Afterword:

# Spindles

## Prof. Manuel Schabus
The University of Salzberg

SLEEP AND ITS DISTINCT STAGES are defined according to criteria based on the occurrence and amount of specific phasic activities seen in the electroencephalograph (EEG). The EEG records the electrical activity of the brain along the scalp – specifically voltage fluctuations resulting from current flow within the neurons of the brain (currents caused by neurons 'firing' individually and becomimg visible on the scalp when in sync with many other neurons). These scalp measurements, together with eye (electrooculogram) and muscle (electromyogram) activity, are the only way to actually determine what sleep state somebody is in.

During a night's sleep, EEG recordings typically show the brain moving, cyclically, up and down, through different strata of sleep – stages defined by the average frequency and amplitude of brain waves – faster and shallower amplitude waves for light sleep (when large numbers of neurons are firing independently of each other), slower and higher amplitude waves for deep sleep (when greater numbers of neurons are firing in sync; see also Introduction, pp v-xvi).

Sleep spindles are a particular type of brain wave activity that occur mainly in Stage 2 sleep; so their appearance marks the transition into what feels like 'real' sleep (many people misperceive Stage 1 as wakefulness), where the brain 'shuts down' its processing of information from the outside world and presumably switches to a more internal processing mode. This shutting down generally occurs after muscle-twitching (the so called 'hypnagogic jerk') and, as Claire's story notes, the appearance of spindles coincides with a period of sleep where external stimuli, like sounds, are effectively 'blocked out'.

Interestingly, there is scientific evidence (Dang-Vu, et al., 2010) that shows individuals who generate more sleep spindles during a night of sleep exhibit a higher tolerance for disturbing environmental noise such as loud trucks passing by on the street. It can be speculated that these individual differences in resilience to disruptive stimuli are also reflected in better learning over the night and ultimately perhaps even higher 'intelligence' over a lifetime.

On EEG recordings, sleep spindles appear as waxing-and-waning oscillations at a frequency of about 11-15 Hz; they appear on the EEG graph as short bursts of activity, that spike in the middle and are usually tapered at both ends:

Spindles were first described by Berger (1933) with the term being introduced by Loomis and colleagues in 1935. In deeper stages of sleep, these kinds of oscillations are progressively replaced by lower frequency, high amplitude slow waves. In addition, spindles 'couple' with these slow oscillations in the sense that slow oscillations group spindles together; that is to say, spindles are more likely to be present during the positive, 'up-state' of the slow oscillation (i.e. the top half of the slow wave) – when most neurons fire – as compared to the negative, 'down-state' of the slow oscillation, when most neurons are hyperpolarised and silent.

The thalamus, a structure buried deep in the brain between the two hemispheres, is a central structure that has been identified as the generator of these sleep spindles and is often referred to as the 'gateway to consciousness' (Crick & Koch, 2003), as it is a central relay station in distributing incoming sensory information to appropriate regions of the cortex.

Within the thalamus, specific neurons have been found that are now regarded as the 'pacemakers' of spindle oscillations, what we call the thalamic reticular neurons (RE). Although spindles can be generated within the thalamus in the absence of the cerebral cortex (the brain's outer layer), the neocortex is essential for the induction, synchronisation and termination of spindles (Steriade & McCarley, 2005). In the intact brain, spindles are produced through complex thalamo-cortico-thalamic loops involving three types of neurons: thalamic reticular neurons, thalamo-cortical neurons, and cortical neurons (Steriade & Deschenes, 1984).

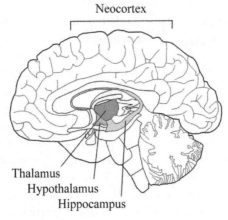

Neocortex

Thalamus
Hypothalamus
Hippocampus

In humans, EEG recordings are only able to characterise non-REM sleep oscillations in terms of scalp topography. Although they are detectable on all EEG scalp positions, spindles are mostly prominent over central and parietal areas (the central and posterior top parts of the head) with a peak frequency of about 13-14Hz (De Gennaro & Ferrara, 2003). A second cluster of spindles is visible over frontal (more anterior) areas, with a frequency of about 12Hz. This topographical segregation of spindles has led to the hypothesis that the two types of spindles are mediated by distinct biological mechanisms. Both types of spindles are also differentially modulated by age, circadian and homeostatic factors, menstrual cycle, pregnancy, and drugs (De Gennaro & Ferrara, 2003).

My own research, which combines EEG with functional resonance imaging (fMRI; a measure of 'energy consumption' in the brain) during human sleep, supports the existence of these two subtypes of spindles (Schabus, et al., 2007) although different spindle types are not described in the animal literature, so far.

In particular this simultaneous EEG/fMRI data revealed that – besides *increased* brain responses in the lateral and posterior aspects of the thalamus, as well as in paralimbic (anterior cingulate cortex, insula) and neocortical (superior temporal gyrus) areas – the fast spindle type is associated with increased haemodynamic activity (blood flow) in hippocampal and sensorimotor regions. This finding also indicated a possible differential functional significance of these two spindle types, with the fast spindle being more closely associated with cognitive functioning (Milner, Fogel, & Cote, 2006; Morin, et al., 2008; Tamaki, Matsuoka, Nittono, & Hori, 2008) as the hippocampus is one of the most prominent regions for memory. Yet more research is needed in order to unravel the functional significance of these two spindle types.

Sleep spindles are of special interest for cognition as they have been directly related to the repeated reactivation of thalamocortical or hippocampocortical networks after learning. Specifically in rats, hippocampal ripples were found to occur in temporal proximity to cortical sleep spindles, indicating an information transfer between the hippocampus and neocortex (Siapas & Wilson, 1998); a process which is vital for permanent storage in the brain. This neuronal 'replay' in turn has been suggested as the basis for reorganisation and consolidation of memories (Buzsaki, 1996; Steriade, 1999). Steffen Gais and colleagues were the first to demonstrate that sleep spindle density is also enhanced in human subjects after declarative learning (Gais, Mölle, Helms, & Born, 2002).

Furthermore, studies by Zsofia Clemens and her

colleagues in Hungary suggest task-specific topographic distributions of sleep spindles, suggesting that spindles occur predominantly over regions where actual memory 'replay' takes place. In accordance with known functional specialisations, Clemens and colleagues reported spindle foci over left frontocentral areas for verbal declarative memory (Clemens, et al., 2006) compared to parietal spindle focus after spatial declarative learning (Clemens, et al., 2006). Even more interestingly, there are several studies that link the above described fast spindle to motor learning overnight (Milner, et al., 2006; Morin, et al., 2008; Tamaki, Matsuoka, Nittono, & Hori, 2008), which is surprisingly well in agreement with the activation of vast sensorimotor regions during the presence of fast sleep spindles (Schabus, et al., 2007). When we talk about 'learning during the night' it is important to mention that in the declarative memory domain (that is, conscious knowledge and retrieval of 'facts', like the fact that Vienna is the capital of Austria), the forgetting of such facts is very common and likely over very short periods of time. In this sense, it is astonishing that sleep succeeds in strongly slowing down or even eliminating this forgetting over extended time spans (8 hours and more). Procedural learning or 'unconscious' learning of motor skills (such as mirror tracing or bicycling), however, might show actual improvements over time while the subject is awake. Yet, here sleep seems to add an additional 'boost' to the subject's motor performance: subjects who have slept after learning perform better than those who have been awake for the same length of time (Walker, et al., 2002).

Meanwhile, there is also plenty of evidence that an individual's learning potential or 'intelligence' might be well reflected in certain sleep features like sleep spindles (cf. Schabus, et al., 2006; Bodizs, et al., 2005; Fogel & Smith, 2011) as they allow an indirect view into the brain's connectivity. For this reason it is also possible that sleep spindles might be quite informative after brain lesions or degenerative diseases and allow us to estimate residual learning capabilities. The attempt to stimulate spindles as a way of improving memory, sleep or brain restoration has already begun (Marshall, et al., 2006; Hoedlmoser, et al., 2008; Schabus, et al., 2014), but further exploration is still needed before it can be applied in specific treatments.

# References

Berger, H. (1933). 'Über das Elektroenzephalogramm des Menschen.' *Archiv für Psychiatrie und Nervenkrankheiten*, 99, pp 555.

Bodizs, R., Kis, T., Lazar, A. S., Havran, L., Rigo, P., Clemens, Z., & Halasz, P. (2005). 'Prediction of general mental ability based on neural oscillation measures of sleep.' *Journal of Sleep Research,* 14 (3), pp 285-292.

Buzsaki, G. (1996). 'The hippocampo-neocortical dialogue.' *Cerebral Cortex,* 6 (2), pp 81-92.

Clemens, Z., Fabo, D., & Halasz, P. (2005). 'Overnight verbal memory retention correlates with the number of sleep spindles.' *Neuroscience*, 132 (2), pp 529-535.

Clemens, Z., Fabo, D., & Halasz, P. (2006). 'Twenty-four hours retention of visuospatial memory correlates with the number of parietal sleep spindles.' *Neuroscience Letters*, 403 (1-2), pp 52-56.

Crick, F., & Koch, C. (2003). 'A framework for consciousness.' *Nature Neuroscience*. 6(2), pp 119-126.

Dang-Vu, T. T., McKinney, S. M., Buxton, O. M., Solet, J. M., & Ellenbogen, J. M. (2010). 'Spontaneous brain rhythms predict sleep stability in the face of noise.' *Current Biology*, 20(15), R pp 626-627.

De Gennaro, L., & Ferrara, M. (2003). 'Sleep spindles: an overview.' *Sleep Med Rev,* 7 (5), pp 423-440.

Fogel, S. M., & Smith, C. T. (2011). 'The function of the sleep spindle: a physiological index of intelligence and a mechanism for sleep-dependent memory consolidation.' *Neuroscience &*

*Biobehavioral Reviews*, 35 (5), pp 1154-1165.

Gais, S., Mölle, M., Helms, K., & Born, J. (2002). 'Learning-dependent increases in sleep spindle density.' *Journal of Neuroscience*, 22 (15), pp 6830-6834.

Hoedlmoser, K., Pecherstorfer, T., Gruber, G., Anderer, P., Doppelmayr, M., Klimesch, W., & Schabus, M. (2008). 'Instrumental conditioning of human sensorimotor rhythm (12-15Hz) and its impact on sleep as well as declarative learning.' *Sleep*, 31 (10), pp 1401-1418

Loomis, A. L., Harvey, E. N., & Hobart, G. (1935). 'Potential Rhythms of the Cerebral Cortex during Sleep.' *Science*, 81 (2111), pp 597-598.

Marshall, L., Helgadottir, H., Molle, M., & Born, J. (2006). 'Boosting slow oscillations during sleep potentiates memory.' *Nature*, 444 (7119), pp 610-613.

Milner, C. E., Fogel, S. M., & Cote, K. A. (2006). 'Habitual napping moderates motor performance improvements following a short daytime nap.' *Biol Psychol*, 73 (2), pp 141-156.

Morin, A., Doyon, J., Dostie, V., Barakat, M., Hadj Tahar, A., Korman, M., et al. (2008). 'Motor sequence learning increases sleep spindles and fast frequencies in post-training sleep.' *Sleep*, 31 (8), pp 1149-1156.

Schabus, M., Dang-Vu, T. T., Albouy, G., Balteau, E., Boly, M., Carrier, J., et al. (2007). 'Hemodynamic cerebral correlates of sleep spindles during human non-rapid eye movement sleep.' *Proc Natl Acad Sci U S A*, 104 (32), pp 13164-13169.

Schabus, M., Hoedlmoser, K., Gruber, G., Sauter, C., Anderer, P., Klösch, G., et al. (2006). 'Sleep spindle-related activity in the human EEG and its relation to general cognitive and learning abilities.' *Eur J Neurosci*, 23 (7), pp 1738-1746.

Schabus, M., Heib, D. P. J., Lechinger, J., Griessenberger, H., Klimesch, W., Pawlizki, A., Hoedlmoser, K. (2014). 'Enhancing sleep quality and memory in insomnia using instrumental sensorimotor rhythm conditioning.' *Biological Psychology*, 95, pp 126-134.

Siapas, A. G., & Wilson, M. A. (1998). 'Coordinated interactions between hippocampal ripples and cortical spindles during slow-wave sleep.' *Neuron*, 21 (5), pp 1123-1128.

Steriade, M. (1999). 'Coherent oscillations and short-term plasticity in corticothalamic networks.' *Trends in Neurosciences*, 22 (8), pp 337-345.

Steriade, M., & Deschenes, M. (1984). 'The thalamus as a neuronal oscillator.' *Brain Res*, 320 (1), pp 1-63.

Steriade, M., & McCarley, R. W. (2005). *Brain Control of Wakefulness and Sleep*. New York: Springer.

Tamaki, M., Matsuoka, T., Nittono, H., & Hori, T. (2008). 'Fast sleep spindle (13-15 Hz) activity correlates with sleep-dependent improvement in visuomotor performance.' *Sleep*, 31(2), pp 204-211.

# The Trees in the Wood

## Lisa Blower

IT'S NOT THAT I don't sleep. I know I don't *not* sleep. I could fall asleep right now if I wanted to, but that's not what they want me to do. And Mia was fine about it when I asked her, if not a little distracted. But then she's always distracted by something. Her mobile phone rings all the time, then there's the home phone and now her pager. 'It's just that I don't remember giving you my number,' she'd said when I called her again to confirm. She still looks confused when she opens the door to me today.

'What are you bringing me now?' she says pointing to my overnight bag. I try and distract her with my usual offering of wine. She says, 'Laura, what do I keep saying about bringing me wine?' But she still tucks the bottle under her arm – I could see she'd already got a glass on the go – and the bag gets forgotten because then her mobile goes. It's her friend Liz and she's quickly told: 'Not really. Laura's here. It's Tuesday, isn't it?' And it sounds so very unkind.

But then she was all apologies: it was just pasta and pesto for tea because she'd not gone to the supermarket and she was sure that's what she'd given me last week, which she did, but I didn't tell her so. Besides, it was all the twins would eat. And then her mobile goes again and she sighs but when she looks at the number she's smiling. She sticks her head in the fridge to answer it, as if looking for the milk which is already on the side, and her voice is muffled, low, but sweet. 'Hi,' she says, and, 'No, not really, but I can later. Yeah, I'd like that too.' And then she shuts the fridge and says, 'Actually tonight is difficult. It's

Tuesday, isn't it?' And I see that she's not washed yesterday's plates, that the breakfast bowls are still on the table, and that they seem to have acquired a cat because what's down there on the floor by the patio door looks like a bowl of its food.

'Right, drink,' and Mia's back in the kitchen, her mobile back in her pocket, and she's still in her nurse's uniform after a 12-hour shift with her silver grizzled hair tied into a too-tight ponytail that sucks up her face. She fills the kettle, fills her glass and starts to swill out a mug for me. She talks with her back to me, asks 'What's new with you?' and then before I can speak she turns and says, 'Oh my goodness! Did I tell you Rowan made Oxford?' and because she suddenly looks so happy I'm forced to smile and say, 'No.'

Rowan is Mia's eldest daughter and brilliant at science, chemistry her thing, and though this is good, that Rowan will finally be moving out – their relationship is a little fraught to say the least – Mia covers her face with her hands and mutters something about the first from the nest and what will she do without her? I want to say, 'Plenty,' but the hands are removed and she suddenly shouts, 'Oh my God, did I tell you my mother was attacked?'

I look startled. 'No,' I say, and would rather not hear anymore, as I'm sure Mia, if she was thinking straight, wouldn't tell me either given how much she knows I detest the night, but she does and she says, 'Do you know what the worst part is? I'm glad. I'm actually really fucking glad because now I can do what I should've done years back.' And I wish she wouldn't swear because she sounds bitter and cantankerous and she knows I don't like it. But then the home phone starts up and she's hunting it down which I see flashing aside a pile of magazines on the seat of the armchair she keeps in the kitchen by the range which she had fitted almost two years ago and still doesn't know how to use.

Nor does she know how to use the home phone either, because when she answers it's on speakerphone so I get to hear: 'Mrs Onions? Edith Davenport. Davenport House. Just to say that the room is now ready for you and we can send a removal team for a week Friday. Does that give your mother enough time?' And I can see that Mia's panicking about me hearing this because she tells this Edith Davenport to hang on, she's on speakerphone and she doesn't know which button it is to get it off. Edith Davenport laughs and says, 'Technology eh?' and Mia agrees: technology will be the death of her if lack of sleep doesn't get to her first. And I raise my eyebrows at this and glare because she can't have forgotten why I'm here.

Eventually, she asks Edith Davenport to call her on her mobile. 'Because if I didn't know how to use that I'd never speak to my eldest daughter at all,' and she sounds so very sad when she says it. So the call ends and she suddenly remembers I'm here and goes, 'Laura. Shit. Drink. At least let me get you a drink. Things aren't normally like this.' I tell her, 'Actually, Mia, they are.' She gives me the sort of look that makes me feel unwashed, except her mobile is ringing. She says, 'I'm not sure there's teabags but there's coffee so help yourself. You know where everything is,' and goes into the hallway to answer her phone.

This leaves me in the kitchen with the twins, Margot and Henry, who have just turned five and are still in their school uniforms squabbling over jigsaw pieces under the kitchen table where they now also like to eat. I have told Mia that I don't agree with them eating off the floor like dogs, but she says at least they're eating and it keeps them quiet and I spot a few rubbery looking pasta twirls on the floor and a dollop of what looks like hardened ketchup.

I look down at the jigsaw. 'I like a jigsaw,' I tell them. 'A doctor, though I use the word lightly, once prescribed me a jigsaw with a nip of whiskey each night, and diagnosed me as still not grieving, as if that were an actual medical term, then sent me to a counsellor who never spoke. "I'm not the subject Laura, you are," he said to me. So we talked about the art on his walls and his mother's dementia and I tried to have him struck off but apparently depression is now two a penny and there's not enough counsellors to go round.'

I pick up a couple of pieces of the jigsaw and start to fit them together on the floor. Margot frowns at me. 'We were doing that,' she tells me. 'We don't need your help.'

'Of course you do,' I say smiling. 'You need to get the four corners in place which helps you to work on the edges, see? *Then* you fill in the main picture.' I show them what I mean and as I do, I think about what Mia said to me when I told her about the counsellor. How she asked for my pills and looked them up in her medical journal and told me to throw them away. 'I'll help you,' she said to me, and promised to speak to a doctor she knew, but what he said and if she did is something I still don't know.

'That was two years ago,' I tell the twins. 'And I've been on at least six different medications since then, none of which have worked, and now I'm with this new doctor and on this new medication which can't be right because I'm not sleeping at all now, not a wink, and the pills are this funny shape.'

I see that Henry has collected up the rest of the jigsaw pieces and put them behind his back. I ask him what he's doing. He asks me what I'm doing here. 'I'm here because this new doctor has prescribed enforced wakefulness and told me to be wakeful with someone I trust, not sleepless alone,' I say crossly. Though the doctor has warned me it could be short-lived. 'Short-lived positivity,' is what he said. 'That could be lost once you sleep again but at least you will have felt something else that could become the flicker of light in the next darkness.' It had sounded so beautiful I actually cried.

I look down at the jigsaw again. 'You're doing it the hard way,' I tell the twins. 'You're far better off getting your edges in place.' But Henry pulls all the pieces apart and throws them about. I put it down to not enough attention. He's normally such a docile little boy.

I open the drawer that I thought had spoons but find a pile of official looking documents and a plane ticket for the passenger Ms Mia Richer. So I look at one of the letters, it's hard not to see their contents really, and see that she has changed her name from Mrs Mia Onions and accepted a position at a hospital in Christchurch, New Zealand, who are expecting her in February but will forward the files before, and suddenly everything stops and I can't breathe.

I manage to shut the drawer as Mia comes back into the kitchen shouting, 'Right. Pasta!' and just make out her ordering the twins to go and wash their hands because clean hands means ice cream. Then she places a hand on my shoulder and says, 'What am I like, Laura? It's almost six o'clock and I've not even asked how you are. Is this new doctor being a help?' And though I am smiling, I must be because I feel my lip muscles stretch, the words, 'I'm dying Mia,' still drop from my mouth and onto the floor like weights.

But she's too distracted to notice, too flustered about the tea, and she moves from my side to scrub at a pan and starts to tell me that she's got her mother a room in a sheltered accommodation place because this cannot go on and she'll at least know where she is and what she's been doing, because if I remember this rightly her mother, though 80, still likes a drink. And as Mia scrubs at the pan, which I feel down my thighs, it comes out again, 'For Christ's sake, Mia, I'm dying,' only this time I've yelled every word.

She drops the pan and starts rummaging in a drawer for a paper bag. When she can't find one she pulls out what looks like a Hoover bag. 'It'll have to do,' she says, which means it *is* a Hoover bag, and she holds it up to my face and tells me to breathe – *in, out, calm, that's it* – like she does, in that voice, one hand in my hand and the other reaching for kitchen towel which she dampens in the pan she's been scrubbing and places along the back of my neck. She says, 'There are no wasps Laura, only me,' because I've started to swat, and she grabs at my hand and squeezes it so tight I yelp. I yell into the bag, 'Don't leave me! Don't ever leave me!' and she tells me to *Sshh!*

'It's all ok Laura. I am here.'

She leads me to the armchair and chucks the magazines onto the floor where they will remain, I'm sure, until next Tuesday, when I come again, and she helps me sit and tells me to keep breathing into the Hoover bag. She fetches me a glass of water and says she's got to get the pasta on for the kids, and even though she's only three feet away from me, on the other side of the kitchen, she is already on the other side of the world.

As I breathe, I hear pasta rattle into a barely scrubbed pan, the kettle boiling again, the clink of jars and tins as she roots for pesto which she does with a glass of wine in her hand, and I see that under the table the twins have spread out tea towels like picnic blankets, and are holding forks that look like they've been everywhere except the sink. Whilst she drains pasta through a sieve at ten past six, she asks the twins about school: 'Henry, did you do your spellings and was it yoga today Margot or just gym?' Their voices swarm as Henry says he spelt tablet with an i but still got his name on the rainbow and Margot says she tumbled off the high horse and got a badge for landing with both feet. She scurries off to find the badge and Henry spells t-a-b-l-e-t emphasising the *e* and I call out to Mia, '*My* tablets, in my bag,' but the bowls of pasta come first with a squirt of tomato ketchup that comes out like a sneeze, and she places both bowls under the table before she looks for my bag and unzips.

'My clever kids,' Mia is saying as she roots in my bag. 'One day you'll rule the world and look after me!' Henry tells her he will buy her a swimming pool and Margot says they'll go shopping everyday for sparkly shoes, and Mia is on her haunches and ruffling their hair and as they blow each other kisses her pager goes and she takes it from her pocket and sighs.

'Oh dear. He went without me.' Which means one of her patients has really died, palliative care nurse as she is at the hospice where we met, three years ago now, when I was nursing my mother, and where she'd asked for the job to help with her own grief because grief, she had said, was a killer. All I said, after mother finally went, was that I couldn't go home but knew nowhere else, I'd been sat at her bedside for so long.

'Come and have a meal at mine,' she'd said. 'It's only pasta. It's all the kids will eat. But I do make my own pesto.'

Which she did, back then, before the baby, before Rowan got into Oxford, before her husband stopped coming home at a reasonable hour. When I sat at this kitchen table and told her all about my mother, without the phones going, the twins still in high chairs; when she listened to everything I had to say; when I told her it was in my blood, that I had stopped mother, found mother, had mother put away until the death she willed came of its own accord; when, after a year of Tuesdays, I'd become too frightened to sleep, she finally lost her rag and yelled: 'Christ, Laura. Have my life for a day and you'll know what sleep deprivation is. Try losing a child! Have twins at forty fucking four. Work in palliative care for a dying NHS. You think I don't know depression? You think I don't understand why you don't sleep?' And then the worst bit: 'Where's your family Laura? Why do you keep on coming here? What is it that you think I can do?'

What she can do is be wakeful with me. 'I need to be wakeful with someone I trust, not sleepless alone,' I'd explained when I called her up to ask if I might stay overnight. And though she mentioned the twins – 'You know they don't sleep Laura' – mentioned Rowan and her friends – 'She comes in when she wants now. I just count the shoes to know who's here' – reminded me of Paul – 'He works late. He's elephant-footed' – I explained that it was the kind of noises I needed. 'And you have a spare room,' I'd said. 'You won't even know I am there.' But she went quiet at this. She was quiet for a very long time. 'It's not spare,' she snapped eventually. 'But there's the armchair in the kitchen if you like.'

Mia comes from under the kitchen table and looks at the box of pills in her hand. She squints at the label, though her glasses are parked on her head, and tells me she'd rather me take one on a full stomach. Then she checks the time and checks her phone and just listens, and I realise that this is the first time she has thought about the baby since I got here. I want to say, 'He was never here Mia. He never made it home.' But the moment isn't long enough and the spare room remains spare, and then the home phone starts up and she rushes off to answer it because it's half past six which means it's Paul.

She does what she always does: clips her voice, shuts down, reels off stock answers that are the same every week: Rowan is out. The twins are fine. There'll be cold pasta in the fridge. Yes, she's tired but Laura's here. It's Tuesday, isn't it? He offers to call later, I assume, because she says, 'Not to worry. I'm exhausted anyway. Though Laura wants to do that sleepless thing,' and I still don't know what it is that Paul does, just that he works with computers and that he's often in the States now on trips that can last all week.

I trade the Hoover bag for pasta and eat it in the armchair. Not because I can't get up to the table but because I suddenly feel so terribly defiant. I find myself saying, 'You've not asked me a single thing yet about what I'm to do tonight when I'm relying on you, Mia. I can't do this on my own.' And she sighs at me and puts down her fork.

'You know, my mother got attacked by a bunch of kids last Saturday night,' she says. 'They'd followed her home from the pub. "Gold", they said. "Old women always have gold." Even took the earrings from her ears. When the police call me, she's already in hospital. Stuffed in a bed in renal with a fractured ankle and bruised wrists where they'd grabbed her and dragged her about. Christ knows what they thought she had. But they took it all. And do you know what she says to me? "We've all been there, Mia." They're just kids who can't handle their drink."' She stops to drink wine then instructs Margot to eat – 'No, you're not full Margot. I can still see room in your belly' – and as Margot giggles at her mum's tickling socked foot, Mia tosses the pills in my lap.

'Right then, ice cream!' and I watch Mia chisel out ice cream as bright as cheese from a tub with a bread knife. Henry asks for sprinkles and strawberry sauce – she has neither – and Margot wants a flake and a surprise. Mia snaps a flake in half – there's only one – and roots through the cupboards again. She presents them with two bowls of too-cold ice cream with a dusting of hot chocolate, half a broken flake, a squeeze of honey, and they look at their cocktail glasses wide-eyed. There's even little cocktail umbrellas that she's found, like she finds their missing socks, time for cuddles and bedtime stories that go beyond the page, and she says, 'Go on then. But only half the film before bath. You have school.' And they skip into the other room to watch the telly. Then she turns to me sadly: 'I'm crap at this Laura. I'm crap at it all.'

But her pager goes and she's looking down on it and the sadness is replaced with rage. She tells me that they can't move the body until morning because there's no spare porter on shift until 6am and the family are going berserk. 'I leave them for five fucking minutes,' she says, and reaches for her mobile and scrolls through the numbers, makes a call. She's snappy. 'Phone fucking Ken then! You cannot leave him there overnight.' Then she's running her hand through her hair, finds her glasses, puts them on, drinks more wine. 'I'll phone Ken then,' and she's scrolling through the numbers again, finding Ken, and this time she's sympathetic. 'I know, I know,' she says. Pause. Hmmm. 'But do it for me, please?' And he does. I don't know how she does it, but Ken is driving back to work to wheel a man who is 96 to the mortuary and give him the respect he deserves.

*You're amazing*, I think. *How do you not sleep?*

She puts down the phone and downs the wine. She's tired and she looks it yet she smiles at me. At my half eaten bowl of pasta. 'You'll get ice cream if you finish that,' she says, and I find I am smiling back. I pick up the box of pills from my lap and say, 'It's the other ones I want you to look at. They're ever such a funny shape and I'm not sleeping. Not sleeping at all. I mean, I know I'm not meant to be sleeping tonight, and I know I don't *not* sleep. But I don't want to be taking one of my panic pills if that's going to make me sleep when that's not what they want me to do. But when I close my eyes to sleep I fear I will never know life again.'

She runs her hand though her hair and pulls the ponytail loose. 'Laura,' she begins, and rubs at her face hard as if stopping herself from saying something other than, 'Did he give you any information that I should read before we do this?'

'Of course,' I say. 'There's a whole booklet we need to go through. I've read it myself, gone through it a couple of times and made notes. But it's the afterwards that's bothering me and what pills I should take in the morning because I'm going to be very tired but still awake. So I've bought enough clothes for 48 hours just in case, though I can always pop home and get more if you think I'd be better staying here, because it's not the during but the afterwards that he says could be worse...' But the home phone is going again. She throws up her hands – *I don't believe this* – as neither do I, and she leaves the room just as the answer-machine clicks in. It's Rowan. She wants picking up at nine and might have a friend with her. Mia grabs the phone.

'Rowan. No, I'm here. I didn't know you were working, why didn't you say?... Because it's Tuesday, isn't it? Laura's here... What? No. I can't do that Rowan. You'll have to get a taxi.' She sighs loudly. 'Yes, yes, I'll pay him when you get here. Bye.' And then she shrieks at the twins: 'Bath! Now!' Because she's just realised that it's half past seven and she comes back into the kitchen to tell me this. 'Help yourself to whatever,' she says, though I've barely touched my pasta. 'Ice cream, wine. Now get up those stairs before I drag you up them!' And as she heads off to chase the twins up the stairs, I am left thinking of her own mother whom I've never met, not even seen a photograph of, being dragged around by a bunch of kids for her gold. It makes me look at my wrists and I check them over. I think of the pills in my hand, in my bag, those of my mother's which I swallowed one by one by one and how they didn't work, *it didn't work*, and I go to my bag and the panic surges from the back of my throat.

'Now, you *can* call,' this new doctor had said. 'If anything starts to feel wrong you must call.' And I think about using her phone. I could use her phone, couldn't I? Help yourself to whatever, she'd said. She wouldn't mind. So I do.

I don't know what makes me do it. I've watched her scroll through her numbers so many times now I know her address book off by heart. I'm surprised when he answers. 'Hello,' he says, and 'What's up?' He sounds like he's working, he's distracted anyway, and I hear him tap, tap at a computer. 'Mia?' he says. And he sounds decent. He works too much and he stays away from her and they talk on the phone as if cold calling about double glazing, but I also remember Mia once said to me – 'Either I'll have an affair, he will or we will part if I don't start dealing with it.' But they haven't parted, not yet, and he does sound decent. Like he cares. So I tell him: 'I'm a very good friend of your wife who is upstairs bathing your children at almost eight when they should be in bed. Your other daughter is coming home from work in a taxi that she cannot afford and there's a plane ticket in the kitchen drawer. She's accepted a job in New Zealand and it's time you took down that cot from the spare room. There is also someone who calls who makes her smile. I think these are things you ought to know.' I put down the phone.

It's not that I don't sleep. I know I don't *not* sleep. I could fall asleep right now if I wanted to, but that's not what they want me to do. And Mia was fine about it when I asked her, if not a little distracted, but then she's always distracted by something. Her mobile rings all the time, then it's the home phone or her pager. Everyone wants a piece of her. Even though she's incomplete. My mother used to tear pieces off me. For wanting to work here. For taking a job there. For taking up driving lessons. For not coming home when I said. 'It makes me panic Laura,' she would say as I'd stick my fingers down her throat. 'I don't like not knowing where you are. When you're with me, I can get out of the woods.' But she let those trees keep growing.

Mia is gone for a long time upstairs. There isn't much chatter. No arguments or messing, as she calls it. The twins are tired. They will sleep easy but waken, as they do, and crawl into her bed so that Paul will get up and sleep in the armchair aside of the range that they still don't know how to use. Except Mia will stay awake. Sniffing their foreheads, stroking their cheeks, kissing them all over, just in case, just in case.

'You can't keep watching them Mia,' I once heard Paul say over the monitor one evening as I put on my coat to head home. 'They are not Ben. Ben was never going to last the night. We always knew that.' And Mia had wept. She'd nursed all her life, she'd said. If anyone could've saved him, it should have been her. 'I just want to sleep Paul,' she had cried. 'I want to go to sleep and not ever wake up.'

Mia comes back into the kitchen looking weary. She is surprised to see me, as if she's forgotten I was there at all. 'I'm so sorry,' she begins, and she checks the time and fills her glass and asks if she can look at the booklet. 'But you have your coat on,' she points out.

'I do,' I say.

'You don't have to go,' she says. 'I'm more than happy to do this with you. I'll take a shower in a minute. That'll perk me up. Just let me take a look at these new pills so I know what I'm dealing with.' And she holds out her hands. But I don't give her the box. I give her my hands.

'Get some sleep, Mrs Onions,' I instruct and let myself out into the night.

As I walk down the street, a car comes hurtling around the corner as if a life depended upon it. I know it's Paul though I have met him only briefly, but it's him and it makes me glow with the sort of happiness I thought I would never know again. And then a taxi appears, struggling around the bend. Rowan will get out, run in for her mother's money, and then, perhaps, they will talk, the three of them, about Oxford, about New Zealand, about what happens next. Perhaps they will all get some sleep.

I throw all the pills I have stashed in my overnight bag into the next litterbin I see. It's not a big feeling that I have but it's a positive one and I have no idea for how long it will last. That new doctor had said, 'Be wakeful with someone you trust not sleepless alone,' though he did warn it'd be short-lived. 'Short-lived positivity,' he'd said. 'That could be lost once you sleep again but at least you will have felt something else.' Though I'd call it 'short lives'. Mia knows that better than anyone. As I know that I need to start trusting myself that I can sleep alone. And I don't *not* sleep that night. But I do feel like I know where some of the pieces are now. And that's a jigsaw only I can complete.

Afterword:

# The Effects of Sleep Deprivation

## Prof. Ed Watkins
University of Exeter

LISA'S STORY INTRODUCES US to two characters, Mia and Laura, who provide interesting counterpoints and illustrations of the different causes and consequences of sleep deprivation. Although difficulties in sleeping are significant for both Mia and Laura, the way that lack of sleep affects them is profoundly different. This reflects the reality that sleep deprivation itself is complex and has multiple, sometimes paradoxical, effects. One needs to be careful at being definitive at inferring clinical presentations from stories, especially when the characters and their behaviour is described in nuanced and ambiguous ways. Nonetheless, I will make some tentative reflections, in part to highlight some key issues in sleep deprivation.

Mia's sleep deprivation appears to be caused by grief and depression, with unresolved guilt over the loss of her child and the concern that her sleeping might have contributed to his death. In contrast, Laura's sleep deprivation appears to have at its root a fear that if she falls asleep she will not wake up, which is associated with her presentation of panic and anxiety. Both of these reflect two common (and often co-morbid) routes that can contribute to poor sleep: depressed mood impairing sleep and anxiety impairing sleep. A shared mechanism across both routes can be worry and brooding about fears and concerns, with this repetitive, negative thinking maintaining physiological arousal and making it hard to sleep.

It is useful at this point to define sleep deprivation and its different forms more precisely. Sleep deprivation is an extended period without sleep which can last from hours to days. It is important to distinguish between deliberate and voluntary sleep deprivation, such as intentionally trying to stay awake to complete a task, from involuntary sleep deprivation, resulting from insomnia and unwanted difficulties falling asleep. It is also valuable to differentiate acute versus chronic sleep deprivation, and partial from total sleep deprivation. Acute sleep deprivation is when an individual is prevented from sleeping for one night – this would be acute total sleep deprivation if he or she was awake all night. Chronic sleep deprivation occurs when an individual has restricted sleep each night, sometimes defined as less than 5 hours sleep, for an extended period of time. This typically results in chronic partial sleep deprivation. It is not usually possible to have total chronic sleep deprivation as extended loss of sleep leads to individuals falling asleep involuntarily, even if trying to stay awake, often in the form of brief microsleeps lasting seconds and which cannot be avoided, except under exceptional circumstances such as brain damage. Thus, both Mia and Laura report chronic partial sleep deprivation, with reduced sleep over extended periods of time.

Both acute and chronic sleep deprivation have profound consequences on mood, cognitive functioning, and ultimately health. Chronic sleep deprivation can result in sleepiness, fatigue, inattention, poor concentration and clumsiness, increasing the risk of accidents and errors at work. It has also been implicated in poor physical and mental health. Extended periods of reduced sleep are associated with changes in weight and type 2 diabetes. Disturbed sleep impacts on mood and anxiety, and can result in memory lapses and even hallucinations. Poor sleep is a predictor of the subsequent onset of an episode of major depression associated with three-fold risk for depression, with insomnia a prodromal symptom for depression, which predicts increased risk for relapse. Disrupted sleep or reduced need for sleep is also the most pervasive and common prodrome for mania, and often predicts the onset of a manic episode in bipolar disorder. Periods of mania can be characterised by impulsivity, inappropriate behaviour, agitation, racing thoughts, distractibility as well as elevated mood or irritability. Again, with a caveat that we cannot make definitive diagnoses on the basis of the complex descriptions of Mia and Laura in this story, they each display different sets of symptoms arising from sleep deprivation. Mia has poor concentration and distractibility, moving from one topic to another and one task to another during the evening. She is also irritable and, at home at least, disorganised and the insomnia is clearly linked to loss, bereavement and depression. In contrast, Laura's actions during the evening could be characterised as involving some agitation, some impulsivity, and potentially some inappropriate behaviour, such as spontaneously calling up Mia's husband. There is a possibility that she is displaying behaviour on the spectrum towards mania, although the end of the story holds out the possibility that she may have started to take positive steps towards recovery. Both women also share features of depressed mood. More information about their patterns of symptoms over time and in different circumstances would be needed to reach any definitive conclusion as to whether these patterns of behaviour met any clinical diagnosis or simply reflect the normal continuum of effects of insomnia on mood and cognition.

Experimental studies of sleep deprivation have also revealed that reducing sleep can impact mood and cognition. For healthy individuals, restricting sleep to less than 5 hours each night for a week results in increased anxiety, low mood, and reduced positive mood, relative to a control group with normal sleep. It is timely to remember here that sleep deprivation is also used as an interrogation technique, with considerable debate and legal argument as to whether this constitutes torture.

Curiously, the same manipulation of sleep deprivation can trigger an episode of mania or hypomania in a proportion of patients with bipolar disorder. And, paradoxically, for patients with depression, acute sleep deprivation, where they are kept awake throughout the night, can result in marked improvements in mood that night or the following day for 40-60% of patients. This effect of voluntarily preventing sleep on mood is what Laura's doctor has asked her to try as an experimental approach to improve her mood. However, the positive effects of this acute sleep deprivation tends to be short-lived with the majority of individuals who do respond then relapsing back into depression after a night's sleep or a nap. For this reason, sleep deprivation has not become a mainstream treatment, although it has been proposed that combining sleep deprivation with antidepressant medication may produce a more robust and long-lasting treatment effect.

Whilst Lisa's story provides us with a character-driven study that explores the complexity of sleep deprivation and mood, I want to conclude with a wider perspective. Unfortunately, sleep deprivation is increasingly being recognised as a major public health problem, driven in part by societal factors such as round-the-clock access to technology, shift-work, and longer working hours, and also by the prevalence of sleep disorders such as insomnia and obstructive sleep apnea. Sadly, more and more people are experiencing the symptoms that Mia and Laura describe to a greater or lesser extent. Both individuals and society may need to consider how to adjust daily routines to facilitate better sleep.

# In the Jungle, the Mighty Jungle

## Ian Watson

WAKE UP! godvoice tells Nu-la. AWAKE!

So she's alert. Stares into blackest night. Black from which Thing may come. Big as her body's head. Not a spider, no hairs. Stiff jelly. Fat legs. Sticky legs.

Thing puts Thinks behind her eyes.

Godvoice hates Thinks. Thinks can slow Acts.

*Hoomans may never become selfaware in the way of us Octaves. Hoomans may never think abstractly. Non-aware intelligence may be the hooman way.*

*¿Not enough footarms for flexithink?*

Halfmoon rising. Many moons there are. Lessermoon, halfmoon, fattermoon, fullmoon, shrinkmoon, nonemoon. Moons follow one another across sky. Never two at once, never three, never many. Only one travels sky at one time.

THINKS WASTE TIME. LION MAY EAT NU-LA.

Lion not hunt at night. No never. And only wooman-lions hunt. Man-lions lazy.

BAD THINK, BAD THINK!

In next tree a bab awakes, wailing for tit. Second note of wail awakes mother. Tit quick. Milk stops wails.

209

Why babs wail? Why not squirm quiet, why not kick quiet? Wails bring panther, python, wildog.

BAD THINK!

Wails which titmilk never stop equals sick.

ABANDON BAB. PUT NEAR JUNGLE EDGE. AWAY FROM PEOPLETRIBE. DANGER TO PEOPLETRIBE. SICKNESS. WEAKNESS. MAKE 'NOTHER BAB. BETTER BAB.

What if wildbitch carries off bab, not to eat but to give titmilk? Bab may live. To run, to roam, on its fours as wildog.

BAD THINK, NULA!

A bab has no name. Godvoice gives name. She has name Nu-la. Noo-laa.

Others of Peopletribe are Poo-poo and Na-na and Su-su and Mu-mu and more. Noo-la is two-noise. Not one noise two times.

Why is Nu-la awake? Nu-la has no bab. WATCH FOR THING.

Things climb on sleepyheads.

*Yet Hoomans dream akin to ourselves of the Octave. Our palps register their dreamwaves and their undream waves. We try to make Hoomans self-aware.*

Halfmoon rising. Light through vines and branches. WATCH FOR THING.

*We camouflage and match our pace to breezy motions of light, to stay unseen, just as we match our marine speed to the motions of light in water.*

Nu-la's gone bab become snivelsick. ABANDON. PUT NEAR JUNGLE EDGE.

Up here within tree, waking Poo-poo wants put his swelled throb into Nu-la. ENJOY.

Hot throb-cream makes 'nother bab. BAD THINK!

*Ourselves of the Octave learn through our dreams of all the Possibles that may be.*

Branches swaying. Poo-poo grunt-grunt. ENJOY. Soon Poo-poo comes hotwet, slides away. Wet between legs. WATCH FOR THING.

*Hooman godvoice is a jealous god.*

Poo-poo sleeps again. Poo-poo has no self. Poo-poo is no self.

Is two-noise Nu-la a self? What is a self? BAD THINK. WATCH FOR THING.

Movement on jungle floor? Dapple-dark shifts position? Scream alarm so that all tribe wake, seize sticks?

TRIBE SHALL NOT AWAKE ALTOGETHER FROM PEOPLETRIBE'S SLEEP BUT ONLY TO FIGHT OTHER PEOPLETRIBE BLOODSPEARING THIS PEOPLETRIBE, STEALING BABS. THOU SHALT NOT.

Only wake altogether if Peopletribe may die otherwise? Things never kill no one...

BAD THINK!

Halfmoon higher, brighter.

Dark climbs treetrunk darkside?

Trees all connect at tops.

WAKE NA-NA, SU-SU.

'Wake Na-na!'

'Wake Su-su!'

Godvoice of Na-na, Su-su must hear, tell Na-na, Su-su.

'Wha–?'

'Wha–?'

Moon is darkhalf and lighthalf? Always same single Moon? Things come down from Moon as spiders string down from webs?

Things are slippery like wet. Yet Things suck heads tight.

'Things come up trees!'

*^godvoice^ is the best term for what hoomans hear in their heads, telling them to do something. One side of their brain tells the other side. Thus the self does not initiate action; the self obeys the order and is therefore not yet a fullself.*

*Even though fullself may in itself be an illusion, since most of any brain is automatic.*

*But us of the Octave adore our illusion of our selves. Thus we are. Thus have we travelled by the eightfold geometry through the long emptiness, away from our shallow seas, and descended to this world in search of other selfs. We may hibernate long in this world's seas hidden among the semiself octet semblances of us, just as we hibernated during the eightfold paths coming here. Hibernate for octates to the power of octates of orbits until we rise to commune with the farspawn of Nula and her like.*

*We shall harmonise awakings of hoomans from the midst of nightsleep. An interlude of shared nocturnal selfness may be a wedge to break the patterns of their twofold brains. So envisages our Ocularity. So we creep camouflaged through this jungle by night, close to the bright plain of preys and predators.*

*Our toxins quickly taught predators to avoid us. I can kill a lion who only touches me, sniffing. We can also induce a numbness that is more like inattention.*

Halfmoonlight striping darkbark branches bushing leaves. Does Du-du wear a Thing upon Du-du's head? Hard to see, hard to know.

Does Who-who wear a Thing?

Does other Who-who?

'What see, Na-na? What see, Su-su?'

Su-su wears Thing. Her head looks larger, though still like her head. She and her branch sway as she looks around for what is already upon her, out of sight of her eyes on top.

BEAT SU-SU'S HEAD WITH STICK.

*be still be still be still be still*

How can godvoice say otherhow to godvoice?

Nu-la feels Nu-la's head. Tight 'tacles Nu-la never notice drop upon her from higher branch. Hair-cling, skull-cling. Thing.

godvoice silent, peace.

*Think! Awake Nu-la.*

I am Nu-la. I am. I think.

For now, in the awake night hour. By day godvoice commands.

Afterword:

# Bi-Phasic Sleep

## Thomas Wehr MD
National Institute of Mental Health, USA

IAN WATSON'S STORY IS related to experiments that I conducted some years ago, in which I asked healthy, young volunteers to rest and sleep during 14-hour simulated winter 'nights' for one month. I hoped to learn how the human species might once have responded to purely natural light-dark cycles, before the development of artificial light. Curiously, the individuals fell into a pattern of sleeping in two separate 3-5 hour bouts that were separated by a 1-2 hour period of wakefulness. I speculated that this might be the natural pattern of human sleep. Subsequently, this speculation was confirmed by the historian Roger Ekirch, who brought to light many references to 'first sleep', 'watch', and 'morning sleep' in documents from the pre-industrial era.

In my experiment, the mid-night period of wakefulness differed from daytime wakefulness in two respects: Almost invariably, it followed a period of REM sleep, and it was accompanied by high levels of secretion of the pituitary hormone, prolactin. REM sleep is associated with vivid narrative dreams, and heightened prolactin secretion is associated with quiescent states in many animals, and meditation in humans. Thus, our ancestors must have awakened every night into an altered, meditation-like state that differed from daytime consciousness and was suffused with the after-effects of dreaming. In light of these observations, it seems apposite that the mysterious 'we of the Octave' in Ian Watson's story (who speak in italics) gain entry into the minds of 'hoomans' during a uniquely receptive period of mid-night

215

wakefulness, and that these entities attach importance to dreaming as an indicator of potential self-awareness.

Ironically, as with Ian Watson's story, there is an extra-terrestrial dimension to the findings of my experiment. The timing of the two periods of sleep is controlled by two separate biological clocks in the brain. One clock tracks the timing of dusk and controls the onset of first sleep. The other tracks dawn and controls the onset of morning sleep. As the interval between dusk and dawn varies in length over the course of the year, the clocks impose corresponding variations on the length of the interval between first sleep and morning sleep. These adjustments enable the organism to adapt the pattern of its sleep to the changing duration of night. In addition, they are the basis of a mechanism that permits the brain to identify change of season and regulate the timing of seasonal changes in behaviour. The origin of these phenomena can be traced to a cosmic collision that occurred billions of years ago, when the young earth was struck obliquely by another planetary body, whose impact caused the earth's axis of rotation to deviate from its vertical orientation to the plane of the earth's orbit around the sun, and thereby caused the length of night to vary on an annual basis. In light of these facts, one could say that the evolution in humans of an altered state of consciousness interposed between two periods of sleep was fostered by an extra-terrestrial invader.

Ian Watson's story also can be related to Julian Jaynes' theory, in *The Origin of Consciousness in the Breakdown of the Bicameral Mind*, that humans once experienced information coming from a part of their brains as coming from a external god-like source (a voice, presented in Ian's story in capitals), and that self-awareness (presented in plain text) emerged only when humans began to perceive the source as originating within. This theory does fit with current notions that the brain consists of semi-autonomous part-brains that were layered on during the course of evolution, and that much of what occurs in the brain takes place outside of conscious awareness. Psychological growth and higher self-awareness does seem to involve discovering and owning disparate aspects of one's self, making the 'not-me' 'me'.

# References

Ekirch, R. (2005). *At Day's Close: A History of Nighttime*, Weidenfeld & Nicholson, London.

Ekirch, R. (2011). *Evening's Empire: A History of the Night in Early Modern Europe* (New Studies in European History), Cambridge University Press.

Wehr, T. A. (1992): 'In short photoperiods, human sleep is bi-phasic.' *Journal of Sleep Research* 1 pp 103-107.

Wehr, T. A. (1998). 'Effect of seasonal changes in day length on human neuroendocrine function.' *Hormone Research* 47 pp 118-124.

Wehr, T. A., et al (2001). 'Evidence for a biological dawn and dusk in the human circadian timing system.' *Journal of Physiology* 535 (3), pp 937-951.

# A Careless Quiet

## Annie Clarkson

ELKA WAS AT A FESTIVAL so it was just the two of us. She was hardly at home these days and with Sam away at university, it was more often just us. We were still not used to it. No requests for lifts, no friends calling by and staying all evening, no need to stretch food for four into a meal for six. We loved all that of course, but needed our ways to escape. You running or cycling or hiding away in the cubby doing god knows what on the internet, and me with excuses, any excuses to be in the garden or sat at the typewriter one-finger-typing, but always five minutes away from a squabble over the TV or a stroppy daughter upset about one thing or another.

So with time to ourselves, we ate a picnic in the garden, lying on a blanket I found buried at the bottom of the bedding chest. 'Look at this old thing,' you said. 'This takes me back.' And it did, with its crisscross pattern in different shades of green, faded now and with scorch marks and threads along the edges worked loose. It was our festival blanket, our camping blanket from before the girls were born. You laughed and gave me one of those looks. 'What is it?' I asked, and you said, 'Nothing, nothing', but, oh that smile. Just the same as it was when we were wrapped in this blanket in the tent all those years ago. Those days were gone, but that smile was still there, as if you were thinking how we resonate with each other, that no matter where we are we will always feel connected. That's what you said when we met.

Now, grey threaded through our hair, yours silvering, and mine with a mallen streak, life seemed to be creasing our skin more and more. You laughed when I said this, 'Barely a day over 50 and you are beautiful'. 'Bugger off' I said, but you seemed to mean it. We stayed up late and ended up as usual talking about the girls.

You had one of those dreams that night. It was hot, even with the window open, no breeze as we lay without the duvet, only a sheet covering us. We didn't touch. We read, and you told me about a song you used to play on the guitar.

It was later, when I was asleep, your arm hit the side of my jaw, waking me, and you were shouting, and then a second punch, this time with a fist. I sat upright. 'Carl, Carl'. I shook you awake and fumbled for the light switch. You didn't even realise you had hit me. 'Daft sod', I said, 'what were you dreaming about?' Your brow creased as though you were trying to remember. 'I was fighting someone,' you said. 'Who?' I asked. But you didn't know, and that was it, we thought. That was it.

A week later, maybe less, you came home from tiling a kitchen at a house down the coast and something hadn't gone right. A man had complained, you told me, 'Not even the owner', that was what got to you, 'a visitor, some friend of his, saying it was shoddy', and it went without saying that you would put any mistakes right, so we laughed about it. You weren't really annoyed, more frustrated, as you had underpriced the job, which was unlike you. 'Never mind', I said, 'I've made a stew, let's eat it in front of the TV with a spoon each and a beer.'

You fell asleep on the settee early and I flicked channels for a late film, and there it was, *The Piano*, a film I used to watch over and over before we met. You used to play the piano for me, I thought, and glanced over at you sunk into the cushions, your legs on my lap. *Although, you never played for me naked,* I thought as Ava gives a sidelong glance to Baines, while she plays piano for him half-undressed.

As the film came towards the end, the boat being dragged into the sea and all those oars pushing back against the water, you nudged my elbow with your foot, and mumbled incoherently. I said, 'Film's nearly done'. Then you kicked me, a real dig with your heel and I said, 'What the hell Carl?' I assumed you did it deliberately, but you had your eyes closed and I felt a flush of panicked heat when you thrashed out, banging your face on the corner of the coffee table. I almost received another kick but slid out from under your legs and shouted, I don't know what I shouted, but Elka yelled from upstairs, 'Mum, what is it?'

'Nothing, it's fine,' I shouted back. I gripped your arm to shake you, but you were awake already. I could see the shock in your face, when you saw me holding the centre of my chest more in panic than anything and maybe I was crying, I can't remember.

We sat on the step outside with a cup of tea each, and you were sorry, of course, when I told you what you did. Your head pressed into the palm of your hand. You remembered struggling in your dream with a man who was trying to burgle the house. I said, 'You were struggling with me Carl.' You shook your head, speechless. The solar lights in the garden, stars on the wall, dimly lit your face, and I said, 'You've never been like this. Is it stress?' 'I don't know,' you said.

Later that week, I was with Elka at the deli counter in the supermarket. She was watching the assistant fill a tub with olives and asked me, 'What's going on with Dad?' I laughed, thinking she was being funny. She was the cheeky one, and I thought, she's going to tell me about some silly stunt you'd pulled to tease her. Only her lips were pressed together in that worried way that meant something was bothering her. 'What do you mean Elky?'

'The fits', she said. That's what she called them and I felt a lump in my throat. 'The fits?' 'Yes', she said, 'those things in his sleep where he shouts and moves about.' I frowned because we had agreed not to tell the girls. 'When you were at Gran's,' she said, and passed me the olives that the woman behind the counter was holding out for me, and I noticed we had created a queue of people wanting to be served. 'He shouted in his sleep,' she said. 'It wasn't nice. He had this angry look on his face, Mum, and he was hitting out in his sleep,' she said. 'It frightened me. He told me not to tell you.'

We went to the doctors. A morning when it was teeming down and barely light with all those dark clouds, and the spray on the road and those wipers making that awful squeaking noise, because so many times we said they needed changing without doing it. The doctor was supportive. I made a joke about you beating me up in your sleep, and she just looked straight-face-serious at us. She realised it was our sense of humour, our way of coping, our way of playing it down, because it had been upsetting, and your hand was sore and I had a bruise on my thigh the size of a donut. But she made it clear she didn't share my joke and said she would refer you.

You slept better for a few weeks, no hurting yourself or me, but you were twitchy in your sleep and I was woken sometimes when you made sudden movements, almost like jolts. 'Someone tried to take the girls,' you said. 'I was falling down the stairs,' you said. It was strange, all these dreams, mostly in the mornings, in the half-light before you had woken.

You went to a clinic to be monitored, and Sam came home. It wasn't the holidays, but she wanted to be with us, and our girls sat like they were ten again, one of each side of me, not too grown up for a cuddle it seems, and they had questions, some of which I didn't have the answers for. 'Why Dad?' 'Why now?' 'What's going to happen?' 'Is he going to be alright?' Elka and Sam had been talking on Skype and were worried. I explained what I could, what the doctor had said about sleep disorders, and how you weren't doing it on purpose, it happened to people sometimes, especially men your age, and how there was medication depending what exactly it was. There were things they could do to help, and it would all be fine, of course, it would all be fine.

You decided to sleep in the spare room. There was an empty half-bed in our bedroom for the first time since we were together, and I knew you didn't like it either, but you said it was for the best until the medication worked. But, even after taking the tablets for a while, you said it was better to sleep, 'Just to be sure'.

'But it's better to sleep together,' I said, 'because I can wake you from it. Please Carl, what's a bruise between people who love each other?' You seemed sad and distant when I said this, but not as sad as I felt watching you take your book into the spare room.

Some nights I crept in when you were already sleeping. I slipped under the covers, because I was used to your breathing and those noises you made, those mumbles and shouts and words sometimes, although the words didn't always make sense. But I wanted the incoherence, your warmth, our closeness.

It took months to persuade you to come back to our room, but the tablets did seem to be working. They suppressed things, not the dreams, but you didn't react to them the same. So, life slipped back into some kind of normal.

We were distracted by Sam failing her exam at the end of her first year and we had all those conversations about re-sits and told her not to worry about one exam, how it didn't count towards her final degree. But she was adamant she was leaving. There was a musician called Colin. They wanted to travel, she said. I raised my eyebrow, and there was a moment when I could see you wanted to laugh, and I knew I must have raised my eyebrow like my mother had when I told her about you all those years ago.

We talked quietly just the two of us, sitting on the step outside wrapped in cardigans and scarves because there was a chill and a damp in the air, and we agreed Sam would make her own mistakes and successes and stubborn as she was, she would never listen to us if we said any different. We agreed you would take her for a drive and ask her, 'Is this what you *really* want?'

Elka was going through that stage. Dyeing her hair all those colours and a ring in her ear, widening her lobe in a way that I thought she would regret, but you told me to hush and said you kind of liked it. 'She's got a style that girl of ours,' and you were right. Those little dresses with skulls on or bright red cherries, and all her dark eye make-up which managed to get rubbed into the carpet near her mirror.

I never forget the look on her face as we walked up the path that day she was hanging out of the window smoking, and not one word was said by either of us, but oh, did she do everything we asked for days. You suggested we exploit it, but I said, 'Come on, we all did those things once'.

There were times when you did hit out in your sleep, of course. But the details are gone now. Times when your medication didn't work or maybe you were sick, or you missed a dose or forgot to pick up your prescription, I can't remember. It became normal like washing up after Sunday dinner, or bringing the clothes off the line when it was raining, or taking the car to the garage to be serviced. We each sometimes got bruises. But, after a while, I tried not to think about it, and soon the girls were both living elsewhere, Sam with Colin in a flat not too far away, and Elka at arts college staying with your cousin, and not as many visits as we'd have liked from either of them.

You decided to retire. The economy partly and you were finding the work more demanding. There were a few complaints, not serious ones, but grumbles about the quality of your tiling not being as good as expected, how your work was slow, and word gets about in a small community. 'It's time to call it a day,' you said.

You cycled and played guitar again. I didn't like to say that your playing was not quite as deft as it had been once. Your hands seemed to fumble on the strings and play bum notes, but it made me smile because you loved playing. 'I should join a band,' you kept saying, and you should have done. Seriously, while you were well enough, you should have done.

Sometimes in the night, I would feel you leave the bed, and you would come back sometime later. 'I made hot milk,' you said, 'and read for a while downstairs.' I said, 'You're getting old', and we laughed about the naps in the daytime, how life was slowing down and how sometimes just occasionally you forgot what you were doing and had to stand still for a while and try to grasp from your memory what it was.

I started taking students for additional money. I sat in the back room preparing them for exams, and you went out for walks, coming back up the drive slowly, your legs tired, you said after walking so far. I liked how active you were in retirement, how you worked to keep yourself fit and healthy.

Although, you slept a lot and I thought perhaps those dreams were making you feel down, or frustrated because you couldn't quite do everything as well as you used to do, and you seemed restless sometimes, hands trembling a little. 'It's your age catching up with you,' I said, 'Let's see what the doctor says.' But you didn't want that, no you didn't want that.

We planned a stay with your brother for a few weeks, their house in the middle of nowhere. It had been unsettled weather, one day sandals, the next an umbrella, and I drove because you didn't feel like it, thought you might like to sleep on the journey, and I played some Alan Bennett CDs, the ones with the monologues, and actually it livened you up a bit, you seemed more with it, as we listened, and I said, 'I like that Julie Walters', and we started laughing because you said, 'Yes, I love that film, she's in, what's its name again?' It was like a recurring joke between us, memory harder to find these days, and we settled with agreeing we both liked that film, whatever it was, because we couldn't think of a film she'd been in that we hadn't liked.

Your brother and his wife had made a meal and we sat down almost as soon as we arrived. Lots of wine and talking, and he put on some old records, and we danced to some song or other.

In the bedroom, I unbuttoned your shirt. You were all fingers and thumbs, and I did it slowly pretending it was a strip tease, but me undressing you instead of myself. We laughed and laughed, and they must have wondered what we were doing, but it had been such a relaxed evening with the wine especially, oh how many glasses we had. It was a sticky night, the air close and damp with a storm due, and we lay together only a sheet over us, and we touched, your hands tender as they always were, not grabbing or hungry, just tender, and we barely moved for a while. We just held on to each other, and you said, 'How long have we been together?'

It was nearly morning when you fell out of bed. Running from something in a dream, I thought. The noise woke me, and I saw you hunched on the floor in the dawn-light, and your brother must have heard the thud because I could hear someone stirring in the hall and a knock on the door. I can picture the scene now: you crouching next to the bed and me looking down at you. I laughed and said 'I didn't push him out of bed. Too many drinks, or one of those dreams, Carl, who were you fighting off this time?'

But your brother, he didn't make a joke or ask what happened, he just said, 'It's time we told her', and Carl, you just shook your head, and I asked, 'Tell me what?' and your brother said, 'We need a drink. We need to talk'.

So we went downstairs at five in the morning and you sat there restless, clearly annoyed with your brother, telling him it didn't need to be a problem and the blinds were still closed, it was half-dark so I couldn't see your face. I felt as if I was missing a day or a week or maybe something had happened in the night while I was sleeping. That was the feeling. I thought, aren't we always connected? That's what you said when we first met, and I looked to you for reassurance, and oh for that smile, but your brother was just standing there waiting for someone to speak and when we didn't he said, 'It's Parkinson's' and that was it.

There was a clock ticking and the dog snuffling in its bowl and the wind outside sounded like waves in the trees, it was huffing and shushing. There must have been a window open, because a draught from somewhere made the door creak.

'It's a sleep disorder,' I said. 'it's just Carl, it's what he does. You know that. He acts out his dreams in his sleep. It's his medication,' I said. 'It might need changing.'

You were silent and the central heating clicked on and there was a whoosh and trickle in the pipes, the hissing of the kettle coming to the boil.

We stood outside in your brother's garden where the trim lawn edged onto a brambled fence, trees overhanging so that everything seemed that much quieter as you told me about your visits to a neurologist, how you didn't want to tell me, and after you were diagnosed you thought if you just kept on as usual, I wouldn't notice and this would protect me, protect the girls.

I wanted to know when you were diagnosed, but your eyes refused to meet mine and I knew it had been a long time. I asked, 'How many months Carl?', and your head dipped lower. You said, 'About two years,' and my breath caught in my throat. I reached out and gripped your jaw a little too hard. I made you lift your face to look at me. 'Two years?'

I decided to drive home early to give you some time with your brother, and to be honest, I needed time for me. I wasn't sure whether you understood how your silence, the lack of words all those years, felt almost as bad as the illness.

On the drive, I thought about the little I knew about the disease, about Muhammad Ali, who we saw on a chat show once when he was old and slow and shuffled and seemed to struggle for words and his eyes had seemed blank. That's how I remembered it and all I could think about were shaking limbs and stilted slow shuffling-walks, and wheelchairs and memory loss.

I tried to list in my head any symptoms I could have noticed, all these instances where you dropped something, or stumbled or fell, or shook a little, or couldn't keep up, or when your foot went to sleep that time a few months ago and the sleeping in the day and the dreams. I didn't know what was just age or tiredness or coincidence, or something I could have picked out from everything else, and said, 'Something is not right here Carl, let's get this checked out'.

I stopped on the way home, near where the motorway reaches its highest point, where the moors on either side seemed to stretch out eternally darkened by clouds, and the motorway cut through the hills with its snake of traffic, sidelights on to lift the gloom of the day. I stopped in a lay-by and sat with my hands on the steering wheel, thinking, *I don't know how this happened*, the words your brother said repeating over and over in my head. 'It's Parkinson's. It's Parkinson's'. It was as though the repetition of the words might help me make more sense of it, or accept it, or just feel something other than this overwhelming sense of our life together driving away from me like the cars speeding past so close I could feel our car swaying in their wake. I stayed there for what felt like hours, holding the steering wheel wanting to scream, 'Fuck this Parkinson's fuck it fuck everything,' but I stayed silent watching the traffic, until the police pulled up behind me, and an officer started walking to the car. Then I had to roll down the window and say, 'I'm sorry, I just didn't feel well and wanted to stop until I recovered myself.'

They moved me on, of course, as life seems to always move us on, and I drove home to find you there with your brother. We had dinner as usual, the knives and forks clinking against the plates as we struggled for words. I washed the pots carefully, taking longer than needed, wiping each one deliberately avoiding that moment when I knew I had to step outside and join you on the garden step so we could talk, so we could work out what might be next for us.

Because life was no longer everyday or something we joked about, pretending that a bruise on your arm from when you hit the bedside table in your sleep was where I had hit you, with a wink to each other and a straight face to everyone else. We had to find new ways forward, not our stupid careless way of making it less than it was.

Afterword:

# REM Sleep Behaviour Disorder

**Dr Paul Reading**, MA, MB BChir, PhD, FRCP
The James Cook University Hospital, Middlesborough
President of the British Sleep Society

ANNIE'S STORY IS A BEAUTIFULLY poignant account of a couple dealing with a significant sleep problem, Rapid Eye Movement Sleep Behaviour Disorder (RBD), and the associated neuro-degenerative condition, Parkinson's Disease. It reads as an entirely plausible clinical scenario and one that is increasingly recognised in sleep clinics as sleep medicine becomes more established as a specialist discipline. RBD is a fascinating phenomenon that was only formally described as a specific disorder of rapid eye movement (REM) sleep in 1986. Intriguingly, however, French neuroscientists back in the 1960's had unknowingly created an animal model of RBD in cats following minor operations in a part of the brain called the pons, a region known to be involved in REM sleep control. These cats were observed to display discreet episodes of aggressive behaviour during sleep even though brain wave monitoring showed they were firmly in the state of REM sleep. During REM sleep in humans, a large part of the brain is highly active, giving rise to vivid dreams or nightmares if a subject happens to awake during REM. Indeed, some authorities refer to REM sleep as 'paradoxical sleep'. However, in the face of this increased cerebral metabolic activity, excepting movements of the eyes and diaphragm, there should be virtual complete paralysis of peripheral voluntary muscles during REM. In the last 20 years, it has been convincingly shown that a small area of the brain, the part damaged in the unfortunate French cats, switches on in REM sleep, sending impulses to all the voluntary muscles thereby inhibiting their activity and making a dreaming subject completely floppy.

RBD is classically a disorder of late middle-aged men who literally start acting out aggressive or violent dreams, frequently causing injury to themselves or bed partners. It has been increasingly studied in recent years but many questions remain unanswered. For example, the male preponderance is unexplained, as is the curiously violent nature of the sleep disorder which often contrasts to a very peaceful waking demeanour. A subject will frequently awaken or be woken during the nocturnal disturbance and will typically recall dream activity. Characteristic themes include defensive punches thrown towards a perceived attacker, human or otherwise, or active sporting activities. I have seen several elderly men who have broken their hips falling out of bed, thinking they were scoring a winning goal at Wembley. Bed partners will often be hit as innocent bystanders. The events occur with variable severity, potentially on a nightly basis each time the sufferer enters REM sleep, four or five times a night. Medication is usually effective at minimising the disorder, typically converting a punch to a jerk or a profanity to a mumble.

Perhaps the most intriguing fact about RBD is the close association with Parkinson's Disease and similar serious movement disorders. Long-term follow-up has indicated that the majority of those presenting with isolated RBD will eventually develop the neuro-degenerative disorder, often more than 5 years down the line. It is very likely that the pathology causing Parkinson's disease affects the brain areas producing REM sleep paralysis. The clinical pattern of disease progression in an individual patient reflects precisely which parts of the brain happen to be affected first. The typical tremor and slowed movements of Parkinson's are due to pathology in the areas controlling movement with consequent depletion of the neurochemical, dopamine.

At the end of the story, we learn that Carl has received a diagnosis of Parkinson's Disease two years earlier as a result of seeking help for his sleep disorder. The fact that his wife was unaware of his underlying movement disorder is not particularly surprising. The characteristic and recognisable tremor of Parkinson's is sometimes absent and motor symptoms simply reflect slowed initiation of movements or reduced dexterity. His deteriorating work performance and clumsiness with buttons obviously reflect these aspects. These types of symptoms, along with increased daytime sleepiness and mild memory impairment, are often mistakenly attributed to the adverse consequences of normal ageing.

Isolated RBD is clearly of great interest to neurologists given that it is a relatively specific and reliable marker for future development of a neuro-degenerative condition. Specifically, it provides a potential window of opportunity for preventing or slowing down the progressive motor and cognitive symptoms associated with Parkinson's Disease. So-called 'neuro-protection' in all neuro-degenerative conditions, such as Parkinson's and Alzheimer disease, remains a vital unmet need as our knowledge of the precise mechanisms underlying the pathological progression remains rudimentary. One further major problem has been the lack of a measurable marker for disease progression in any potential treatment trial which RBD may provide.

RBD is also of great interest to those rare breed who study dream sleep, oneirologists. For example, it seems clear that the violent dreams of RBD are acted out in 'real time', a fact that would otherwise be hard to prove. It is of debate whether studying RBD furthers our knowledge of the ultimate question of why we dream. Clearly, humans evolved to have REM sleep in their distant past when the daytime environment was very different and daily survival was a major goal. This perspective has led to the interesting idea that REM sleep has evolved to allow the 'flight and fright' parts of our brain to become hyperactive during sleep in an otherwise peaceful daytime existence – this has become known as the ludic theory. Potentially this acts as play or rehearsal for life threatening scenarios and better equips the individual for real threats when and if they occur. Furthermore, this might explain why REM sleep is so prevalent in early life during active neuro-development. A newborn baby spends at least half of the 24 hour period in a form of REM sleep. Although dreams, as we recognise them, are clearly not associated with this brain state at this time of life, the emotional areas are certainly working hard and will potentially be more efficient in the baby's future.

# The Raveled Sleeve of Care

## Adam Roberts

I MET DR SLECHTERSCHLAF three times. It was on the third occasion, when he told me he wanted me to become his son in a more than symbolic sense, that I knew he had finally lost his sanity.

Our first meeting was in 1960, in Buenos Aires. At that time B.A. was still a shabby and sprawling place, before the money transformed it into today's skyscraper-pegged neon and glass metropolis. Nowadays of course it is merely another of the world's interchangeable 24-hour cities, like any number of others around the globe. But back then it was its own place, with its own flavour. Of course, I must concede that part of that flavour was *fear*. Only a few years earlier the military had bombed protestors in the Plaza de Mayo, and some 350 civilians had been relieved of the burden of their lives. The Junta worked for many months with military stubbornness, if not with finesse, to purge the country of its love for the Peróns. As a foreigner, and a man of some means and reputation, I had, of course, no particular fears.

My passage across was not comfortable: there was an international chess tournament in the city, all berths were full, the bar always busy, the deck cluttered with folk. Accordingly I was in no good humour when my friend Moses Ozier met me off the boat. I had arranged for rooms in the Alvear Palace Hotel.

That first evening dined with Moses, and he took me to a number of bars, mostly cellars, where electricity strained against the clammy gloom and wide-faced Argentine men drank in silence.

I had come to complete my novel *Faust in Paris.* Doubtless you know it, for it won the Farfelu Prix Littéraire in 1962, and if you have no interest in my writing then I cannot imagine why you would be reading this memoir. The point is that being *in* Paris as I wrote *about* Paris was, in some strange way, preventing me from realising the truth of my vision. Moses called Buenos Aires 'the city that never sleeps'; but I had come there precisely because it was a city that *did* sleep. Away from the main roads, with their crossly chaotic South American traffic, the place was constantly dozing. Even the counter-coup that had ousted Perón had barely woken the beast. It slumbered in the sunshine; its citizens ambled like sleepwalkers, its rhythms were slow. This soothed my writerly sensibilities in a way the distracting irritations of Paris did not. Moses asked me why, in that case, I hadn't moved to a countryside retreat. I tell you what I told him: because I am not a barbarian.

So I settled, as best I could, into my new routine. I wrote a little, I pondered much, I lunched and slept and walked.

I first met Dr Slechterschlaf at a bar on the Recoleta.

It was a bright, sunshiny day in May, and the outside tables were all busy. Everyone else was coupled off and hunched over checkered boards. Oh, the city had gone chess-mad. It has never been a game that appealed to me, suited more to machine minds than human ones – as subsequent developments in computing have conclusively proved. But the crowding at the restaurant had, at least, this consequence: that the good doctor, unable to find a table of his own, and seeing that only mine possessed a single empty chair, asked me stiffly in Spanish whether I minded if he join me. 'Provided only,' I stipulated, 'you do not wish to play me at chess.' He nodded, ponderously, as if taking my pale joke in earnest. But he sat down. We made introductions and, I confess, gratifyingly so far as my ego is concerned, he had heard of me. 'Last year your novel I read,' he told me. 'I do not know the name of it in French; but in my land it was with the title *Ein Begriffener Gott Ist Kein Gott* published.'

'*On Ne Peut Point Comprendre Le Bonne Dieu*,' I said. 'Might I trouble you for your opinion?'

'I cannot gauge whether the translation accurately reflected the original,' he told me, switching languages to French, which was clearly more fluent than his Spanish. 'But I admire the book. It is, as a work of art, pre-eminently *awake*.'

'Thank you!' I replied.

I ran my gaze along the elephant-trunk drapings of the rubber trees in the square, each one leaning against another, in places requiring man-made props to hold them up where they sagged. They cast a rather fishlike green shade onto the ground.

The lazy waiter emerged, and took down the Herr Doktor's order: a salad, a glass of wine. I suggested we share a bottle and he, again with ponderous seriousness, nodded his consent. 'A medical doctor?' I asked him, and he replied that he was. A word, here, as to his appearance: I would not have cast him, were I filming a melodrama about a German doctor. He did not look the part: no wire framed spectacles, no kettle-shiny bald forehead, no agitated precision of movement. He was amply supplied with black hair, which his hair oil made shine like liquorish. His face was wide and his features rather coarse. His eyes, small and slow-blinking, were surrounded by rings of blue skin that looked almost exotic, like the iridescent indigo of a beetle's shell. His moustache was as black as his hair, trimmed very neatly, and combed precisely, such that the lines of hairs in its oblong slab reminded me, oddly enough, of the black vinyl grooves of a phonograph recording.

He insisted he spoke better Spanish than French, but I do not believe he was correct in this. At any rate it was in the latter tongue that we communicated. I enquired as to whether he specialised, or was a general physician.

'It was as a physician in Heidelberg,' the Doctor said, 'that I encountered my *first* case. According to the latest study in the *Berliner Medizinblatt Verlogenheit*, there are eight German families with a proneness to the condition, compared to only two British and one French. There are more, it seems, in Italy. These, you understand, are postwar diagnoses...'

I was unsure the relevance of this latter datum, but nodded anyway. The somnolent waiter shuffled to our table, and I ordered a second bottle of wine. 'And new glasses too, *y más rápidamente esta vez, señor.*'

Flies snored through the air. In the distance a car backfired, like a single drumstroke. 'Sporadic Fatal Insomnia,' Dr Slechterschlaf murmured. 'Such is the name by which physicians classify it. A rare but fascinating disease, as far removed from conventional insomnia as a heart attack is from indigestion.' He pointed an index finger skyward, for some reason. Birds flickered through the shadows, hurled themselves like mortars over the roofs. The blue of the sky was essence of May. The sunlight warmed the back of my hand upon the table. A man riding a horse, of all things, trotted briskly past, and behind him the same man – presumably his brother, perhaps twin – drove an open-topped automobile. The noise of the engine died away, and all I could hear was the tick and tock of chess pieces being moved about the various boards at the other tables. A drip, drip sound. The waiter finally returned with a chilled bottle of Chenin Blanc.

'I have never heard of this condition,' I said. 'Indeed, the insufficiency of my medical knowledge is a source of continuing regret. A novelist,' I added, pouring the wine, 'who does not understand the workings of the human body can never really understand the workings of the human spirit. Or at least not wholly.'

'You do yourself an injustice, sir,' grumbled Herr Doktor. 'I have read a number of your works and have yet to encounter any egregious medical errors, of the sort that, alas, disfigure the writings of Thomas Mann or Ernst Jünger.'

I toasted my interlocutor to thank him for this compliment. It struck me, rather awkwardly, that this action might look as though I was vaingloriously toasting myself. But the Doctor seemed lost in thought. 'Where was I?'

'You were telling me of Sporadic Fatal Insomnia.'

'The age of onset of the disease varies, though it is more common in later life than in earlier. Death usually occurs twelve to eighteen months after onset, although some patients have lived as long as three years. But it is invariably fatal, and the quality of life of the sufferer degrades very rapidly and very substantially. During the first six months, patients doze often but never enter the slow wave sleep that, we now know, is its most vital portion. Accordingly sleep never refreshes them, and they begin to manifest panic, paranoia and derangements of reason. In the second phase, hallucinations are common, and attacks of sudden panic. Normal life and work is impossible for them. Weight gain – people erroneously think weight loss the consequence of somnolence, but the reverse is true – muteness and a general somatic unresponsiveness follow, after which death is not long in arriving.'

'We must be glad such a ghastly sickness is so rare!' I said.

The doctor had not exhausted his list of symptoms: 'patients sweat profusely, their pupils shrink to dots, men become sexually impotent and constipated. Faux-narcolepsy, incessant convulsions in the hands, trunk, and lower limbs while awake. My first patient died at the age of 51. Naturally I conducted an autopsy and found the frontal lobe of his brain withered, which I believe the proximate cause of his demise.'

'Secret police forces commonly use sleep deprivation,' I noted. 'To force confessions.'

'The brain *must* sleep,' Herr Doktor said, simply. 'It is wired that way. But,' and he ran the top of his yellow forefinger up the side of his wine glass, mowing a path through the droplets of condensation, 'what if it could be *re*-wired? What if a human could be created who needed never to sleep?'

'An intriguing notion.'

'You mean, intriguing for a novelist?' He parted his lips just enough to show me the irregular line where his top teeth met his bottom. I don't believe I ever saw him smile more fully than this.

'A world in which the need for sleep were done away with?'

'A world,' he said, '*cured* of sleep.'

'Ah, but your cure would rob us of one of life's pleasures. Do you know the English writer De Quincey? He says somewhere that his purest bliss would be to sleep a million years and wake only long enough to know that he was falling asleep again.'

Herr Doktor frowned. 'A foolish notion,' he said. 'It is – how do you say? Babyish. An infantile abdication of the responsibilities of life.'

Clearly Dr Slechterschlaf was in no mood for my treating his premise whimsically. 'Very well,' I said, matching my brow furrows to his. 'I suppose, were sleep banished altogether, there would be *some* benefits for mankind. Think how much more productive we would all be! Workers could build twice as many tractors, artists paint twice as many beautiful canvasses. Progress would be inevitable on a hundred fronts. Is this why you speak of a cure?'

'Practical advantages are legion' he agreed. 'But we must not neglect the spirit – the soul, and man's unclouded view of the Holy.' This seemed like an odd direction for the medical man, but mystics and theologians abound in every profession.

'Does the spirit ever truly sleep?' I pondered. 'Interesting. Perhaps its vitality comes into its own when we slumber. Hence – dreams.'

'Preposterous!' spluttered Slechterschlaf. Then he reined

himself back, apologised in *court* French, and added: 'Dreams have a purely mechanical function in the operation of sleep as a physiological necessity.'

'Excuse me,' I said. 'I took your remark about the spiritual advantages of sleeplessness to indicate a religious sensibility.'

'No excuses are necessary,' he said, sitting back. 'God is alive in me. I see him every day, and speak with him. He speaks to me as one of the elect. I will never die.'

Clearly I was dealing with a religious monomaniac. He was frankly *glowering* at me now, crushing his moustache between a pushed-up upper lip and two flaring nostrils, as if daring me to contradict him. I was in no mood to provoke Old Testamentary wrath. Still, the wine was pleasant and the air fragrant. I excused myself, went into the low, dark cave of the bar itself in order to locate *los sanitarios*. When I returned the good Doctor had relaxed, it seemed. He favoured small cigars, and was smoking one now.

Our conversation turned to politics; rarely a well-chosen topic between gentleman who have only recently met, but perhaps safer ground than religion.

'People talk of tyranny,' said Slechterschlaf. 'But there *is* only tyranny – or more precisely, tyranny and anarchy are the only options for political nature. Tyranny by an elite, or by one man. Tyranny by the mob, which we call democracy. It is not the fact but the *nature* of this tyranny that is important.'

'Tyranny is not usually seen as being compatible with elections,' I demurred.

'Oh the agents of the tyranny are replaced from time to time. The tyrant is the demos; he never alters. And as I say, this is not the important thing. The important thing is whether the tyrant is awake, or asleep.'

'I have honestly never considered political matters in this light before,' I told him.

'Too many nations dawdle and slumber,' he insisted. 'Too many suffer under King Log.'

'Preferable, though, to King Stork?'

'If a little terror is required to wake people *up*,' said the Doktor, smacking the table with the palm of his hand, 'then all the better. The future will belong to those who are awake! Nations can be narcoleptic, just as individuals can!'

There was a good deal more in this vein.

Eventually I excused myself and made my way back to my hotel room. I felt sleepy, naturally, after my bibulous lunch; yet when I closed the slats that hung across my window and lay down sleep did not come. After a while I got up and tinkered with my writing. I found it hard to settle.

I did not sleep that night either. By dawn I was in a fever, my mind afire with insuppressible trivia and anxiety. I called a doctor, who attended me in the hotel room and prescribed me tranquilisers. Desirous of fresh air, I walked out to collect these myself – a mistake.

The sleepy city had become a place of strange nightmare. The people seemed to have dog faces. Their hats were alive. I saw a toad the size of a car squatting in the middle of the road, and every time it opened its ghastly green-dustbin mouth flies swarmed out blood-red and stinking. The clouds convolved over my head into grotesque eidolons of female secondary sexual characteristics. Windows seemed to burst into shrapnel as I passed them and the savage confetti blow at my face like snow in a blizzard, such that I kept screaming and crouching down and covering my head. People came to assist me, but I struck out at them. For a while I ran, as the pavement behind me turned to faecal quicksand, threatening to suck me under. I saw a horse biting chunks large as cabbage-heads from the flank of another horse. I saw a gypsy woman withdraw her eyeballs into her sockets leaving only dark caves, and then spit those same eyeballs at me from her mouth. I stumbled, fell, and took skin off my palms against the ground, and when I looked at my stinging hands I saw worms crawling in between the fibres of my muscle. A policeman approached me, but his eyes were four times the size of normal human eyes, and I whimpered and fainted. When I came to, I was being lifted onto a stretcher by, as I believed, goblin-aliens from a cheap science fiction movie. I kicked and kicked, and each time my foot made contact it went straight through, as if these ambulance men were made of papier maché. They backed away, and I jumped from the stretcher.

I tried to sprint off, but instead ran face-first onto a brick wall. This stunned me long enough for the monsters to restrain me.

I was taken to the *Hospital Francés de Buenos Aires* and there I stayed for three nights. The first night I remember sweating so much the sheets had to be changed six times, and the drip that hydrated me constantly renewed. I also vomited, and expelled waste matter from my lower quarters with distressing liquidity. The second night I don't recall: I believe I slept twenty hours straight, and then woke only fitfully. The third night I felt myself again, and although the doctors wanted to keep me in for observation, I discharged myself.

I was shattered, exhausted, and for a week could do little but loll on the balcony of my room and watch the world go by. I slept ten hours every night, and napped in both morning and afternoon. And then the strangest thing: a surge of energy and – *mirabilé!* – inspiration. A fortnight, and *Faust in Paris* was completed.

As for my strange and sudden sickness: at the time, it simply didn't occur to me to connect it in any way with Dr Slechterschlaf. Why would I? Medical opinion pronounced itself baffled by the suddenness and the nature of my indisposition, suggested perhaps that I had ingested something poisonous. I myself suspected food poisoning, and pointedly did not return to the bar on the Recoleta. Accordingly I happened not to bump into the good doctor again during my stay. Indeed, it was by pure chance that I saw him at all in that city, as the boy was loading my suitcase into the taxi to take me to the airport (after my experience on the boat over, I had decided to fly back to Europe). He was strolling past the hotel at that moment, and performed a slight, Germanic bow. 'You are well?' he inquired. Simple courtesy required I not burden him with any detailed account of my hospitalisation, so I replied I was. 'Sleeping well?' I took this to be a reference back to our lunchtime conversation, and replied, smiling, that indeed I was. He looked at me blankly, shook my hand and passed on.

I did not see him again for more than two years. *Faust in Paris* enjoyed, as you know, a certain success, and I was persuaded to write a stage play – it became my celebrated *The Works and Days and Weeks and Months*, staged at the Théâtre Mogador, which won the Critics' Golden Bough and the European Wand.

It was at the first-night party for this play that I met Dr Slechterschlaf a third time. The producers had booked the entirety of *Les Halles Des Folles* on the Avenue Gabriel; people came and went, much champagne was drunk, and it was well past midnight when I was introduced to an American 'diplomat' (one could clearly hear the inverted-commas around this job title) and his charge. I recognised him at once, although he was travelling under an alias. For obvious reasons. 'This is Doctor Bestrafer,' said the American, adding 'a *most* eminent neurologist from Bonn.' The Doctor smiled and shook my hand, holding my gaze with his. I had no desire to challenge his disguise, or make any kind of a fuss, but I suppose he wasn't to know that. Then his American spoke to him in rapid German, and the doctor replied. My German is not fluent, so I could not be sure, but it sounded as if he said that I had proved unsuitable. Naturally this intrigued me. 'It is good to see you again, Herr Doktor,' I said, in my poor German, and he put his head fractionally to one side.

'Gentlemen!' said the American, in French. 'Shall we all sit down? Share in the loving cup? Friends altogether?' There were many empty tables, and in moments we were seated, and the waiter had left a new bottle opened before us. I poured. It was my play, after all.

'I understand,' said the American laying his two arms flat along the backs of the two empty chairs on either side of his, ostentatiously relaxed, 'that you have yourself already been lucky enough to receive the Doctor's revolutionary treatment.'

Slechterschlaf – or 'Bestrafer' – shuffled in his seat and rounded his eyes at his companion. It was not a glare; but neither was it a normal look. They exchanged babbled words in *Deutsch*. The penny, as they say in English, dropped. Indeed, I would have had to be an unusually dim individual not to have added two to two. I said to the doctor: 'You drugged me.'

He nodded very slightly. 'You wish me to apologise and I will not apologise. Should a doctor apologise to a blind man for curing his blindness?' He took a miniature sip of champagne, and peered into the flute as if into a crystal ball. Light prismed through the glass and drew little vertical lines on his face. 'Or attempting to cure,' he added.

'I appear,' grinned the American, 'to have falsely stepped. Hey!'

'It doesn't matter,' said Slechterschlaf. 'Although I believe our friend, here, is a,' he almost spat the word, '*democrat*.'

'By no means,' I replied, a little shocked. 'I have dedicated my life to the best that can be thought and known. No true artist can pander to the mob.' This was a little pompous of me, I confess; but I was annoyed. I added: 'If I suffer from blindness, it is of a kind of which I am perfectly unaware. And I can hardly thank you, for several days of intense discomfort, including a period of hospitalisation.'

Herr Doktor was immediately interested, at least, to discover what had happened. Professional fascination, of course. I explained the course of events, and, oddly, my little narrative seemed to cheer him considerably.

'My researches have advanced,' he said, as much to the American as to me, 'considerably. Sleep is an intensely individual matter – it is remarkable, really, that the soporim is so carefully adjusted. Looked at as a proportion of the whole population, the number of those who do not succumb to it is remarkably small.'

'I like to think,' said the American, showing me 32 white teeth, 'aliens. You will say that it is because I come from the land of science fiction movies and UFO sightings. But I can't get the good doctor to state in unambiguous terms *whom* he thinks behind it.'

'Behind what?'

'Drugging homo sapiens – no, no,' and the American put his palm upright between himself and Slechterschlaf, 'I know what you'll say. Drug implies some physical contaminant. Like particles in the water or something. No, no, I *know* what you'll say – there's no such material. But doesn't that just mean we haven't *found* it? Who knows what advances these aliens might have made?'

'I'm confused,' I admitted. 'What aliens?'

'There are no aliens,' said Herr Doktor. 'My friend has a fanciful imagination. He will grow out of it.'

'I will!' laughed the American, and then he did a strange thing. He leaned forward, put his large lips all the way around the rim of the champagne flute, and jerked his head backwards. His hands were under the table the whole time, the glass was entirely upended and its sparkling contents disappeared down the trapdoor of his gullet. Then he replaced the glass on the table, still without touching it manually, sat back up, and beamed at us.

'With what did you dose me?' I asked Slechterschlaf.

'Look at me,' the doctor said. 'Do I look tired?'

His eyes were surrounded by folds of bagged skin. They looked like black olives nested in rings of pastry. He looked, in truth, exhausted. 'A little,' I told him.

'Not so tired as I should. I have not slept since 1946. I

do not mean,' he added, as his companion alternately opened his eyes very wide, and then closed them very tight, in, I suppose, dumb-show foolery designed to express amazement – he broke this off quickly and chuckled to himself, and returned his attention to his wine glass. 'I do not mean,' said Herr Doktor, 'I have suffered from conventional insomnia, dozing half an hour here and half there, lying awake and feeling sorry for myself. I do not go to bed. I do not *own* a bed. I am awake all day and all night. In point of fact I have freed myself from the stupefaction imposed upon the rest of humanity.'

'Ah, but imposed by whom?' the American wanted to know. Then he laughed like a kid.

'So you have taken some potion, some powder, and it has had this effect,' I said. 'Moreover – *without* my permission – you dosed my wine with the same, back in Buenos Aires?' I should have been angry; yet somehow the rage did not come. Not that I believed his strange tale. I suppose I assumed him within the normal human range of madness, somewhere between eccentricity and mania. But whatever he *had* given me had certainly had a most malign effect upon my health. I had read reports of LSD and other hallucinogens. I assumed it was something of this tribe. Distantly I wondered if I should report him to the police. If he was in the habit of dropping his crazy bedroom-chemistry-set concoctions into the drinks of strangers, he should probably be detained in a secure institution.

'The principle is sound. I tried to free you and I admit I failed. I admit my failure freely. But now I know how to adjust the treatment so that it addresses itself to the specific internal coordinates of consciousness. There are seventeen distinct varieties of sleeper, you know. And I have finally been able to train myself to spot, simply by looking at someone, what type they are.'

This talk of *knowing now how to dose me* gave me a little jolt, I won't deny it. I stared at my champagne. I had yet to taste it, and the glass had not been out of my sight for a moment; yet I found myself disinclined to touch it. 'You, sir,' I said to the American. 'You are eager to try this treatment?'

'We,' said the American expansively, 'are in negotiations with the good doctor. I represent – look, I don't suppose there's harm in me telling you. I'm military. We're interested in what a corps of soldiers might do if they never got tired –'

'No!' barked the doctor, sharply. 'How many times! You *will* get tired, and you will need to rest your muscles. This is not what my treatment achieves. It is only the addiction to *sleep* that can be cured. It is your brain, not your body, that will become fatigueless.'

'He's a stickler for sure,' said the American, in English. Then, in French: 'It hardly matters. The crucial thing in war is having the edge. An army of men who didn't need to sleep would have a most obvious advantage over an army that did. Not in the short-term, but as the days and nights added up. Anyway, my government is interested.'

'You will try it yourself, personally? I feel I should warn you: my experience was of nightmare and fever, a grotesque horror-show that lasted until I vomited and sweated the last of the toxin from my trembling body.'

Herr Doktor was blithe about this. 'Indeed, the dose was not well calibrated to you, back then. But now…'

'Sleep deprivation produces nightmare hallucinations,' I insisted. 'One need not be a specialist doctor to know that. We need sleep.'

'We need,' the doctor returned, 'to *wake up*. Sleep is there to keep the human race in chains, to render us malleable and easy to control.'

'Though not by *aliens*,' the American laughed.

'We are all addicts. All of homo sapiens – alcoholics, blotting out reality with this daily *fix*.' He used the French *se drogeur*, which reinforced my belief that he was talking about some conventional narcotic. But I had got this the wrong way about. When Slechterschlaf said 'drug' he meant sleep itself, not whatever potion he was offering the US Military. 'Weaning oneself from this drug entails all the agonies of the most deeply bedded narcotic-withdrawal symptoms. Indeed, so severe are these withdrawal symptoms that, hitherto, they have invariably proved deadly. What my new treatment does is ease that transition. One must push on through – to the other side – one must open the door to eternal wakefulness. God is always awake. Or did you think the Almighty *dozes*, from time to time?'

'That might explain a few things,' said the American. 'About the messed-up world.'

'No!' Slechterschlaf was in no mood for levity. 'No! All the mess in the world is because we humans sleepwalk through our existence! Literally so – as often asleep as awake, drugged and soporific, clarity and vision and purpose impossible!'

'Alright, Doc,' said the American, slipping back into English. 'No need to fly off the handle. We're all on the same team.'

'Gentlemen,' I said, standing, speaking English also. 'You must excuse me. I am so severely addicted to this drug called sleep that I fear I must go and *me drogue* without delay.'

Two days later, as I emerged from my hotel, I was placed into what amounted to arrest by the Americans. Naturally I found this a very disagreeable state of affairs. It was, they assured me, an informal arrangement, although it was one with which the Conseil d'État had been apprised, and endorsed. 'National security,' said the American who invited me to step into his large black car. 'I'm sure you understand.'

I was taken to the American Embassy and given quite good coffee. The American I had met at the *Folles* that night joined me, and introduced himself formerly: Hank Bannett. 'I'll come straight to the point. We would like an assurance that you will not share the information to which you were privy, at the meeting between we two and our esteemed mutual friend.'

'I am offended at this treatment,' I insisted. 'I am a French citizen, an internationally respected writer, and a gentleman.'

'Happy to apologise,' grinned Bannett. 'Believe me, it was not an action we took lightly. And I should stress, it is your word as a gentleman we seek. There's no question of any official sanction or pressure. We ask, as representatives of one friendly nation to the greatest living writer of another.'

'Your flattery is crude and contemptible,' I said.

'Doctor Slechterschlaf's researches are top secret. We ask you to respect that.'

'And if I do not?'

Bannett looked very serious. 'As a friend, we can use our influence. Visas for visiting the States become extremely easy to obtain. Government subventions can help your American publisher disseminate translations of your writing to a wide audience. We can talk to the Swedish Academy about the Nobel prize; and believe me, we can be very persuasive.'

'You are talking nonsense,' I scoffed.

'On the other hand, as an un-friend, we can make visas extremely difficult to obtain. Translation opportunities might dry up. Your Anglophone readership would be, sadly, starved of your new works. The Nobel Committee might prefer the work of Monsieur Sartre…'

Naming my famous enemy in this way was so clumsy an approach that I almost laughed. 'I owe a duty to art and the truth,' I told Bannett. 'What kind of worm would I be to kow-tow to your threats? Although, having said that, I can be honest and say the strange fairy-tale of Doctor Slechterschlaf has no interest for me, artistically. If I were to tell people, they would not believe me.'

It seems a strange thing to say, but after this inauspicious start Bannett and I became quite good friends. We would meet up, at irregular intervals, throughout the 60s, and the occasions were always pleasant ones. He was frank with me, and I with him. I daresay I served some official purpose for him, because I was very well connected amongst the higher echelons of French society, the more so after I won the Nobel in 1964 than before. ('Nothing to do with us,' Bannett assured me, laughing). I even dedicated one of my minor pieces to him – *La Joie*, which emerged in the long interlude between the brouhaha occasioned by the appearance of my *Un Dossier Coordonné* and the international acclaim that greeted *Puissance Charismatique* in 1970. From time to time I would ask after the eccentric old German, and his impossible researches, and sometimes Bannett would brush me off with jokes. But sometimes, depending on how much alcohol was in his system, he would grow more serious.

'We had a bad experience with the first troops treated with Slechterschlaf's technique.'

'Nightmares?' I said. 'Hallucinations?'

'Oh, the treatment worked,' said Bannett. 'We put a couple of hundred sleepless soldiers into a specialist company, deployed them to East Asia during the ongoing unpleasantness. They did good work for us, for about three months. Then they went – savage. We lost contact with them. There were… atrocities. People, both enemy combatants and civilians, were executed by having their arms and legs cut off and swapped about. Arms sewn to hips, legs to shoulders. The bodies would be hung in the trees, or nailed to fences. Hundreds and hundreds.'

'Great God!'

'Indeed. Then they went AWOL. We picked up their Captain in Hong Kong. God knows how he got there. He was at the heart of a new cult – claimed he was the Messiah. We took him back to Fort Bragg, interrogated him for six days and nights straight.'

'He wouldn't talk?'

'He wouldn't *stop*. But it was all mystical babble.'

'What did the good doctor have to say to all this?'

'He's gone AWOL too. Down to the Argentine, we think. We're washing our hands of the whole business. It's turned a simple hearts-and-minds campaign into a drawn out bloodbath.'

'Vietnam?'

'Laos, Cambodia.' He shrugged. 'The wildfire spread is directly a result of this experiment.'

'No more sleepless soldiers,' I said. 'I am pleased.'

I fear this was not the whole truth, though. It may or may not be the case that the US military deployed their infamous 'Devil Platoons' to the Sudan, to Central and South Africa and various other places. The President always denied it, of course. I was in New York when he won his third term, after that controversial change to the constitution. Duck-bill nose, flat line eyes, insincerely wide smile: his face was inescapable, from every TV screen and billboard. I was in a bar in Lower East Street when the news of his landslide came through. My fellow drinker declared: 'He'll be President forever, now. President until the year 2000.' And then he took a swig of vodka. And then he burst into tears.

I was unmoved. I felt more European, in that place at that time, than I ever have before.

It hardly needs saying that the title character of my novel, *Gustave Van Dorm*, was based on Slechterschlaf. As you will know if you have read it, my character is researching not sleep but human aggression; and his work at curbing the destructive urges of humankind is perverted by the authorities. I was surprised by its success – my New York trip was publicity associated with its appearance in the US. I gave talks at bookshops, universities, and flew from NY to Chicago, across to Los Angeles and back to Boston. It was exhausting.

Bannett met me after my last engagement, and took me to a restaurant located at the top of one of the city's iconic skyscrapers. His wide smile faltered a little when he met my eyes. This was unlike him. 'Eat what you like,' he boomed, as the waiter slid my chair underneath my descending derrière, as if chair and I were some single, elaborate folding machine. 'The government is paying.'

'Such generosity!' I said, picking up the wine-list.

He looked grave 'I'll be blunt: we have a very large favour to ask you. We being the US government, in consonance with the United Nations Security Council.'

'Good gracious,' I said.

'We know where Slechterschlaf is. Argentina. In a large compound, out in the grasslands. Garrisoned with, there's no other way of saying it, a private army. Quite a big one, in fact. A large body of loyal troops.'

'He was always mad,' I said, wonderingly. 'But it seems he has gone, as you say, the whole seven yards.'

'What I'm telling you, it's nine by the way, is top secret.' We were conversing in English, which is not my most fluent tongue, so I had to concentrate. 'Any suggestion of affiliation between the bad doctor and my government will be strenuously denied. Though such denial is made trickier than it should by the fact that many of Slechterschlaf's private soldiers are ex US special forces.' He shook his head sadly.

'And the Argentine government is comfortable with this armed fort on its territory?'

'Money's no object,' said Bannett, and for a moment I wasn't sure if he was talking about US government funding or about Slechterschlaf. 'Friends in high places. A large following amongst the humble, some of whom consider him a, well, messiah. Or so it is said. But the bottom line is: the way to winkle him out would be direct assault, and that would be costly, in men and money and worst of all in bad publicity. They, and we, would prefer a less martial solution.'

'Diplomacy,' I said. It was really not a bad glass of Chateau Somnier. I held the glass stem between thumb and forefinger, and electric light made the reds shine like stained glass saint's-blood with the sun behind it.

'He won't accept an embassy from us. He won't accept an embassy from the Argentines, or even the U.N.'

'Oh dear.'

'He will, however, see you.'

My stomach twisted. I saw where this was going. 'Me?' I

replied, slipping into French.

'It is as I have said, now,' said Bannett, following me into my mother tongue. 'He has read your book, *The Doctor Van Dorm*. He recognises its portraiture.'

I put the wine glass down. 'And? He is – offended? Many are, when the artist works them into his art. Flattered? I would not have thought him the type susceptible to flattery. Why *me*?'

'We want you to visit him. There are certain propositions we would like to put to him, by way of – as you say – diplomacy. There is a last-chance failsafe, and we really have no desire to invoke it.'

'I'm guessing, from the doom-y way you utter the word failsafe, it involves aeriel bombardment? Missiles? Atomic ones, perhaps?'

He shook his head at this latter, but didn't deny the rest. Then he leaned across the table. 'I don't know why he wants to see you, and I don't care. But we have to reach out to him. There's no question he has developed his treatment – his cure for sleep. His antidote. He wrote a book too, you know: *Die Wahrheit über Schlummer*. It's not been widely noticed, because it reads so very like the work of a crank and a crazy. It reads that way because that's how it *is*. But if you read it you get a desperately clear sense of his mission. He plans to cure humanity of sleep. All of us! If we like this or do not like this, he will do it.'

'But how?'

'I don't know. Dosing the rivers with his... potion? Putting it into bombs and air-bursting them over major cities? We don't believe he has the capability yet, but we don't want to wait either. Remember what he did to you.'

I remembered it only too well. 'You never took his treatment, yourself?'

Bannett slipped back into English. 'Never. I supervised the soldiers we dosed, though. It's a traumatic transition, and not all of them made it. The ones that came out the other side were... changed, though.'

'Driven mad,' I said, grimly.

Surprisingly Bannett did not accede with this judgement. 'I wouldn't say that. They talked and acted perfectly sane. Within, you know, the parameters of soldiers. They were more religious, I guess. But they were mostly that before. No atheists in a foxhole, after all.' He had to explain this phrase to me.

At any rate, I resisted his urging that I fly down to the Argentine. I told him: absolutely not. I said I was returning to France, after an exhausting book tour. I was going to take a well-deserved holiday, perhaps on the Côte d'Azur. It was out of the question.

I went, though.

Sitting on the plane flying down to Buenos Aires, I interrogated myself, incredulously, in a lengthy internal stichomythia. What was I *doing*? What did I think I was *playing at*? I was met at the airport by one American and one Argentine bodyguard. These two gentlemen loaded my suitcase into the back of a black official car big as a boat, and drove me straight out of the city. None of us talked. I had been briefed by Bannett, in company of one of his superiors, a fat bald man in a suit the colour of a raincloud.

The automobile was fitted with a cooling system, thankfully counteracting the great heat outside. Azure overhead, like a sky that was in the process of calcifying into some deep blue and perfectly smooth stone. The landscape all grass: first, on the highway, margined by low barbed-wire and home to great herds of brown cows with bright white faces, as if they had been painted with zinc powder. Then we reached the pampas proper, where the grass was dry spaghetti yellow, freckled with cowpats, and stretched flat to the horizon like a stage set. Every now and again I caught sight of a centaur, its human component wearing a broad-brim leather hat, always smoking a cigarette. But cowboys were few and the cows uncountably many.

Several hours into the journey we left tarmac and slowed right down to shudder up a dirt road, drawing a dirty comet-tail of dust behind us. The grass here was paler still, with a grey sheen to its parched yellow. No cows here, although I did see goatish-looking deer. Giant anthills littered the plain like dry heaped blancmanges. A chain of round-shouldered hills appeared over the horizon, teal and barren as suede. I thought I saw a hamster close beside the car, and realised with a start that it was actually a capybara in the middle distance. Then, with a prestidigitator's flourish, the landscape revealed a valley hidden in its folds, and we drove down into sharp greenness, bushes and then trees, and finally out into a wide space with a lake in it and grass the colour of England, not Argentina.

We had arrived. The compound was, as I expected, large and fortified. A double-set of fencing twice as a high as a man enclosed the acreage, and there was a large gate and a guardhouse. Two men stood, hatbrims wrapping their eyes in shadow, rifles slung over their shoulders.

There was a long exchange at this gate between my driver and these two guards. The result was: neither the car nor my companions were to be permitted inside the compound. They could sit in the heat, or return to Buenos Aires and collect me another day. No amount of remonstrance changed the guards' minds on this point; and they confirmed it with many hiss-clicky conversations on their walkie-talkies. So I had to step out of the car into the oven of the day, and carry my own heavy bag the mile or so from the gate to the main building. At the beginning of this process my shirt was eggshell blue, and ended wet mauve. Lean brown cows looked up at me from their grazing: their horns fat and short like ears, their ears long and thin like horns. Impassive, wedge-shaped faces. Then back to the grass, than which I was, clearly, less important.

Insects made a dental-drill noise in the hot air. I wished I had packed my case less heavily.

The front of the compound's main building reared up, like the cliff in that Wordsworth poem – like guilt, like a prison, like death. There were more guards lolling in chairs by the main door, rifles in their laps. One nodded at me, and I went in.

The cool inside was like a drink of water. An elderly man popped out from a sideboard door and stole my case without a word. I wiped my brow with a handkerchief and watched him lug it up the central staircase. I was about to follow when another elderly man, so alike the first as to suggest twindom, appeared from stage-right with an actual glass of water on a tray. This I drank, thankfully.

'The Awakener is ready to see you,' said this second fellow, in Iberianly-accented French.

'I should freshen up,' I said. 'Has my luggage been taken to a room? I should go and…' I plucked my damp shirt away from my chest with a small sound. But the factotum looked at me as if I had spoken (as we say in France) 'le charabia'.

There was to be no up-freshening. I was led to the back of the building, through a door and down a corridor before which my guide stood in silence. We waited, for who-knows-what. Finally, just as I was about to say 'should we knock?' the fellow – knocked. 'Da bin ich!' boomed the familiar voice.

The door was opened to the accompaniment of an invisible violin, sliding up a semitone.

'Monsieur,' said Slechterschlaf. He was seated behind a desk, and did not get up. I stepped though the door and walked up to the desk, the factotum sealing the door behind us with a reverent hunch in his frame. 'You must sit,' Herr Doktor told me. I was obliged to fetch a chair from the side of the room and bring it closer to the desk, and as I performed this Slechterschlaf watched me with his usual scientific dispassion. I sat, and he continued to stare at me. I glanced about his room – shelves clutched neatly-packed arrays of books. There was a single image – a portrait photograph of exactly the person you would expect to find in Slechterschlaf's study. The glass doors framed a most attractive vista of green grasslands leading down towards the lake. I looked back to the Doctor, and he was looking calmly at me.

On a whim I asked him: 'What do you see when you look at me so intently?'

He answered without hesitation: 'I see a soul tangled in the daemonic dread like a fly swaddled in spider-silk, yet not even aware of it. I see God, God, God in every direction and in every moment. I see choirs of angels singing a song so pure that not even mathematics might comprehend it. Holy holy holy holy holy holy holy. *Diese irrationale Momente als damit verbundene Gefühle sich der rationalen begrifflichen Fassung entziehen und nur durch hinweisende Ideogramme bzw. Deute-Begriffe aufgezeigt werden können. Die irreduziblen Momente dieser Erfahrung mysterium tremendum und mysterium fascinans sind.'* He spoke this little speech in a low, calm voice, and betrayed not the slightest intimation of enthusiasm.

'Good gracious,' I replied, almost in a whisper.

'You wrote a book about me,' he said.

'An artist,' I began, 'draws his inspiration from many sources. It is never the case that a character…' But I dried up. 'My friend,' I said. 'The Americans are worried.'

'Worried?'

'They are… scared.'

'They have good cause. I am flattered to have inspired a book by so eminent a writer.'

'I am in turn flattered by your high estimation of my work,' I said, insincerely. 'My friend,' I tried. 'Why will you not agree to talk to the Americans? To the Argentinian government, at least – its representatives?'

'My kingdom is not of this world,' he said.

'Yet,' I pressed. 'Here you are – in this world. Along with the rest of us. If you are not of this world do you really need an army?'

He blinked, as if he could not understand a word I was saying. Then he said to me: 'You will become my son.'

'What?'

'Not symbolically. I do not mean a legal adoption, or any such nonsense. You will never be my heir, for I shall never die. But I am now the all father, and you are my ratio inferior, and so must be my son.'

I digested this statement.

'I would,' I said, falling as I often do at moments of great stress, into undeliberate literary quotation, 'prefer not to.'

'Your preference is neither here nor there. The truth of sleep is that it wraps protective cotton-wool about the minds of the weak. Without sleep to drug us, we see the cosmos as it is – divine and eternal and beyond time. For what is sleep, but the pendulum that tick-tocks away the cattle-lives of humans with calming regularity? Purged of this we become like Gods. This is the truth of the knowledge of good and evil, and this is the function of its fruit. My research has advanced beyond all mortal science. No longer do I need to produce a powder or drafts. Now it is in my mesmeric voice. Now the air bristles with microscopic points of light. *Ich bin der väterlichen Gott. Ich bin der väterlichen Gott.* You are my son, in whom I am well pleased.'

'You're insane,' I cried, running to the door. The quality of the light inside that room had changed – not darkening so much as thickening, growing sluggish.

Slechterschlaf did not rise from his chair, or even move, yet somehow he reached across to me. My fingers slipped from the door handle. I could not gather the strength to turn its dodecahedral crystal knob. My muscles became watery and feeble, so that I slumped against the wall. I struggled to speak. My world was nought but a piece of paper, scrunched into a ball and tossed into the bin to creak, still alive, and weakly strain to unscrunch itself. My world had always been this. The doctor was speaking, his voice not loud or emphatic yet nevertheless inexpressibly forceful and compelling.

'Sleep veils us from God. The sleepless man sees God face to face, and it drives some to lunacy, yet it opens to others the truth of great power. The sleepless man sees me, for I am God. And you will become my son in whom I will be very proud. *Sie können ein Kind verzaubern. Sie schaden mannigfaltig.* I command the sun to rise and it rises! I command the Americans to assemble a mighty force in the air and compel it to rain down fire upon me, and they oblige! What,' he was, abruptly, yelling: 'what! Can! I! Not! Do!'

All the hairs of my pelt were bristling. My intestines writhed like dying serpents. I had the weird sense that my own tongue had lengthened and thinned, and was snaking up into my sinuses and exploring the inward cavity of my nose – nonsense. The walls shimmered with life. Every atom an angel.

I gathered my will. I do not believe, either before or since, I have ever wrenched such effort out of my poor bourgeois soul. I flopped my right hand onto the doorhandle, twisted it, and half-pulled, half-fell back. It opened, and I was at the threshold.

'Monsieur!' Slechterschlaf called; and all the majesty and terror had gone from his voice. By opening the door I had broken some seal, or punctured some magical reservoir, and his words no longer had their power over me. 'Monsieur!'

'Goodbye, Doctor,' I said, without looking behind me. 'We shall not meet again.'

For a third time he said: 'Monsieur!' And, despite myself, I could not help but look over my shoulder. The doctor was there, behind his desk, looking much reduced in stature.

He said: 'I had a son.' There was a new quality to his voice, one I had not heard before. Was it – human emotion? 'He was killed in the Struggle, the Great Struggle. He died in the Ukraine, and his mother died one month to the day after, of her grief.'

'Goodbye Doctor,' I said.

I left my bag. I could not exit the house rapidly enough. Squeezing my eyes mostly shut against the sunlight I jogged gasping, or sobbing (one of the two), along the long path, flanked on both sides by long green grass that kept telling me the old, old news concerning Midas and his ears, whether I wanted to hear it or not. All the way along that road I half-expected to feel the killing impact of a bullet in my back.

The guard at the gate was surprised to see me, but let me out. I walked for, perhaps, another hour – my mouth parching, my shirt slapping wetly against my torso, before I saw the car that had brought me, parked in the shade of some Lenga Beeches.

I fell onto the back seat, and lay there panting and gasping whilst the driver fetched me some water. The American was on his walkie-talkie, and I suppose I overheard what he said, and I suppose I chose not properly to understand.

Soon enough the car was rolling slowly back towards the main road, rocking ponderously on its suspension and the air conditioning had cooled me to the point where I had regained a little dignity.

'It didn't go well, then,' said the American.

'The doctor is,' I replied, rummaging for the right word. 'Mad,' I said eventually, because I could not leave the sentence unfinished. Professional pride. But of course this was the wrong word. This was absolutely the wrong word.

Three jets roared over our heads, trailing a bridal train of prodigious noise after them, heading back in the direction we had just come. A little while later I heard thunder, and remarked on the prospect of a storm, and the American agreed that storms could be sudden and overwhelming on the pampas lands. But the sky was flawless blue in every direction.

I returned to Paris. I have not slept from that day to

this. Not so much as a cat-nap. There is something to see now, and I have deliberately and consciously shut my eyes. I shall have to open them I suppose, but there is no hurry, and I have no desire. I shall see, face to face. I shall see his face. I shall face the face. No glass, nothing dark, no dark of any kind, but face to face to face.

Afterword:

# Living Without Sleep?

## Dr Penelope A. Lewis
University of Manchester

THE QUESTION OF WHY we sleep, and what would happen if we didn't, has haunted psychology for well over a century.

A lot of the work examining impacts of sleep deprivation has been done on animals, and most commonly rats and mice. A key study by Alan Reschaffen, one of the fathers of sleep science, showed drastic health effects, with sleep deprived animals quickly losing control of their body temperature, developing infections and skin lesions, losing weight, and eventually dying (Rechtschaffen & Bergmann, 1995). Unfortunately, it is difficult to interpret these findings, as the animals in question were almost invariably kept awake through extremely stressful procedures. We do not know, therefore, whether the outcomes were truly due to sleep deprivation, or instead relate to the prolonged periods of stress they endured.

For obvious ethical reasons, work in humans tends to focus on either acute, total sleep deprivation, lasting just a few nights, or chronic, partial sleep deprivation, lasting for much longer periods. Acute sleep deprivation for a few days has been shown to cause moodiness and impairments in memory, attention, and complex decision making as well as a general slowing of mental processes and general loss of motivation (see Lisa Blower's story and Prof. Ed Watkin's afterword, pp185-201, also Harrison, 2012). In terms of longer periods of voluntary deprivation, the most famous is probably the story of Randy Gardner, a 17-year-old who voluntarily stayed awake for 11 nights in 1965 (a record at the time). By the fourth day Gardner had experienced memory loss and minor hallucinations. His speech had become slow and slurred after a week, and by days nine and ten he developed signs of paranoia. However, he also won a game of pinball against a non-sleep-deprived interviewer on the tenth day, and although he had lost about 90 hours of sleep, Gardner only overslept by 11 hours after the experiment, and showed no evidence of long-term side-effects (Boese, 2007). The impacts of chronic sleep restriction remain to be fully understood, but there is growing evidence of long-term negative impacts on health. Impaired vigilance, daytime sleepiness and weight gain due to a craving for carbohydrates are known side-effects. This topic is of obvious importance to our contemporary 24/7 society.

In the 'Raveled Sleeve of Care' Dr. Slechterschlaf attempts to develop a serum which will completely remove the need to sleep. While I am unaware of any bona-fide attempts to do this in the scientific community, the story is highly reminiscent of the unratified tale of the Russian Sleep Experiment (Begin, 1979). This is an urban legend which may be entirely fictional but likely has some basis in fact. In this experiment, the Russian special forces supposedly tested out a stimulant gas as a method for keeping people fully awake for 15 days. The participants were unwilling political prisoners who were told they would be freed if they could complete the experiment. According to legend, however, the results were beyond disturbing, as while the participants apparently did stay awake for the full duration, one of them died of unknown causes in the process and the others became deeply psychologically disturbed to the extent that they tore their own bodies to shreds, lifted their own organs out onto the floor around where they lay, and apparently ate chunks of their own flesh. There is no evidence that this experiment ever really happened – and even if factual it would be impossible to say how much this dreadful outcome was due to sleep deprivation and how much due to the unknown stimulant that these people inhaled. What we can say for certain, at this point, is that no drug exists which will safely remove the need to sleep in the long-term.

Having said this, exciting work from Vlad Vyazovskiy at the University of Oxford has recently demonstrated a new phenomena – local sleep. His work shows that small networks of cortical neurons can go 'offline' in sleep deprived rats who are otherwise apparently awake and performing the fairly stimulating task of reaching for sugar pills. These localised microsleeps are brief (~80 ms) but very frequent (~40 per minute), and the more often they occur the more mistakes the rats make in the reaching task (Vyazovskiy, 2011). The fact that networks of neurons in our cortex can apparently 'take a break' while we are awake may explain a lot about why we survive sleep deprivation as well as we do. It seems that our brains have a way of getting at least *some* of the sleep they need even when we don't explicitly allow time for it, or put ourselves in the kind of situation where we'd expect to get it. One might speculate that a mechanism for boosting this ability could potentially allow people to stay awake for longer without needing sleep, however I expect that the resulting wake would be a sort of fugue state, in which the brain was somewhere between wake and sleep due to large populations of cortical neurons being offline. Given that Dr. Slechtershlaf's 'cure' had a lot of side-effects, we could hypothetically imagine (with a bit of poetic license) that it might have worked along these lines.

Although complete removal of the need to sleep seems unrealistic, the new science of Sleep Engineering offers ways by which we can optimise the sleep we get so that it has the maximal positive impact in the minimal time. Thus, we can deepen slow wave sleep and increase its benefit to memory and cognition, and we can also trigger the replay of target memories in order to enhance their consolidation and the extent to which emotions are processed. (See Introduction, pp v-xvi). Maybe this is the start of new technology that can at least shorten and optimise our sleep?

# References

Begin, Menachem (1979). *White Nights: the story of a prisoner in Russia*. San Francisco, Harper & Row.

Boese, Alex (2007). 'Eleven days awake' in *Elephants on Acid: And Other Bizarre Experiments*. Harvest Books. pp 90–93.

Harrison Y. (2012). 'The Functions of Sleep' in *The Oxford Handbook of Sleep and Sleep Disorders*. Morin, C.M. and Espie, C. (Eds.). OUP USA.

Rechtschaffen, A. & Bergmann, B. M. 'Sleep deprivation in the rat by the disk-over-water method' in *Behavioural Brain Research*, 69, pp 55-63 (1995).

Vyazovskiy,V., et al. (2011) 'Local sleep in awake rats' in *Nature* 472, pp 443–447.

# About the Authors

**Martyn Bedford** is the author of five novels for adults, including *Acts of Revision* (Bantam, 1996), winner of the Yorkshire Post Best First Work Award, *The Houdini Girl* (Penguin, 1999) and *The Island of Lost Souls* (Bloomsbury, 2006). He has also written two novels for young adults: *Flip* (Walker, 2011), which was shortlisted for the Costa Book Award and won four regional prizes, and *Never Ending* (Walker, 2014). Between them his novels have been translated into 15 languages. Martyn is a senior lecturer in creative writing at Leeds Trinity University.

**Lisa Blower** is an award-winning short story writer and novelist with a PhD in Creative & Critical Writing. She won The Guardian's National Short Story competition in 2009, was shortlisted for the BBC National Short Story Award in 2013, and has been Highly Commended in this year's Bridport prize. Her work has appeared in *The Guardian*, *The New Welsh Review*, *The Luminary*, *Literary Salmon* and on Radio 4. Her debut novel *Sitting Ducks* is out Spring, 2016 (Fairacre Press) and she is working on her first short story collection, *It's Gone Dark Over Bill's Mother's*.

**Annie Clarkson** is a writer and social worker. Previous stories have been published in Comma anthologies, *Brace* (2008), *Litmus* (2011) and *Lemistry* (2012) as well as various anthologies and magazines.

**Claire Dean**'s short stories have been widely published and are included in *Beta-Life* (2014), *The Best British Short Stories* (2011), *Murmurations* (2011) and *New Fairy Tales: Essays and Stories*, (2013). *Marionettes* (2012) and *Into the Penny Arcade* (2012) are published as chapbooks by Nightjar Press. She lives in Lancashire with her two young sons.

**Zoe Gilbert**'s short stories have appeared in anthologies and journals in the UK and internationally. She is currently working on her first collection of stories inspired by folk tales, and is studying for a PhD in creative writing at the University of Chichester. Her story 'Fishskin, Hareskin' won the Costa Short Story Award 2014.

**Andy Hedgecock** has written reviews, essays and non-fiction for 30 years for the likes of *The Morning Star*, *The Spectator, Time Out, Penguin City Guides, The Oxford Companion to English Literature* and a number of SF magazines and academic journals. He is a writer, researcher and co-editor of *Interzone*, Britain's longest-running SF magazine.

**M.J. Hyland**'s first novel, *How the Light Gets In* (2003), was shortlisted for the Commonwealth Writers' Prize. Her second, *Carry Me Down* (2006), won the Hawthornden and Encore Prizes and was shortlisted for the Man Booker Prize. Her third novel, *This is How* (2009), was longlisted for the Orange Prize and the International IMPAC Prize. Her short fiction has previously been shortlisted for both the BBC's National and International Short Story Awards in 2011 and 2012, respectively. She worked for seven years as a commercial lawyer, and a lecturer in criminal law, and is currently a lecturer at the University of Manchester.

**Deborah Levy** is a novelist and a playwright and lives in London. She trained at the Dartington College of Arts and was a Fellow in Creative Arts at Trinity College, Cambridge from 1989 to 1991. Her novels include *Swimming Home* (2012), *Beautiful Mutants* (1986), *Swallowing Geography* (1993), *The Unloved* (1994) and *Billy and Girl* (1996). She has also published several collections of short stories, including *Ophelia and the Great Idea* (1985) and *Pillow Talk in Europe and Other Places* (2004). In 2012, her story 'Black Vodka' (later to be the title story of her 2013 collection) was shortlisted for BBC International Short Story Award. Deborah has written for the Royal Shakespeare Company and, in 2001, was awarded a Lannan Literary Fellowship in the US.

**Sara Maitland**'s first novel, *Daughters of Jerusalem*, was published in 1978 and won the Somerset Maugham Award. Novels since have included *Three Times Table* (1990), *Home Truths* (1993) and *Brittle Joys* (1999), and one co-written with Michelene Wandor — *Arky Types* (1987). She is also the author of *The Book of Silence* (2008) and *Gossip from the Forrest: A Search for the Hidden Roots of Our Fairytales* (2012). Her short story collections include *Telling Tales* (1983), *A Book of Spells* (1987) and *On Becoming a Fairy Godmother* (2003). Her short story 'Far North' was adapted for the screen by Asif Kapadia in 2007 and starred Sean Bean and Michelle Yeoh. Sara's previous science-inspired stories (written specially for Comma Press anthologies) were collected in *Moss Witch* (2013).

**Adam Marek** is the award-winning author of two short story collections: *Instruction Manual For Swallowing* and *The Stone Thrower*. He won the 2011 Arts Foundation Short Story Fellowship, and was shortlisted for the inaugural *Sunday Times* EFG Short Story Award. His stories have appeared on BBC Radio 4, and in many magazines and anthologies, including *Prospect* and *The Sunday Times Magazine*, and *The Penguin Book of the British Short Story*.

**Adam Roberts** is an academic, critic and novelist. He has a degree in English and Classics from the University of Aberdeen and a PhD from Cambridge University on Robert Browning and the Classics. His novel *Jack Glass* (Gollancz 2013) won the John Campbell and the BSFA Awards. His latest novel is *The Thing Itself* (Gollancz, 2015), a sciencefictional novelisation of Kant's *Critique of Pure Reason* via John Carpenter's *The Thing*.

**Sarah Schofield's** stories have appeared in several Comma Press 'science-into-fiction' anthologies: *Lemistry*, *Bio-Punk*, *Beta-Life* and *Thought X* (forthcoming). Her prizes include the Writers Inc Short Story Competition and the Calderdale Short Story Competition.

**Lisa Tuttle** is an award-winning author of science fiction, fantasy and horror. Her first novel, *Windhaven* (1981), was written in collaboration with George R.R. Martin, originally published in 1981. Her latest novel, a tale of detection set in late Victorian London, is *The Curious Affair of the Somnambulist and the Psychic Thief,* scheduled for publication in 2016. Born and raised in Texas, she has spent the last twenty-five years living in a remote, rural area of Scotland.

**Ian Watson** taught in Tanzania, Japan, and Birmingham's School of History of Art before becoming a full-time writer in 1976 after the success of his first SF novel, *The Embedding*. 40 books followed; he is translated into 17 languages. 2014 saw *The Best of Ian Watson* from PS Publishing. His 13th story collection, *The 1000 Year Reich*, debuts from NewCon Press, Easter 2016. 10 months eyeball to eyeball with Stanley Kubrick resulted in screen credit for *A.I. Artificial Intelligence* (2001), filmed by Steven Spielberg. Nowadays Watson lives in the north of Spain. www.ianwatson.info has fun photos as well as words.

# About the Scientists

Professor **Russell G. Foster**, CBE, FRS FMedSci (born 1959) is head of Nuffield Laboratory of Ophthalmology and The Sleep and Circadian Neuroscience Institute (SCNi) at the University of Oxford. He and his group are credited with the discovery of the non-rod, non-cone, photosensitive ganglion cells in the mammalian retina which provide input to the circadian rhythm system. Foster was elected a fellow of the Royal Society in 2008 and a member of the Biotechnology and Biological Sciences Research Council in 2011. He is the co-author, with writer and broadcaster Leon Kreitzman, of two popular science books on circadian rhythms, *Rhythms of Life: The Biological Clocks that Control the Daily Lives of Every Living Thing* (2005) and *Seasons of Life: The Biological Rhythms That Enable Living Things to Thrive and Survive* (2009).

**Isabel Hutchison** is a PhD student studying the role of sleep in emotional memory at the University of Manchester. Her research involves manipulating sleep – through sound and elictrical stimulation – to investigate the respective roles of REM and slow-wave sleep in emotional memory processing.

**Dr Simon Kyle** is a Senior Research Fellow in the Sleep and Circadian Neuroscience Institute (SCNi), Nuffield Department of Clinical Neurosciences, University of Oxford. He is also course director of a new postgraduate MSc, the Oxford Online Programme in Sleep Medicine. His research interests focus on the etiology and treatment of sleep disturbance and the mechanistic links between sleep disturbance and mental health. Dr Kyle also serves as Associate Editor of the journal, *Behavioral Sleep Medicine*.

**Penelope A. Lewis** is a neuroscientist at the University of Manchester, where she runs the NaPS (Neuroscience and Psychology of Sleep) lab. Her research investigates the impact of sleep on memory, cognition, and health in general. Currently, her main interest is in 'Sleep Engineering', or manipulation of sleep's properties to enhance its beneficial impact on health and cognition. She is the author of *The Secret World of Sleep* and has also written for popular science publications, including *New Scientist, Scientific American*, and *BBC Focus*. Her research has been featured on the BBC, and received funding from the UK research councils, the Wellcome Trust, and Unilever.

Following a neuroscience PhD thesis from Cambridge University, **Dr Paul Reading** completed his neurological training in Edinburgh and Newcastle before moving to the James Cook University Hospital, Middlesbrough, to work in a multi-disciplinary sleep unit. He has been running regular Neurology Sleep Clinics for 12 years alongside his general neurology workload. His particular interests are narcolepsy, abnormal sleep in neurodegenerative disease, and parasomnias. He is President of the British Sleep Society, the largest body in the UK for professionals involved in sleep medicine and science.

**Stephanie Romiszewski** holds a BSc in Psychology and an MSc in Behavioural Sleep Medicine and works as a Sleep Physiologist. She started her career working at Harvard Medical School Sleep Division working on NASA-funded sleep studies. There she had the opportunity to work on some infamous studies such as the affects of blue light on sleep. She came back to London and started working for the NHS diagnosing and treating a wide range of sleep disorders. She now directs her own practice 'Sleepyhead Clinic' in Exeter where she treats insomnia and provides training and workshops. She also works for the Royal Devon and Exeter Hospital where she is piloting one of the first NHS funded insomnia treatment services in the UK.

**Robert Stickgold** is an Associate Professor of Psychiatry at Harvard Medical School and Beth Israel Deaconess Medical Center. A preeminent sleep researcher, he has dedicated his life to understanding the relationship between sleep and learning. Having worked with the prominent sleep researcher J. Allan Hobson for many years, he has been a proponent of the role of sleep in memory consolidation. His research has focused on sleep and cognition, dreaming, and conscious states. He is also the author of two novels *Gloryhits* (1978) and *The California Coven Project* (1981), both published by Del Ray.

**Manuel Schabus** is Professor at the University of Salzburg, Austria, and is head of the 'Laboratory for Sleep, Cognition and Consciousness' research. He habilitated on 'Residual Cognitive Processing in Altered States of Consciousness' (covering sleep as well as coma related topics) and has expertise in Cognitive Neuroscience as well as Psychotherapy (being a client-centred psychotherapist and family counsellor). He is currently working on a comprehensive study on 'disorder of consciousness' patients and non-pharmacological treatment of primary insomnia. Altogether he has published over 60 articles in peer reviewed journals.

**Ed Watkins** is Professor of Experimental and Applied Clinical Psychology at the University of Exeter, co-founder of the Mood Disorders Centre, and director of SMART (Study of Maladaptive to Adaptive Repetitive Thought) Lab. He is a chartered clinical psychologist specialising in cognitive-behavioural therapy and psychological research to improve treatments for depression. He has published over 70 peer-reviewed scientific papers, funded by the Medical Research Council, Wellcome Trust, and European Commission. He was awarded the British Psychological Society's May Davidson

Award 2004 for outstanding early-career contribution to the development of clinical psychology, and is a member of the current NICE Guideline Group for depression.

**Adam Zeman** is Professor of Cognitive and Behavioural Neurology at the University of Exeter Medical School. He works clinically with patients with cognitive and sleep disorders. His research focusses on the effects of epilepsy on memory (http://projects.exeter.ac.uk/time/) and the neurological basis of visual imagery and its disorders (http://medicine.exeter.ac.uk/research/neuroscience/theeyesmind/). He is the author of *Consciousness – a user's guide* (Yale, 2002) and *A Portrait of the Brain* (Yale, 2008).

**Thomas Wehr** is a psychiatrist and Scientist Emeritus in the Intramural Research Program of the National Institute of Mental Health, where he was Chief of the Clinical Psychobiology Branch. He has published extensively on his group's research on effects on human biology of wakefulness, sleep, darkness and light. This work led to the discovery of seasonal affective disorder and its treatment with light, and to manipulations of sleep that improve depression and prevent mania. Dr Wehr discovered a brain-mechanism that tracks dawn and dusk and creates a biological 'day' and 'night' within the human body. He showed that the actions of this mechanism, which generates seasonal cycles, have been suppressed in humans by artificial light. Dr Wehr received a degree in English Literature and training in psychiatry at Yale University.